BLACKBEARD'S FREEDOM
BOOK 1 OF:
THE VOYAGES OF
QUEEN ANNE'S REVENGE

JEREMY MCLEAN

POINTS OF SAIL
PUBLISHING

Points of Sail Publishing
P.O. Box 30083 Prospect Plaza
FREDERICTON, New Brunswick
E3B 0H8, Canada

Edited by Ethan James Clarke
http://silverjay-editing.com/

Cover Design by Kit Foster

ACKNOWLEDGEMENTS

I could not have done this novel without the support of my friends and family for their patience and belief in me throughout. To my friend, David Burrows, your guidance after reading the first draft helped make this novel better than it could have ever been without. To my editor, E.J. Clarke, if there is any semblance of order and coherence to this, you are the reason.

Thank you all.

I dedicate this novel to my parents, who brought me into this world and taught me that hard work will reap rewards. The greatest reward that I have ever received is their love and respect. This is for you.

TABLE OF CONTENTS

1. Edward Thatch 1

2. Mutiny 11

3. Port Royal 17

4. Push VS. Shove 33

5. A Trip To The Gallows 45

6. Battle-Proven 48

7. The Map And The Woman 55

8. Forbidden 68

9. The Two By Two Islands 80

10. Between A Rock & A Current 92

11. The Doctor And The Dials 98

12. The Ambush In The Den 105

13. The Weight And The Chest 112

14. The Fifth Island 117

15. The Lost And The Left Behind 122

16. The Musician's Incident 126

17. Into The Storm 137

18. Black Bart & The Pirate Commandments 142

19. The Jungle 155

20. A Sacrifice 165

21. A Leader 170

22. An Uninvited Guest 184

23. A Warrior 194

24. The Revelation 202

25. The Princess And The Pirates 213

26. The Smell Of Blood 225

27. The Bodden Town Bandits 235

28. The Prince & The Pauper 245

29. What Matters Most 249

30. Freedom VS. The Family 257

31. The Crossed Swords Flag 264

32. The Hunter And The Hunted 272

33. The Predator And The Prey 283

34. Honouring The Deal 292

35. The Arm Sword 299

36. The Past And The Relapse 306

37. The Third Island 312

38. A Ship Out Of Water 321

39. A Captain's Resolve 330

40. No Regrets 337

1. EDWARD THATCH

Salt water and sweat mixed as it fell from Edward's hair and forehead. The drops went down his cheek, falling onto his lips and leaving a sickening taste in his mouth. But it was not the hot sun which caused him to perspire so. No, it was the twenty marines, in their stark blue uniforms, with their rifles pointed at him. He steadied his shaking hand on the flintlock pistol he had pointed at the back of their captain's head.

Oh Father, what am I doing?

"Think about what you're doing, boy. The way you're going, there's no ending with you free. We can negotiate here. You have a choice to make: one can lead to a happy life… and the other never ends well."

No… no, I will be free. And I won't let you stand in my way. It's too late for choices.

Edward cocked the gun against the captain's head, his mind clear on what he needed to do. "Listen carefully," Edward said aloud for all to hear, "for I'm only going to say this once."

Five Hours Ago

Edward Thatch breathed deep, taking in the full scent of that salty sweet air he so loved. He held that breath far longer than normal, like a jealous lover who thinks he could lose his love at any moment. He had to let go, but with another breath it was back again.

"Still don't feel real, does it?" A man came up beside Edward and placed his arm around Edward's shoulder. He glanced sideways to see Henry Morgan, a third generation Welshman and his best friend.

Henry was not as tall as Edward, but he made up for the height with might. His straight brown hair was in a ponytail, and his rolled sleeves displayed his farmer's tan.

"Well, it has only been a few days since we started whaling," Edward replied. "Any man would be hard pressed to come back to earth after too much heaven."

Henry laughed with vigor. "We need you here on the ship, Captain."

Edward smiled. "You know me, Henry. You couldn't keep me from this beauty with a loaded pistol."

Edward and Henry watched the crew of the ship called *Freedom* from the raised aft deck. The men milled about, performing various duties aboard the three-masted ship.

On the aft deck there were some fixing the sails and rigging. On the quarterdeck the helmsman concentrated on changes in the skies and sea with help from a cabin boy. On the main deck some were checking on the main mast while others cleaned. Far ahead on the raised foredeck there were men loafing about as far from their captain's eye as possible.

"Despite the oddness of how Benjamin Hornigold sold us the vessel," Henry said, his eyes wandering the floorboards of the sole, "... it is a fine ship."

Edward cringed. "Let us never speak of the incident again. My stomach churns with the mention of his name."

"Come now, it's not every day that one buys a warship while tanked off whiskey." He slapped Edward on the back as he laughed.

"Yes... but as we are trying to be whalers, we've no need—" Yelling from the waist of the ship stopped Edward's voice and called their attention.

"Ye lilly-white kencracker. You stole me money, I know ye did!" Sam was yelling to another crewman on deck.

Samuel Bellamy, the apparent aggressor, was a young man of around five feet eleven inches, but like a true cockney Londoner he acted as if he were ten feet tall. Despite his prettiness, which no doubt made women ogle, there was darkness in his jet-black eyes.

"I stole nuthin' of yers," the other crewman yelled back. "Why don't ye check it again? All that black hair gettin' in yer way."

"Stop yer lyin' and give back me money!" Sam rushed up to the man and pushed him hard, sending him sprawling against the starboard railing.

This can't be good, Edward thought, before bolting down to the waist of the ship. Henry followed a few steps behind him.

The other crewmembers gathered around in anticipation of a fight. The crewman accused of stealing pushed Sam back, and then they circled each other as the rest chanted. Edward pushed through

2

the throng. Sam threw the first punch straight in the face of the other man, who countered with a right upper to his chin.

Sam's head snapped back, but he seemed unfazed by the blow. His lips drew back in a cruel smile, and his eyes glistened as if he were enjoying himself. He burst like a cannon with a punch to the crewman's gut, and followed it with a downward right against his jaw. The crewman fell to the floor, unconscious, but Sam kept beating on him. Edward still had not reached them.

William, the crew's boatswain, jumped from the main mast and slid down a rope to the deck. He grabbed Sam by the arm, flipped him over on his back, and pinned him to the deck.

William was mature in demeanor despite his young age. His eyes and face were devoid of expression, and he seemed incapable of smiling. He could blend in with anyone else among the ship, but, upon closer inspection, revealed a man sharper in mind and stronger in body than most.

Sam struggled and writhed but was unable to escape William's grip. Edward, finally at the centre of the throng, shouted, "Let him go, William." William rose to his feet just as Henry forced his way to the front of the crowd.

Henry glared angrily at the beaten and bloodied crewman and at Sam, who had just gotten to his knees. "You bastard!" He leveled Sam again with a thunderous punch.

Edward stepped between Sam and Henry. "Henry, stop! I will have no more fighting aboard my ship!" He pointed to the unconscious crewman. "Someone help that poor sod." Two crewmen carried the injured man below deck.

Edward walked to Sam, still stretched out on the deck, and looked daggers down at him. His dark eyes pierced Sam, carrying a force greater than Henry's punch.

"Another incident like this… and you're off my ship, and maybe I won't wait for us to make port," he said.

"That rat bastard stole me money, I knows it!"

Edward knelt and leaned close to Sam's face. Henry and William stood on either side of him. "We'll question the man when he's well again, but my warning stands. You are not to get into another fight. Understood?"

Sam tried to stare down Edward, but the intensity of Edward's gaze made him turn away. "You got it, Chief."

"What was that?"

"Captain," Sam replied with emphasis.

Edward offered his hand, but Sam ignored it and picked himself up off the floor before stalking off.

Edward watched Sam go. Then he looked at his officers and the crowd of seamen. "Back to work," he ordered.

The crew resumed their duties with a fresh reminder of who their captain was. They also knew now to stay away from Sam.

Edward turned to Henry and William. "William, keep an eye on Sam. I don't want him causing problems again. You stop him at the first sign of trouble."

William saluted in his no-nonsense way. "Yes, Captain." He was about to turn and walk away with his orders, but something caught his keen eye. "Captain, there's a storm approaching. We must warn the helmsman," he stated in his perfect English, so unlike Sam's cockney twang.

Edward searched the sky. In the east, the clouds were practically roiling, already black and heavy with a promise of rain. "Hard to starboard!" he called out. "Keep this ship beating to the wind. We don't want to be here when that menace hits!"

Henry stopped Edward before he went to help the crew prepare. "We'll never escape that storm without releasing the foresail."

Edward glanced to the front mast and the sail Henry mentioned. It had been stuck in place since he'd bought the ship, and whenever they tried to find the reason it was an exercise in futility.

I've never seen a storm come in so quickly without warning... Henry's right, this ship is too slow with only two sails.

"I need five strong arms with me now!" No sooner did Edward yell the command than Sam, Henry, and William joined him on his way to the bow of the ship. "We're unfurling the topsail one way or the other. Our lives depend on it. We need to find the reason it's stuck and make it unstuck. Go, go, go! No time to waste!"

Darkness was descending upon them as the smell of the sea air faded and clean rain flooded in.

The group of sailors inspected the rigging and climbed up to the sail by the ropes. They checked the knots, pulling and tugging on whatever they thought might be holding the sail down. Before they made any progress, the rain began. Everyone knew what this meant, and they worked all the harder to accomplish their task. Many of the rest of the crew broke out the oars and started rowing to make the ship move faster.

Sam was in the middle of the mast checking the rigging when he suddenly yelled, "I found it!" He pointed excitedly to a spot on the mast where a metal notch held a rope down. "I need a knife!"

Someone on the foredeck heard his cry and tossed him a small knife. He placed the knife in the notch and pried at it. He went this way and that as the rain worsened and the wind picked up. Slowly the notch inched its way out of the wood. Minutes passed like hours as the storm grew worse. Edward and the crew watched, their lives in the hands of the one who had almost killed a mate not minutes ago.

With one final snap, the metal hook flew out and hit the deck with a clang. Several men released the restraining ropes and the topsail unfurled.

The crew of the *Freedom* started to cheer, but those cries of victory died very quickly in every throat. Painted on the topsail was a black skull with two crossed bones beneath it. Lightning flashed a brilliance of white light and a crash of thunder followed soon after. Sounds of astonishment rippled through the crew. The Jolly Roger, the sign of a pirate, was painted on their sail.

Edward couldn't believe what he saw. He felt sick. Sweat broke out on his brow, mixed with the rain and ran down his face. He stood still as a statue. *What is that doing on my ship?*

"There's no time to worry about that right now, Ed!" Henry shouted. "Hold it together!"

Edward blinked his eyes back into focus. "You... you're right. We must hurry." Edward ran to the edge of the foredeck. "Pull those oars in before they get taken away. Soon we'll be moving too fast for them to do any good." A mate nodded and yelled back something in the affirmative before issuing commands to the other men. "This storm will not beat us, gentlemen! We're sailors, not craven landlubbers."

Edward joined in hoisting the heavy oars onto the deck and securing them. "Do not yield, men. This storm cannot topple us!"

The crew ran this way and that, keeping the sails and the ship together in the strong winds. Edward stayed in the thick of it with the other crewmates, and soon his arms legs burned with the strain.

After what seemed like hours, the wind and rain had abated somewhat, and Edward knew from his father's teaching that this was a crucial time. If the sails were left up now the ship could be blown in the wrong direction.

"Secure those sails before the wind changes!" Edward shouted while he ran to the aft sail. He and the other free crewmembers rushed to pull up the sails. The rain had made the ropes slick and harder to work with.

Edward pulled on the rigging with all his might. His arms burned with the struggle. The rough grain of the rope dug into his calloused hand, but he gritted his teeth to push away the pain.

Edward finished raising the aft sail, but noticed the crew still furling the foresail. "Hand that foresail!" Then he looked beyond the sails, beyond the bow, and saw a thing more shocking to him than the sight of the Jolly Roger.

A ship was heading straight for the *Freedom*.

He removed a spyglass from his coat pocket and peered through it. Judging from the new ship's size, it was a frigate much like the *Freedom*. It was a marine vessel and, unlike the *Freedom*, was equipped with cannons. The name emblazoned on the side was H.M.S. *Pearl*.

He spun on his heels and shouted, "Everyone! Finish what you're doing, and raise your hands in the air. A marine vessel is approaching off our bow! Someone bring me something white tied to a plank!"

In a flurry of frantic activity, the crew rigged the sails and a cabin boy brought Edward a white shirt fastened to a pole. He ran to the front of the deck and waved it in the direction of the oncoming vessel. Everyone else did as ordered and raised their hands in the air in submission. Henry had come onto the main deck, ready for the inevitable. Sam was trying to hide behind others, but still had his hands raised. William was also trying to hide, but was doing a better job of it than Sam. Edward kept waving the pole as the marine ship pulled up beside them. He then dropped the pole and went down to the main deck to join Henry. He opened up a hinge on the railing of the ship to allow a gangplank to be placed down and the marine officers to board. He then backed away and raised his hands in the air.

We'll talk our way out of this. They have to believe us...

Marines tied the ships together with grappling hooks, and extended gangplanks over the water. The officers and guards boarded with muskets raised. Their leader was a man of no more than average height who nonetheless carried himself with the deadly grace of a lion on the prowl. He had the clean-shaven face of a youth, but his uniform revealed him to be an accomplished military captain.

"Who is your captain?" He glanced around at the ragged crew, who stood frozen in poses of surrender. "And would you put your hands down? You've already lost any credibility as a threat."

Everyone obeyed. "Now, which one of you is the captain of this ship? Speak up!"

"I am... sir." Edward stepped forward.

The marine commander looked Edward up and down. Edward was much taller and imposing than the captain, being six foot four inches, but the battle-hardened marine didn't appear fazed. An amused smile flitted across his face and then disappeared. "A fine ship you have for a pirate."

"We're not pirates!" Henry yelled from behind Edward.

"I did not ask you, powder-monkey."

Edward turned to Henry. "Henry, I can handle this." Henry pursed his mouth and did his best to be quiet.

"Your man says you aren't pirates, yet you bear the mark of them on your sail. You own a high-class warship, and clearly are not marines or any merchants I've ever seen. If you aren't pirates, and this ship isn't stolen, then I must be the son of Davy Jones himself." The captain's men laughed.

"I told you we're not pirates!" cried Henry. "We're whalers. This is a misunderstanding. Edward paid for this ship fair and square!"

The commander signaled to one of his men. The marine walked over and smashed the butt of his musket into Henry's face, sending him crumpling to the deck.

Henry! Edward struggled to resist the impulse to rush over and help his friend, and fought hard to control his anger and panic. *God damn him! How will we get out of this?*

"Order your men to tend to him," the captain commanded.

Edward turned to some of his crew. "You heard him, take him downstairs." Then he met the captain's eyes. "Despite my friend's... outburst, his word is true. We are no pirates and I purchased this vessel fairly."

"Can you produce papers of sale or title of ownership to prove your man's claim?"

Edward felt his stomach turn. "N-no. The previous owner forgot to entrust the papers to me."

"Of course he did." The captain glanced over his shoulder at his men and smiled.

"I-it has only been a few weeks since the sale, if you just return with us to Badobos I'm sure we can find him to corroborate my story. His name is Benjamin Hornigold."

At the mention of Hornigold's name, the marine captain's eyes widened and he missed a step. "Do you take me for a fool?"

Edward was taken aback and tried to stammer out a response, but couldn't think of any.

"I am Captain Isaac Smith of the Royal Navy, and I am hereby taking control of this vessel. You will all be brought to Clarendon Parish where you will be jailed until your trial."

"Trial! W-we haven't done anything! We're simple whalers. Look at our equipment, look at us, we're not pirates. My name is Edward Thatch. I... I was raised in Badobos by the Hughes family. You can ask them about it." Edward hated to flash his adopted family's name around, but he was overcome with desperation.

"Save it, pirate. We're onto your deception. It's obvious you were damaged during the storm and wanted to try talking your way out of a fight."

"Are you even listening? We live on Badobos a few days southwest of here. I just bought this ship and I didn't even know about the sail."

"Enough excuses. Your story is as vaporous as the deed you seem to have misplaced. I'm claiming your ship as my own. You will be tried and executed in a court of law, which is more than you deserve."

Edward's mind raced. *Executed? ... I can't die, not now, not like this!*

Captain Smith turned and motioned for two of his men, who walked over to Edward, sheathing their weapons and pulling out shackles. He noticed a pistol on the captain's belt. *We're not pirates. We don't deserve to be treated like this! I won't let him have his way!*

Edward put Smith in a choke hold, grabbed his gun from its holster, and pointed it at his temple. "Nobody move or I shoot!"

The marines all aimed their firearms at Edward as his crew watched on in horror. "Drop your weapons, you fools!" commanded Smith. "Do as he says."

He walked backwards with Smith in tow, his elbow tight around the captain's neck. He felt like he should be breathing rapidly, but his breaths were steady, calm almost.

"Now you have my attention, boy, but you're not doing yourself any favours," Smith said, his hands held up to calm his men. "If you didn't want us thinking you were pirates you're doing a piss-poor job of it."

"Shut it!" Edward glanced swiftly back and forth to the marines in front of him. He thought out his options, and came to only one conclusion. "Sam?" Edward called.

"Yea?" Sam was only a few feet away.

Edward pushed Smith forward, but kept the pistol trained on him. "Bind the captain's arms and feet," Edward commanded.

Sam followed the order without question. He grabbed spare rope from the foot of one of the masts, then tied Smith's arms behind his back in a handcuff knot. He wore a wicked smile as he made the captain kneel down, then used the slack from the handcuff knot to tie Smith's feet to his hands. The more Smith pulled against the knots, the more they tightened.

"Think about what you're doing, boy. The way you're going, there's no ending with you free," Smith whispered with a pause for Edward to consider his words. Edward cocked the gun in response. "We can negotiate here. You have a choice to make: one can lead to a happy life... and the other never ends well."

It's too late for choices, Edward thought before echoing the words into Smith's ear.

"Listen carefully," Edward said loudly for all to hear. "for I'm only going to say this once. Drop your muskets, pistols, and other equipment near the mast and then back away to the starboard railing with your hands behind your backs."

The marines seemed unsure of what to do, but they were quick to action. They followed his order immediately, eyeing their captain nervously.

Edward's crew stared in rapt attention as the soldiers delivered their weapons and gear without a murmur. They were in awe of him, he could feel it; him, the man who, not two weeks ago, had not even met the lot of them.

"Take their weapons, men." The crew's eyes went from Edward to the guns as if they didn't know what they were. "Do it!" he shouted. They obeyed. Then, to Smith, "Now order your crew to gather up all the food, supplies, and weapons aboard your ship and bring them over here."

Edward knew he was pushing his luck—the marine crew looked uncertain, offended even—but fortunately Smith applied his own pressure. "Do it," he ordered.

"Leave enough food so you can make it back to port."

Some of Edward's crew pointed the muskets at the marines and some held them like foreign objects, filthy and wrong in their hands.

"This will never work," Smith whispered. "My men will have your portrait posted at every port from here to the Bahamas by next month. Think this through! I'll cut you a break if you stop this madness right now."

"Just like you were going to cut us a break earlier? Ha!"

A few minutes later the marines walked back with bags and barrels filled with supplies: swords, muskets, pistols, a few rifles, and barrels of gunpowder. They also had more spices and food than necessary for a short voyage on a small ship. They dropped them in the centre of the *Freedom* and returned to the starboard rails, awaiting the next commands from Edward.

"Now tell your men to head south until they've lost sight of us. Their lives depend on it. I'm a deadly pirate, remember? You don't know what I'm capable of." *How is my voice so calm? My heart's about to explode!*

Smith examined the man in front of him once again, as if he was re-assessing his first impression of Edward. "Men, I want you to sail away from here," Smith commanded. "Sail until you cannot see this ship any longer…"

"But, Captain—"

"Don't worry, I'll be fine. These men are whalers, remember?" As his men were leaving, he muttered to Edward, "I'll make you pay for this humiliation, Thatch."

"We'll see about that, now won't we?" *I'm a dead man.*

The marine crew pulled the gangplanks back into their own ship, cut the grappling hooks, and released their sails. The enemy ship headed south, slowed by the wind against them.

Edward cried out, "Men, I want those sails unfurled and this ship underway!" No one moved. "That's an order!" Those who had guns dropped them where they stood and went to work unfurling the sails again. The ship moved fast with the wind, and in no time at all the marines were out of sight.

Edward now took hold of Smith's arm and dragged him to the side of the ship. He pulled a knife from his pocket and cut the ropes binding Smith, then backed away a short distance. After Smith rose, Edward pointed the pistol at him. "Now jump."

Smith's face froze in astonishment. "You cannot be serious!" He looked at the water, then at Edward, then some crewmembers who stood watching.

Edward didn't lower the pistol an inch. "Get off my ship."

Smith slowly climbed up the port side of the ship. "You can't hide from me, Thatch. The stench of a pirate is all over you. We will meet again, and then the tables will turn." Smith spat on Edward's ship as one last act of contempt before he jumped off the side.

Edward and the crew watched as the marine did his best to stay afloat. "Throw him a plank!" Edward commanded. A cabin boy obliged. Smith grabbed onto it and floated there, the waves pushing him up and down.

Edward and his crew kept staring at the marine captain until his tiny, bobbing form could be seen no longer.

What have I done?

2. MUTINY

Henry sat with two men on a pier, their legs dangling into the water, looking out to the ocean. They sat watching the sun set in silence; it would be the last sunset they would all see together.

"Let's make a promise," Robert Maynard said.

Robert was sitting in the middle, with Henry on the left and Edward on the right. He was younger than the other two and of smaller stature. He had wispy blond curls and a smile that made women swoon and men envious.

"Let's promise that we shall meet again when we fulfill our dreams and have something to show for it. We will reunite either right here, in Badobos, or out on the open seas." He looked up to his taller friends and placed one hand on each of their shoulders.

Henry looked to Robert and Edward, smiling to them both. "It's a promise," Henry and Edward both replied in unison.

...

Henry woke with a start. He took deep breaths through his mouth; his nose hurt something fierce. The crew cabin's wooden plank ceiling and swaying hammocks were spinning, but he could see Edward and two other crewmembers. They were arguing over something.

"Can you all shut it? The devil's knocking on my brain."

Edward's face turned to Henry, and he flashed a small smile. Then he turned his attention back to the other crewmembers. "We'll discuss this later." The men shook their heads and left the crew's quarters.

Henry leaned up on his elbows so he could see everything. "What happened? Did you convince the captain we were whalers?"

"Yes, about that..."

Edward described what had happened. As he listened, Henry's expression changed from interest, to shock, to disgust, and finally to anger.

"What in the devil's name were you thinking, Edward? You... you pulled a gun on a marine officer? You fool!"

11

"I am no fool! Any man would have done the same thing!" he argued. "He wasn't listening to reason; I did what I had to do to secure the lives of the crew... Your life," he said while pointing at his friend.

Henry sighed as he ran his fingers through his hair. "What are we to do now? Where are we to go? Where *can* we go? From what the marine captain told us, he'll make sure you're infamous before we next reach port."

"Yes, and judging by his character he'll embellish the story and make us out to be the truest of villains to cover his blunder."

"He'll probably say we were the devil's own children and we used our deadly powers to compel him and his men to do our bidding." Edward and Henry shared a grim chuckle.

Edward looked over his shoulder and noticed their quartermaster, John, trembling as he paced. He was a somewhat plump man, the type who had seen action in their glory years and then rested on their laurels for too long.

"John," Edward said, and the older man jumped in fright. "You're just the man who we need to talk to. Come," Edward commanded. John dragged himself over to Edward and Henry, adjusting his rounded glasses nervously. "Do you have any idea where we could escape to after this nasty business?"

Edward and Henry awaited their quartermaster's response, though he seemed to be on the point of breaking at the light questioning. John glanced back and forth from one of them to the other, as if he were at gunpoint. "I... I... don't know of anywhere, Edward." He was almost cowering with fear as he replied. He ran a shaking hand through his salt-and-pepper hair.

Edward glanced at Henry, then back to John. "John, what's wrong? You won't look me in the eyes."

"It's nothing," John said, still not looking up.

"No, please, John. You're from Badobos; you know us. You know that you can tell us anything," Henry reassured the man.

John gained confidence at Henry's reassuring words, then focused on Edward. "Wh-when you had the marine hostage, there was something a-about your eyes. They were dark like the devil's, and you had a smile on your face, like it was all a joke. The men are saying you seemed like you were having fun."

"What? I think I would remember if I was smiling. I don't remember doing that. Why would I smile? I didn't smile!"

"Ed, calm down. We know you wouldn't do that. They're probably mistaken. Right, John?"

John looked at Edward and then back at Henry. "Y-yes… They must have been s-seeing things, Edward."

"Yes… they must have."

"Well," said Henry, trying to cut the tension, "this still leaves open the question of where we can safely land."

"We'll have to discuss it with the crew. John, call everyone to the deck. We'll see if anyone has a good suggestion."

"Right away, Captain." John left and went straight up the stairs, telling everyone he saw along the way to meet on the deck.

Edward wanted to make sure Henry was all right before heading upstairs. He could walk fine; his nose was the problem, and they weren't able to do much about it.

The two walked up to the top deck where the crew was waiting, then moved to the quarterdeck. John followed them up soon after.

The sun was high in the sky after the harsh storm. It was almost as if the storm had never happened, but the remnants of the wind and rain remained as a reminder. The smell of the gunpowder and spices on the deck gave the crew a memento to the second storm that happened.

Edward stood there for a minute, staring at his men. He didn't know what to say, and the number of people confronting him was already working on his nerves. Speaking to crowds was always a problem, but Henry had been trying to help him get better. He slowed his breathing and did what Henry had taught him to do: focus on one person in the audience at a time.

"You all know of what has happened, and, unfortunately, there's not much we can do. That is why I ask you, men, what should our next course of action be?"

The crew murmured to each other. Some had raised brows in a questioning manner, and others tightened their fists as they talked in hushed voices. No one knew what to say until an angry-looking crewman spoke up. His name was Frederick. A fisherman by trade, he had worked in Badobos all his life. Edward knew him well and wasn't surprised to be hearing from him.

"You got us into this mess and now you're asking us for help? Because of you, the marines think we're pirates! Why should we help you at all?"

Henry's technique wasn't working any more. Edward started to panic. His breathing became more rapid, and his eyes flitted to all the other men looking at him for an answer.

Henry came to the rescue. "We're all in this mess. Fighting over who to blame won't solve anything."

13

"Why can't we just sail home?" another crewman asked. Several more agreed with him.

"The marines know where we're from. That will be the first place they inspect. We can't return home, at least not now. We might be able to revisit when we figure out how to clear our names, but for now we need something else."

Frederick spoke up again. "I think we should seek out the marines and explain the situation to them. Maybe if they hear the words of a few sane people then they'll understand." Many in the crew agreed loudly.

Henry sighed. "Oh, you think they'll understand? Like the last marines did? You think when they hear the account from Captain Smith they'll let the charges drop? Don't be a fool. They'll never believe our word against his. We can't go to the marines." Henry was trying his best to protect Edward, but Frederick was having none of it.

"I think you're afraid of what they'll do to your friend the 'Captain.' *He's* the one pulled the gun on Smith; *he's* the one who ordered him around. He's the one they want, not us." Frederick turned to face the men. "If we take him to the marines, then they'll absolve us of his wrongdoing! I say we tie him up and put our lot in with the authorities! Who's with me?"

Half the crew yelled in agreement and started making their way up to the quarterdeck.

"This is insane!" shouted Edward. "You think they'll treat you differently because you bring me in? They'll think you're trying to save your own skin."

"Don't listen to him, men! The captain is the one who's labelled a pirate, and he'll be the one put on trial if we turn him in."

At least fifty men crowded onto the quarterdeck, and thirty more waited on the stairs, ready to beat the tar out of Edward, Henry, and John. "Any suggestions?" Henry asked Ed as they put their backs against each other.

"Not unless you count fighting off eighty sailors as a suggestion."

William ran up the railing leading to the quarterdeck. He had four swords in hand, taken from the marine ship. He leapt over to Edward, Henry, and John and handed them each a sword. Then he pointed his own at the ringleader, Frederick.

"You dare direct your anger at the man who saved your lives? He is your captain. You owe him your allegiance!" William yelled above the rising din.

"He didn't save our lives. He put us into this situation, and he's going to get us out of it, one way... or the other. You can't take on all of us! Surrender so we can return home."

Edward gritted his teeth. "I had already tried to explain to him how we were whalers and he didn't care. You think he'll change his mind because a different person tells him?"

"Well... I'd rather take my chances with a marine who believes in justice than live the rest of my life as a pirate! We'll be able to cut a deal with him over your life."

The standoff held for a whole minute, with neither side willing to budge. The mutinous crewmembers didn't want to risk injury, and the four armed men didn't want to hurt them.

Then a loud bang sounded from the main deck, causing everyone to duck for cover. They turned their attention there, where Sam stood, brandishing a pistol.

"You should all stop what yer doin'. Captain's right. Whatever you do it won't do a lick o' good in your situation. You'd be right old fools to take 'im to the marines, and even bigger fools if ye kill 'im."

"Oh yes? And how would you know?"

"I know 'ow the marines think. If you off the captain, they jus' find the ship and execute you all at sea. If you take 'im in, they really will think you're jus' tryin' to cut a deal and you'll be chained before the piss stains yer pants. If the lot of us'd been put on trial, you'd have been found guilty regardless of what you said and then executed. We all be alive 'cause he was bold. The best thing you can do now is take the ship to a good port, and go our separate ways. The marines only have 'is name and this ship to go by. Edward Thatch is the one they're after."

Frederick considered Sam's words as he peered at the crew and Edward. After a moment of thought, he lowered his sword. "Let's stop, everyone. Sam's right."

Despite the attempt at placating the situation, the crew was reluctant to stand down. They talked to each other in loud whispers, debating whether they could take Sam's words at face value. When they convinced themselves, or at least calmed themselves, they lowered their weapons.

Edward, Henry, John, and William all let out a collective sigh of relief as the crew lowered their weapons. The clang of swords falling on the deck meant their throats were safe for another day.

The threat over, the crew who had started the mutiny returned to the main deck, and Edward turned to Sam.

"So what are you suggesting we do?"

"We're close to a port soft on pirates. Dole out a little coin to the harbourmaster and he won't say a word."

Edward thought it over for a minute. "We need to be in agreement on this. All those in favor of following Bellamy's plans, raise your hands and say 'aye.'" The whole crew did so. "All opposed?" No one spoke up. "Right. Then move those weapons into barrels and into the corners of the steps. Move any excess to the crew's quarters. Put all the gunpowder in the crew's quarters for the time being. Lay aloft and loose all sails! Sam, what's the name of the place we're sailing to?"

"Port Royal."

3. PORT ROYAL

"This is my decision, and that is all that matters," Edward said, arms folded.

"Why stay with the ship, Ed?" Henry objected, his melodic Welsh accent undercutting his obstinate tone. "We can leave it and never be seen again. If we stay with the ship, it'll be like a target on our backs."

"I bought this ship, Henry. It took me a week just to say I'd keep it, and now... I'm attached to it. I can't explain it, but I feel bound to this ship. Besides, as I told you, Smith knows my name and my face. No matter where I run I'll be hunted like a pirate."

Henry folded his massive arms in front of him. "And should they find you? You'll fight them?"

"If I must, yes."

"And what if it's Robert chasing after you? What then? He plans on becoming a marine to stop pirates. Would you fight him too?"

The words hit Edward like a shot to the chest. Edward, Henry, and Robert had been best friends since childhood. "I guess... I never thought about it."

"No, you didn't. I can tell from the look in your eyes that no matter what I say you'll keep the ship. But it's not worth dying over, or killing."

"Maybe to you the *Freedom* isn't worth dying over, but to me it is. I don't want to kill anyone... but if someone tries to take my *Freedom*, I will fight them. I don't care how long I'm chased. I will not relinquish this ship."

"Even to Robert?"

"Robert would understand. He would believe our side. He's still our friend. Besides, we're not killing and stealing from anyone."

Henry sighed. "Well I can't leave you on your own. I'll stay with you... to whatever end," he said with a melancholic smile. "Besides, you know you're lost without me."

"Ha! I bet you just can't stand the thought of being apart from me," Edward said with a playful push.

Henry rolled his eyes. "Yea, I sure do love gettin' my face bashed in and being bossed about by a tosspot like you." They laughed together a moment, but then grew silent as the swaying

17

hammocks caught their attention. They could hear the splash of waves and the shouts of orders above them. "You know, it's a bit like one of them books your Dad had. The tattered ones with the heroes who get into a spot of trouble, enemies chasing them down, but they outsmart them at every turn. You think that could be us some day? And with pirates there's supposed to be treasure, right? What do you think?"

Edward scratched his face. "I guess."

The two sat thinking of the past, and what they left behind.

"Have you thought about Lucy?"

The mention of that name brought Edward back to the small Caribbean island of Badobos. Aside from his friend Robert, Lucy was the only person he missed from home.

Edward fondly remembered Lucy as fair and gentle, demure in bearing and dainty in appearance, but with a fire inside her. Edward had not found that spirit in any other woman, nor did he think he would. Her sky blue eyes filled him with joy more so than the sea air.

"You know I have," he replied.

Henry gave him an exasperated look. "And? You're just going to leave her behind, no so much as a letter explaining what's happened?"

"She's better off not knowing. It will make letting me go easier."

"Ed, she will find out one way or another. At least if you send her a letter explaining that you aren't a pirate it will be better than the alternative. You owe her that."

"I will be the one to decide what I owe her or not, thank you." Edward knew Lucy. If she thought there was any way she might be able to help, she would not hesitate to find him. Better she thought he left her than to hold out hope to find him again. That way they could both move on.

Henry rubbed his eyes in frustration. "At least tell me that you will think it over. The poor girl will be worried sick when you do not return."

"I will think it over," Edward lied. "I'm going to check on things above deck."

Edward left to head upstairs, and Henry went into the mess hall to have something to eat. It was turning into a nice day with a full sun, and the wind in their sails was bringing them to Port Royal at a quick pace.

The salt air was back and Edward could smell it stronger than ever. He thought he should feel bad with all that had happened, but there was no weight on his shoulders.

Edward noticed William brooding on the main deck next to the weapons they had procured from the marines. He surveyed the arms, running his fingers down the length of a rifle in a familiar way.

"Best be careful. The sparks from your gaze may ignite the gunpowder," Edward joked.

"Gunpowder is added prior to firing, not while in storage," William pointed out.

Edward's face flushed and he coughed. "Right." He stood there for a few more seconds with nothing to say as the wind swayed the ship and the crew walked about on the deck. "William, I was curious of your decision to stay with me at the risk of being labelled a pirate. You seem like one who would brook no such thing."

"I know the truth of the situation. You were in the right. You are my captain now, so I follow you. If you wish for me to leave, I will. If not, I will help you however I can."

"Good to know." Edward nodded, and William returned the gesture.

"I have a query," William said a few moments later, when another uncomfortable silence threatened to settle between them. "I notice that some of the doors on the ship are locked and we are unable to access certain sections."

Edward's mouth made a line. "Yes, that. Well, after purchasing this vessel, the previous owner, Benjamin Hornigold, only left a few keys for us. Thus our locked door predicament."

At the mention of the name Benjamin Hornigold, William, for the first time, showed a hint of shock on his face. He turned speechless for a moment.

"What's wrong, William?" Edward asked, looking over his own shoulder.

William recovered quickly. "Nothing. Did you meet with this Hornigold personally?"

Edward grinned. "I believe so. It's an amusing tale, actually. After a particularly... eventful celebration with Henry, I awoke the next morning with my life savings gone and a note explaining the sale of this ship in my pocket." Edward laughed, until he noticed William staring at him with a straight face and his arms crossed.

"Perhaps a list of the doors locked would be prudent. We can have some of the crew attempt forcing the locks later."

"Right, I'll get on that right now. Good idea, William."

Edward turned around, but glanced back at the other man. He seemed lost in thought once again, but this time he wasn't looking at the marines' guns. Edward decided not to pry and returned to his task.

He made a mental note of the two cabins aft and fore of the main deck, as they were among the sections locked off.

Edward moved on to the bow to descend to the lower decks. The gun deck was first, but was currently only used to access the crew cabin as the doors in the hallway were locked as well.

Edward gazed at the doors on either side of the hallway. *How are we to ever open you? I suppose a locksmith could give picking it a try.*

Sam walked up the stairs from the crew cabin and noticed Edward. "Isn't that just the rub, mate? A full set of cannons and no way ta fire 'em. Jus' like when you're about ta get with a girl and she leaves before ye can clank yer rocks, eh?" He laughed at his own crude humour.

Edward ignored the comment. "Sam, I wish to thank you for the other day. You saved my skin."

"Just returning the favor, mate."

"I'm curious why you're choosing to remain aboard. Why aren't you leaving?"

"Well… I guess it would have come outta the woodwork sooner or later. I used ta work on a pirate ship a few years back. Got away and managed ta stay away from the gallows. I wasn't no one special, s'no one cared about me. From then on, it's been port to port fer me. And here ye come, yer labelled as a pirate, and I'm back in the same spot. Figure I'm destined for this life. It be a sign if there ever was one."

Edward thought it over. "I guess that makes sense." *To a madman.*

"I knew you'd understand. Ya do what you've gotta do, right, mate? And boy, when I saw you take that marine's gun, then force 'im to give you all his stuff? I said to meself: this guy's one to watch. Figure I'll set eyes on a great show if I tag along fer a while. Y'understand. Right, mate?"

Edward nodded as he walked away. "Glad to have you aboard, Sam," he said over his shoulder. *He is mad.*

Edward moved on to the crew cabin, just below the gun deck. The crew cabin was empty now, and he couldn't see Henry anywhere.

Perhaps Henry is still in the mess hall.

Hammocks lined the crew cabin bow to stern—two hundred forty-eight altogether. A few beds were also built into the side of the hull at intervals. At the stern was a door leading to the mess hall, and at the bow was another door locked from use.

Five in total. I have half a ship thanks to that Benjamin Hornigold. Edward gazed at the dim wooden estate he now owned, taking in the smells and sounds of his ship. The vessel creaked and groaned as it swayed over the waves. The smell of pine and salt air mixed in his nostrils; it was distinct, and familiar, as if he had smelled the same thing before somewhere.

Well, he did provide me half a beautiful ship at least. Edward leaned against the wall of the crew cabin deck, gazing at the *Freedom.*

His ship. His *Freedom.* His home.

"You look so much like your father, Edward," a voice said behind Edward.

He turned to see John, feeling a stab of melancholy at hearing John's compliment and thinking of his father. He managed a small smile. "Was there something you needed, John?"

"Uhh… yes, Captain. There is something that we should discuss in p-private, if you please."

"Certainly." Edward followed John a short distance to the only spot on the ship they could have a private conversation—the galley.

The galley had a swiveling door for easy entrance to the mess hall. Various pots and pans hung on hooks overhead, and plates were stacked on closed shelves. On the port side was a pantry filled with plenty of food; lemons, limes, salted meats, and exotic spices were some of the treasures left by Hornigold or taken from the marines.

"So what is this about, John?"

John reached into his pocket. "This," he said as he pulled out a piece of paper folded in quarters. "This slipped my mind until it fell from my pocket. I found it nailed to the front of the quarterdeck after our mysterious friend Benjamin left me the keys to the *Freedom* for you."

Edward took the paper, unfolded it, and read: "To whomever owns this ship—Salutations. I am the previous owner of this fine ship and to you I present a game to prove yourself worthy. On the back of this paper is a clue to finding the first missing key to one part of the *Freedom* along with a bit of 'incentive' to sweeten the teeth."

Edward turned over the paper, and sure enough, there was more writing. It was in the form of a cryptic puzzle.

From two ports of two crescent moons, two and two islands north and north northwest. Two by two islands, two by two tests. Two by two crews, one of wit, one of grit. Each test gains one key for the chest. Bring the keys and find the chest in the belly of the fifth.

Edward lowered the paper and frowned. "John, I don't want you to tell anyone about this, all right?"

"I promise I won't tell a soul, Captain. But... what does it mean?"

"I don't know..." *A riddle to some treasure, probably.* With misgivings, Edward pocketed the paper. "Let us forget about that for now, as a question came to me that I've been meaning to ask. Why are you deciding to stay with me, after what has happened?"

"It was because of you I joined this crew, Edward, and it is that same reason why I am still here."

"Me! Why me, John?"

"Because you're your father's son. He was my captain years ago, and now you are my captain. Besides, now that we're in this mess you'll need me even more. I promised your father I would protect and help you in any way I could."

"John, are you sure you'll be able to handle being on this ship? There will be battles if we have to escape from marines."

"Edward, I know sometimes I can be a bit... timid. But it's different when I'm in an actual battle. I was in the Nine Years' War, you know?" He seemed lost in thought for a moment. "I know how to load and shoot a gun, and you can count on me outside battle as your quartermaster as well."

Edward paused a moment, seeing John with different eyes. *It is true. When the crew was in their mutinous phase, he held his sword even steadier than I did.* "All right then, John. You can stay. Don't let me regret my decision."

"Yes, Captain."

"So what was my father like as a whaling captain?"

"That's right, you were too young to join us back then. He was a true man of the sea. No matter what storm came, your father held everything together. He was an inspiration to the crew, and some say he was the best captain they ever had."

"So what happened?"

John's nervousness set in again. "N-no one knows. He had been acting odd, and then one day he left his regular crew and went on a journey with another group of sailors. They say a storm caught them and killed the whole crew." Edward's face fell at the words. John pulled the younger man's chin back up. "If you ask me or anyone who was on his crew, they'll tell you there's no way your father would have died. He was too stubborn. He's p-probably out there somewhere, trying to find his way home."

Edward scrubbed at his nose and clapped the quartermaster on the back. "Thank you, John." *I'll find you, Father. I'll bring you home, wherever you are.*

John looked for a moment like he wanted to say something else, but instead he gave a grin and a sloppy salute, and then left to let him have a moment alone.

...

Henry was on the main deck and Sam was passing by with a piece of cheese in his hand. "Sam?"

"What is it, mate?" Sam asked before taking a bite of his cheese.

"When we reach Port Royal, I want you off this ship. Permanently."

Sam snorted, a bit startled but unfazed. "No," he answered in a flat tone, starting to walk away, but Henry grabbed his arm.

"Why don't you drop your hand from me arm before I remove it meself?"

"I want you gone," Henry seethed. "You're more trouble than you're worth, so find another ship. I don't care what you do afterward, but I don't want to see you again."

Sam leaned in. "Well, mate, you ain't the captain, now, is ya?" he said with a grin. "You got a problem with me, take it up with him. Otherwise, piss off. I don't got time for nancies like you."

Sam pulled his arm away and sauntered off to the foredeck.

"You'd better watch it, Sam," Henry called after him. "The next time you decide to take your frustration out on someone, I'll be there. You won't like it when that happens."

Sam looked back over his shoulder. "Oh. I'm sure I will, mate. I'd like to see what you think you can do." Sam tore another piece off his cheese and shot Henry a cocky smile.

Henry watched the younger man walk away. Moments later Edward walked up to him from the crew cabin.

"What were you talking with Sam about?"

"Oh, nothing… You wanted to talk with the crew about the spoils today, didn't you?"

"Yes, but there's something else."

Edward pulled out a piece of paper he had folded up in his pocket. It was the paper John had found on the ship when he first tried to sell it. He handed it to Henry.

"What's this?"

"Open it up and take a look. John just showed it to me. He found it on the ship before we set sail."

Henry unfolded the sheet with care and examined it, back and front, all the while muttering to himself. "Sweeten the teeth... Two by two islands, two by two tests... One key for the chest... Belly of the fifth?" He cocked his brow. "You know what this is?"

Edward whispered, "It's the location of one of the keys to the ship. Seeing as how this is a pirate ship, it might be a safe bet there's treasure too." He smiled at Henry's widened eyes.

"This is..." Henry started to say, but stopped himself. "This is unbelievable, Edward! Do you know where it's talking about?"

"No idea."

Henry read the cryptic message over once more. "Well, since our current helmsman plans to leave, we won't bother showing him. Our new one will have to make sense of it."

Edward smiled widely. "Go gather the crew together, would you?"

Henry nodded and, with William's assistance, gathered the crew on the main deck. They and John then joined Edward on the quarterdeck.

Henry did the talking.

"It will take John a little more than a week to sell everything we acquired, and then we can divide the spoils. You will all receive a share regardless of your decision to leave or to stay, but you have to be here if you want the money. You can wander around town, but if you're not here when we hand it out, you're given nothing."

The crew of the *Freedom* shouted gleefully their understanding.

"Also, for those who do not want the shares, we would appreciate it if you keep your mouths shut. You know Edward did what he had to; he's not a pirate. For the sake of those who wish to have their fair share, some of whom you no doubt know from Badobos, please leave the authorities out of this."

Edward spoke up at that. "I hope it's clear to you all that I... I didn't mean to bring any of this upon you. You've been a fine crew and... I mean to say, you've earned your reward. All I ask is your understanding."

Many in the crew nodded to Edward, with a fair number of sympathetic looks. Henry dismissed them, and they returned to their duties in a buoyant mood, the thought of money no doubt speeding their hands and feet.

Edward turned to Henry after the crew went back to work. "Let's talk in the galley. We have a few things to discuss in private."

Edward took Henry, John, William, and Sam downstairs to the crew cabin. They walked past the swaying hammocks, past the pine benches and tables of the mess hall, and into the stone and metal kitchen. Sam guarded the door as Edward opened the conference.

Edward leaned against the stove. "We'll leave right after we divide the shares. No later." Edward fixed them all with a grim frown to emphasise his seriousness.

"Do you think someone will still try to turn us in?" asked Henry.

Edward stroked his chin in contemplation. There was one plain-looking sailor in particular he had in mind.

"Frederick. He seems to want retribution."

"It makes sense. He was like that in Badobos too," Henry agreed. "I remember one time he and James had an argument. James' house burned down later in the week. Everyone suspected it was Frederick, but no one could prove it."

"William, would you be able to keep an eye on him? All you'd have to do is stay out of sight, and if he talks with anyone, let us know."

"Yes, Captain."

Edward turned to Henry. "What about the crew? Who will we need?"

"We'll need new able-bodied seamen all around. We should purchase cannons as we could run into a fight on the sea, and we'll need gunners to support them," Henry said. "A new sailing master too, as our current one is leaving us." He scratched his chin, and then ran his fingers though his hair. "A surgeon is a must if we will be getting into battles."

With care, John wrote down everything Henry proposed; he was becoming famous for keeping lists and not neglecting any detail.

"That's a good point, we'll want to keep the guns and gunpowder, but only sell the spices and our bounty from our brief time as whalers." Edward chuckled. "And we can't forget the... disposition... of these crewmembers. They need to know this has been labelled a pirate ship and be so branded when they come aboard." Edward glanced at the door. "Sam mentioned he knew some people who might join."

"I don't trust him," Henry stated, folding his arms. He didn't care that Sam might be listening right outside the door. "He's a troublemaker, and the same goes for anyone he would have join us."

"He scuffled with another crewmember. It's not as if you've never had a temper problem before."

"I don't care. I don't think we should keep him aboard."

"We don't have the luxury of choice. He stays," Edward declared with finality. "Now, anyone else have suggestions?" No one came forward. "Well, Henry and I can first ask around for surgeons when we have his nose examined."

"What? My nose is fine! Never been better. See?" Henry took in several large breaths through his nose, but Edward could tell he was suppressing a wince. He moved from the stove, walked over to Henry, and then flicked his nose. "Ow! Damn you, Edward! That hurts!"

"See? You need to see a surgeon. Everyone else clear on what they are doing?" They nodded in agreement. "On to Port Royal!"

With their plan of action in place, it was a straight sail to Port Royal. After the marine incident had passed they were not far away from port, and soon after they docked the *Freedom* at the farthest end of the harbour of Port Royal. Long before landing they had furled the foresail so none would see the Jolly Roger, and they planned to replace it later when they had new canvas and no prying eyes. Rowers brought the ship in, then retracted their oars at the command of the sailing master to let the *Freedom* slip the rest of the way into port.

They were quite a sight to behold. To begin with, it was most unusual for a frigate to be in the Port Royal harbour. If Edward was a captain of a wealthy merchant ship, he certainly didn't look the part, clothed as he was almost in rags. The crew, if anything, looked even worse.

From the pier, Edward could see much of Port Royal itself. It was midday, and the bazaar was bustling with activity. The smell of meat and vegetables cooking wafted in all the way to their ship. Edward heard vendors hawking their wares, buyers trying to haggle, and locals catching up while shopping. The island was green and lush, and had an abundance of swaying palms contrasting against the stone streets of colonisation.

As the crew was preparing supplies to sell, the harbourmaster met them at the west end of the pier where they had docked. The crew placed gangplanks out on the pier and the harbourmaster boarded without an invitation. Edward went to greet him.

"Hello, and welcome to Port Royal, sirs. No doubt you are in a hurry, so may I have your name, please?" the harbourmaster asked.

Bollocks! What do I tell him my name is? "Edward Hughes. Pleasure to be in your town." Edward shook the harbourmaster's hand.

The harbourmaster returned the handshake while glancing at the ship, the haggard crew, the muskets, and the whaling equipment. Edward could tell that at each glance the harbourmaster became more wary of the newcomers. "There is a docking fee of a piece of eight."

Edward called John and took from him two pieces of eight. He gave both to the harbourmaster with a smile. "Here you are, one piece of eight," he said with much emphasis on the word 'one'.

The harbourmaster looked at the two coins with delight, pocketing one. "Welcome to Port Royal," he said with a smile and a bow.

"Thank you," Edward replied. The man left without another word, writing something in his ledger regarding their ship.

"Captain, are you sure it was wise to b-bribe the man? We don't even know him." John shifted his gaze from the harbourmaster and then back to Edward in quick succession while wringing his hands.

"We ensured his silence."

"How c-can you be sure?"

"Did you see the way he pocketed the money? He won't say anything." Edward turned around to speak to the whole crew. He took a few deep breaths and focused on a few people in the crowd. "Everyone, listen please. I know because of all that has happened some of you want to leave, but I want you to know I appreciate your help in everything you've done here. I'd have any one of you as a drinking mate across the Caribbean and back again."

The crew was silent until Sam yelled, "Hear, hear!" and everyone joined in with a shout. Then they were back at the task of unloading the cargo and piling it up on the pier in preparation for sale.

"Captain, may I make a suggestion?" William asked in his usual formal tone.

"Yes, William, what is it?"

"If we are purchasing cannons, you should buy smaller ones."

Edward folded his arms. "Why would we do that?"

"It makes more sense to have smaller ones on deck. They can be operated by one person rather than the two or more required to operate the larger ones. You can have more cannons in total, and still have money left over. I estimate we can fit ten cannons on each side of the ship. Given market pricing of the whaling equipment, blubber, and spices, you should have money to spare."

Edward thought it over a minute. "John!" John came running. "When you buy our cannons, make them small so one crewman can operate it, ten for each side of the ship. And the necessary ammunition, of course."

"I'll put it on the list, Captain."

"Now, come, Henry. We need to find you a surgeon."

Edward and Henry walked into town and headed to a surgeon who, Sam claimed, didn't ask questions. They wanted to make sure they recruited a person they could trust, as well as one who might be willing to join the crew.

As they moved through town, they could smell the sweet salt air of the sea, grass, perfumed women, and the aroma of roasting meat wafting from various establishments. The closer they got to the surgeon's shop, the less sweet the smell became. They passed shabby houses, dank bars, and ruddy-faced roughs loitering about drunk at midday. Some structures were falling apart and seemed like a strong breeze might push them over. By the time they reached the farthest side of the town, no longer could they smell the salt air, the grass, or the meat, and instead they smelled some foul concoction of mud and rotten food.

"Do you see it anywhere?" Edward asked.

Henry was still rubbing his nose with care. "No… Wait, I think I see it. Over there." He pointed to a doorway in the middle of a stone alley with a sign hanging in front. The dirty, rusted sign read *'barbier chirurgien'* and as it swung in the breeze it made a horrible screeching noise. The door was also in a dilapidated condition with what appeared to be bullet holes strewn about on its surface, and it hung crooked on its rusty hinges. "Are you sure about this, Edward? Sam's information was second-hand. I don't know if we can trust it."

"Only one way to find out." Edward grabbed the handle and pushed at the door. Before he had opened the door a quarter of the way, someone pulled the door inward with his hand still latched to the handle. It dragged him forward and soon he was looking straight down the barrel of a pistol.

"Who sent you, knaves? Speak or be shot. *Tu comprends?*"

Edward spoke as quickly as he could, his hands in the air. "We are here of our own accord, sir."

The eyes of the man holding the pistol darted back and forth between Edward and Henry, and then, popping his head past the doorway, outside to the alley. He pulled the gun away and stepped back.

"Come in, gentlemen."

Edward and Henry shook their heads to each other, and then entered the establishment. "My friend has a—"

"Broken nose," the man said dismissively. "I know this already. Sit down. I need to *expérimenter* something first."

"How did you know his nose was broken?"

"I am observant where others are not," the surgeon said as he worked with something at the back of the room.

Edward and Henry got a good look at the room. It was small and almost barren, and not well kept in the slightest. The wood on the walls was rotting, the floorboards were broken beyond repair, and the only chair in the room was old, dirty, and falling apart.

There was a peculiar smell, like vinegar and pure alcohol, and something else that Edward couldn't put his finger on. He had to cover his nose for the first minute to stifle the smell.

Henry sat down in a tall chair with wool spilling from holes in the upholstery. "I noticed the more than casual rubbing your friend was doing to *son nez*. The redness and swelling around the bridge and left eye suggest he was struck with a rather large blunt object that hit the right side of the face."

Edward's jaw dropped. "That's... impressive."

The surgeon turned around with a flourish and a bow. "Alexandre Exquemelin, at your service." After Alexandre rose from his bow, he lifted his pistol and shot it at the front of the room.

Edward jumped to the left and ducked down. Henry fell off the side of the chair and took cover behind it. "Ed, are you all right?" Henry yelled.

"Yes, I am fine. Were you shot?"

A moment passed. "No."

Edward rose back to his full height of six feet four inches, flexing his muscles in an attempt to intimidate the Frenchman in front of them. "What are you bloody doing, man? You could have hit us!"

"Relax, *mon ami*. I added rifling in the barrel, it's perfectly safe." Alexandre loaded another bullet into the pistol.

Edward looked to the front of the room and noticed a dead pig hanging from the ceiling. The pig was riddled with bullet holes and cuts that appeared to be from a fencing sword.

Alexandre aimed once more at the pig and fired. The noise of the gun was deafening in the small room. Edward was already having trouble hearing after the first shot, and the second compounded the problem. "To answer your question, I am trying to make a *balle* that is piercing and more accurate. So far, the *expérimenter* is going well."

Edward took a better look at the Frenchman. His thin jawline was clean-shaven and he had a prominent nose, but his eyes were what Edward noticed most: Baggy, dark, sullen eyes, set deep in his bony face. They gave the impression he would as soon slice your neck open as shave your beard. Those eyes were wild and unpredictable, and it made Edward's skin crawl almost as much as the place in which he now found himself.

I suppose that attribute is perfect on a pirate ship.

Henry sat back in the chair at Alexandre's beckoning, but eyed Edward with worry. Before he could voice his concerns, Alexandre was on him.

Alexandre grabbed Henry's nose and yanked it hard to the left. There was a distinct cracking noise, followed by a range of colourful expletives from Henry. "Ow! Ahh that hurt, you bloody git! I thought you were a surgeon! Bugger! That *smarts*!" Henry kept rubbing his nose as he muttered some Welsh curses for good measure.

"There, that should heal properly now. Is that all, *messieurs*?"

Henry gave Edward the evil eye, saying without words that he didn't want this man on the ship, but Edward shrugged his shoulders. "There is another matter which we would like to discuss with you."

Before Edward could continue, Alexandre held up his hand to silence him. "Let me guess. The salty, sweaty smell on you means you were recently at sea. You want me to join your *rassemblement?*"

Edward's and Henry's jaws slowly dropped as they listened. "That's… exactly right. How did you…?"

"How did you do that?" Henry finished, dumbfounded.

"*Je viens se dire cela.* I'm observant." Alexandre's strange face softened into a smile of satisfaction. "Now: to answer the question you have no need to ask… You have to tell me what type of vessel you're on and what I'll be treating onboard. That will determine my answer."

"Why?"

"Because I want excitement. I want *défi*. I want to see things you cannot see in normal everyday work. Can you provide, *messieurs*? The smell of gunpowder on you tells me you can."

Edward and Henry looked at each other. "You want to tell him?" Edward asked.

"Me? Why don't you tell him?"

"I don't want to tell him, you tell him."

"You're the captain, you tell him."

"Tell me what, *messieurs*?" Alexandre jumped in.

Edward sighed. "Fine. I'll tell him," he said. "We are the right people for you, Alexandre." Edward whispered as if someone might hear him and place him under arrest. "We've been labelled pirates. More than enough excitement, I'd say."

"*Vous plaisantez*! I've been dying for a chance like this! I knew moving here was the right idea. So much excitement! It will be *un grand plaisir* to join you."

Alexandre took a large bag from under his desk and loaded his surgical and barbering equipment into it. He also grabbed a sack to hold an extra set of clothes and his experiment with bullets, excluding the pig.

"You'll be labelled as a pirate after this, you know."

"Oui. I know that, *monsieur…*?"

"Henry."

"*Monsieur* Henry. Labels mean nothing to me. I merely wish to enhance my skills and keep things interesting. Caring for the elderly or *les enfants*, it is boring. The life of a pirate is full of excitement and danger. I have no incertitude caring for you while in the midst of battle will also be exciting. Now if that is all, we should be leaving quickly. What is the name of your ship in case we are separated?"

In case we get separated? "It's called the *Freedom*. Why would we be separated?"

No sooner had the words left Edward's mouth than Alexandre's door burst open with a crash and fell off its hinges. Two burly men, thugs who seemed to be used to heavy drinking, busted through.

"That's why," Alexandre answered.

"Alexandre, you filthy French pisspot! You stole all our money!" The man on the right, closest to Edward, pointed to Alexandre as he spoke.

Edward turned to Alexandre, his brow raised. "What's he talking about?"

"I'll tell you what I'm talking about. That arsehole put something in our drinks that made us fall asleep, and then he stole our money. Now he'll pay. *You'll* need a surgeon after this, Alexandre!"

"It is a simple *malentendu* really. It was an experiment, and *messieurs*, you were excellent subjects." The man walked to Alexandre, not swayed by his words. Edward and Henry were ready to fight, but didn't know what to do, as they weren't the ones being targeted. Alexandre kicked the man's groin hard, sending him to the floor. Then he punched the other, knocking him back. "*Courons!* Run, *messieurs!* The experiment has gone awry!" Alexandre yelled as he rushed out the door.

Edward and Henry ran out the door as well. "Let's split up. I'll go to the right. Meet at the ship!"

"Right!" Henry yelled, and then he and Alexandre headed back to the main street and on to the *Freedom.*

The men who were after Alexandre ran out soon after, but they didn't see Henry and the surgeon leaving on the main street. They saw only Edward, stepping off onto a side street. They chased after him, hot on his heels.

Damn! Why are both of them chasing me? I thought they would split up!

Edward ran as fast as he could. He bobbed and weaved in and out of the streets, darting around people and wagons and vendors' stalls. He was making good speed, but the two large men kept pace with him. They were light on their feet for their size, and smashed and shoved anything in their way. Edward tried to pass between buildings to lose them, but they didn't slow down. He didn't dare look back, but the grunts and shouts from bystanders told him they were still at his heels.

And then he tripped over a rainwater barrel in an alley.

They were on him at once, picking him up off the ground and throwing him against the nearest wall. There was no one around to help him.

"Where's Alexandre? You obviously know each other. Where do you hide out?"

"We arrived in Port Royal not a few hours before and just met him. We needed the work of a cheap surgeon and then you busted in."

"Yea, and I'm the Queen of England," one of the men said with sarcasm dripping from every word. "We'll just have to make you talk." He punched Edward in the stomach, and Edward doubled over and fell to the ground. Then the two of them cracked their knuckles and smiled.

"Welcome to Port Royal."

4. PUSH VS. SHOVE

Edward was staring into the faces of men he didn't know, for a theft he didn't commit, involving a man he had met not ten minutes before.

When I get my hands on Alexandre, he will pay.

"You'd better start talking or we start breaking bones."

Edward said nothing as he struggled to find a way to escape. It was then that he noticed Henry sneaking up behind the men. Henry grabbed an empty glass bottle from the ground in his hands and nodded to him.

The thugs were about to pounce on him when Henry smashed the bottle down on the head of the one on the right. The other man turned to the noise, and Edward took his chance and punched the second man straight in the jaw. The man's head was flung to the side, and down he went.

Before it had even started, the fight was over.

Edward clasped hands with Henry and thanked him for the help. "I thought you and Alexandre were headed to the ship."

"We were, until I noticed that we weren't being followed. Alexandre said he could find the ship on his own, so I came back to save you. Just like I always do," Henry added, folding his arms.

"Yea, yea, rub it in." Edward pushed his friend, then thanked him again. "Let's head back to the ship. I want to have some words with this surgeon."

When they returned to the ship, they found Alexandre there, sitting pretty on the port railing. When Alexandre noticed them he rose to his feet.

"Ah, *mon Capitaine*, I trust you are well?"

Edward glared at Alexandre. "No thanks to your friends. I was trapped in an alley but Henry saved me. Do you mind explaining why those men wanted your head?"

"*Toutes mes excuses.* As I mentioned to them, it was merely a misunderstanding. I made a... *préparation* causing the men to fall asleep. It worked and my experiment was *complète*. However, when I left, someone must have stolen their money. It was not I, but the men assume. *Incorrectement*, I might add."

Edward shook his head, exasperated. "It matters not. Find a place for your things in the crew cabin."

"*Votre souhait est mon commandement*," Alexandre said with a flourish, and then descended into the lower decks.

"So now what?" Henry asked.

"We'll rent a room at an inn and stay there for the time being. Tomorrow we can search for a sailing master."

"Pray to God everything else goes smoothly, friend." Henry patted Edward on the back. "I know I have."

"Pray he fixes your nose. I would like to have a first mate that at least looks intimidating. Right now a slight breeze could break you."

"Oh? And who saved you from a couple of drunkards? At least I took my punishment."

Edward slowly brought his hand up in a manner suggesting he was going to flick Henry's nose again.

"Don't you dare."

Edward and Henry had a good chuckle before leaving the ship to find an inn. They found many just above the harbour, and Edward decided to look at one alone first and left Henry standing outside. He emerged not ten minutes later and motioned Henry on without a word.

"What was that about?" Henry asked.

"I secured us a room at this inn for the week, but we'll find another to stay at."

Henry cocked his brow. "Why?"

"This way, with William on the prowl and ready to notify us when Frederick makes his move, we can slip into this inn. Frederick will think we're at the next inn, which we'll stay at for the next few days, but he won't find us there."

Henry dwelled on it. "I have to admit, that is clever." Edward smiled at the praise. "For you," he added, for which his captain punched him in the arm.

They both went into the next inn and Edward rented them a room for the next ten days.

The room was what they might have expected for the price: small, well-worn beds, no furniture, rats and bugs everywhere. The smell of sweat and even less savoury fluids emanated from the floors and sheets.

"This is a fine choice a lodgings you've found us," Henry remarked as he scanned the room.

"No one claimed the life of a pirate was glamorous."

"You would do well not to utter the P-word. We aren't pirates, remember? The marines only think we are. Besides, someone might hear you."

"And what of it?" Edward took off his boots and lay down on his bed. Henry did the same and flashed Edward a nasty look.

"So you're fine with it? You're fine with having people think we are pirates?"

"There are some advantages to it."

"This is what I was talking about before," Henry said, his melodic Welsh accent appearing with his anger. "What would Robert think of this? You stole from those marines. You can try and gussy it up however you want, but taking something that isn't yours is theft. Before, I could understand your stance, but now you should stop saying you've been labelled a pirate as though it was unjust."

"I'm not a pirate. We needed to make sure they wouldn't attack us afterwards. Taking their weapons was the only way. If we could have taken their cannons, I would have."

"If you say so, Captain."

Edward ignored the jab and laid his head down. *I shouldn't have to justify my actions. He's a part of this too.*

The two laid in silence as the noises outside the inn died down, and all they could hear were the occasional drunkard and night-birds singing a song. They drifted off to sleep and it washed away the tension between Edward and Henry. After they voiced good mornings, Edward got down to business.

"We only need to find ourselves a sailing master and our job will be done." He touched his hand to the pocket that held Benjamin Hornigold's mysterious gift. *Then we can start on this.*

"We need one who's not only willing to take the position, but has the necessary fortitude for it. Where will we find a man of such disposition?"

The salty air blew at Edward's face, and the sun hit his eyes as it inched up on the horizon. "Well, we are near the pier. What say we start our journey here and work our way up?"

First they returned to the ship and told some trustworthy crewmembers where they were staying. They were to keep it secret from all except William, should he need Edward or Henry. Then the two traversed the entire pier, asking if anyone knew of any sailing masters craving work. Finding no success, they took their search to town, but after three days they still hadn't found anyone for the position.

Everything else seemed to be proceeding according to plan. John was nowhere to be seen until the fourth day, but the results of his efforts were apparent. New crewmembers were showing up by the dozens. From riggers to gunners, more showed up with each day's passing, and each one was more capable than the last. Some appeared shady, but hardy and eager to leave shore nonetheless.

Also new to the ship were the cannons. Just as planned, they were able to buy twenty small ones and still had a good chunk of money left over.

When Edward and Henry weren't searching for a sailing master, they familiarised themselves with the new crewmembers. They wanted to know who the newcomers were and what skills they had. Edward thought certain men might be trouble later on, but he couldn't be picky about the crew at this time.

Close to night on the fourth day, John and William both returned to the ship with urgent concerns. Edward, Henry, John, William, and Sam all met in the galley once again for a private meeting.

John and William said simultaneously: "We have a problem." They looked at each other, but William nodded to John to go first.

"I heard in t-town that Port Royal has anti-piracy laws that are s-strictly enforced," he said, wiping sweat from his bushy brows.

"Anti-piracy laws?" Edward frowned.

John nodded. "Port Royal isn't the p-pirate safe haven Sam made it out to be. The new governor appointed in Jamaica set up anti-piracy laws. If we're found out, we'll all be h-hung, Captain." The man was shaking.

Edward turned to Sam, his arms folded.

"Don' look at me! I 'aven't been 'ere in years. Not since the war ended."

"That's exactly when it happened. Queen Anne appointed him specifically to rid Jamaica of pirates after the war ended."

"How soon can we leave?"

"This very minute should it please you, Captain. We've sold everything and bought all we need; all that remains is to divide the spoils among the crew."

"Very good. We'll divide the spoils as soon as we find a sailing master, and then leave immediately. No one knows about us except the harbourmaster, and as long as he continues to cover for us we'll be all right."

John moved to speak, but William cut him off. "That is where my problem comes in. Frederick made his move. He knows of where you're staying in Port Royal, and the marines plan to arrest you tonight. He's hoping to avoid having to send them to the ship, but I think they plan to make either him or you talk."

"Bollocks! How long would you say we have?"

"Provided you and Henry aren't captured tonight… a day or two at most."

"We have need of a sailing master before we leave. There's no other way. None of us are skilled enough to read the seas." Edward stood and paced the room.

"C-Captain?" John said meekly.

"We need options. Plans to abscond."

"Captain?" John repeated a little louder.

"How are we to make it to the next port without someone to guide us? I need suggestions, mates. If you have any ideas now would be a good time."

"Captain!" John yelled.

"Yes, John, what is it?"

"I may have a solution. I happened upon a sailing master who may be willing to leave these shores, but…"

"Great! John, you've proven yourself time and time again! William, Sam, prepare everything for departure in the morning! Tomorrow at the break of dawn we set sail!"

Edward, full of purpose, left the ship to find John's sailing master. He had John guide him to the man's house, and dragged Henry along. He didn't want to waste any time in this place which was suddenly so dangerous to men like them.

They approached a rather secluded home at the peak of the hill on Port Royal. With bare walls and a flat roof and only one level, it looked more like a warehouse than lodging. The lawn was unkempt, grass growing everywhere, and the windows were caked with dirt.

"This is the place?" Edward asked, unimpressed.

"Yes, Captain, this should be the one, if my information is correct."

"How can we be sure he'll join us? Aside from the upkeep of his home, he seems like a normal everyday citizen, from what John mentioned." Henry peered at the fading sun. Night was creeping up on them. William would be dividing the spoils at that moment, and Sam letting everyone know when they'd be leaving. Most would stay the night on the ship, Edward hoped.

"We'll have to do our best to convince him, won't we, Henry?" Edward knocked on the door to the house. He waited a minute, and then knocked again.

"Who is it?" a voice asked from behind the door.

"My name is Edward. I have heard there is a sailing master living here. I'd like to speak to him."

There was a pause on the other side. "What about?"

"I'm a captain. I'm here to discuss a position on my ship. May we enter?"

Another pause, and then: "Please wait a moment." Edward could hear someone shuffling and picking something up, then a clicking noise. "Come in."

Edward shrugged to John and Henry and then opened the door, only to walk right into the barrel of a musket. *Oh shit!* He dropped to the floor and covered his head. The noise of a gun firing filled his ears. Then he heard a struggle and the same voice he had heard from behind the door saying, "No! Let go!"

"It's all right, Ed, you can get up now."

Edward pulled his arms down from atop his head, hoisted himself up from the floor, and looked the shooter over. It was a young man, about the same age as Edward and Henry, sitting slumped in a wheelchair. Ragged, tatty clothes covered his small frame. His legs were thin, but his arms appeared strong. He had dark circles under his eyes, and Edward thought that the man had long ago lost his hope in this life, and over time it had given him a perpetual slouch in his chair.

"Why did you shoot at me?"

"Humph." The young man folded his arms and pursed his lips.

"Fine. John, Henry, clearly we won't meet a decent sailing master here. Let's leave. If we're quick we can find someone else. Good day, sir." Edward left, with Henry and John following right behind.

"What? That's it?"

Edward turned back to the man. "You shot me! You expect me to stay and have tea with you?"

"No, no, that's not… I'm sorry. This is a misunderstanding. Please, sir, let me explain," he said. The young man looked genuinely contrite, and upset with himself over his anger.

Edward was dubious and furrowed his brow. "Fine, but this better be a damned good explanation, mate." He walked over to a low table in the house, and the others followed. The man motioned for them to sit down in the—to put it nicely—*modest* couch and chairs available.

"So you truly are a captain?"

"Yes."

"And you're really looking for a sailing master to guide your ship?"

"Yes. Now can you please explain yourself?"

"I'm sorry. I... I'm in debt, and I thought you were collectors. I don't have many visitors. As you can tell, I've had my share of hardships. But my biggest problem is no one will hire me. So if you are here to offer me a job, I would be more than willing to take it."

Edward waited a moment before speaking. "How long have you been in debt to these... collectors?"

"Not long. But for these types 'not long' is too long."

"So why should I hire you to sail my ship?"

"I've studied the science of sailing in great detail, I pride myself on my ability to read clouds, and I know everything needed to run a ship." The man's eyes lit up with a hope long suppressed. "If you take me on, you'll never find a better sailing master. No one has more knowledge and intuition than I have. And no one could be more loyal or more dedicated."

Edward thought for a moment. "Any specific conditions for joining?"

The man thought on the question a moment. "Yes, there is one... My fourteen-year-old sister has to come with me. I can't leave her here."

"Done," Edward announced before Henry and John could object. "But I have two conditions of my own."

The man was smiling and almost on the verge of tears. It was clear he hadn't had a job in some time, and sailing was his passion.

"Name them," he said.

"First, I know not how my men will react to having a woman aboard. It's a common superstition that it's bad luck to bring one out to sea. Not mine, but I'm not the only person aboard. Dress her in boy's clothes, cut her hair, whatever is necessary. Second, you'd best not have any objections to you and your sister being in battle, as we've been labelled pirates."

"Edward!" Henry yelled.

"A pirate ship? You're pirates?"

Edward threw his hands up at Henry. "It's easier just to say it!" Then, to the young man: "Not exactly. We were *accused* of piracy, and we may end up in danger because of it. If you've no desire for the life, then you're free to stay here and await the collectors. The choice is yours: the freedom of the seas, or slavery to money."

The man thought about it for a while. His struggle was evident. "I have one more condition."

"Oh?" Edward asked with raised brow.

"If we meet the pirate Calico Jack, or any of his subordinates, we will kill them." He spoke of killing as if it were a business transaction.

"And why are we to kill this Calico Jack and his men?"

"My reasons are my own. I need for you to promise me if we meet him or any of his men, we will kill them."

Edward thought about it for a moment. "Done." They shook hands, sealing their deal of death.

"Pack your things, only essentials, and be ready to leave in the early morning. We're setting sail at dawn."

"Understood… Captain." The man smiled.

"Oh, and it would be good to have your name."

"Ah. My name is Herbert Blackwood. My sister's name is Christina Blackwood."

"All right then, Herbert, I'll be back here early in the morning and we'll escort you to our ship. Be ready."

"Understood, Captain."

Edward stood and left the house without saying another word. As he left the house, the last rays of light shining upon him, he felt elated that they now had a sailing master.

"What the hell are you doing?" Henry said on their way back to town.

"What are you talking about?" Edward kept walking as the others followed.

"What am I talking about?" Henry counted off the offences on his fingers. "I'm talking about hiring a cripple, bringing a girl aboard our ship, and agreeing to kill a ruthless band of pirates? Are you out of your bleedin' mind?"

Edward stopped and turned to Henry. "I'm helping this man and his sister. My father never had a problem with women aboard as long as they pulled their weight, and neither do I. Besides, we need him. We need to leave right away, and this man appears to be an expert sailing master. Shall I remind you that I make the decisions here, Henry, not you?"

"You think they'll be safer? On a pirate ship? The man's a cripple, Edward. What do you expect will happen during a battle? What if he falls over? Who will pick him up? What if we're in a storm and he can't stick to the wheel?"

"Enough, Henry." Edward resumed walking.

"And what about the girl? I don't care if your father was fine with it, you know it's bad luck to have a woman aboard. If the crew finds out, she'll be thrown overboard at the first sign of trouble. Either that or they'll rape her. You think the crew we've gathered is as noble as you? Don't be a fool, Edward!"

Edward turned to Henry once more. He pointed his finger in his face. "I said enough, Henry! Both of them are joining the crew and that's final. If you don't like it, then maybe you're on the wrong ship!"

Henry's expression changed from anger to surprise to hurt. After a few moments, he walked away. Not in the direction of the inn, and not to the pier either. Edward stood and watched him leave. John stood with his mouth agape as if he wanted to say something, until Edward motioned to resume their walk to the inn.

"W-what do you want me to do, Captain?"

"Leave him. If he wants to have a fit right before we set sail, then fine. He knows when we weigh anchor. Prepare some men to escort Herbert and Christina to the ship in the morning. Make sure they're armed."

"Yes, Captain. B-but what about you? Do you need someone to watch over you tonight? You know, with Frederick and all?"

"No, I'll be fine. I want to be alone anyway." *Henry just needs to cool off ... And maybe I need to cool off as well.*

• • •

Edward watched from his room on the second floor as the marines went into the other inn. He could tell they wanted to be silent and catch him by surprise. But Edward was ready. He wouldn't be found in that inn. He was down the road, at the inn he had set aside at the beginning of the week.

After Edward watched them enter the decoy inn, he went back to sleep, satisfied that they were not onto him. In his slumber he did not hear the screams from the other man they *had* found there.

• • •

Early the next morning, William, John, and four other crewmates went to Herbert's house and helped him back to the ship. Edward met them on the pier by the *Freedom*. He could see Herbert in his wheelchair and a young one at his side. *That must be Christina.*

Edward waved to them and turned to William as they approached. "You didn't see anyone suspicious on your way here, did you?"

"Nothing worth noting, Captain. None are up at this hour. We chose a longer route back, but it kept us away from prying eyes."

Edward nodded in satisfaction. *I expected nothing less, William, but these skills make me wonder who you were before joining our crew.* Edward walked over to Herbert. "How are you feeling? Must have been a while since you were last on a ship."

Herbert smiled. "And a fine ship it is…" he said as he gazed at his new home. "You are right, it has been a while. My brother Christopher and I are a little nervous."

Edward stroked his chin. *Christopher… Nice touch.* "Don't worry, everything will go smoothly. Excited, Christopher?" Edward asked to the young one beside Herbert. The girl nodded, but didn't say anything. Edward could see blue eyes and short blond hair sticking out from beneath a cap. *She is young. I hope I haven't made a mistake.* Edward felt a pang of regret at the fight he'd had with Henry over this, but suppressed it. "Come, let's get you on board."

Edward, Herbert, and Christina went up the gangplank onto the main deck. They were greeted by various men of the *Freedom*'s crew loading supplies, packing things away, and arranging the rigging. Some were reeling in the anchor, while a few stragglers were just arriving.

"Well, Herbert, what do you think?"

"It's beautiful. Thank you, Captain." Herbert's gaze travelled the length of the ship, but then went back to shore. He scanned the pier and docks with a noticeable look of concern.

"As long as you're aboard this ship, you'll be free. They won't find you here," Edward reassured him quietly.

"I know. You live one way for so long, it's tough to change."

"Well, you're part of our family now. We'll take care of you."

"You're different, you know."

Edward laughed. "What do you mean?"

"A regular captain wouldn't want someone like me aboard his ship, especially after I shot at him. I know I wouldn't."

Edward knelt down next to Herbert and smiled. "Well, I'm not a regular captain then, am I?"

"No, I guess not." Herbert smiled back. As he boarded, he wheeled his chair straight to the aft stairs and stopped.

Edward saw the problem. "Need someone to help you?"

"No, I have someone." Herbert hopped off his wheelchair, and his sister grabbed it and carried it to the top of the cabin.

Several crewmembers watched as Herbert climbed the stairs, one by one, accompanied by what they took to be an adolescent boy. They shook their heads as they carried on with their work, some making rude comments to each other. Herbert pressed on, ignoring them. After a few moments of hard labour, he made it to the top, sat back in his wheelchair, and took his position at the ship's wheel. He showed Edward his thumb, saying he was ready to work.

We need to find a better system for Herbert to move across the ship. Edward became lost in thought trying to think of something that would help Herbert manoeuvre around.

John grabbed Edward's attention. "Captain, I have something to show you."

"What is it, John?" Edward followed John's prompts into the crew's quarters.

"This."

John pointed to a set of clothes hanging against the wall. They were garments meant for a man of the sea, and a man of rank: a pair of long boots, black breeches, a white tunic with half-length sleeves, a black leather vest, a knee-length black coat and, to top it off, a black tricorn hat befitting a captain. The smell of new leather accentuated the quality.

"John! These are incredible! Wherever did you find them?" Edward examined the clothing, amazed at the workmanship.

"I bought them at one of the local shops. I thought it would be appropriate for you to have something good to wear as captain. You have to be a figure of authority and an inspiration to the crew. I hope they fit you well."

"These are… for me?"

"Why yes, Captain. No one should wear that hat but you."

Edward picked up the hat and examined it, smiling. "I'll put it on right away!"

"Hurry, your crew awaits." John left Edward to change into his fine new clothes.

Edward soon emerged from the lower decks wearing the clothes, feeling that he would be able, for the first time, to present to his crew the visible image of authority.

"It suits you," John said.

"Thank you, John." Edward inspected the assembled crew for someone he had not seen since the day before.

"Looking for Henry, Captain?" John asked.

"I guess he's made his decision…" he said.

His eyes were cast to the sole of the ship, and he felt a wrench in his heart. The two of them had been inseparable for many years, and in a few short moments it was over. They might not see each other ever again, and over a foolish argument. Edward thought to run out looking for Henry, but his pride steadied his feet.

Edward let out a shaky sigh. "Ready the sails before anyone else makes the same decision. Or before we're discovered."

"Right, Captain."

Edward heard a couple of crewmembers boarding at the last minute, talking about something that drew his attention.

"You there!" Edward shouted.

"Yes, Captain?"

Misplaced anger welled within Edward. "What is so important that you were almost late for departure?"

The two men explained hastily. "Well, beggin' yer pardon, Captain. It was about a hangin' they suddenly announced. It's set for noon today. They say some unlucky sod of a pirate was caught. At least the ones like us know not to be flauntin' our nature about."

Edward felt a pang in his stomach. "Who is it being hanged?"

"Uhh, I think it was two actually. Fred something, and... who was the other? Henry, I believe."

The words pierced like a knife. Edward spun around and looked at John, who had heard every word. They both knew beyond doubt the Henry the men were talking about was their Henry.

Edward's best friend, Henry Morgan, was about to be hanged.

5. A TRIP TO THE GALLOWS

The sun was nearing noon over Port Royal Point. The point was a finger of land projecting out into the sea, ending in a high bluff. It was much like the one Henry, Edward, and Robert had climbed as boys in Badobos. Today a crowd of more than three hundred gathered inside the stone enclosure at the peak, with still more spilling out of the arches and onto the grassy hill. Henry and Frederick stood on a wooden platform at the back of the square, nooses around their necks, waiting for the inevitable. The hot sun beat down on them and the salt air blew in their faces. Adults and children alike were jeering and throwing vegetables and fruit at them.

Ironic it would end at a place like this, Henry thought, remembering the bluff and his friends back home. He scanned the crowd, and he could see the disgust and rage in their faces. *I didn't even do anything, and yet they hate me. I wonder how many innocent people have stood here like this. There wasn't even a trial.* Someone threw a cabbage and it hit him square in the jaw, missing his nose by an inch.

Frederick was right beside him, stone-faced but shaking. "I'll haunt you after I die," he threatened.

"This was your doing," Henry spat. "William followed you and saw you talking with the authorities. What I don't understand is how you ended up here if you sold us out."

"I refused to tell them the name of the ship you were on because some of my friends were still on it. So they accused me of conspiring with pirates. But if it wasn't for your friend Edward, we wouldn't be in this situation."

Henry clenched his teeth, hot fury on his cheeks. "If you had kept your mouth shut then we wouldn't be here either, now would we?"

A marine rammed the butt of his rifle into Henry's stomach. Frederick smiled, but the officer did the same to him. "Stow it, you two!"

Damn! Why did Edward and I have to argue over something so stupid? If I hadn't of been so angry I would have remembered to leave the decoy inn.

Someone in the mob caught Henry's eye—a man dressed in black garb like a captain of a ship was strolling through the crowd. He bore several weapons, but no one seemed to notice or care. The man stopped just shy of the podium and then lifted his face.

Edward? Is that Ed? What the hell is he doing here? He's going to get himself killed! Henry stared at Edward, and the man smiled and winked at him. Then he disappeared into the crowd again, weaving ever closer to the stairs of the podium. *No, you stupid sod! Leave me! I'm not worth it!* Henry searched the crowd and could make out a few other familiar faces. John, William, and Sam were all there. *There's probably more of them too, the bleedin' idiots! They'll die trying to save me.* Henry forgot about his own plight and could think only of the danger to his friends. *What are they planning to do?*

The militia prodded the crowd to part so the magistrate of Port Royal could walk to the podium in front of the gallows. The militia kept the crowd at bay while he climbed the steps. The magistrate was a large man accustomed to a life of ease. He carried himself with an air of superiority to the rabble gathered for the show, and especially to Henry and Frederick.

At a gesture of his hands, the crowd grew quiet and he began his speech. The man droned on about the supposed villainy that Henry and Frederick had participated in—none of it true, but it riled the crowd up regardless. It culminated in the magistrate sweeping his arm through the air in a grand flourish as a sign to the executioners. They stepped up to pull the levers that would spell Henry's and Frederick's doom.

Before they could reach the levers, someone in the crowd yelled "Now!" Henry saw Edward and William strike the two guards standing at the foot of the stairs unconscious. There was a loud bang and Henry felt the noose around his neck loosen. Then Edward jumped up to the railing, sprang to where the astonished magistrate stood, and placed his sword at the magistrate's throat.

"Nobody move or this man dies!" he yelled.

The authorities on the wooden podium made a move towards Edward, but William appeared brandishing a pistol, and backed them into a corner

"Tell all your men to move away from the podium!" Edward hissed into the magistrate's ear.

"I'd rather die than help you escape!" the magistrate hissed back.

"I had a feeling you might have that attitude… so I took some precautions to ensure your cooperation. Look toward the eastern entrance to the square."

The magistrate turned his head to the right and noticed his family there. A middle-aged woman in a nice dress of green held two children, a boy and girl of the same age, close to her. Sam was standing behind the three.

"You see that man? He's with me, and he has a gun pointed at your wife right now. If you don't cooperate, she'll die first. Don't push me." Edward pressed the sword harder against the magistrate's throat, drawing blood.

Sweat poured down the magistrate's face and neck. "Men, move away from the podium now!" The guards hesitated in confusion, but then slowly drew back, providing a wide berth around the platform.

"W-what is it you want here?"

"I'm here to save my friend. The one whom you were about to hang."

"Y-you're pirates in league with him? I should have known."

"We aren't pirates, and had there been a trial, that would have become apparent. Instead, you would condemn an innocent man on the word of one you were also going to hang? A fool if I ever saw one."

William went over to Henry and Frederick and released them from their bonds. Then they all walked down the podium with the magistrate in tow. Sam herded the magistrate's family forward, and they all went to the edge of the bluff with the officers following every step of the way.

"What do you plan to do? You're surrounded. Give up," the magistrate said.

"Ha! You think I'd yield now you prat? Don't worry, Magistrate. If I can help it, no one will die today. Not even you."

When everyone reached the edge of the bluff, William nodded to Edward, and he moved right up to the edge, until the magistrate whispered: "Who are you?"

Edward laughed an almost maniacal laugh. "My name is Edward Thatch." Then he shoved the magistrate back into the crowd of shocked soldiers—and he, followed by his companions, jumped off the edge of Port Royal Point.

"Are they insane? Those fools will never survive the drop!" the magistrate yelled as he and the guards ran to the edge to see the pirates plummeting—but not to their deaths. For right there, beneath the bluff, the *Freedom* drifted in the water—and on the aft deck the ship's crew had a sail stretched out for Edward and the others to fall into. Everyone on the bluff was in awe and disbelief.

The crew let Edward and his companions gently down onto the deck. Edward stood up, stretched his muscles and shook his head; he raised his eyes to the people gathered far above on the bluff, and laughed as he waved to them.

The sails of the *Freedom* were dropped soon after, with the foremost sail still showing the Jolly Roger. The pirate ship sailed away, their stolen crewmates in hand.

6. BATTLE-PROVEN

"Captain, they're sending ships out to pursue us." John pointed towards the port.

Edward turned around, a smile still on his face. "I have the notion it's best if we leave, wouldn't you agree John?" Without waiting for an answer, he walked to the edge of the deck overlooking the rest of the ship. "Gentlemen, we've overstayed our welcome in Port Royal. Put those sails in a broad reach and get us out of here!"

The new crew—Edward's new crew—rushed to work in a frenzy. The ship pitched and rolled with the waves, and the men without sea legs were having a hard time navigating the deck. That, coupled with the men not knowing what their duties were, was like too many cooks spoiling the broth. Men were bumping, tripping, and falling on top of each other as they ran to adjust the sails. Soon everyone was yelling and fights were breaking out.

Edward, Henry, and William went straight into the thick of it in an attempt to bring order to the chaos. The three were frantic in issuing orders, breaking up fights, and focusing the crew on the task at hand to save their lives.

A three-masted ship with at least twenty-six cannons was gaining on them from the rear. It didn't have any affiliated markings that denoted it being part of the British Navy and was most likely part of Port Royal's militia. The ship was smaller than the *Freedom* and thus faster and likely more maneuverable.

Edward was fighting to stop two crewmates arguing and to focus them on rigging the sails when he noticed the pursuing ship approaching broadside.

"Cannons!" Edward bellowed, jumping to the floor of the ship and dragging the crewmen he was arguing with down.

A thunder like none he had ever heard before erupted. It sounded very much like the real thing, only quicker, more uniform, and almost hollow. A second volley followed soon after.

A hail of cannonballs hit the *Freedom*. The large, speeding iron ripped and crushed the wood in its path. One hit the starboard railing right next to Edward, breaking the wood to splinters and showering the pieces over his head.

Edward rose on unsteady hands and feet amid the new sounds, moving at a snail's pace. Once on his feet, he glanced about at the other crewmates. Some were still in shock, but others who had been through battles before were quick to man the cannons themselves. Edward couldn't see any injured.

John came over to Edward and shook him by the shoulders. "Captain, we need you on earth! We need to counter."

"Yes," Edward replied. "Yes," he repeated, coming to his senses again. He turned to his crew. The men were still running around with no idea what to do, and Edward's anger was rising. "Men!" he yelled at the top of his lungs. His voice seemed louder than the cannons and the crew stopped what they were doing to look at him. Only then did he notice all the eyes on him, but his anger fought off his nervousness. "Prepare for battle."

With their captain's simple decree, the crew was brought to heel. The gunners gathered powder and cannonballs and manned the cannons. Others grabbed muskets and loaded them with balls, and the rest worked on moving the sails to fill them with wind and regain lost speed.

"Herbert!" Edward called. The new sailing master was sitting at the helm in his wheelchair, and from the look on his face he was well aware of what trial by fire awaited him now. "Keep those cannons from harming us," Edward commanded.

"Aye, Captain," Herbert replied with a grin.

Herbert swung the wheel hard turned the *Freedom* starboard to the south until its stern faced the other ship, presenting less of a target. He shouted to the crew to adjust the sails so they were running with the south wind, and then ordered some other crewmates to lower the jib sails to ease the fore mast.

Edward went up to the stern and pulled out a spyglass. He examined the other ship and could see that its name was *Gentry*, and it was turning forward to renew the chase against the *Freedom*. It would not be long before it caught up. Beyond the enemy ship, Edward could see other ships at the dock of Port Royal preparing to leave.

Damn! If those other ships catch up to us, we're done for. If only our gun deck wasn't locked. Curse you, Benjamin!

Edward ran back down to the main deck and grabbed a musket. *Wait a minute. I don't even know how to load this.* He glanced at the other crewmates, who loaded their muskets as if they were experts, and he could not help but feel like he'd have very little to contribute were it to come to a battle.

John, noticing his captain's plight, came to his rescue. "Here, Captain," he said, gracious enough to offer his own musket. Edward traded his empty weapon for the loaded one. "Keep your wits about you Captain; the other ship is approaching."

Edward turned to see the other ship gaining on them. Herbert had managed to coax enough speed from the sails to slow the *Gentry*'s progress, but soon the smaller ship would overtake the *Freedom*.

Edward went for cover behind the stern stairs. John went behind some barrels lined up against the starboard railing. Henry, musket in hand, crouched near the bow, ducking behind a cannon and peering at the approaching ship.

"Full and by the sails. Prepare to fire starboard!" Herbert yelled.

Fire starboard? Why are we firing? We aren't even close.

As if in answer to Edward's thoughts, Herbert gritted his teeth and flung the wheel hard to port. The ship lurched to the right as the crew gave the sails some slack, easing the turn. With the wind full in the sails, the *Freedom* passed in front of the *Gentry* before they could fire another broadside volley.

"Fire starboard!" Herbert commanded.

The gunners complied; the thunder was more distinct this time, louder, and it hurt Edward's ears.

Most of the iron balls met their mark, hitting the *Gentry* on the bow and starboard side. Some of the cannonballs hit the sea and splashed water into the air around the other ship.

Herbert pulled the wheel back to starboard, turning the ship to port. The *Freedom* evened back out, heading south from Port Royal again. The *Gentry* was still following on their heels, on the port side this time. Soon it would be in line to deliver a volley, despite Herbert's gambit.

The hot, metallic smell of burnt gunpowder tickled Edward's nose and mixed with the salty, sweet sea air and the *Freedom*'s pine planks. The smell of war overpowered the smells of nature, and the combination was unlike anything Edward had smelled before. His heart was pumping as fast as a storm wind turns a weather vane and it invigorated him. He wouldn't easily admit it, but he was enjoying it; the smells, the situation—all of it filled him with the excitement of battle, a thrill he had never known until now.

The two ships were closer now, close enough for bullets. The sound of small pops filtered into Edward's ears, and he noticed the crew on the port side ducking behind cover. He crawled over to the port side and peered out from behind cover. A bullet nicked the railing right next to his head and he dropped back down behind the stairs in an instant. When there was a lull in the pops of bullets hitting the ship, he ventured out of cover once more. This time, no stray bullets came at him. He lifted the musket, a far cry from the whaler's harpoon he was used to, and copied his neighbours in peering down the barrel. He moved the musket around until he was staring at someone down the sights.

As he watched the man down his sights, Edward couldn't pull the trigger. *I have to.* He gritted his teeth. *I will not let them take Henry. I will not let them take my* Freedom. *If I want to keep my* Freedom *and save my crew, this is something I have to do.* He stared down the barrel another moment. *Sorry.* He pulled the trigger and closed his eyes from the sudden burst of light and smoke in his face. The muzzle flared as the bullet left the chamber. When he opened his eyes, they stung and watered from the smoke. He was still staring down the barrel, but he'd lost sight of the man he was aiming at. *Did I hit him?* He would never know for certain.

A rain of cannonballs crashed into the *Freedom*, decimating part of the port-side railing. Edward fell back from the blast of wood splinters in his face, and a cannonball skimmed across the deck five feet from him. It churned up the wooden planks of his home before falling off the other side.

Edward landed on his back and dropped the musket. His face and chest and eyes hurt. He thought he tasted blood in his mouth. The coppery warmth slid on his tongue, and he spat red onto the deck.

Henry ran up next to him. "Are you all right, Ed?" he asked as he grabbed Edward's hand and lifted him up to his feet.

"I am well. Just a scratch. What of the crew?"

"No serious injuries, but we can't keep going like this," Henry said.

Edward nodded in agreement. "We need to escape, and we can't do that unless we take the wind out of the *Gentry*'s sails."

Henry looked like he had been hit in the face. "That's it! We need to take the wind out of their sails."

"What?" Edward asked, dumbfounded. "How?"

"Focus our fire on the sails. No ship can be quick with holes in the canvas."

Edward smiled. "Brilliant." He turned to the crew. "Men! Focus cannon-fire on the sails. We're getting out of here."

The gunners responded with a yell and began raising the mouths of their cannons. The small cannons were easy to use, just as William had predicted, but with an extra hand they were able to fire that much quicker.

The *Gentry* was returning fire at will, and the shots were more erratic now. Where before they took the time to line up the shot and fire as one, now the enemy gunners seemed to be hastier in their aim. Cannonballs fell into the water in front of the *Freedom*, splashing waves onto the deck, or overshot and went between the masts and into the water.

Edward noticed the same thing happening with his crew. They weren't taking time to aim, and their shots were wild. A few grazed the masts of the *Gentry* here and there, but nothing did too much in the way of damage.

Edward thought he recognised the issue. "Herbert," he called, "why is the *Gentry* not circling around us if they're faster?"

Herbert glanced at the enemy ship, then at Edward again. "They've chosen to match our speed, Captain. They must feel they have superior firepower."

Damn! Edward thought. *They must have noticed how we haven't fired anything from the gun deck. We'll never hit the sails with this angle.* Edward used his spyglass to peer at Port Royal once more. He could see ships almost ready for departure. *We need to end this now.* "Crew, listen up!" he yelled. "Move all the cannons to the starboard side and ready for a broadside volley on the enemy sails."

The crew stared at Edward as if he were mad. They had a right to, given that the enemy ship was on the port side, and this was their first time with him in battle. He hadn't earned their trust yet.

We don't have time for this. His anger again pushed through the nervousness he felt at everyone staring at him. "Move it, men!" he bellowed. Despite his youth, his height made Edward an imposing figure and he had a deep voice, and the crew reacted accordingly.

They hopped to their task, helping the gunners move the cannons to the other side of the deck. Being on wheels helped, but they were heavy, lumbering pieces of iron and steel. Edward pitched in and pushed a cannon over to starboard as water and bullets continued to rain down on the crew. The *Gentry*'s aim was improving by the minute, and the ships were inching closer.

As soon as the cannons were secure, Edward looked at Herbert, who nodded in a knowing way.

"Full and by!" The crew changed the alignment of the sails for a close-haul to the wind at Herbert's command. Herbert threw the wheel to starboard, and the *Freedom* obeyed by moving to port and closer to the *Gentry*. "Ready starboard!" Herbert commanded. The gunners loaded the cannons and readied to take aim. The *Freedom*, slowed by the change in sails, moved up behind the *Gentry*. *Freedom's* starboard side faced the enemy's stern, but they weren't parallel. *Gentry* was already starting to turn, anticipating *Freedom's* plan of action. The crew of the *Freedom* understood what was coming next, and knew they had only one chance. "Fire!" Herbert commanded.

Twenty cannons went off almost at once. The sound reverberated off the floorboards of the deck, shaking the ship as it did so. Crewmates with their ears perked soon heard the sound of tearing fabric. Tiny rips opened one after the other in the canvas as the balls went through sail after sail. Not all the cannonballs hit their mark, but enough did so to render large parts of the sails useless.

Herbert straightened out the *Freedom* to be in line with the wind as much as possible while still moving away from Port Royal. "Broad reach the sails," he commanded.

The *Gentry* tried to turn back to give another volley and continue pursuit, but the wind wasn't helping them as it had before. Almost all its sails had holes; the ship was crippled, and there was naught the crew could do about it. By the time it had turned enough to fire cannons again, the *Freedom* was too far away, and they would not catch up again.

Other ships from Port Royal were just leaving dock, but were too far away to even bother taking up the chase.

Edward put away his spyglass and went to the quarterdeck, happy they had been able to escape with Henry and their lives. He patted Herbert on the back. "Good job, Herbert. You've proven yourself to be more than capable today, and I hope the crew realises this as well."

"You are too kind, Captain. I had a reputation to uphold. Best crippled helmsman in the New World." Herbert chuckled at his own joke.

There was significant damage to the side rails and small holes from bullets here and there, but for the most part the crew was unharmed. Henry, John, and William were helping bring the injured over to Alexandre for care, with Sam first in line with a grazed arm. Edward could hear him cursing as Alexandre applied some sort of salve with no concern for his patient's comfort.

Edward's ship was no longer pristine, with broken pieces and smaller chips of wood littering the deck. *Poor* Freedom. *This battle was probably the first of many. We'll need a carpenter to help you with all this damage.*

A crewman began to cheer. His friends joined him, and soon the majority of the shipmates were sharing in victorious revelry.

As each second of the hoots and hollers and pats on the back continued, Edward seethed with more anger. His knuckles went white as his fingernails dug into the quarterdeck railing, and he clenched his teeth together.

Herbert looked concerned. "Uh… Captain?"

Edward ignored Herbert. "Enough!" he shouted. The crew stopped what they were doing, their happiness draining away. "You think you ought be proud of what just happened?" Edward asked without waiting for an answer. "You think your actions are praiseworthy?" He let the question hang in the air. His nerves at public speaking were not able to creep in at all past his ire. "That battle was pathetic. You ought to be ashamed. We could have avoided that battle altogether if you had worked together on the sails and followed directions. Instead you trip over yourselves and fight with each other. I am disappointed in you all."

Some of the crew had the decency to lower their heads in shame, but others did not. The man who started the celebration was one of the men who did not.

"We wus just—" he started.

"Silence," Edward commanded with a look in his eyes that did not allow for discussion. "Your excuses mean nothing to me. If we are to survive on this ship, we will do so as a team. We cannot let what happened today happen again." His words sunk in, with the crew all nodding in agreement save the one he cut down—that one looked angry and embarrassed. "Be prepared. Tomorrow we start training for battle."

7. THE MAP AND THE WOMAN

Henry punched Edward in the arm. "You stupid git! You could have been killed up there! What were you thinking?"

Edward rubbed his arm. "Ouch! I was trying to save your bleedin' arse. If I was privy to the thanks I would get, I would've left you there."

Henry pulled Edward close and embraced him. "Thank you, Ed. You saved my life, and after I had that stupid argument with you, I didn't deserve it. I'm sorry."

Edward patted him on the back. "Don't be foolish... I'm the one who should be apologising. I shouldn't have said the things I did... I'm sorry. And if you're willing to forgive me, there is a position available on the ship for you."

Henry smiled. "First mate?"

"What? Swabbie? Did you say you wanted to be a swabbie? If that's your desire, then that's well and good, but I was going to say first mate."

"I said first mate," Henry said, his tone dry.

"Swabbie it is! The poop deck needs some shining, so get to it!" Edward chuckled.

Henry punched his arm again. "Thanks, Ed. Really."

Edward smiled. "You're my best friend. I would have fought all of England to save you. Even if your sorry arse didn't deserve it."

They laughed together as they watched the crew trim the sails. The *Freedom* was already far enough out, so they wouldn't have to worry about their pursuers overtaking them.

Sam passed by Henry with a grin on his face. He had refused to quit the crew as Henry had told him to, and now was one of the people who had saved his neck. Henry ignored him.

"So what shall we do with him?" Henry motioned to Frederick, standing across the deck from them. Edward walked over to him.

Frederick looked away from Edward's gaze. "Thank you for—"

Edward punched Frederick, sending him to the deck. Then Edward extended his hand. "Now we're even."

Frederick accepted the hand and Edward pulled him up. "I suppose I deserved that. You didn't have to save me, and yet you did. Thank you."

"We can drop you off at the next port if you wish. I won't keep you here against your will."

Frederick opened his mouth, but he said nothing for a moment. "I... I don't know what I want to do anymore. Can you give me some time to think it over?"

"Take all the time you need, but as long as you're on this ship you must earn your keep."

"Yes, Captain." Frederick went straight to work with the other crewmembers, trimming the sails to the wind.

Henry walked over to Edward and they both watched from the stern as the ships from Port Royal shrank into the distance. "So what now? Any plans?"

Edward reached into his pocket and took out the folded piece of paper, once more showing it to Henry. "A few. I want to see if anyone here is able to open the locked doors before we leave on some wild goose chase."

Henry nodded. "There's probably no shortage of people who can pick locks here. What do you think of the crew so far? Despite your reprimand, they pulled through when we needed them." He turned to look at the lot of them.

Edward was watching them too. "They're brigands and thieves. Just what we need. I hope they can follow orders..."

"It will be a test of your will, now won't it?"

"I'll no doubt have to punish some to set an example, but for now I think we should focus on making this ship fully functional. We need to find us a carpenter to fix the damage from the previous battle."

Henry folded his arms and nodded his head curtly. "Agreed."

The ships from Port Royal had abandoned the chase, and Edward commanded the third sail, the one with the Jolly Roger, changed to the new canvas. He then asked the crew if anyone was a carpenter or knew one nearby who might join them. When no one spoke up, William said that he knew a man who might join, and who lived at a port not too far away. William worked with Herbert on the heading and they made for port straightaway.

Along the way, Edward requested anyone with deft hands and experience picking locks to try gaining access to the gun deck. Many tried, but none succeeded; even the most extreme measures failed. Several men actually tried to ram the door down, but could not.

"Thanks, men, but we're done here," Edward said at last with a sigh. He leaned against the door and closed his eyes. "How is this possible?" he asked aloud. "Maybe William's carpenter will help us with knocking the walls down."

"Perhaps the locks are magical, Captain."

Edward opened his eyes to see a young boy in front of him. He was taller than most, a teenager by Edward's reckoning, but the sound of his voice was perhaps a bit higher in pitch than would be normal for a teenager of his age, and the accent was almost too formal. His clothes were baggy and layered, the top a thick calico cotton print dyed brown with a leather vest overtop, while the dusty leather pantaloons were at least two sizes too big.

"Care to explain your meaning?" Edward asked after looking the boy up and down.

"Some things in this world cannot be explained, Captain. The locks might be protected by magic."

Edward narrowed his eyes and smirked. "Sorry, boy, but I think you've read too many stories. What's your name?"

"Jim Johnny, sir."

Edward examined the strange boy closer. His face was smooth and dotted with small freckles, and he had a thin jawline and eyes the colour of the green ocean. He also noticed a few loose ends of red hair sticking out of a leather cap Jim wore. There was something odd about the boy Edward could not put his finger on.

"Yes… Well… Back to work, Jim Johnny…" Edward said with his hand under his chin.

The boy turned and ambled back to the crew cabin.

Very strange. I'll have to keep my eye on this one.

Edward's went back up to the main deck to see the *Freedom* just pulling into the port of a tiny village. The town obviously did not see much aside from the occasional merchant ship, so a frigate was drawing all sorts of attention from the villagers. Edward did not allow shore leave, as they would not be staying long. William went to find his friend, and came back an hour later with two people.

"I have brought the carpenter, Captain," William said, gesturing to one of his companions. "His name is Nassir."

Edward examined the man next to William. He was a tall black man, as tall as Edward, with muscles bigger than Henry's. His head and face were clean-shaven. A small boy, almost the miniature version of Nassir, stood at his side.

The man extended his hand to Edward. "My name is Nassir, sir. This is my boy, Ochi." Nassir spoke in a thick accent, gesturing to his son with his other hand.

Edward took the man's hand and gave it a firm shake. "William tells us you are a fine carpenter, sir. Have you worked on a ship before?"

"Yes, I have sir, many times. I am very skilled. Here is a sample of my work." Nassir removed a pack slung over his shoulder, then pulled out an item covered in cloth and handed it to Edward.

Edward unwrapped the item to reveal a figure of what appeared to be Queen Anne in fine detail. "This is lovely," he said. "If it was a bit larger I would love to have this as a figurehead. The eyes are mesmerizing. So lifelike."

Nassir smiled at the praise. "I can certainly work on one for you if you'd like, sir. There is but two small matters I must address before the deal is final. I wish to bring along my son, as I cannot leave him and I understand that this vessel will not be returning," Nassir pulled his son in close to him, as if guarding him even from the thought of leaving him behind. "The other matter is payment. Sir, I am a free man, and I will be compensated fairly for my work. If these are not problems, I will join you."

"Payment is not an issue. You will be given a fair share, just as the others."

"Edward!" Henry whispered, pulling Edward aside. "What are you thinking? He may be a free man, but that doesn't mean he should receive the same as everyone else."

"He'll be working on the same ship, won't he?" Edward replied. "He deserves as much as everyone else." He turned back to Nassir. "So, as I was saying, your wages will be the same as the other mates. Your son is another matter… We may see battle on this ship, and I am loath to see him put in danger."

"Battle?" Nassir questioned, glancing to William, and then noticing the damage to the ship.

Edward looked at William, then back to Nassir. "Did William not tell you the nature of this ship?" Nassir shook his head, and Edward glanced about to ensure there were no eavesdroppers. "We've been accused of piracy."

"Piracy!" Nassir nearly shouted. "What is the honourable William doing aboard a pirate ship?" He looked at William, but all the stoic Englishman could do was lower his gaze in shame. "I'm afraid my services will be better used elsewhere, sir," Nassir told Edward firmly and then turned to leave.

Edward pulled Nassir back by the shoulder. "Please, let me explain." Nassir hesitated, his eyes narrowed, and Edward continued in a rush. "I said we have been *accused* of piracy, not that we *are* pirates. William is the honourable man you know him as; I even owe him my life. You have my assurance that I will do whatever is in my power to keep you and your son safe, but I cannot promise that this journey will be free from danger."

Nassir measured Edward with an intense scrutiny, weighing his words. He glanced back to William for assurance, and then nodded. "If William trusts in you, I shall too. I also owe him my life. Perhaps I can repay the debt aboard this ship."

Edward smiled. "Then I welcome you to the *Freedom*, Nassir." He turned his gaze to Nassir's son. "And you as well, Ochi." He looked at Nassir once more, his expression serious. "Will you be able to fix the railings on the go? I'd like to shove off as soon as possible."

"Yes, sir. As long as the supplies are on board, it should not be a problem."

"William, please show our newest crewmate around."

William nodded and led Nassir off. Edward glanced around as the three walked about the decks of the ship. There were more than a few looks of disgust cast at Nassir, and some even spat on the deck as he passed by.

I hope my crew doesn't give Nassir any problems.

Before Edward could give the order to depart, he heard the sweet sounds of music nearby. He turned to see a musician playing the fiddle on the waist of the ship. As he played, the crew danced and sang along. Even Edward began tapping his feet to the jolly tune. When the song ended, he walked over to the musician.

"Hello, sir," Edward said. "I thank you for the tune, but we are about to depart. I would appreciate it if you could see your way back to shore."

The man turned around when Edward started talking. "Captain Edward, I presume?" He gripped Edward's hand before he could respond, and shook it with great vigor. "Thank you for allowing me to stay aboard this fine vessel! It will be an honour to serve you and entertain your crew."

The man was of average build, past middle age, but spry. He spoke with an accent which Edward thought might hail from the Provincial colonies, and there was a faint smell of alcohol on his breath.

Edward shook his head. "There seems to be some misunderstanding. I thank you for the brief music, but this is not a transport vessel. You are free to leave."

"But Captain, I have no home to return to. If you'll just take me to the next port I will be eternally grateful. I will even pay you, if that will help."

"I'm sorry, but that's not my problem. Besides, as you can see, this vessel could see battle in the future. You could be risking your life. It will be better for you to find another ship to travel on." Edward turned to leave.

The man stepped forward, grabbing Edward's sleeve. "I am used to being on ships of this… nature. Please, sir, I can be useful to your crew."

"How so? We have no need of a musician."

Henry cut in. "Edward, aren't you being a little harsh? Look at the crew, they love him." He motioned to the crewmembers who were still singing the song even though the fiddler had stopped playing.

"Captain, if I may?" Nassir interjected. William had just finished the tour of the decks when they came by again.

"Yes, Nassir?"

"On my days on a ship, ones I generally do not wish to recall, one thing was able to keep my mind on happier times. Every day, the musician on board the ship would come to our quarters and sing us a tune to remind us of home. It gave us hope, and the strength to carry on. If it wasn't for him, I would have broken, and I would not be the same man before you today. If I were you, I would allow this man to stay. You are the captain, however."

Edward watched the crew still singing the song for another moment, and then turned to the musician. "Maybe it's not such a bad idea. What's your name, sir?"

"Jack Christian."

"Well, Jack, I'm sorry for my unkindness. You may remain aboard. But don't make me regret my decision."

"I promise you, sir, you will not. We'll all be dancing together before the cows come home." Edward stared at him with an odd look. "Ah, sorry, I sometimes forget my company. I mean that we'll be the best of friends before long."

Best of friends? Hmm. "Jack, I have my first order for you. This is Nassir and this is his son Ochi. The men seem to like you. Maybe you can introduce these two to the crew."

Jack took a gander at Nassir and his son. "I can try, Captain. But I'll cook up no promises. You know how some are with Negros. Just plain don't like 'em."

"Do you dislike them, Jack?"

"No, Captain, perish the thought. Come, Nassir, let's introduce you to the crew."

Nassir held his boy's hand tight. Edward gave a reassuring nod, and he returned it. Then the Negro took his son and followed Jack to meet the other crewmembers. They stopped singing, but after a small speech from Jack and a moment of brooding, they started alongside Jack's fiddle again. It wasn't total acceptance, but it was a start.

"Smart move, Captain," Henry said as they both watched.

"This should make things easier. The sooner everyone starts working together, the better off we'll be." Edward turned to Herbert. "Herbert, sail us out of here."

"Aye, Captain." Herbert shouted orders to remove the mooring lines and move the ship away from dock. Despite their brief stay at the small port, the departure of the large ship was a spectacle. The villagers waved to the crew as they left, and children ran up the pier to see them off.

Once back on the open sea, Nassir began repairs on the railings with Ochi by his side. Jack was playing music as the crew cleaned and worked, and the sun shone on them. It was becoming a nice day.

Edward talked with Nassir about repairs to the ship. Nassir said that with the gun deck locked he couldn't fix the holes. When Edward asked about whether they could tear down the wall, Nassir expressed doubt. He admitted that the construction of the wall was like no other ship he had seen, and it might be load-bearing. They risked damage to the rest of the ship if they tore it down. He explained he only found three holes in question and none would put the ship in danger if left alone. Edward trusted Nassir and let him handle the matter.

I suppose our only way to open the ship is to play Benjamin's game. "There is another matter I'd like you to look into, Nassir," Edward said.

"Yes, what is it, Captain?"

"Could you try and make something to help Herbert, our sailing master, up and down the decks? He's crippled, so it's more difficult for him to go from deck to deck."

Nassir looked up at Herbert, who was preparing maps and instruments at a table built into the quarterdeck. He had to have noticed the odd looks some of the crew gave Herbert—so similar to the way they looked at Nassir himself. Despite proving his mettle in battle, some of the crew still couldn't quite accept Herbert. "You are a strange one, Captain. It is refreshing."

After a slight pause and an odd expression taking over him, Edward replied "My thanks?"

Nassir chuckled. "I will see what I can do for you, Captain."

With his first and second plan of action for the locks exhausted, Edward called a meeting between the *Freedom*'s senior members. He would have done it in the galley, but he needed Herbert to examine Benjamin Hornigold's map to see if he could discern anything. To ensure privacy, he ordered all the crew to stay away from the quarterdeck.

Herbert, Edward, Henry, John, Sam, and William were all present. "What I'm about to tell you"—he looked specifically at Herbert, Sam, and William—"does not leave this group. Understood?"

"Yes, Captain," they said in unison.

"When I first purchased this ship, this note was left with it." He took out the note and allowed those who hadn't seen it to read and examine it. "Parts of this ship are locked, and on one side of the note it states that if we follow the clue on the other side it will lead us to the keys. We've tried picking the locks to no avail, and Nassir believes tearing down the walls could damage the ship, so following this clue is our only option."

"What's its meaning?" Herbert asked.

"I know not, exactly. That's why we're having this meeting. I want your take on the first part: 'From two ports of two crescent moons, two and two islands north and north northwest.'"

Herbert gazed at the paper and thought for a few minutes as the others watched his face. "It must refer to some islands shaped like crescent moons, but why two? Maybe there are two islands north and north-northwest of each crescent moon. It doesn't make sense."

"Why? Are there any ports shaped like crescent moons in the Caribbean?"

Herbert laughed. "Yea, there are countless crescent-shaped ports depending on how you view their shape to be. And if we believe this ambiguous message, we'll be searching for months. I consider this is a farce played by the last owner."

"No, I'm sure he wants us to find the keys through this game of his. We only have to narrow down the choices of the ports. Let's bring out a map of the Caribbean."

They placed the map on a table built into the quarterdeck. The wind being slight, there was no need to place weights on the map to hold it down. They pored over the map, scrutinising it for clues to reveal which of the twelve possible ports were the right ones.

"Well... the ports must be good to pirates, this bein' a pirate vessel," Sam suggested.

"No, that's too much of a stretch," Edward guessed. "As we've experienced with Port Royal, allegiances can change swiftly. Unless Benjamin created this not two months ago, we wouldn't be able to say these ports are pirate havens. However, I think it is safe to assume the ports have a decent amount of sea north and northwest of them so it's possible for islands to be there."

"That leaves six." Herbert reached over the table and marked the relevant ones.

"Anywhere just colonised within the last few years probably doesn't belong," John interjected.

"Five." Herbert took one of his markers off the map.

"He says 'ports *of* crescent moons,' not ports *like* crescent moons. That would mean islands, not just ports, shaped that way." William tapped on the note a few times. "*Of* implies the whole port and island is a crescent moon shape, whereas *like* would mean it looks similar and is part of a larger piece of land."

"Three." Herbert updated the map. "I think that's as far as we'll be able to narrow it down without more information," he surmised.

One island was in the middle of the Caribbean, one in the Cayman Islands, and one close to Costa Rica. Edward pointed to the first of these.

"This one is the closest to us. We'll check north of it first. Good job, everyone. Herbert, lay the course. Everyone else resume normal duties." Edward walked over to Herbert, who was turning the ship north-northwest. "So, Herbert, how are you doing on the ship so far? Too soon to tell?"

The helmsman paused before replying with, "Well and good, Captain. Well and good."

"You're a terrible liar, Herbert. Tell me your troubles. I'm the captain, I'm here to help."

"Well, some have been ignoring my orders. In battle they were fine, and perhaps fear had a part to play in that, but since then it's changed. They should know the sailing master takes precedence over the captain in certain situations, yet they don't take me seriously. Luckily it has been small things, nothing consequential.

But if we were in a storm, I fear it would be to the detriment of the whole crew if they continued to ignore my warnings."

Edward placed his hand over Herbert's shoulder. "Do not worry, friend. When the time comes, I will make sure they listen."

"Thank you, Captain."

"How is your sis— brother doing aboard the ship?"

"He's doing fine. But he's afraid of being seen, and he's unsure of what exactly to do aboard a ship, especially one of this nature…"

"Tell him not to worry. This is a pirate ship in name only—and a name bequeathed to it by others, in fact. To me, the *Freedom* is a regular ship. Tell your brother to think the same and everything will truly be well and good. And of course he can help you out like he's been doing. Maybe have him swab the deck from time to time as well." Edward chuckled.

"I'll be sure to let him know," Herbert said with a smile.

After the conversation, Edward could hear the sweet music of Jack Christian on the main deck. He left Herbert at the helm to go listen to Jack for a spell. In Jack's short time with the crew Edward had noticed that he kept the men relaxed and entertained. That in turn made them less likely to take out their frustrations on their shipmates.

I suppose my initial assessment of the man was wrong. I don't think I've been more fortunate to be wrong.

Edward listened as Jack played a tune he had heard as a child growing up, as well as others he had only recently learned, and all were a delight to hear. Before he realised it, an hour had passed with Jack not stopping his music once. Edward dispersed the crew listening, to the dismay of many.

"Jack, I think you need a break. I haven't seen you take a day of rest since you've come aboard. The crew won't revolt because you aren't there with music on one or two days."

"Ah, but Captain, this is my job. My life! I'm used to playing for long periods without rest. Besides, the crew loves it."

"I understand, but even you need to rest every once in a while. Will you force me to order you to take a break?"

Jack laughed. "I think perhaps yes. Otherwise my colleagues will pull me back in. I cannot resist the urge."

"Then I order you to take time to yourself at least once a week. And you can tell anyone who doesn't like it to take it up with me."

Jack laughed again. "Yes, Captain."

Edward left Jack to help some crewmen secure sail rigging, and noticed one of them was Jim Johnny. After the crew tied the rope down, they thanked the captain for the assistance, but Jim left immediately without so much as a thank you.

That's it! Jim has been avoiding me ever since the incident on the gun deck. I'm going to find out the secret of this Jim Johnny once and for all! Edward walked over and pulled Jim aside. "Galley, now!"

Jim tried to find a way out, but could not avoid Edward now. "Yes, Captain." And so both of them went to the lower deck and into the galley area.

Some crewmates were there, preparing the next meal. "Leave us," Edward ordered. Once the room was empty, he began his interrogation. "You will be straight with me right now or I'll make you leave at the next port, Jim Johnny!"

Jim panicked. "Uh, I don't know what you are referring ta, Captain!" Jim said in a broken attempt at a cockney accent.

"You're hiding something and I know it! Now what is it? Are you a marine spy? Answer me true or I'll see to it someone else makes you to talk."

"I… I have a condition. I can't be near captains or I get deathly ill."

"You take me for a fool?" Edward grabbed Jim by the neck and slammed him up against the wall, pinning the boy's chest down with his forearm. "You will tell me the truth or—" Edward felt something odd around his forearm and saw something on Jim's chest that shouldn't have been there on a man. *What the…?*

Then Jim grabbed Edward's arm and twisted it behind his back with ease. He tripped Edward to the ground and put his boot on the back of his neck.

Edward tried to scream, "You're a woman!" but it only came out as a muffled squawk.

"You were not supposed to find out about that." Jim's voice had resumed its normal pitch, and his—her?—accent was suddenly formal English.

The galley door burst open and the senior officers, Henry, John, and William, emerged. They all carried swords and pointed them at the young deckhand.

"Release the captain!" Henry yelled.

Jim let out a dismissive snort before releasing Edward, who rose and stood with the others. "I'll have my men lower their weapons if you promise not to do something foolish."

"Very well!" Jim said through clenched teeth.

Edward nodded to the others to put their weapons down, but they kept them in hand just in case. He walked over to the galley door and locked it.

"Take off your hat."

Jim did as commanded. Then she took a pin out of her hair, letting loose long, curly red hair that shone in the dim light. She was frowning, feminine in appearance but with fierceness in her green eyes.

The others dropped their jaws at the sight.

"He's a... she's a... It's a woman!" Henry stammered. "Did you know Jim was a woman?"

She's beautiful. Edward had to shake himself to get back to the situation at hand. "I... uh... I had my suspicions, but I didn't expect this. What's your name? Your real name?"

"Anne... Anne Bonney."

"Well, Anne, you mind telling me why you attacked me after I discovered your secret?"

"Humph! I know what your kind does to women. Either you use them for play-things or kill them at the first sign of trouble. I disguised myself as a man so I could stay aboard the ship. I warn you, gentlemen, if you try to take advantage of me, I will make it so you do not have the capacity to do so to anyone ever again."

Edward smiled. "Bold words for one so outnumbered..." She took a fighting stance. "That wasn't a challenge!"

"We need to decide what to do with her," said Henry. "She can't stay on the ship."

Edward scoffed. "And why not? She's been capable so far in doing regular duties. Let's test her mettle and see how she'll do in a fight. Then we can decide."

Henry rubbed his forehead in frustration. "Why? Why are you allowing her to stay aboard? This is foolishness."

"I agree she was foolish in attacking first. But we already have one lass aboard. What's the harm in another?"

Anne stepped forward. "You have another woman on the ship? Who is it?"

Henry glared at Edward, ignoring the question. "I swear, someday all the trouble you've visited on this crew will rain down like a storm, and then you'll be wishing you'd listened to me."

Edward laughed. "You know you wouldn't miss this for the world. William, Anne, do a little swordplay." William was sweating bullets and couldn't keep his eyes off Anne. "William, what's wrong? Have you never seen a woman before? Come now, ready yourself for a little test." Edward handed Anne a sword and William slowly unsheathed his.

The two sized each other up. William was still sweating and he looked on the verge of collapse. Anne attacked and he deflected the first blow, but then she managed to pass his guard to his neck, stopping short of actually hitting him.

"That was a lucky shot. William was distracted."

"Henry's right. William, you must at least try."

William nodded and got into position. Anne struck first, thrusting her blade at his face. He slapped her sword away with his, but didn't strike back. He stepped away and circled her. She slashed towards his gut, but as he brought his guard up she stopped short and went to knee him in stomach. He used his free hand to stop her knee. They continued fighting, but from what Edward could tell they were evenly matched.

"I've seen enough. You can clearly hold your own."

"Humph!" Anne turned away from William and handed Edward's sword back to him. He took the grunt to indicate defiance and contempt for his doubt.

"You can stay aboard on one condition: You must continue dressing as a man and no one must find out about you. Continue your regular duties and help the crew as before. Agreed?"

"Agreed," Anne responded without hesitation.

"And as for everyone here, it will be the same with the other girl. You are all sworn to secrecy about the true nature of this crewman. Understood?"

"Yes, Captain," they all said in unison.

"Now, let's all leave before the crew thinks something has happened." Edward left the room followed by Henry and John.

William lingered a few seconds, and Anne confronted him as soon as they were alone. "Do not think me an imbecile! Why did you hold back? You know I am skilled."

"Yes, I do know it. I could not strike against you without guilt."

Anne's eyes widened, fear mixed with cold rage. "Then you know who I am?"

"Yes."

"Then I order you to stay silent about your knowledge. I shall have none know of this. It is 'Jim' from now on. Understood?" Anne tied up her long red hair and covered it again with her hat.

"I saw the command on your face before you even had to say the words." And he knew the orders issued from her were higher even than a captain's.

Anne and William left the room, their bond secured, their secret hidden between the two of them.

8. FORBIDDEN

"Father, do you have to leave?" the young boy asked.

The father tucked his son into bed with a sad frown on his face. "I'm sorry, son, but I have to do this." He smiled. "I need to make enough money to feed you. It's like Davy Jones' locker in there." He tickled his son. The boy laughed and fought against it, tousling the blankets once more. The father tucked his son in yet again and got up to leave. "I'll be back before you know it."

"Father?" the boy said, expectation in his eyes.

His father turned back before leaving. "Hmm? What is it, son?"

"The song."

"Oh. Sorry. I almost forgot." The father sat down on a stool and began to sing a lullaby to his son as he did each night he was home.

Edward awoke with a start in the darkness, the recurring dream lifting his slumber. The dream always ended the same: His father left and never came back. That part his mind couldn't change, because that's how it happened in reality.

He rose from his bed in the corner of the crew cabin and lit an oil lamp. He could see and hear the crew in their hammocks, swaying with the ship. It was peaceful to see all those men sound asleep in their new home.

He walked up the stairs to the next floor. There was a lit lantern on each end, letting a little light into the darkness. *Soon, we'll open you up. We just have to find your keys, don't we, girl?*

When he reached the main deck the smell of salt air mixing with the pine of the ship greeted him. That heavenly scent made him want nothing more than to sleep up here each night, if not for the cold. The wind whipped against the ship with a howl, and water splashed the hull. Then he heard singing. It was Jack's voice. He was stumbling about, drunk.

I should help him back to his hammock. Edward walked closer, but the sight of Jack's profile and the song he was singing stopped him. *He's crying.*

Jack was singing a familiar lullaby. It was the same song Edward's father had sung to him as a boy. It was a joyful song about a boy growing up to be a great and splendid king. But the way

68

Jack was singing it made it seem like a funeral dirge. Edward felt tears in his own eyes. He waited there until Jack finished the song, and then turned and drifted back to the crew's quarters.

Edward went out there on several occasions, and he heard the same thing each time. Sometimes Jack was singing a different lullaby, but still in the same way. Edward couldn't bring himself to disturb the man's time of grief. Despite his determination not to interrupt, he still went up to listen to Jack whenever he had that dream.

And he had the dream most nights.

...

Ever since the day Anne's identity as a woman was revealed, William was not far from her side. He was always watching over her, no matter where they were. She noticed this sometimes, and delivered words sending him away—but for a time. He always resumed his guard when her attention was elsewhere.

What is William thinking? He's been following Anne from the moment of her revelation. Perhaps he fancies her? I can't let this affect his performance as my boatswain. "William! Here! Now!"

William ran over in an instant. "Captain!" He saluted.

Edward leaned in for a whisper. "William, you need to stifle your affection for… Jim. The crew is starting to notice."

"Sir?" William looked confused.

"Jim, remember? The one with the secret? The crew will uncover the ruse if you keep this up."

There was a small pause as William processed what Edward was saying. "Yes, Captain. It shan't happen again. I shall do my best to restrain myself." William remained as stone-faced as ever.

"Good. Now back to work."

"Yes, Captain." William saluted and left the aft deck.

Edward watched as William passed by Anne with nary a glance. She looked up at Edward from her post and saw him watching. She gave him a grateful nod, and he returned it.

"Captain," Herbert called. Edward went to the quarterdeck to see what he needed. The helmsman pointed off the bow to a small dot in the distance. "There's Half Moon Cay."

"Excellent," Edward exclaimed. He pulled out a spyglass and looked at the island in front of them, but wasn't able to see much. "At least now we can start this blasted search. It feels more like

69

we've been chasing the wind, and the crew is restless for some action. I fear Jack's music can placate them only so much."

Herbert had nothing to add to Edward's comments, so he changed the subject. "With your approval, Captain, I'll have us move north-east for time, then north-west, then mirror the direction on our return. That should provide us the most complete view of the area."

Edward nodded. "You are the expert here, so I will defer to your judgement, Herbert."

Herbert smiled. "Aye, Captain." He turned the ship starboard to move them north-east of Half Moon Cay and start the search.

The search was long, even with the *Freedom* sailing at full sail. Everyone available was watching the ocean, many with spyglasses or regular glasses, and the rest with the naked eye. Some men hung off the rope ladders leading to the masts, others stood atop the mast bars holding the sails in place, and a few were even in the crow's nest. No matter how much they explored, however, they were never able to see any islands.

"I don't understand," Henry complained one day. "They were supposed to be here. It feels like we've been searching for a whole month."

"Don't be so dramatic, Henry. It's only been a week or so... I think." Edward counted the days off on his fingers.

"We've been gone long enough that you've been growing a beard. You could have Alexandre shave you."

"I like it. It makes me look more distinguished, and older." Edward stroked his black chin hairs, which were, at this point, little more than stubble.

Henry rolled his eyes as he ran his fingers through his brown hair. "Well, the crew is becoming impatient regardless. They long for what we were meant to do, and someone told them it would involve riches and piracy."

"Well, *I* never told them that. I clearly stated we've been *labelled* pirates, not that we *are*. We're headed to Luna Bay next. They'll be able to have some shore leave for a few days once we arrive. Until then, we'll just have to keep busy."

Nassir approached Edward and Henry, interrupting their conversation.

"Captain," he started in his deep, accented voice, "I have something to show you." Edward nodded and Nassir led him to the aft deck.

Nassir had modified the deck railing on each side of the ship by cutting out a section and reattaching it with hinges to make a gate. The gates opened up right next to the stairs, where Herbert could grab onto a rope and shimmy up or down the decks. Someone still had to bring him his wheelchair, but Nassir placed chairs right where Herbert would land so he could sit down while he waited.

"This is ingenious, Nassir! Just what I wanted for him."

"This is nothing. It is only the first part of what I have planned," Nassir said, but he sounded happy for the praise.

"What do you have planned?"

Nassir laughed. "I cannot say. It will have to remain a secret for now."

Edward grinned. "All right, keep your secrets then!" He turned toward the helm. "Herbert?"

Herbert wheeled himself over to the edge of the quarterdeck. "Yes, Captain?"

"Have you tried out Nassir's invention?"

In answer, Herbert opened up the gate in the railing, jumped out of his wheelchair, climbed down the rope, and sat in the chair waiting for him.

"Yes, I have tried it." He grinned. "It's amazing! And I love the chairs; they make it a lot easier. Thank you, Nassir! I really appreciate it."

"Do not thank me; the captain wanted me to make something to help you." He smiled in spite of himself.

"I'm not the master builder. You deserve the credit." Edward held his hands in the air as if backing away from receiving the praise.

"It's a great thing regardless of who thought of it. I thank you both. Now, I need to get back up there before we're blown off course." Herbert climbed up the rope to his wheelchair and manned the helm again.

"Great work again, Nassir. I'm glad to have you aboard. Even if we are scoundrels, like you think we are."

"I am starting to rethink my position on that."

"Glad to hear it. If anyone gives you trouble, point me in their direction and I'll assist in any way I can."

"Aye, Captain."

Ochi walked by with something in his hands. Nassir stopped him and asked him what he was doing.

"Kenneth wanted me to take this black powder to him," the boy replied.

Edward heard the words and turned around. Herbert's interest was also piqued. "Black powder? Ochi, let me see that bag."

Edward took the bag and examined it; sure enough, it was gunpowder. *Why does Kenneth need gunpowder, and why did he make Ochi bring it to him? Kenneth has been making trouble ever since he started the cheering after our failed first battle at Port Royal.* Edward told Ochi and Nassir he would handle the matter, and then hurried to the foredeck where Kenneth and his group were waiting by the cannons.

"Kenneth, why did you make Ochi bring you gunpowder?"

Kenneth let out a sigh as he turned around. He was a tall, nasty-looking man with crooked, discoloured teeth, shaggy hair, and a flagrant disregard for general hygiene. "Me 'n' the boys 're workin up the cannons. We wanted ta practice our shot, 'n' the boy was jus' bein' useful."

Out of nowhere Herbert appeared, jumped on Kenneth and punched him.

"Herbert, stop it! Yield, yield I say!" Edward pulled him off Kenneth.

"That cripple hit me. Get 'im, boys!"

"Stop right there or I'll hit you myself," Edward flared. "That's an order." He turned to the helmsman. "Herbert, explain yourself. Why did you attack Kenneth?"

Herbert was on the floor of the deck, holding himself upright with his hands. "You might not realise the weight of this, Captain, but I do. He was trying to use Ochi as a powder monkey. They have them on ships with cannons like this, little boys meant to bring bags of gunpowder from the holds to the cannons. So many young ones have died from accidents." Herbert almost had tears in his eyes. "It's because of that I... No one should have that kind of job, Captain. Least of all a child." There was a seething anger showing on Herbert's face, and Edward could tell this situation meant more to him than just a passing fancy.

Edward knelt down to Herbert and whispered to him, "I understand your frustration, Herbert, but you can't beat anyone who does something you don't agree with. I stopped it before anyone was harmed. I'll take care of this. If you have a problem, you come to me, all right?"

Hebert pursed his lips, but after a moment replied, "Yes, Captain."

"Now back to your post. Some of your shares will be withheld because of what you did."

"Understood." Herbert crawled back to the rope and shimmied back to the main deck.

Edward went to Kenneth and grabbed him by the scruff of the neck. "If I had known the whole story I wouldn't have been so easy on you. From now on, if you want the powder you grab it yourself, end of story. If you had done that during an actual battle I would've thrown you overboard, but seeing as you didn't, I'll be lenient and diminish your shares. Don't let it happen again. Understand?"

Kenneth managed a defiant grunt.

"I'll take that as a yes. All of you are at half shares until further notice," Edward commanded as he walked away.

...

Kenneth had only been a nuisance before Edward cut his shares, but now he seemed contentious and volatile. As the days passed, his mood became fouler, towards Edward most particularly. He never directly disobeyed an order, but he made a point of voicing his complaints to anyone who cared to listen. Few did care to—least of all Edward, who, so long as he did not actually cause trouble, paid him no mind.

By contrast, Frederick was being more than accommodating to Edward. He followed orders and did the required work and then some. He was a mate skilled at running things on a ship; that was why Edward had let him on board when he first started whaling.

One day when Frederick was swabbing the deck, Edward made a point of speaking with him about his stay. "Frederick, I'm sorry, I meant to take you straight to the next port, but it slipped my mind. We'll be in Luna Bay soon and you'll be free to go."

Frederick stopped what he was doing. "Are you ordering me to leave the ship?"

"No... Why would I need to order you? You're free to leave."

"Well, I've changed my mind. I'll stay aboard—if you'll have me."

"But... I thought you hated me. And why do you want to stay on a ship full of pirates?"

"You saved my life at the gallows when you could have left me to die. It helped me realise that's all you were trying to do from the start. I was wrong, and you were right. Besides, it's not so bad on board. You have yourself a fine crew, I'd say. Some have a rather... salty disposition, but it's not much different from the crew before the split in Port Royal. And I know you aren't really a pirate. I'd be happy to repay my debt to you aboard."

Edward extended his hand and grasped Frederick's. "Glad to have you with us."

Edward had also felt ambivalent towards Sam at first, but the young man's relationship with others aboard the *Freedom* improved over time. In general he was less inclined to fight and argue, and even got along with William to an extent. The two now shared a no more than passive resentment towards each other, more like rivals than enemies. Henry, however, still didn't like Sam one bit.

Edward found Sam alone one night, drinking out on the deck in the dark, and joined him.

"Having a good time?"

Sam laughed. "Aye, a pirate's life for me." He took a swig of rum and graciously passed the bottle to Edward, who accepted it and had a few sips.

"So why are you a pirate, Sam? Why stay with us?"

"I've been here since the beginning, mate. At first I thought you wus a pratter so focused on rules you had 'em up yer bunghole. But when your *Freedom* was threatened, you took charge against that marine. No hesitation. That's why I'm still 'ere, Captain. Someday, something's gonna happen with you, or many somethings, and I wanna be there to see 'em."

"Mmm." *I don't know what it is he sees in me.* Edward continued to drink in silence with Sam for a bit longer, until he became tired. "Thanks for the drink, Sam," he said before heading below deck to sleep.

"Any time."

During the dull days of sailing, in spite of his reluctance to practice, Edward was also able to improve his public speaking abilities thanks to Henry's techniques. His nervousness was still there, and he still panicked after a time and had to stop, but that eventuality arrived later and later. He made speeches in the mess hall in front of ever larger groups. Sometimes they were discussions about their finances or supplies, and other times they were stories from Shakespeare, or the news.

The Shakespeare bits gave Henry an idea.

"You know what? We should do that."

Edward laughed at that. "Do what exactly?"

"We should have plays on the ship. I think it could help with morale, and it would be fun."

"That is a most foolish idea if I've ever heard one. These are pirates, not some high lord mollies. That's silly—and if you think I'll do more than a soliloquy, you are mistaken, sir!"

"Come now, you know it would be fun. And who's to say no one here would enjoy it? They enjoy listening to you do it."

"I'll think about it."

Henry scoffed. "No you won't."

He was right. *There's no way I'll make a fool of myself more than I already have.*

Edward, however, continued to do the readings, and improved over time. He used gestures and moved around, talking to certain people as if they were a true audience. Henry smiled as he watched his protégé.

...

Edward invited Anne into the galley for a private talk to see how she was adjusting to life on the ship. She let out her hair and untangled it when they were alone. Edward began to stare.

She's gorgeous.

"What?" Anne snapped.

Edward coughed. "Uhh... nothing... How are you adjusting aboard the ship?"

"What do you mean?"

"Well, it must be hard, I imagine."

"Why? Because I'm a woman? Do you need me to remind you of our first encounter here?" she said, tightening her fist into a ball.

"Peace! Peace! I only meant your previous life. It must be hard to switch to pirating."

"What about my previous life? What do you know?" Anne moved closer to Edward, her finger pointing at his face.

Why is she so defensive? Edward let out a sigh. "I know nothing. That's why I'm asking. I'd like to know more about you."

Anne lowered her hands. "Oh... Sorry. I thought you... Pay that no mind. Truthfully, I don't find it hard here at all. My life at home was simple... easy, even. I like to work hard, and I have always had a romantic fascination with being out at sea. I never viewed pirates as the brigands and rogues everyone else did. If you knew the political mishaps of the privateers after the last war, you would understand why pirates do what they must."

Edward had lost focus halfway through what Anne said.

Anne explained further. "What I mean to say is that they were commissioned by the crown, but they only knew how to fight and steal. The crown left them without jobs after the war ended. They were not even given half-pay as the normal military has. It is not fair the way… the way the queen treated them."

Edward shrugged. "I guess you understand it better than I. All I know of pirates is the rumors of horrible deeds spread about."

"That is all they want you to see. And why pirates are hated so. What I cannot understand is why you are a pirate. You are young. Were you on a privateer ship when you were younger?"

Edward leaned against the galley's stove. "No, my father was a fisherman… a whaler in truth. I wanted to follow in his footsteps and bought this ship… Well, I suppose I bought it. I don't remember it exactly as I was quite drunk at the time." He laughed at the situation, which is one thing he thought he never would do. "It turned out to be a pirate ship, and we happened to be in the presence of a marine ship when we unfurled a sail that had a Jolly Roger on it. I pinned the captain, Isaac Smith, and used his life as bargaining to get us out of there. That's how we ended up in Port Royal. We've been on the run ever since."

"Truly? Well, that is unfortunate for you. I have heard the name of that captain. They call him 'The Hound' in some circles. He is an excellent tracker."

Edward nodded. "Yes, he seemed one who wouldn't yield easily." He shuffled a bit, and thought of another question to fill the silence. "So, what made you choose this ship? Hadn't you already heard about how we'd been labelled as pirates?"

Anne shook her head. "No, I found out after."

Edward folded his arms. "And it didn't bother you?"

"Well, at first I was going to leave at the next port, but when you found out my secret, things took a much different turn than I'd expected. I decided to stay because you are not like other pirates. And now that I have heard the whole story, I suppose you are not pirates at all."

"Just on the run like pirates." Edward chuckled at his misfortune. "Well, for what it's worth, Anne, I'm glad you're here with us. It's nice having you aboard."

"Does this mean you'll tell me of the other woman on board?"

"Not a chance."

"Come now. Just a hint?"

"No. You'll have to find out for yourself."

Anne sniffed and pouted. "Fine then."

Edward chuckled. "You're cute when you're angry..." He stopped, frozen.

What did I just say?

Anne blushed, and they stared at each other for a long moment, neither of them knowing what to say.

"I have to leave," Edward said quickly.

"Me, too." Anne began tying up her hair and Edward moved to help her, but it only made the process more awkward. She managed to put her hat back on, but as she was about to rise from her seat on the stove, they stopped and realised the situation they were in.

Edward was pressed up against Anne's chest. He could feel the rapid thumping of her heart next to him. His hands were around her shoulders. He closed his eyes and leaned forward. Their lips touched. They stayed there for a few seconds, the warmth of each other just registering before Anne pushed him away and slapped him. The image of another woman invaded Edward's mind. *Lucy.*

"How *dare* you!"

"I... I know. I'm sorry. I don't know what came over me."

Anne went to the door and then turned back to him. "Maybe I was wrong about you. You are like the rest of them." She whirled around and stormed out through the mess hall.

Edward was left thinking of Lucy, his former flame from Badobos, and of Anne. *I can't believe I did that. How could I be so stupid? But why did Anne slap me? I swear she leaned in... unless I was imagining it.* Edward couldn't know for certain, so he left the galley and headed back to the main deck.

Anne and Edward never spoke of the incident, and avoided each other at every turn for the rest of the day. By nightfall the tension abated, but others noticed the awkwardness between them. Henry approached Edward about it when it became obvious, which didn't take long.

"Ed, is there something going on between you and... and Jim?"

"What? No, don't be silly. Let's talk about this later, shall we?" *Please take the hint, Henry.*

"All right, Ed. Let's meet an hour from now in the galley."

Their arrival at the galley frustrated the galley crew, who didn't appreciate all the impromptu meetings, but they followed the captain's orders and left, grumbling under their breath about frequent interruptions.

"So what's going on, Ed?"

"I kissed Jim... I mean, Anne."

"You kissed Anne?" Henry said, incredulous.

"It just… happened. But now I can't stop thinking about Lucy. I feel like I betrayed her. And Anne's mad at me as well."

Henry pinched the bridge of his nose. "You're still thinking about Lucy? Edward, it's already been past a month, and it was only a kiss. You chose to leave her behind without even a letter explaining things. By now she's probably heard about what happened. Besides, you're better off without her—or Anne, for that matter…"

"What's that supposed to mean?"

"I… I just think that you can do better."

"What was wrong with Lucy?"

Henry shuffled around and scratched his face. "She hangs around with those prissy bints. It doesn't matter if she fancies you. She's the same as them. It's not as if we can return home anyway, remember?"

"I know, but I don't care for your attitude. She's different from them. And what about Anne? What's your problem with her?"

Henry shook his head. "Since when did this become a serious discussion about your love life, Edward? I thought we were discussing how this was a mistake?"

"We are."

Henry ran his fingers through his hair. "She has a smug attitude about her. She thinks she's better than others. Just listen to the way she talks. Like some high-class Englisher born with a silver spoon in her mouth."

"I disagree there as well. First off, why would she be on a ship like this if she was rich?"

Henry held his hand up to stop Edward from continuing. "Of course you disagree, but our opinions on her eligibility are moot. Remember how we're trying to keep her secret just that? A secret? You go gallivanting about like two lovers, and questions will be raised."

"Yes, yes, I know. What do I do about it?"

"You apologise, you say it won't happen again, and you don't let it happen again." Henry emphasised the last part. He grabbed Edward's forearm and glowered at him. "Involving yourself with her is a whole mess of trouble waiting to happen."

Edward let out a long sigh and shook his head. "You're right. I'll do what you say." He still couldn't shake the thought of Lucy out of his head.

He sought out Anne later in the day. Walking up to the aft deck, he noticed her and William talking in hushed voices. When she saw him, she tried to leave, but he grabbed her by the arm, causing William to straighten in surprise.

"I wish to speak with you."

"I have nothing to say to you."

"Please." The hint of pleading in his face was meant only for her.

Anne let out a sigh and said, "Fine, but make it quick."

Edward and Anne left William standing on the deck in complete bewilderment. They returned to the galley to commandeer it from the crew, who were quite fed up with the constant shuffling by now and actually voiced their anger. Edward managed to calm them down by telling them this would be the last time. When the crew was out of earshot, he sat down with Anne to talk.

"I wanted to apologise for my actions again. I don't know what came over me, but I promise you it won't happen again."

"I should hope not."

"Please don't leave the crew."

"I shan't. But if you ever kiss me without my permission again, I will make sure it is the last thing you ever do. Am I clear?"

Edward gulped. "Understood."

Anne rose without another word and left Edward sitting at the table. He let out a breath, then stood and followed her.

After they parted ways, Henry had his own talk with Anne when she came back up to the main deck. "Hey, Jim?" She came over to see what he wanted. Henry spoke in a hushed tone. "I want you to stay away from Edward. He doesn't need someone like you."

Anne laughed at him. "Whatever makes you think you can tell me with whom I can and cannot associate? Edward can think for himself, surely. As can I. What happens between us is of no concern to you, understood?"

"Sorry Jim, but it does concern me. Edward and I have been best friends for almost our whole lives. He hasn't been with anyone before, and he doesn't know what type of woman is best for him. I have his best interests in mind."

Anne straightened at that, her eyes narrowing to slits. "Oh, and how many women have *you* been with?" Henry pursed his lips and didn't respond. "I thought so. Edward is a man, not a boy. I understand his need for a confidant, but he does not need you to protect him from what *you* are afraid of," Anne said haughtily.

And with that, she left Henry silenced and embarrassed, standing alone on the deck.

From then on Edward and Anne continued their lives aboard the ship as if nothing had ever happened. Now and again one of them would steal an unseen glance at the other and smile. And every night, in their separate beds, they recalled the kiss that never should have been.

9. THE TWO BY TWO ISLANDS

The *Freedom* reached Luna Bay without incident, and Edward allowed the crew some shore leave for a couple of days. They restocked food, ammunition, and general supplies to last them for the next few months. John was keeping track of everything and made a note to Edward that the next time they resupplied they would be out of money.

Let's hope there will be more than just a key on those islands. Either that or we'll have to start acting the part of pirates. I don't want to, but if we're left with no choice...

Edward stayed on the ship, having no inclination to leave. He and a few crewmen kept busy by checking the ship and making sure John hadn't missed anything.

While their speaking relationship was strained, Anne and Edward always had the courtesy to greet each other in passing.

Edward watched her as she was tying up the sails. The riggers were ashore, and everyone else was too afraid to do it. *Anne certainly is intriguing. Lucy never would have done something so bold as to join a group of pirates in disguise. At least, I don't think she would.* The thought of Lucy brought him back to himself. He still felt guilty about the kiss, so he kept his distance from Anne as best he could.

After the two days ashore, the crew returned. Frederick was among them, eager to work. It was as if he had become a different person.

When everyone was present and accounted for, they left Luna Bay, circled around the island, and headed north.

As they had done with the first island, they followed a diamond course far north of Luna Bay to cover the most ground. Edward was sure they would find something this time.

They searched in the same manner as before, travelling for days until they almost lost hope, until one day an excited cry from the crow's nest lifted Edward's spirits again.

"Land ho!"

"Where?" Edward yelled as he ran to the quarterdeck railing and gripped it hard as he looked to the crow's nest for an answer.

"North and starboard."

Edward looked off to the right side of the ship, and there it was: a small island in the distance. He began to laugh out loud at the sight of it. *Finally! We found one of them!* "Herbert, turn the ship north. Head for that island."

Herbert, along with many, caught Edward's buoyant mood. "Aye aye, Captain!"

Henry jumped up the steps leading to the quarterdeck. "Is it the one? Is that the island?"

"It must be, Henry! There's nothing else it could be. Are you as excited as I am?"

He was. It appeared that they were finally about to solve the next part of the riddle. Once they came closer to the island, however...

"What kind of a cruel joke is this? The devil himself must be laughing at us!" Henry suggested bitterly.

The island was nothing but a large sandbar. There didn't appear to be anything on it at all.

"There must be more to it... We should search the whole thing."

"For what, Edward? There's nothing there!"

"There must be something. A trip door, a secret entrance, *something.*"

"Very well, we'll search."

They took a few teams and scoured the whole "island" for a hidden passageway or a clue, but found only sand. Edward and the crew returned to the ship in a foul mood, still confused as to what they were searching for and why.

They continued sailing in the prescribed pattern. Each day passing left them feeling more restless than the last. Tension mounted amongst the crew, and the captain's dark mood was infecting the others.

On their return approach to Luna Bay, John approached Edward. "C-Captain?"

"We need to rethink this whole business, John. We're not reading the map right. There's some kind of trick to it we're overlooking. I'm sure of it."

"Captain?"

"I want to have a meeting with you, William, Sam, Herbert, and Henry again. Another look at the riddle could be useful."

"Captain?" John uttered for the third time.

"What is it, John? You have your orders."

John recoiled, but went on regardless. "Captain, the c-crew is angry with what's been happening recently. Th-they would like to know what we're searching for."

"They want to know what we're doing? Call everyone together then. I'll tell them what we're doing!"

"Aye aye, Captain."

John traversed the ship and gathered everyone to the main deck, where Edward was waiting to speak to them.

"So I hear you all want to know what we're searching for."

The crowd murmured in the affirmative.

"Well, I think you should be more concerned with performing your duties than why you're doing them, don't you? Keep to task and you'll know soon enough."

A ripple of whispers washed over the crew.

"Does anyone have an objection?"

A crewman spoke up. "I think we 'ave a right to know why we're doin stuff!" Others voiced their agreement.

Edward was reaching the level of nervousness where he would soon panic. His public speaking practice sessions had not prepared him for objections. He tried to say something, but stammered while another crewmember spoke up.

"We should have a say in what we'll be doing as a crew," the man claimed. "Aye, we should vote on it," another added.

Edward's eyes went out of focus and he could feel his heart beating through his flushed cheeks. "Henry!" he yelled and motioned for him to join him. When Henry arrived, he whispered for him to take over. He handed him the paper and told him to explain the keys and the possibility of treasure.

"Very well then. We'll let you know exactly what we're here for." Henry held up the paper. "This is what we're after."

The crew looked at Henry, confused. "Paper?" someone asked.

"What? No. You may have noticed some of the doors on our ship are locked and you're unable to enter those sections. We don't know exactly what some of them hold, but this piece of paper will lead us to the keys to unlock them. And there's another reason to find these keys: treasure. There may be something more than just keys if we manage to find the location where they are stored."

"You mean you don't know where it is?"

"No, that's why we need you all to help in this. There's a riddle on this piece of paper that leads to some islands. On those islands is the treasure. So far, our attempts at solving the puzzle have come to naught. If you vote to search for them, we can hold a meeting to find out what the riddle means. This vote is a vote of trust. If you trust in the captain and me, as you have already, we will find these islands and we will find the treasure."

The crewmembers muttered and whispered to each other, debating Henry's words.

Edward came back into the conversation. "All in favor of searching for the keys?"

Edward raised his hand and several in the crowd followed. On the quarterdeck, Henry, Herbert, Christopher, and John raised their hands. On the main deck, William, Sam, Anne, Nassir, Alexandre, and Jack all voted in favor. A few more began raising their hands while nudging others to raise theirs. Anne watched this hesitant response with growing impatience and finally ran to the stairs.

"You want adventure, don't you?" she yelled, to which many responded in favor. "You want treasure beyond your wildest imaginings?" More replied to her in the affirmative. "Then raise your bloody hands, because treasure and adventure are what we will find!"

The vast majority now put up their hands, and Anne went back into the crowd. Edward smiled at her, and when she noticed she turned aside, a slight redness on her cheeks.

"All opposed?" Edward asked.

A few people raised their hands, but not enough to call the vote. Among them were Kenneth Locke and his group.

Edward stared straight at Kenneth. "The majority rules. We search for the islands." Then he addressed the whole crew. "Now we will have a meeting to see if we can figure out the riddle. If we cannot, then each of you will be called to try your wits at it."

As Edward had requested, Henry, John, William, Herbert, and Sam joined him on the quarterdeck. Edward set up the maps and everything they needed.

"Sam, do you have any new thoughts on the riddle?"

Sam took the paper from Edward's outstretched hand and read it over, front and back. "I have nary a clue, jus' as last time. I be a simple man, Captain."

Henry scoffed and said, "That figures."

Sam gave him a death stare and continued. "There is something I reckon is important. This bit about the 'wit and grit.' Maybe there be traps on the islands for both smart and dumb people."

"Well, you have a good point there, but we can worry about it later. We know from what we discussed earlier that it's two of these three islands, but we need to find out how they're connected."

They went over and over the puzzle for a good few hours with some reasonable ideas proposed, but nothing approaching a definite solution. They brought other crewmembers in, but none of them could make heads or tails of it. Impatience and irritation set in. Arguments broke out.

This is ridiculous. Can no one figure this nonsense out?

Edward turned away from the table to get away from the noise.

Maybe we're thinking about this the wrong way. It's probably something so simple it's right in front of our eyes. It has to be that. Some sort of trick to catch people off guard. Edward was deep in thought when he heard someone say something that drew his attention.

"Wait... What did you say?"

Herbert spoke up. "Henry's being a fool. He thinks north means straight from where the island is pointing. It doesn't, Henry! It refers to magnetic north. That's why we have compasses." That renewed the argument once more.

The words sparked something in Edward. He went over the riddle in his head once more. "*From two ports of crescent moon, two by two islands, north and north northwest, wit and grit...*"

He jumped up and shouted, "I've got it!" causing everyone on the ship to stop what they were doing and look at him. "I know where the islands are!"

"What?" Henry said with a blank stare.

"I solved the riddle of where the islands are located. It's because of the two sides to everything. The riddle isn't just a test of how smart you are. It's also a test of how dumb you are!"

Everyone looked at him as though he had been dropped on the head as a child. "Maybe you need some rest, Edward. You're not making sense."

"It makes perfect sense, Herbert. It's the perfect way to throw us off. Everyone's first inclination is magnetic north of the islands themselves. That's what each person we brought up here kept asking which way north is. And if you keep thinking nautically, then you'll never see the true picture. It took Henry's comment of going straight from how the islands are pointed that helped me work it out. Here, I'll show you."

Edward took the map they had of the Caribbean and drew lines on it according to how each island was oriented. He used his knowledge he was learning from Herbert and drew two lines, one for north and one for north-northwest from each. Not magnetic north, but north as in straight out from the curve of the half moon formed by the island.

The lines Edward drew went out from the islands almost like a V. The first island they'd gone to, Half Moon Cay, had a V going past the west side of Jamaica. The second island, Luna Bay, had a V that went south to Panama and the Isla de la Providencia, nowhere near the lines from the first island. The final island, Slivers Isle, went southeast and intersected with the lines from Half Moon Cay.

The intersecting lines from both Vs created four points in the middle of the Caribbean Sea.

"We used our smarts to narrow it down to three islands, but after we couldn't move forward. We would have never figured it out if we didn't look at it from both perspectives. The island we were just at, Luna Bay, leads nowhere—it's something to try and throw us off the trail to the real islands. The two true ones have two lines each and they both intersect in the middle of the Caribbean Sea. Four points, two by two islands. That's the riddle, and those are the islands we've been searching for."

Everyone inspected what Edward had put on the map and considered his explanation. As they realised the logic in it, their eyes lit up like his.

"He's right! It makes perfect sense, in a foolish sort of way," Henry said.

"I have to admit, I never would have seen that. Good work, Captain." Herbert sounded a bit downhearted at not having been able to solve the riddle.

"I never would have figured it out if not for all of your help. Sam pointed me in the right direction with his remark on the two parts of the tests. Then Henry's comment about where the islands were pointed provided the rest."

Everyone began to feel excited; they had finally solved the puzzle, and soon they would be swimming in treasure.

"Let's not become too exuberant yet. We have a long road ahead of us." Edward went to the edge of the quarterdeck where the crew was still waiting. "Everyone, we've solved the riddle! This ship needs to be seaworthy before we can proceed. Weigh anchor! Release the sails! Everyone back to work! Herbert, set the course! Let's find us some treasure!"

"Aye aye, Captain!"

...

The days came and went at a quick pace. The crew was appeased, indeed happy, since their purpose had been made clear.

No one knew what adventures awaited them at the islands, but the mystery heightened the thrill.

Treasure proved a fine motivator.

Then, one day, a familiar cry signaled the end of their search.

"Land ho! Dead ahead!" a crewman yelled from the crow's next.

"How many islands do you see?" Edward yelled to the scout above.

"One."

Damn!

"No... wait! I see another one... And another... Four islands! Four islands off the bow."

Ha-ha! Yes! "Excellent! Good job!" Edward saw Henry and John staring at him, looking as if they were about to explode. "As you will, gentlemen. Let it out."

Henry and John, along with the rest of the crew, let out loud whoops, and cheers erupted from every nook and cranny of the ship. Edward couldn't help but join in; having his solution to the riddle proven true in reality was almost reward enough.

Almost.

When they reached the islands, Herbert took the ship between them. The four islands were almost bare; they consisted of small rocky hills covered by tall grass and a few scattered trees.

Herbert pushed himself up with his arms for a better view. "They're closer together than the map you made indicates, but it's certainly an ingenious riddle."

"I can see why people would pass these islands by," said Henry. "There's nothing on them to speak of."

"Well, Henry, let's hope you're wrong. Take her in to the port side island, Herbert. John, gather a small landing party. Tell them to bring weapons. I don't want to take any chances."

Herbert and John set about carrying out Edward's orders. When the ship had made landfall, Edward, Henry, William, and a few others disembarked on the island.

"Be on the lookout for anything out of the ordinary."

They searched the island, examining everything they saw with care. The group stayed close together; it was a small island, but they had no idea what to expect. They climbed a grassy hillside, checking the ground for a clue to their next step, but saw nothing remarkable. Then they went down the other side of the hill, which was rocky and covered in moss and vines.

"I don't understand. There's nothing here, but these *must* be the islands," Edward said to no one in particular.

"Maybe there's some trick. Do you have the paper still?" Edward pulled it out and handed it to Henry. "There must be something in the next part of the riddle about these islands." Henry sat down on a rock and read it with a furrowed brow. "'Two by two tests'. Do you think this is the test? Finding the spot on the islands where the key is located?"

Edward thought for a moment. "Nah, that's too easy. I think there's more to these islands than there appears to be. There's mention of a fifth island in there too, but do you see another island around here? There must be something else here…"

"Captain!" William called out. "I believe this is what you are looking for." He was pointing at the entrance to a cavern in the rock face.

Edward and Henry rushed over. "How did you find this?"

"I was walking along the side of the rock face and felt a cool breeze and picked up an odd smell, so I investigated. The opening was concealed by the moss and vines, so I cut them down and this is what I found."

"Genius!" Edward commented. "Let's return to the ship."

"What? Aren't we going to journey inside?"

"Not yet. We need to figure out exactly what we'll do for these tests."

When Edward and the others arrived back at the ship, the men wanted to hear about everything. The questions came one right after the other.

"Did ye find the treasure?" "Where's the entrance?" "Did ye get a look inside?" "Is it haunted?"

"Haunted?" Edward chuckled. "No. We haven't gone inside yet, so calm yourselves. I'll let you know what we're doing when we're ready to do it."

Having fielded enough questions, Edward went to the quarterdeck so he could consult first with the senior officers and then the entire crew before he proceeded.

"Find anything, Captain?" Herbert asked.

"We found the entrance to a cave, but we didn't enter. I imagine there are similar entrances on each island. But we have something else to consider. Henry, the paper, if you please?" Henry handed him the paper which held the riddle on it. "See this part about the tests? 'Two by two islands, two by two tests. Two by two crews, one of wit, one of grit. Each test gains one key for the chest. Bring the keys and find the chest in the belly of the fifth.' There's probably a clue inside each island, which leads to a fifth island where the chest is. Each island holds a cavern, and each requires both smarts and strength."

Henry shook his head. "No... The way it sounds to me, it seems like two will require wit and the other two strength."

"Maybe you're right, Henry, but we can't afford to take any chances. What if we send a group of people in who won't be able to complete the task? We don't know what's down there. They could die."

"What will we do?" John asked.

"We have to separate into four groups and have each choose an island. Each group needs individuals with a range of skills, capabilities, and knowledge. They need to be able to deal with any eventuality." He turned to Henry. "You, John, William, and I will be the team leaders. I'll take the last island, the rest of you can choose accordingly."

"So we will split the crew into who is smart and... well... who isn't?" Henry asked as he folded his arms.

"Somewhat. Everyone has their strengths and weaknesses. We have to make sure each group has the best chance of success."

They proceeded to divide the company into four parties. Each party consisted of some who could read and write, some who knew how to use a compass, some who could do math, some who possessed exceptional strength and dexterity, and so forth. Which qualities of wit and grit would actually be tested by their expedition, no one could guess at.

I'm sure everything will go smoothly. Benjamin wants us to have the keys. It won't be that hard. Will it?

Jack was to be left in charge of the remaining crew who were not to participate in the expedition. Edward trusted Jack, the men liked him and would listen to him, and he could keep them entertained with his music.

The process of choosing members for the four groups went, for the most part, smoothly. But when Edward picked Anne to join his group, William spoke up.

"Jim should be with my group, or I will join yours."

"No, William. It will cause an imbalance. I need his skills with me. You don't have to worry, he'll be safe."

William took a moment, and, seeing Edward's point, conceded.

"So I guess I'm staying here, am I?" Herbert's eyes were stuck on the deck and his chin sunk into his chest.

"What are you talking about? You're in my group. Nassir will carry you along, provided you wish to come." Herbert's face lit up.

"I'll take that as a yes, but I'm sending you back at the first sign of trouble. Understood?"

"Understood!" Herbert said with a salute.

After explaining the situation to the crew, and how they would be split, they voted on the proceedings. The crew was in agreement, so they let everyone off. They began with William's group on the island they landed on. Alexandre was with him at the southern island.

The crew in the first group exited the ship by rope ladders, with some jumping from the deck to the sandy beach below. Others took their time stocking with weapons and supplies in case the need arose.

After the first group disembarked, they went with Henry's group, which included Sam, to the west island. John's group, with Frederick and Kenneth Locke, amongst others, took the north island. Lastly, Edward's group took the east island.

"Well, this is it. Stay alert, everyone."

Edward's group made their way from the ship via ladders or leaping over the side onto the small island. They took in the surroundings while they waited for the captain and the rest of the men to land.

"Captain, I'm not sure if you've noticed, but there is something odd about these islands."

"What is it, Herbert?"

"Well, there are shallow parts around the islands at the ends. The four may be connected. It's almost like a compass, they seem to be connected like a cross."

Connected like a cross? Belly of the fifth? "Maybe we'll meet up with the other groups at some point."

"It's plausible. Look in the middle of the four islands, I know it's hard to see, but the water is very shallow there. I guess we won't know what it means until we head inside our island."

"Speaking of heading inside. Nassir!" The tall Negro walked over to Edward. "Can you help Herbert down? The rest of you get his wheelchair."

After nodding to Edward, Nassir helped take Herbert down the side of the ship while another crewmate lowered his wheelchair to the beach.

It was intended that Nassir's son, Ochi, and Christina, Herbert's sister, would stay aboard ship in the care of Jack. But now that his father was actually leaving, the boy was afraid, and he desperately wanted to go with him.

Edward noticed Ochi watching his father at work. "Ochi. Come here, boy." He trudged his way over to Edward. "You scared to be alone?"

The boy nodded. "Yes, Captain."

Edward chuckled. "Now you needn't worry. You remember Jack?" Edward pointed to the fiddler. He saw him pointing and walked over. "Your Uncle Jack here will protect you while we're away."

"You can count on me, Ochi." Jack knelt down to the child's level.

"We're going to find us some treasure and your father will be back in no time. You won't even notice he's gone."

Ochi had tears in his eyes as he nodded again.

"Hey, Ochi! I have something important for you to do. See, when I leave this ship, I won't be a captain anymore. A captain is only a captain on a ship. I need someone to take over for me while I'm away." Edward took off his tricorn hat and put it on Ochi's head. "Do you think you can be captain for me? Can you keep the ship safe for me and your dad?"

Ochi's face lit up. "I sure can!" He played with the hat and then put it back on. He was in awe of that hat.

It'll be nice to let him play for a bit.

Jack took Ochi's hand. "Let us man the helm, Captain." He smiled as he led the boy away.

Edward noticed those remaining behind were talking in a group. "Keep an eye out, gentlemen, and keep the ship safe." They all replied with an "Aye, Captain."

"Captain?" a tender voice said from behind Edward.

It was Herbert's sister, Christina. *I barely noticed her; she's so quiet all the time. She rarely leaves Herbert's side.* "Yes, what is it Christina?" he whispered so that the others could not hear.

"What will I do while you're gone?"

Hmm. "Well, you see Ochi?" Edward pointed to him. "He's captain while I'm away, but he needs a first mate to help him out. Without a first mate, the captain is lost. You think you're up to the task?"

Christina smiled and nodded her head.

"Well, you'd better hurry before he casts off without you." He pushed Christina off in the direction of Ochi and Jack and she ran up to them. He had seen them playing together before. It was nice to see they got along so well. Jack also seemed right at home with the children and was smiling and playing right along with them. *I promise I'll bring your family back soon, little ones.*

When Edward was certain he had packed everything necessary for the expedition, he disembarked. They fanned out in smaller groups to investigate every part of the island. Nothing looked promising until one of the groups found a hole beside a knocked over tree. The tree itself was gnarled, decayed, and a shell of its former self. The opening it left led almost straight down and was wide enough for several people to climb down the abundant vines covering its walls.

"It's pitch black down there, Captain. You don' mean fer us to climb down into its depths, do ye?" one crewman asked.

"That's exactly what I mean for us to do, gentlemen." Edward and his crew steeled themselves for their journey into the abyss.

10. BETWEEN A ROCK & A CURRENT

The climb was treacherous for the lot of them. The moss was slippery and some vines broke, but luckily the rock face allowed for plenty of footholds. They kept climbing down until no light reached them from overhead and all was darkness.

When Edward reached the bottom, he noticed a faint light. As his eyes adjusted, he could see they had entered a long underground cavern, and the light was coming from far ahead of them. The whole cave, save the twenty square feet of rock they were standing on, was filled with water. It was moving forward in a swift current, and seemed too deep and felt too cold to swim across. A fair-sized boat capable of holding ten to twenty people was secured to the bank with a rope. However, using the boat posed a problem.

Rocks of all shapes and sizes protruded from the surface of the water going as far as Edward could see in the dim light of the mossy cavern. A crossing could be treacherous with the current.

"Blimey, ow're we suppos'ta get by wif all those jagged rocks there?"

Anne walked up behind Edward while everyone else was gawking at the water. "You believe that to be dire? Take a closer look at the boat," she whispered.

Edward almost blushed at her closeness as he turned to the boat. What he saw caused him to dash up to the boat, examining the rear.

"What's wrong?" Herbert asked.

Edward turned to him. Nassir held Herbert in his sturdy arms, and he seemed hardly to notice the weight he was carrying. "The rudder's broken on the boat. There's no way we can steer it."

"Let me examine it," Herbert said. "Nassir, could you bring me closer, please?"

"Certainly." Nassir carried Herbert over to the back of the boat.

The helmsman made his assessment. "You're right, Captain, it's broken. It can't be fixed. As far as I know, we don't have anything with us we can use to create a makeshift one. We also don't have oars of the proper size back on the *Freedom*. We could break the ones we have, but then they would be useless to us after this."

"What are we to do then? We need to keep moving forward."

"All hope is not lost, Captain. We can use whoever goes across as our rudders and oars. It's not the best way, but it's all we have at the moment."

Edward cocked his brow. "What do you mean?"

"I'll sit in the bow of the boat issuing orders. Depending on where we need to go, ten people on one side and ten on the other can put their arms into the water to either turn or slow down the boat. It's tricky, but it should work."

"Should work, or will work?"

There was a small pause before Herbert said "It will work," with confidence brimming in his eyes. "You can count on me."

"That's what I wanted to hear. Uhh…" *What was Anne's fake name again?* "Jim…?" Edward uttered the name in a half-questioning drawl as he turned to look at her.

Anne arched her eyebrow. "Yes, Captain?"

"Gather everyone together. We need to move on."

Anne did as commanded, and Edward's group moved to the boat at her beckoning. Edward explained what they would be doing, and asked for volunteers to continue onward in the boat.

Edward wanted Anne, Nassir, and Herbert on the boat as a matter of course. Others were reluctant to join after seeing the current and the rocks, but with some persuasion, seventeen volunteered. Herbert explained what would happen and what commands he would deliver for various manoeuvres. When he finished, Edward reiterated everything to make sure it was clear to everyone.

"Now, everyone who's crossing, board the boat. The rest of you head back to the surface and board the ship." *I hope this works.* Edward watched Anne as she boarded the boat. *It will work.*

Herbert made his way to the bow and positioned himself so he could see everything. Edward was near him on the left side with Anne right beside him, and Nassir was on the right side. Everyone piled in, except the last two who waited for the order to shove off.

"Wait, what about my chair?"

"The other crewmembers will have to take it back; it's too big to take with us, and if it should fall out it would be lost. Nassir, you'll have to take care of Herbert from now on, yes?"

"Understood, Captain," Nassir said in his deep, accented voice. Edward had no doubt Nassir would have assumed the task— whether ordered to or not—with a smile on his face.

Edward turned to the crewmembers waiting at the end of the boat. "Let's shove off!" They pushed the boat farther into the water and jumped in.

The current immediately took them in its cold grasp. The crew soon realised how difficult it would be to control their course—and how easy it would be to die by smashing against jagged rocks—and it unnerved them.

"Full!" Herbert yelled over the noise of the rushing water.

Everyone put their hands into the water and did their best to hold them straight as the water pressed against them. This slowed the boat a good deal. A rock came up on their port side. "Left!" Those on the right side took their arms out of the water, making the boat turn to the right. "Full! Stroke!" The whole crew put their arms back in and synchronised their movements to Herbert's commands. They were able to move well out of the way of the rock in time.

They kept on, with Herbert issuing commands and the crew following to the best of their ability. Every time they took their arms out of the water they rubbed them to bring the warmth and feeling back. The water was not bitterly cold, but the continuing exposure did take its toll.

Edward and Anne were right beside each other, with her body pressed up against him. He couldn't turn his gaze to her, but he could have sworn when they weren't rowing he felt her touch his hand.

Herbert was successful in guiding the crew in avoiding all obstacles—if at times by the skin of their teeth—and their initial fear was subsiding. The rocks around them stood out of the water like giant moss-covered fingers. The remnants of the sea stuck to the skin like dirt under the fingernails. Salt water, seaweed, and crabs scattered between the cracks and crevices. It was almost a pleasant ride.

Then the current grew stronger.

Herbert shouted orders to everyone in a frenzy to avoid the multitude of rocks in their path. Full! Left! Right! Stroke!—the commands resounded one after another over the roar of the gushing water. But the boat creaked under the force of the current, and nothing they tried seemed to do any good.

My arms are burning! I don't know how much longer I can take this!

"Do not worry," Anne's voice said from behind Edward. "I know we can make it." The force behind Anne's words seemed to give him the strength he needed, and he was able to keep going.

Herbert continued to yell out orders one after another, until Edward felt he had used up his last ounce of strength; from the looks on the faces around him, they all had. Then, without warning, the orders ceased.

Is it over? Edward looked up, and he understood why Herbert had stopped. Two large rocks, a short distance apart, loomed dead ahead. There might have been enough time to go around them, but it would have been risky. The only alternative was to pass between them. *But will the boat fit through?*

"Herbert!"

"I know, Captain! We can make it! Arms in!" Everyone pulled together toward the centre of the boat and away from the sides.

They were moving a lot faster now that there was no resistance. The rocks were inching closer by the second.

The crew watched in helpless terror. The rocks were immense; if they hit them, there would be nothing left. A collision was seconds away, but time seemed slowed to a standstill.

Edward held his breath and closed his eyes in silent prayer.

A scraping sound from the starboard side caused several people to gasp aloud. Edward opened his eyes and saw the boat was intact. He could breathe again. He smiled at Anne and then looked toward the front of the boat.

What he saw brought terror to his eyes. They were on a collision course with another rock. The crew had no time to save themselves. It was too late.

"Brace for impact!" Edward yelled, seconds before the boat smashed against the rock.

Everything was a blur as bodies flew this way and that. Some were flung from the boat and into the water. Others, including Edward, hit the rock first and then fell. He smashed his left arm against the rock and then slid into the depths. The current took him tumbling downstream. He flailed his arms and legs in a panicked struggle to orient himself in the swift-moving water, every conscious thought vanishing save one: *Anne! Where's Anne?* After a few seconds of stumbling about, Edward was able to right himself as the current died down. He could see other crewmembers surfacing. Off to his right was a small dock, no doubt intended for the broken boat; he noticed Nassir helping Herbert and some others up onto it. Edward searched every face in desperation, but the one he wanted to see was missing.

Damn! Where is she? After another few seconds, he dove into the water again, the light from the exit giving him at least something to see by. *Rocks! Nothing but rocks! She can't have drowned; she's too stubborn for that to happen. Wait... There!* He noticed movement beside a large rock and swam over to find Anne struggling to free her leg from a crevice between the large rock and another. *There's no way we can lift the rock... No! We have to try. I won't let her die!* He moved in close beside her and tried to push the rock with his feet while bracing himself on the bedrock beneath. No matter how hard he pushed, it wouldn't budge. Anne tried to help by lifting as best she could in her awkward position.

I need more air, but she needs it more than I do. He turned her face to his, and for the second time their mouths touched. Edward granted her the last of his remaining air before returning to the surface for more.

As soon as Edward was ready he went back down. Anne was struggling to move the rock on her own. Edward gave her more air, and they continued the struggle together. They pushed as hard as they could without stopping, sometimes changing angles, but all to no avail.

He looked into her eyes, and she into his. He could see the anger, and the fear.

I'm not letting you die, Anne! Edward leaned with all his might against the rock and he could feel it budging. Then Nassir, the giant of a man, appeared out of the darkness, swam over to them and added to their efforts all the strength he had. With each push, the rock nudged ever so slightly forward—and, in a few seconds, Anne was free.

Yes! Thank you, Nassir!

They rushed to the surface at once, the murky waters providing their last resistance to salvation. When they broke through the surface, all eyes were on them. Edward and Anne were gasping for breath as they made their way to the dock with trembling arms and legs.

Edward climbed up first, and, in an instant after seeing Anne's loose hair, turned himself around to face all the eyes upon him. "My God! Is that crewman all right?" Edward thrust out his arm and pointed at the far wall of the cavern.

Everyone turned to where he was pointing. With the precious few seconds they had, Nassir took out a cap from his back pocket and handed it to Anne. She shoved her soaked hair into the wet leather before everyone looked back at Edward in confusion.

Edward shrugged. "Oh, I guess it was nothing."

Anne stifled a cry of shock. "Edward! Your arm!"

"What?" His left arm, the one that had hit the rock after the crash, was limp, and he wasn't able to move it. During his effort to rescue Anne, he had been unaware of anything wrong, but as soon he saw his dangling arm the pain returned in full. It felt torn and broken. "No need for concern," he said with a grimace. "I'll have Alexandre inspect it later."

"Are you sure? It could be broken."

"Worry not, it's trivial at best. We have to press on." Edward walked up the wooden dock and counted the crew as he went. The cold of the water also hit him. He was chilled to the bone and his teeth were starting to chatter. "We're missing three people."

"They're lost to Davy Jones, Captain. They couldn't swim."

Edward stood straight and motionless. It was the first time anyone in his crew had died. He closed his eyes and he felt numbness in his limbs and his mind, but it was not from the cold of the water. He was weary, and when he spoke his voice was low and hollow. "We'll hold a ceremony tonight in their honour. For now, we must move on. Let us hope their deaths are not in vain..." *They died because of me. If I were stronger, if I had only been paying attention...*

"I'm sorry, Captain."

Edward turned to look at Herbert. He was holding his weight up with his arms; his body spoke more to the weight he felt than did his words.

"It was my fault," the helmsman said. "I should have noticed the danger in time. I should have had us go around those rocks, but I foolishly thought I was good enough to guide us through. I won't let it happen again."

Edward knelt down to Herbert and lifted his chin. "Those men died at my command, not yours." Then Edward turned and walked away, his body sore and his footsteps heavy—but his determination set like stone.

11. THE DOCTOR AND THE DIALS

William and the other members of his party walked down the sloping corridor into the depths of the cave. It was the very one he had found when they first landed at the "two by two" islands.

The air was stagnant and smelled of rotten wood and the burning cinders of their torches. The corridor they traveled through was wet with dripping seawater, and slick with green and brown moss.

"This is quite *l'aventure*, yes, William?" Alexandre commented.

"Yes." William seemed in no mood for talk, but that was usual for him.

They took care in watching their step, trying to avoid the slippery moss. William strode forward with purpose and was always ahead of the others, except for Alexandre.

"You are quite *rigide*, William. *Se relaxer, mon ami.*"

"I cannot relax. Not right now."

"Are you worried for your *fille?*" Alexandre said with a long, drawn-out smile. "Ah! I should not have said that. Now I have let *le chat* out of the bag."

William stopped in his tracks and turned to Alexandre with eyes of cold stone. "Cut the theatrics. What do you know?"

The other crewmembers were catching up, so Alexandre motioned to keep walking down the sloping corridor. He began to whisper in French.

"I'm an observant man, William. I know how to identify a woman in hiding when I see one. The way she walks and acts, the way she tries to mask her voice. It's all about observation. She is not the only one either. There are two more on board."

"Two?" William knew about Anne and Christina—but who was the third?

"Yes, three altogether. The third is good at hiding. I must say, even I had trouble spotting her, but I have no doubts. But enough of that. I know you are not in love; you are too formal and protective. It is obvious by your mannerisms that you were in the military; I seem to recall a high-ranking youngster named William—

rather famous, too, for some… shall I say, less than reputable actions?

"And as for the girl, she's decent at hiding herself, but too protective of her red hair, and of a certain ring I've seen before. Very hard to make a forgery.

"Taking those factors into account, I deduce there is only one person she can be. I admit even I was surprised when I reached the conclusion myself. Why, having the daughter of—"

William slammed Alexandre against the stone wall. "You keep your mouth shut about who she is! I will kill anyone who threatens her safety!"

Alexandre laughed a weary, emotionless laugh, unfazed by this outburst. "My dear William, I am merely an observer. I will simply watch until her mask shatters. I enjoy the game. Where is the fun in telling everyone?"

William let Alexandre down when he noticed the crew approaching. "Remember what I said."

"Of course," Alexandre said. "This confirms one thing for me though…" he commented as William walked away. "That you remain loyal to her means you are innocent."

William walked off into the dark of the corridor, alone, ahead of everyone else, as he had five years ago.

…

William's party caught up to him and left the corridor for a large craggy dome. William had placed some torches in sconces, allowing the crew to see their surroundings better.

Twenty feet from the sloping corridor was a sharp drop to water below. There was a pegged wooden dial, almost like a large stonemill, in the middle of the standing area. In front of the dial, five feet from the edge of the cliff, stood two cannons, ready to be fired into the darkness. On either side of the cave was a large stockpile of gunpowder and cannonballs.

The crew could see nothing else but craggy walls and ceiling. No way to cross the cliff, and, as far as anyone could see in the darkness, nothing even on the other side of the gorge.

"Is this it?" one crewmember asked.

"There's no way across," said another.

"*Pas necessairement*," Alexandre refuted. "There must be something we can do with the cannons. Try turning the dial."

A few of the men went to the dial and began pushing. As the wheel turned, the cannons swiveled on some mechanism set into their bases. Once they reached a certain angle, they stopped moving and the wheel could not be turned any farther.

"Hmm. Now *renverser, s'il vous plait.*" At Alexandre's command, the men turned the wheel the other way, and the cannons swiveled left. They stopped turning before the cannons would be able to hit the wall.

"Aha, as I thought!"

"What? What do you see?" William asked.

"Search the walls for a target."

William examined the cannons. "You heard him. Search the walls."

Several men took torches and inspected the accessible parts of the wall. Sure enough, on both sides of the craggy dome wall hung two wooden planks with rope tied around them.

"If those are hit, they must release something so we can cross the gorge." William peered behind each cannon to the target on the left wall. They were moved as far left as they could be by the dial. "The angle of the shot is wrong. We can't hit the target. Can these cannons be taken apart?"

Alexandre sighed. "*Non, non, non.* They are fine. Leave them."

"What do you mean? They'll never hit like that. And we can't shoot the rope with our guns, it's too far away."

"*Avoir confiance en moi.* I know what I am doing. I need but a moment."

Everyone waited as Alexandre took out a stick of graphite and a piece of paper, on which he scribbled various pictures and annotations. He went at it for a few minutes while everyone watched him pacing back and forth in thought. His leather shoes made a distinct tap tap that rebounded off the cave walls.

When he finished and put the paper away there was a glint of determination in his eyes and furrowed brow. "Start the dial, *si'l vous plait.*"

William nodded to the crew. They turned the wheel, making the cannons move right about five inches.

"*Arreter!*"

They stopped as commanded. "Why here?"

"Fire *les canons* in sync and you shall see," he replied with a smirk.

William smiled in spite of himself; he thought he could see what was happening now. "Do as he commands."

"But Will, it don't make no sense to be firin' 'em. They won't hit nuthin'."

"I have a feeling we're in for a surprise. Just make sure you fire them at exactly the same time."

The crew gathered gunpowder and cannonballs from the stockpiles, loaded the cannons, and prepared to fire.

Alexandre bestowed upon himself the honour of the firing signal. "*Tirer!*"

The cannons fired with tremendous force. Some of the onlookers were able to see, or hear, the two cannonballs ricochet off each other. The impact caused one to hit farther to the left than it normally would have. But this had been Alexandre's intention. When the dust cleared, the target and the rope were gone.

The crew stood there wide-eyed and slack-jawed. Even William was awestruck by the spectacle. "How did you do it?"

"Simple *mathematiques, mon ami*. Now, the other target."

The crew immediately turned the wheel to the other side until Alexandre told them to stop. They fired the cannons once again, with similar results, and a dusty drawbridge dropped down in front of them.

They all cheered and congratulated Alexandre on his genius; even William freed himself of his black thoughts and praised him for his ingenuity. The company crossed the bridge across the gorge together.

But whatever it was they expected to find, what they actually encountered only confused them. They stood at the brink of another rocky ledge ten feet long and another gorge, which they could neither cross nor see beyond. At the bottom of the chasm, they could see water flowing forward, ahead of them.

"Will, there be another one of them dials," a crewman said as he pointed to the right side of the cave.

In an alcove along the wall was another wheel similar to the one at the entrance. The alcove almost seemed to be there to protect the dial from something. The question was: from what, exactly?

Will noticed a rope running along the ceiling. He followed it forward and it went across the second gorge, presumably where another drawbridge was. The other end went to another wooden plank target, on the ceiling this time. A matching target was twenty feet from the first, also on the ceiling.

Alexandre noticed the same thing. William issued a command: "Four of you return to the other side and examine the cannons; everyone else help me turn this."

Half of the group went to the first section, with the first dial, and a few joined William at the second dial. When everyone was in position, he yelled out to the side. "Ready?" he asked the crew at the cannons.

"Aye."

They turned the wheel as far as it could move.

"What did it do?" yelled William.

"It be moving up, Will. They be aimed at the ceiling. One is aimed a bit lower than the other."

"As I thought." William turned to Alexandre. "The second dial, on this side, will allow us to hit those planks on the ceiling. The first dial allows movement left and right, and the second allows movement up and down. Let's fire a shot after turning the cannons to the centre."

Alexandre nodded as he stood in the middle of the cave watching the planks with attentive eyes.

William cupped his hands and shouted across the first gorge to the team and the first dial. "Move the dial until the cannons are facing the centre. Then fire them at the same time."

After a moment to grasp the situation, the group at the cannons replied with an "Aye."

The crew came out from the second wheel and began to watch with William and Alexandre. They could hear the other team turning the cannons and then loading them. The sound of the blast punched their ears and reverberated off the walls.

The cannonballs bounced off each other as before, but this time it made one ball jump higher. One cannonball almost hit the plank, but the ball was too low from the ceiling.

They had another problem as well. The cannonballs were heading across the gorge, right at William, Alexandre, and the others. The cannonball hit one of the crewmen in the chest, sending him flying into the abyss with a splash. The others jumped to the edge to see if he could be saved, but he was dead before he hit the water.

"Dammit!" William slammed his fist against the stone ground.

The crew watched the water in desperate hope the man would surface again, but he was gone.

William turned to see Alexandre watching, his baggy eyes glassy and emotionless as usual, almost as if nothing had happened.

"You are a surgeon, dammit! Can you not even feign caring?"

"*Je suis désolé.* I keep a detachment from patients and others alike."

William understood, but in that moment his anger would not subside. "Come, everyone, we can mourn later. Alexandre, hide in this alcove so you aren't killed either."

"*Non.* I must stay here."

"What are you talking about? That's suicide."

"If no one watches the *trajectoire* then we won't be able to adjust the position. Do not worry. *Je serai bien.*" One side of Alexandre's mouth curled into a hollow smile.

I cannot tell whether he is insane or if he really does care. "Very well, be careful."

William and the rest went into the alcove and began to turn the dial so the cannons were aimed a touch higher.

"Move the cannons a bit to the right," Alexandre shouted across.

"Aye," the crewmen replied, and they set to the task.

"*Tirer!*"

No sooner was the order issued than they heard the loud bang of gunpowder. This time the ricochet was closer to the target, but the height still wasn't good enough. Alexandre observed one cannonball fall, without worry, as it smashed into the ground ten feet from him. He took more notes and then relayed orders to William's group.

The next shot was dead on, and the rope was released. This time the cannonball had missed Alexandre by only five feet. One target remained.

Alexandre instructed the other group to move the cannons left. He counted the seconds on his fingers and then told them to fire. He must have counted wrong, because something went awry.

The cannonballs hit each other and bounced. One shot up, hit the ceiling, and then headed down with the other to where the surgeon was standing.

"Look out!" William yelled.

Alexandre took a casual step out of the way and the cannonballs passed him before smashing into the stone floor. He made some more notes and then yelled orders to the other side again. He counted down once more.

The crew watching from the second dial in the alcove were holding their breaths from the tension. Some were sweating, on the tips of their toes, others bit on their nails, and still others closed their eyes, but every few seconds opened them again.

The cannons fired. The cannonballs hit each other. One went to the ceiling and hit the target dead on before plunging into the gorge with a splash. The rope released and another drawbridge lowered.

The crew ran over to Alexandre, jumping up and down in amazement. Alexandre himself smirked, not displeased with the adulation.

"*Pas besoin de louanges*. Let us move on before my head swells with praise."

"Come on, boys!" William yelled to the other side, and his group began to make their way across the second bridge. He turned to Alexandre. "Why did you do it?"

"What do you mean?"

"I mean, why did you decide to stay and watch the angles? We had plenty of cannonballs; we could have tried to guess at the timing. We would have gotten it eventually."

"Hmmm. *C'est quoi le mot?* Ah, yes! Duty. It was my duty, and no one else's. With all due respect, you could not have accomplished the task with guesswork. I am the only one who could have done the calculations. I am not totally heartless, William, despite what you may think."

"Perhaps not." William paused, gazing upon the sullen-eyed man in front of him with a new light. "Let us press on. They are waiting for us."

Alexandre nodded, and they both walked across the bridge and into the heart of the caves, not knowing what further trials might await them.

12. THE AMBUSH IN THE DEN

Henry and his team found themselves in a spacious subterranean room, having found the way into their assigned island's cave. They had had to rappel down a deep shaft, and had left the end of the rope tied to a large rock in case they needed a way back up.

They could see by the light from the opening that the chamber was roughly square, and the walls were smooth to the touch. At the end of the room was a wall the crew could climb up to another level. Henry couldn't see the far end of the chamber very well, but it appeared as if the higher level might provide an exit.

Up the wall on the left and right sides of the room ran thick ropes attached to the floor by heavy iron pegs. The ropes went all the way to the ceiling, but because of the angle of the room he couldn't see where they were attached.

I wonder what those are for?

"So, First Mate, what're your orders?" Sam asked with a slight mocking tone.

Henry gritted his teeth and let out a deep breath. "We continue. Be careful, everyone."

They set out to cross the room, inching forward, with Henry and Sam leading. There didn't seem to be any traps, and they were able to move at a good pace. When they reached the middle, Henry took another look around the room. He was now able to see each of the ropes went straight up the wall to the ceiling, then snaked forward to the upper ledge. Presumably, when they climbed up to the ledge, they would find out what the ropes were for.

Henry noticed something odd about the walls on the level they were on. There were little circular notches, like someone had carved them into the rock. Both walls were covered with them.

As Henry turned to start walking again, he noticed a raised section on the floor. It was too smooth and clean cut to be natural. Before he could examine it further, a crewmate who wasn't paying attention stepped on it. The raised stone pressed down, and the circular notches on the wall opened, transforming into dark, round holes.

"It's a trap! Run!"

Everyone reacted in a different manner. Some ran forward, some ran back, some ducked, and some stood there wondering what the fuss was about with foolish expressions on their faces.

Bolts shot from the holes in the walls without a discernible pattern. They hit men caught unawares in the legs and they dropped them to the ground immediately. Henry had a head start and was able to reach the end of the room, along with some others, without incident. Sam took a bolt to the shoulder but kept running. He stopped, started, and watched his step as he tried to reach the far wall. Sam pulled back when a bolt whizzed by his face but another hit him in the thigh. He fell to the ground, clutching his thigh.

"Dammit! Get up, Sam! Everyone, you have to make it to this end where it's safe! Crawl if you have to," Henry yelled.

"What're we gonna do, Henry?" one crewman asked.

Henry glanced at the ropes attached to the ground. He just knew that they were somehow related to stopping the bolts from firing.

"Everyone climb to the top!"

Those who had made it all the way across steeled themselves, turned their backs on their brothers, and climbed the wall. They tried their best to ignore the screams of pain and pleas for help from the ones who could not follow them.

The crew climbing used the uneven stone as handholds and footholds. One man grabbed a raised stone, activating another hidden trap—and before he could react, a pendulum axe swung down and sliced him in two. His body crumpled and fell to the floor in a shower of blood.

"No!" Henry cried as he and the others looked on in helpless horror. They were losing men by the minute, and there seemed to be nothing Henry could do. *No! There must be a way to stop this before anyone else dies!* "Keep moving! If you feel anything move from under you, jump away or fall to the ground."

The men all seemed like they wanted to immediately jump off and not risk going any farther. "Move!" Henry's command impelled them back into action and they began climbing again.

They were climbing a little slower now, but that was proving to be a good thing. The crew checked each handhold and foothold for suspicious cuts in the stone. Once Henry found himself close to a premature end as another pendulum swung down and past him. It thrust into the stone wall, sending small pieces of rock flying everywhere with the force.

Then Henry heard the unmistakable sound of stone rubbing together to his left. He saw the horror in his comrades' eyes.

Not this time!

Time seemed to slow. Henry saw everything stand still, almost as if it were a painting. The crewman's eyes widened as he turned to see the impending doom. Henry reached over and grabbed his hand. The huge pendulum was falling, the razor-sharp axe threatening them both. He yanked the crewman out of its path, and the axe sliced into the rock wall in his place, sending chunks of rock and dirt everywhere. He was holding the crewman by one hand, dangling him in the air. He placed him back on the wall where he could find a foothold again.

How did I do that? Henry stared in amazement at his palm.

"Thanks, Henry. I thought I was a goner."

"Huh? Oh, you're welcome." Henry's eyes darted to the scene below. There were still crewmen trying to crawl to safety. *Now's not the time for questions or pleasantries.* He began his ascent again, carefully avoiding the traps. The climbers were able to make it to the ledge without further incident.

Henry could see nothing up on the ledge suggesting a solution to his dilemma; he had saved some of his men, but how could he help the rest from up here? The two thickly twined ropes he'd seen earlier hung from the ceiling on both ends of the ledge. He followed the rope once more as it snaked its way across the ceiling to the middle of the room, then all the way down the wall, where it was tied to the floor. He rushed to one of the ropes and gripped it in his large hands.

"Half of you take hold of the rope on the right, the other half grab the left one with me!"

They rushed into two lines, knowing exactly what needed to be done. They pulled hard, stretching the ropes taut, but whatever was at the other end was too heavy. They kept pulling and pulling, but nothing moved.

"Come on, you bastard!" Henry let out a grunt, gritted his teeth, and pulled as hard as he could. His muscles bulged from the strain. The rough twine dug into Henry's hand and pulled against his skin, close to drawing blood, but he kept pulling.

The bottom ends of the ropes, attached by iron pegs to what had appeared to be the floor, were actually attached to thin slabs of stone. As the men pulled with all their might, the slab near the left wall moved upward, covering the holes the bolts were firing from. Now that the sheet was moving, it wasn't hard to bring it up the rest of the way and stop the bolts on that side completely.

Now the other side. "Hold on to this side! I'm going to help the others!" Henry held on until the men with him nodded for him to let go. The weight of the stone sheet caused them to skid a little, but they were able to hold on and keep it from sliding all the way down. Henry ran over to the other group. They had moved the slab a few inches, but it seemed to be stuck halfway. Henry's added strength was able to bring it all the way up so the onslaught of bolts was completely stopped.

Henry frowned at the sight of his men who lay wounded in the chamber below. He addressed those who were still strong and mobile. "Help those who are injured back to the ship. We can handle it from here."

The terrible episode had left everyone shaken, but with the immediate danger gone they were able to come back to the here and now.

The crewmates who escaped harm helped their brothers up and carried them back to the entrance of the trap. Their boots crunched the leftover bolts as they walked, and they left pools of blood in their wake.

They'll be safe now. We have to find a way out of here so we can reach the other groups.

On the platform with the ropes there was a large gap in front of them and a drawbridge that somehow needed to be lowered if they were to keep moving. Henry searched everywhere, but he couldn't see any way to lower the drawbridge. They needed to figure out a way of keeping the ropes in place so they could proceed with exploration.

It took Henry a moment for an idea to surface. "Everyone, we can tie these ropes together so we don't have to keep holding onto them. Who's good at knots?"

"I am," Sam said as he pulled himself up with a heave. He was sweating and ragged. The bolts were gone from his shoulder and thigh, but there were two dark red holes and fresh blood running out in their place.

"Sam, what are you doing? You're injured."

Sam laughed. "Maybe this'd stop a child like you, but for me it be a flesh wound. I'm fine. I can tie the knot while you hold it in place."

The two teams pulled the ropes closer together, and they had enough slack to make a knot. Sam tied the ends together, and then the teams released their grip one by one. The now single rope snapped taut at about chest level, held by the iron pegs embedded into the rock, and everyone was free to move.

"I'll send you back to the ship if you are harmed again," threatened Henry.

"I'd like to see you try!" replied Sam.

Henry gestured toward the hoped-for exit. "We have to find a way to release that drawbridge. I don't see any rope holding it in place, so there must be a switch somewhere."

"Henry, what about that over there?" A crewman pointed towards the wall across the lower level where they'd entered.

"What are you talking about? I don't see anything."

"Come over here and look."

Henry walked over to the crewman; everyone else crowded around them, trying to see in the dim light. By squinting his eyes, Henry could make out something made of wood which, at first glance, appeared to be suspended in the air above the entrance. Upon closer inspection, a ledge protruding from the wall held it in place.

"That must be the way to release the bridge," Sam guessed. His breathing was still heavy and he was holding his shoulder with one hand.

"Yes, but how can we get to it? We don't have any way of securing a rope to the other side."

They all thought it over, but no one was forthcoming with any suggestions.

We need a ladder or something to climb across... Henry glanced around at the room once more. *Wait, we have one of those.* "I can cross by shimmying on the top of the slab we pulled up."

"Are you sure that's safe?"

"Safe or no, it's our only option." Henry walked to the slab without waiting for an answer. He put his back to the wall, stepped onto the stone slab, and inched his way across it, careful not to lose his balance. *This is a lot narrower than I thought.*

"Don't look down," Sam said.

Henry's gaze immediately shifted to the floor below, and he lost his grip on the wall. *Oh God!* The weightless feeling hit his ears. He pushed with his toes and brought his balance back.

Sam exhaled. "I told you not to do that, you git."

Henry closed his eyes for a second and let out a sigh. "Well I wouldn't have if you hadn't mentioned it! Shut it, all right?"

Henry's body was rigid and his breathing rapid. He took his time, but no matter where he directed his gaze he could still see some of the floor. It was making him sick. His hands were against the wall, gripping with as much friction as it would allow. Then he reached the centre of the slab where the rope was attached.

I'm at the halfway point. Good. Good. I can do this.

He grabbed onto the rope and turned himself around so he could maneuver around it. He lifted one foot over and onto the other side of the rope, straddling the twine now, and he could hear some of the crew gasp. He put his other foot over and it slipped with an unmistakable scraping noise. He fell. A collective yell echoed from the crew. Henry tightened his grip on the rope still in his one hand. It burned as he fell to the top of the slab. That one last tug on his arm almost cost him his grip, but he didn't let go.

Henry was dangling in the air, and the only thing between him and death was a few fingers and a thumb. His body had twisted and contorted with the fall. He hung against the slab facing outward, and could see the crew yelling for him to climb back up, as well as the high drop right in front of him.

His eyes went wide. He turned himself around and caught his breath before reaching up and placing his right hand on the top of the stone slab. He pulled himself up, and with his left hand grabbed higher up on the rope. He inched his way back up to the top until he had both feet safely back on that small ledge of stone.

He let himself have a minute to steady his breathing. The crew had gone silent now. When his heart finally stopped pounding in his ears, Henry continued his trek across the stone slab. He reached the other side without further incident, and finally stepped over to the ledge with the lever. He took another few seconds to rest before walking over to the contraption.

Henry gripped the large wooden stick in both hands and pulled it with all his strength. It worked as expected—but as the drawbridge began to lower, two large pendulum axes dropped out of nowhere and onto the ropes holding the slabs. One of them sliced through the rope, but the other jammed in place, almost suspended in the air. The slab Henry had walked across shot down to the ground from the rope being cut, uncovering the wall and allowing the bolts to fire once more. The other slab stopped partway.

The knot they had made caused the rope to stop in its place, but it was almost to the bottom of the floor. Henry couldn't jump to it, nor move back to the other side. "You need to pull the rope back so I can get across."

The crew's eyes went from him to the rope, and then the jammed axe ready to fall at a moment's notice. With obvious trepidation, they gripped the rope and began to pull it back as far as they could.

The second axe hovered overhead, seeming to shake a little, as if with the slightest nudge or breeze it could fall.

"You have to hurry, Henry. That axe will drop any minute!"

Without further deliberation, Henry ran to the stone slab. He moved onto it and shuffled across, his mind empty of all thoughts and focused solely on making it to the other side in one piece.

Pendulum axes began appearing out of nowhere. One of them slammed into the wall to Henry's left, inches away from him. One after the other they fell, intent on killing him. Henry was moving as fast as he could, but they kept falling faster and faster.

He reached the halfway point. *Almost there. I'm almost there, dammit!*

Henry tripped again. He fell off the slab with no rope to hold onto this time. Everyone watched in shock and terror. Henry reached out and grabbed the ledge, arresting his fall.

"Get up, Henry!" Sam yelled.

I can't die here. Not now! Ed still needs me.

Henry put his other hand on the stone slab and pulled himself up. After his back was against the wall again, an axe descended and slammed down inches from his fingers. His feet moved of their own volition. He was nearing the end, but the axe that had stopped in midair fell again, heading straight for the rope the crew was holding onto, the same rope keeping him alive.

No time for prancing about!

Henry bent down and leapt into the air. The rope was cut at the same time and the slab fell with a thud. Henry landed on the ledge with the other crewmembers. He had one foot on the edge, and the other in the air. As he tried to place the other foot down he fell backwards. Henry was flinging his arms wildly as he tilted backwards over the ledge to certain doom, when a dozen arms caught his and pulled him to safety.

When he was safely back on the ledge with them, the crew let out a collective sigh of relief. Sam even smiled.

"Nice work, First Mate," Sam said, this time without sarcasm.

"You weren't so bad yourself."

The crew's gaze returned to the floor below. The dead crewmembers they had been unable to save still littered the rocky ground along with the multitude of bolts which caught them.

I hope the other groups had an easier time than us... I hope Edward is safe.

Henry and the others crossed the drawbridge and headed, once again, into unknown territory.

13. THE WEIGHT AND THE CHEST

John, Frederick, and their men entered a cave and immediately found themselves in a narrow, spiraling corridor. The walk was endless, the cramped corridor was oppressive, and one crewman in particular was becoming quite agitated.

"What the hell is this anyway? Why we be goin' in this blubberin' cave? We be pirates. Why ain't we attackin' ships and pillagin'?" Kenneth Locke yelled in his thick cockney accent.

Kenneth and his friends were, as usual, making trouble, and made a miserable situation more uncomfortable for everyone.

"I can't believe him!" Frederick shook his head. "The captain has saved our lives, and this is what he thinks about what we're doing? He sounds more like a common thief."

"Well, we are pirates, after all, or at least that was how it was sold when we were looking for crew in Port Royal. He does have a point," John replied.

"Yea, but he makes it seem like it's something we *should* be doing. Edward hasn't actively attacked anyone. We've only defended ourselves."

"And broken the law in doing so."

"Are you agreeing with him or disagreeing, John?"

"Neither. We've all been branded pirates whether we like it or not. We must become accustomed to taking what we can to live. But that doesn't mean you have to listen to that fool prattle on. Ignore him."

"All right, I'll try. I just can't stand him."

John and Frederick decided to push farther ahead so they wouldn't have to listen to Kenneth anymore. Soon they reached the end of the spiraling corridor and emerged into a small room containing a statue on a pedestal, and a hallway on either side.

"What is this?" Frederick asked no one in particular.

"This must be the trial the riddle talked about."

John walked to the statue. It was a figure of a ship, a frigate very similar to the *Freedom*, carved in precise detail. The bow was tipped upwards, and behind it was a set of scales built into the stone. Like the ship, the right side of the scale was tipped high in the air. John could see engraved words in the stone pedestal below the ship and scales, which he read aloud.

"The eight pieces of the Spanish pride bring balance to the scales and reveal the true path." John reached into his pocket and pulled out a few coins and placed them on the right side of the scale. The scale tipped down and the ship's bow moved down in tandem with it. The bow was now pointed down and the stern raised high in the air, but nothing more happened. "I need five more pieces of eight."

"What for, John?" Frederick asked as he pulled a few coins out of his pocket and handed them to him.

"I'm trying to balance the scales, and the message on the bottom calls for eight pieces of eight. I need two more." John turned to the group gathered behind him. "D-does anyone else have any?"

No one responded; they only stared at John and Frederick with curious looks.

Frederick decided to provide an ultimatum. "Whatever this is, it's probably important. The sooner you give John the two pieces of eight, the sooner we can move on. He'll return them after."

Two men each pulled out a coin and handed them to John. He took the coins and put them on the scales. He tried various combinations of the coins on either side, but nothing worked; no matter how he distributed the weight, the scales never balanced. Halfway through his attempts, the rest of the crew emerged from the spiral walkway, including Kenneth.

"Hurry up, old man. I'm bored here," Kenneth said.

"I'm tr-trying," John stammered.

"Shut it, Kenneth," Frederick retaliated. "I don't see you contributing." Kenneth made a defiant sound and then walked down the left corridor alone. "What does it mean? You've tried everything."

"I think it means we're using the wrong pieces."

"But how? It's standard currency."

"Yes, but these must be sensitive scales that need to be balanced with precise weight. There must be pieces of eight scattered about in this room."

A thunderous crash from the left corridor shook the room.

"What was that?" Frederick yelled as he ran in the direction of the noise.

Around the corner they saw Kenneth sitting on the floor nursing his elbow. In front of him was a large square slab of stone, studded with spikes thrust into the ground.

"W-What happened?"

The other crewmembers tried to help Kenneth up, but he shoved them away. "The damn place is alive an' tryin' ta kill me."

"You must have done something to trigger it. What did you touch?" Frederick questioned.

"I ain't touched nothin', you git! Nothin' that don't be worth takin', anyway."

Frederick, bigger and more aggressive than John, picked Kenneth up off the ground and slammed him against the wall. "What did you take, Kenneth?"

"Get offa me, you little tosspot." He struggled and squirmed, but couldn't escape. "Fine! I took a single piece of eight, all right? It was jus' lyin' there on a rock sayin 'take me please.' Whut's wrong with that?"

"What's wrong is we need that coin to leave, and you could have died, or worse, hurt someone else with your recklessness." Frederick let Kenneth down. "Now give me the piece of eight."

Kenneth spat on the ground before submitting and handed the piece of eight over. Frederick pulled a pouch from his side pocket, emptied its contents, deposited the coin Kenneth found, and passed the bag to John.

"We need to locate seven more pieces of eight like this one in this room. Obviously, they are guarded by traps, so be careful. If you find one, return to the statue and scale and give the coin to John. Understood?" Everyone nodded. "All right now, split up."

"Thanks to you, Frederick. I'm terrible at speaking in public."

"No problem. I guess that's something you and the kid share in common. He's better, certainly, but he still needs a kick."

"I'm always so nervous, especially around p-people like that. You'd think I would be more used to public speaking than to bullets... At least all those years in service weren't entirely wasted."

Frederick laughed. "You'll be used to it soon. Wait here, John. I'll be back after I help the others."

As the crew went about the search, they began to realise the whole room was a maze. The tall stone walls, straight and plentiful, seemed to have no discernible direction to them. There were hallways that led nowhere, and turns that went to dead ends. Everyone lost their way at one point, traversing places previously visited and already explored. And then there were the traps. Each one was designed in such a way that one needed excellent reflexes to avoid them, and few were left untriggered.

Frederick spotted a piece of eight at the end of a corridor and was about to walk to it when he stopped himself. It occurred to him to examine the floor, and sure enough, it was dotted with raised sections. They were distributed in a pattern, however, and once Frederick realised this he was able to step in the safe zones and grab the coin.

Luckily, no one was hurt too badly by the traps, and in no time they had found seven out of eight of the coins. They had one left to locate.

Kenneth was sauntering around the maze, but wasn't checking where he was going despite the fact that he almost died earlier.

"Stupid git Frederick thinks he can boss me around. I'll show 'im and Edward who the real pirate is."

Full of smug swagger, he turned a corner and saw a sight most pirates could only dream about. It was a medium-sized chest filled with about one hundred gold pieces. Without wasting a moment on common sense, he bent over the chest and ran his fingers through his treasure.

Kenneth cackled with glee. "With all this gold I could buy my own ship, maybe two!"

Kenneth dug in and tried to remove a handful of coins, but before he could clear his hand of the chest, the lid closed on his wrist. With a clicking noise, the chest was locked on his hand. No matter how he tried he couldn't move the small chest or open the lid. His hand was stuck in the chest's belly with the golden coins tickling his fingers and taunting him for his greed.

"Dammit! Someone help me! I need help," he pleaded.

The crew heard him screaming and followed it to his location. He was digging at the seam of the chest, trying to open it again, but he was only making himself tired.

Frederick watched him for a moment. "What did you do this time?"

"I reached into this chest and the blasted thing locked on me arm."

Frederick laughed and the others with him joined in. "We warned you about the traps, you even triggered the first one, and now you have a chest stuck on your hand. Maybe we should leave it on you and teach you a lesson."

"Dammit, Frederick, stop flappin' about and help me!"

"Yea, yea, I'll help you. No need to throw a fit." Frederick walked closer until he noticed the last piece of eight on a rock pedestal beside the chest. He grabbed it and handed it to another crewmember. "Take this back to John. I'll be fine here."

The crew obliged and left the two of them alone.

Frederick examined the chest. "I don't see anything that will open the chest at the moment, so let's focus on removing the chest from this pedestal."

"Hurry it up. I ain't got all day."

"Would you rather I leave you here? Shut it while I work," Frederick said as he searched. "...Actually, since you not talking is a long shot, why don't you tell me why you have such a poor attitude? Even I know when to let go."

"He ain't nothin' special. I be movin' up in the world. The first chance I get ta jump ship I'm takin' it. I be the captain then. Now hurry up and pull this off me!"

They heard a loud sound like rocks moving, and the ground trembled. After a few seconds, the noise was gone and the ground stopped shaking.

"John must have solved the puzzle. And I think I found the release mechanism for this. I... just... have to... reach it." Frederick pushed a panel at the base of the pedestal holding the chest, and Kenneth was able to lift the chest off, which was a start. But when the panel was pushed, it triggered something else. Rocks shifted on the walls around them and small holes appeared. Kenneth realised they had set off a trap, but Frederick was just standing up and didn't notice. Kenneth acted on instinct and pulled Frederick around, using him as a shield.

Bolts fired from the holes. Three of them hit Frederick while Kenneth hid behind him. The bolts stopped firing, and Frederick fell to the floor with a thud.

The other crewmembers, hearing the commotion, rushed over. John went to Frederick and turned over his limp body. Warm blood still flowed from where the bolts hit.

John pulled his friend close and held him for a moment, feeling the heat still radiating from him but knowing it was too late.

"He's dead," John said, his voice sure but hollow.

14. THE FIFTH ISLAND

Edward and his group entered a long hallway after they finished their fight with the rapids. The hallway was dark save for a few torches they found and lit. Seawater dripped into the hallway from above, falling into small pools. The acrid smell of burning oil and rags and stagnant water filled the hallway as they walked.

Edward walked ahead of everyone else. The crew followed him, hurrying to catch up. Anne wanted to say something, but Edward's stern expression made her keep her silence.

Edward was numb from the pain of the icy water and his shoulder, but there was a dull throbbing at the back of his eyes. He clenched his teeth to push it away, but the pain returned whenever he thought on the dead crewmates they had had to leave behind.

At the end of the hallway stood a pedestal with a key resting on top of it and a door beyond. Edward picked up the key and examined it. *This must be for the chest mentioned on the paper.* He walked to the door and placed his hand on the knob. His hand was shaking, and he stood fixed in place for a moment.

Anne walked up behind Edward and whispered, "What is wrong?" The rest of his men were scattered behind him, according him distance.

"Nothing." Edward looked back at the crew. "What are they doing?"

"I think they know how you are feeling right now. They are concerned. *I* am concerned."

"They don't know how I feel," Edward snapped. "No one does. No one is thinking ahead. I could walk through this door and find out..." Edward paused and shook his head. "Find out Henry died." Edward's voice turned soft. "I don't know if I can face that."

"Then let us face it together, Edward." Anne placed her hand on the door handle and waited.

Edward gazed into her green eyes, and he too placed his hand, no longer shaking, on the doorknob, on top of hers. They turned the knob together and opened the door.

What it revealed made them gasp.

"How... How is this possible?" Anne stammered as she took in the sight with wide eyes.

117

In the centre of the room beyond the door there was an island with a large stone pyramid in the middle. Water was pouring in from the ceiling and into a moat between where Edward's group was and the island. The water wasn't high enough to swim across, so from what Edward could see there was no way across. To the left and right of the room there were wooden doors and alcoves similar to the one they entered through. He thought that they would be the exits for the other groups of the crew.

"Why could we not see this when we were above?" Anne asked to no one in particular.

"It must be a trick of the eyes. At a higher angle it blends with the rest of the water. That's why we couldn't see the water pouring in, or the opening," Edward said.

"Yes, but who built this place? All this for some treasure? It must have taken years..." Anne trailed off in thought.

Before she could continue, they heard a noise from the left side of the large room. Another door opened up, and William's group walked through. Edward could see he was holding something in his hand. *Another key...?* He and his men were awestruck by the scene and did not see their friends right away. "William!" Edward yelled.

William, Alexandre, and his group all turned to the noise, and when they saw their captain they let out a cheer. William, seeing Anne, looked relieved.

The cheers went on for a few moments until Edward noticed John and his group entering through the door to his right, opposite William's group. John's face was downcast until he saw Edward and his other crewmates.

I guess everyone had it hard. We'll have to hear about what they went through later. For now, we have to find a way across.

Edward was walking to the edge of the bluff to see if there was a way across when the ground began shaking. He instinctively backed up and the tremors stopped. The other groups were searching as well and seemed just as dumbfounded. *Was that me?* He inspected where he had been standing and noticed something odd.

A small circular piece of rock protruded above the rest of the stone. Edward placed his foot on it again, and the shaking started again, but this time he held his foot in place. A slab of rock slid out from underneath the bluff the crew was standing on. *So this is the way across!* No sooner did Edward think that than the slab stopped moving about one quarter of the way across the moat. He took his foot off the stone but it did not spring back. He tried tapping it again, but nothing happened.

The other two groups noticed what he was doing and searched the ground in front of them. They each found the pressure plates in their respective areas and pushed them down. The slab resumed its movement as they kept their feet in place, reached a point three-quarters of the way to the island, and again stopped.

That leaves one group.

Everyone stood watching and waiting for a few seconds. Then the ground shook, and the slab moved the rest of the distance across the water. Edward's face beamed at the sight. It meant Henry's group was there.

That bastard had better not be dead.

Everyone crossed the stone bridges to the island. The sun became more intense as it shone in from above. When they had all gathered at the base of the pyramid, Edward motioned to John and William, who both climbed the stairs. Before Edward joined them, he had Alexandre examine his arm.

"So how was the trial with your group?" Edward asked.

"*Il était amende,*" Alexandre said as he surveyed the arm. "This is simply dislocated." He tugged Edward's arm hard and it snapped back into place.

Edward jerked his arm away and rubbed it with his good hand. "Ah! That hurt, you blasted Frenchman!"

"You are welcome."

Edward tested his arm and properly thanked Alexandre before climbing up the pyramid. There were four sides to it, with one set of stairs for each of the leaders with keys. When they reached the top, Henry was right there with them, and they were all holding keys.

Edward let out a sigh of relief upon seeing Henry. "I'm glad everyone is all right. Did anyone suffer any casualties?" The others lowered their eyes in shame. Edward knew the answer without needing words. He too hung his head in shame and guilt over the losses.

"Let's focus on leaving, Ed," Henry offered. "We must worry about the living before we can honour the dead."

"Yes," Edward agreed as he shook his head as if to cast the guilt away for a moment.

At the apex of the pyramid, a chest sat on a pedestal, and it had four keyholes. The others nodded to Edward in confirmation, and they all inserted their keys in the locks. They turned them at the same time and heard a click. Edward slowly lifted the lid.

To their surprise, the chest contained another key, a sheet of parchment, and four gold coins. Edward took out the parchment and read it aloud. "Congratulations on surviving the trials. This key is a gift from me to you. It will open the door to a part of your ship. There you will find the details of the next challenge you must face in order to open the other parts of the ship. Good luck." Edward crumpled the parchment and threw it down with a huff. "More trials!"

"Well it's not all a loss." Henry reached into the chest and pulled out the gold coins.

Edward smiled. "Those will come in handy. John, you take care of those. Let's take the chest too; I'm sure we'll find a use for it."

Henry put the gold back in the chest, then John closed the lid and lifted the chest off the pedestal. No sooner had the chest been lifted than the ground began to quake violently beneath their feet. They almost lost their balance and had to hold on to the pedestal to keep from being thrown off the pyramid.

"What's happening?" Henry yelled over the rumbling.

"How am I supposed to know?" Edward exclaimed with a curse.

Edward could tell they were moving up. He thought back to the words of the riddle: '*The belly of the fifth.*'

The whole pyramid, and the island which held it, was rising above the level of the ocean water. After a few moments they were able to see the *Freedom* and the rest of their crew. The crew on the ship pressed against the railing, watching the spectacle unfold before their eyes.

With the island above the water now, the crew turned the *Freedom* around and docked it at the newly surfaced fifth island. They threw rope ladders down for everyone to climb up, and one by one the adventurers stepped onto the deck of the ship that was their home. The trials were over, and the crew was glad to return to the world of wood and rope and sail they were used to.

Edward stood on the deck, scanning the water and the islands, finally settling on the fifth. His eyes drifted to the key he had gained. Despite the hardship and the loss, he hoped it had been worth the trouble. No amount of gold could replace his lost men, but it could bring some help to their families.

He tested the key on the aft cabin, below the quarterdeck and the wheel, but it didn't work. Then he tried the fore cabin. The key turned with a click, and Edward smiled as he pushed open the door. The other crewmembers realised what was happening and followed him into the room whose contents no one had seen.

It was a spacious cabin that seemed to be used for weapons storage. Barrels were stocked with rifles of the highest quality. There were swords, too, each well crafted and razor sharp. But most impressive were the cannons: three decent-sized twelve-pounders that would enable them to attack from the front first, then the sides as they passed a ship.

This will be a good spot to hold meetings from now on.

Edward noticed a piece of paper affixed to the mast pole coming down through the centre of the room. He picked it up and read: "The jungle holds the next key. May this map be your guide to the captain's trial. Look at it with eyes clouded by a pirate's home. Know this: Only the captain may enter, and only the captain may leave." A map was drawn beneath the writing, which represented nothing Edward could recognise. It seemed to show a few landmarks, but nothing significant, and nothing was marked save an X in the middle of the jungle area. *I guess I'll have Herbert examine this later.*

Edward walked out of the foredeck cabin and motioned to everyone on board. "Prepare to set sail. Officers, follow me. We're having a meeting."

15. THE LOST AND THE LEFT BEHIND

"Frederick died?" The news floored Edward. The deaths of the other crewmembers had hit him hard enough, but this was something else entirely. Edward had known him from their hometown. "I cannot believe it. What happened?" he asked.

"He d-died because of a trap. I told one crewman to take his body back while we were in the fifth island. I was so angry with Kenneth after..." John clenched his teeth and fist together.

"Why were you angry with Kenneth? What did he do?"

"Oh, uh... sorry, Captain. It's p-probably best I not tell you."

"I have a right to know, John."

John recounted in detail what had happened: how Frederick had helped Kenneth, and then he used Frederick as a shield, and had the gall to brag about it afterwards. As Edward listened his expression changed from sorrow to rage. Before the tale was complete, Edward stood, grabbed one of the new swords, and rushed out the door.

"C-Captain! Stop!" John yelled, but Edward kept going.

"Kenneth Locke! Where are you?!" Edward screamed to everyone on deck, which made them all turn and stare.

"Ed, you need to stop. Killing him won't solve anything," Henry pleaded, but Edward wasn't listening.

"Kenneth! Your captain requests your presence immediately."

"Edward, this isn't like you. You can't kill one of your own crewmembers."

"Watch me," Edward shot back over his shoulder. Kenneth now approached him. "I heard what you did to Frederick."

"Whut of it? He be dead now, so whut does it matter?"

Edward gritted his teeth together, grinding them as anger washed over him. He thrust the cutlass at Kenneth.

Kenneth jumped out of the way and one of his friends tossed him a sword. Now it was a duel. The medium-sized chest filled with gold was still on his good hand, weighing him down and forcing him to use his left for the cutlass.

They circled each other and the crew gathered around, chanting for blood. Edward swiped and slashed at Kenneth, who was struggling to dodge. Using his off hand and having the other slowing him down was making him more of a target than usual, but Edward's lack of experience made the fight equal.

They clashed swords, and the clang of metal resounded over the hollering from the men around them. Blow after blow was tiring Kenneth, but Edward was still fresh, his anger driving his blade. At times Edward wielded the sword like a club in both hands; it was enough to overpower any man given his size and strength. A last mighty bash from him struck the sword from Kenneth's hand and sent it flying. The tip of the blade pierced the deck with a loud thunk.

Edward pointed his blade just underneath Kenneth's throat. He pushed Kenneth with the sword until they reached the edge of the deck.

Both fighters were sweating and taking in ragged breaths. "Now jump," Edward said, motioning the direction with his chin.

Kenneth was stunned. "Whut? Ye can't be serious!"

"Oh, I am." Edward raised his voice so the whole crew could hear him. "On this ship, we do not use another crewmember's life as a tool to save our own. What you did to Fredrick was a disgrace beyond reckoning. I banish you from my ship. You are no longer of my crew. Now jump before I cut you open. At least on this island you will have a slight chance of survival. It's more than you deserve."

Kenneth turned and placed his hand on the railing, but didn't climb up. He stood there, staring at the beach, for a few seconds. Then he whirled around and went on the attack.

Kenneth used the chest on his hand like a club, swinging it at Edward and at the sword in his hands. Edward jumped back and Kenneth kept swinging, but the chest was too heavy and unwieldy; Edward was able to dodge the blows by taking a few steps out of the way. Kenneth grabbed the chest in both hands, raised it over his head, and brought it down with all his might and a guttural scream. It missed Edward again and hit the ship, breaking a plank in two.

"I be a better captain than you!" Kenneth shouted. "Look who ya got on yer crew. A Negro and a cripple? What a joke." Kenneth was panting. The fight was taking its toll. "This is a pirate ship, ain't it? You're soft. You can never be a true captain. They will chase you and you will break. Because you're weak!" Kenneth took another swing, but Henry and William intervened and grabbed him.

"Throw him overboard," said Edward coldly.

Kenneth thrashed and writhed, trying to escape William's grip, but his strength was ebbing. He shouted obscenities and insults to

Edward again and again as Henry and William threw him overboard and he fell to the sandy beach below. The crew could still hear his shouts when Edward addressed them. "If anyone has any objection to my decision, you can join him; otherwise, know this: I am the captain of this ship, and my word is law. If you disrespect me, or another crewmember, you will be dealt with appropriately. Understood?"

The crew gave a resounding "Aye, Captain!" in response.

"Now set sail. We're heading for Jamaica."

Everyone set to work, and Herbert steered the ship. No one talked to the captain for the rest of the day.

...

"We are gathered to pay respects to our honourable dead."

Edward was on the quarterdeck delivering a eulogy to the crew. They all stood with rapt attention. In front of them was the only body they could bring back: Frederick's. All the others were either lost to the depths or too marred for viewing. He had been cleaned and his clothes changed.

The moon reflected on the waves. A cool breeze blew over the ship. Henry was standing behind Edward with a lamp; other lanterns were scattered throughout the ship.

"Although they are no longer with us, they will remain in our hearts. Their sacrifice will not be forgotten. They were our crewmates, but they were also our friends, our family on this: our ship, our home."

Henry, John, and William had all offered to say the eulogy instead of Edward because of his nervousness, but he had told them it was his duty. He had written it himself, and had practiced to make sure he didn't make any mistakes.

"They, like us, had dreams, ambitions, families, and friends. They, unlike us, had their dreams and ambitions cut short, and now they cannot care for their families. It is our duty, as their crewmates and their friends, to take on their dreams and ambitions, and to care for their families in their place."

Edward scanned the crew. Some appeared in a fog, staring out at nothing, some at Frederick's body, and others intently at him. Over the months they had been living, working, and fighting together they had indeed become like a family, and they all felt the pain of this loss. Edward knew this, but he still felt alone in its sting.

"Do you, as crewmates, as friends, as family, agree to take on these responsibilities?"

They all replied with a firm "Aye."

"Then may they rest in peace, knowing no more worries."

Edward nodded to four crewmembers stationed on the stairs at either side. They trudged with heavy feet to Frederick's body, picked it up off the deck, carried it to the starboard side and placed it in a small boat. They lowered the boat to the water, threw a lighted torch into it, and let the current take it away. It drifted down the broadside, so everyone was able to see the burning pyre.

"Fire!" Edward commanded.

Select crewmembers stationed at the sides fired rifles three times into the air. The noise boomed then faded after each shot, and by the third shot the current had taken the boat a hundred feet off the fore.

With that, the ceremony was complete, and Edward dismissed the crew. He went to the fore cabin and stared out the windows to the shifting seas and the small boat on fire as it drifted away. A minute later, the door opened.

"I'd like to be left alone, if you don't mind," Edward said, without turning to see who it was.

"I wished to see if you were well."

Edward recognised the voice. "Sorry, Anne. I'm tired."

"I'll leave if it please you, but I have something to say first, if that is all right?"

Edward nodded.

"I do not claim to know how close you were with Frederick, but I do know you cared for him, like you care for the others aboard the *Freedom*. You are closer to everyone because of the past months, but right now you are shutting yourself off from your friends."

"Then what am I supposed to do, Anne? Those men died because of me. Maybe Kenneth was right. I am weak."

Anne walked up to Edward and slapped him. Before he could say anything, she wrapped her arms around him and pulled him into an embrace. Edward slowly pulled his arms up and gripped her tight as tears fell down his cheeks.

They stood there together as Edward let himself feel the pain he was so desperately trying to bottle up inside.

"It will be all right," Anne whispered.

And Edward knew it would.

16. THE MUSICIAN'S INCIDENT

Herbert examined the map left in the aft deck again and again, but he couldn't find anything on the ship's maps matching the location on the paper.

When Edward asked him how his search was faring, he answered first with a sigh and then rubbed his eyes. "I'm sorry, Captain. I must take a break, if it please you. I'm sure I'll be able to find out where it is someday soon."

Edward placed his hand on Herbert's shoulder. "It's all right, Herbert. I'm certain you'll solve the riddle in time. Take us into the nearest port for now. I think we all need a break after what we just went through."

"Negril is close, we should be there within the hour if the wind keeps in our favour."

Before the *Freedom* reached Negril, the crew made sure to put all weapons other than the cannons in the fore cabin. If anyone asked, the crew could say they were for defense. As it happened, the arrival of their strange frigate and its motley crew appeared to arouse little curiosity or concern.

"Perhaps this port will provide us with a little relaxation," Edward hoped aloud.

"After all we've been through, I think we well deserve it," said Henry. "How long are we to stay?"

"A fortnight should suffice. The men can have their fun, and maybe by that time Herbert will have figured out where the map is directing us. If not, we can move on. We can't risk staying at one port for too long. Not with Captain Smith still on our heels."

Henry cocked his brow and looked taken aback. "We haven't seen him in so long! What makes you think he's still after us?"

"Just… a feeling. It feels as though we're merely one step ahead of him, and any moment he'll be on us."

"You say some odd things, Ed."

"Shut up, you tosspot." He punched Henry in the arm and he smiled.

"So Captain, what will you do for your leave?" Henry asked.

"I haven't the foggiest. Inspect the local market, I suppose. I should like to buy a few things with the gold we found on the two by two islands. What about you?"

Henry waved his hand. "I'm not sure what we should be doing."

"What do you mean?"

"Well, what do we do on our off time? Back home we had jobs, then the bluff."

"How about we have an honest drink this time? … Mostly honest."

"No more stealing my dad's rum?"

Edward laughed. "Not this time, I'm afraid."

And so Edward, on the first day, oversaw the loading of the supplies John brought in. Food made up the bulk of the supplies, including plenty of fresh lemons and limes, but some necessary gunpowder and bullets as well. The four gold pieces went a long way, so half of the remainder went into a common stock for later, and the other half was divided amongst the crew.

After that, Edward went to the local market and bought a few things for himself. He found some nice local produce he couldn't pass up, and decided he would cook it that night. He also found a nautical supply shop with everything imaginable for a sailor. He decided to buy a star chart and a guide for using it. He supposed it might be useful.

That night Edward cooked up the produce he'd bought at the market for the crew who'd stuck around, including Henry. It was a simple dish, but far different from their standard rations. He packed it full of vegetables and a little meat.

The crew sat in the mess hall. The ship, resting at anchor, rolled gently with the waves. The smell of the stew and the pine evoked a feeling of being outdoors. This was their home, and it felt right eating here rather than in town.

"You astonish me, Captain," one crewman exclaimed. "This is bloody good!"

"I agree, Ed. Nice job. Where did you learn how to cook?" Henry asked.

Edward turned his head, a confused look on his face. "I never told you?" Henry shook his head. "Oh… Well, the Hugheses always had me buy the food and cook for them. I bought spices, but I only used them on my own food. Over the years I've gotten pretty good."

"I guess the captain's a pirate from birth," another crewmember joked, drawing laughs from the crowd.

They ate and joked and told stories for a few hours in the mess hall. In that place, they were free to talk and act as they wished without fear of being overheard.

After dinner, Edward and Henry went out as planned and had some drinks at a local bar. Jack was there as well—and just getting started, by the state of him.

Edward thought he would end up watching over Jack, but it turned out they *all* needed someone to chaperone them. After a few drinking games, Edward was running all over the place like a madman. When Jack entered his singing phase, Edward, Henry and the whole bar joined in. Everything went well until someone bumped into Henry, and Henry in his drunken stupor took it as a slight. He immediately started a fight, which escalated until the whole bar became one huge brawl.

If Jack was good at anything while drunk, it was fighting and running away. He deftly fought four men by himself, jumping over tables, smashing chairs over backs, and throwing bottles—empty ones, of course—into faces. After that, he grabbed Henry and Edward and ran out the door. They made their way back to the *Freedom* in record time.

The next day they woke up on the hard wooden deck. As Edward regained consciousness, he felt the subtle rocking and shaking of the boat inside his stomach, and he immediately ran to the side railing to let out all he had drunk and eaten the night before.

Henry was quick to join him.

"Have a good night, boys?" Jack questioned, as chipper as ever.

"Oh yes, it was jolly until about five minutes ago."

Edward turned and slid to the floor, the railing bracing his back. "I'm never drinking again."

Jack laughed. "All men have uttered those words, but all men return to the drink. Here," he said, handing them cups filled with something dark neither of them recognised.

"What is this? It smells rotten."

Jack sat down with both of them. The morning sun bestowed a bit of heat, but the salty breeze kept them cool. "Rotten? It's coffee, lads. Have you never had coffee? It's been around for centuries, but it's only just starting to make its way across the world."

Edward and Henry took small sips of it and turned their heads in disgust. "It's so bitter! How can you drink this?"

"It does well for waking yourself up in the morning, and ridding yourself of the after-effects of certain indulgences. You grow accustomed to the bitterness."

"Whatever you say," Henry said as he stared into the blackness of the cup with a cringe.

"I discovered it in England back in my younger days. They used to sell it in bars I frequented. While I quit one addiction after another, I've always stuck with the coffee." Jack tipped his cup and guzzled some down. "It goes well with some opium, though I'm of the notion many would claim opium goes with anything."

The word "younger" struck Edward and it dawned on him how different in age they were. Jack was well into his thirties, maybe even early forties. If he had any children, they could almost be as old as Ochi or Christina, or even Edward.

"Did you quit the opium?" Henry asked while taking sips of the hot beverage.

Jack laughed and peered deep into the black coffee. "Yes, none in this cup, I swear it. I suppose I replaced the opium with two addictions back then. I met a girl, as the story usually goes. She wouldn't have anything to do with a bum like me, but I was smitten. I stopped going to the bars, and maintained a steady job as a musician. I saved my money and persisted. Eventually I won her heart, or at least made her acquiesce to my constant advances." They all chuckled. "Those were the best times of my life." Jack finished his coffee and rose.

"Wait, what happened then?"

Jack frowned, grief filling his eyes for a moment, but then forced a smile. "A story for another day, perhaps. I have business I must attend to. By your leave, Captain?" Edward nodded and Jack left the ship.

"I wonder what happened."

Edward thought back to the time he was on deck late at night listening to the tearful songs Jack sang to himself. "I don't know."

Edward and Henry sat there on the deck and drank the rest of their coffee, wondering what Jack might one day tell them about his love and what had become of her.

...

The next day Edward asked Herbert whether he had made any progress with the map.

"Not yet, Captain. Frankly, I'm stumped. I'm sure it's another trick like the last one, but I have yet to figure it out. I've not upset you, have I?" Herbert asked anxiously. "I'm doing the best I can."

Edward chuckled. "I'm not angry, Herbert. Take your time and ask some of the other crewmembers if they have any ideas. I'm certain you'll work it out in no time. How's your..." Edward looked around to be sure no one was within hearing distance, "...sister, Christina?"

Herbert's anxious look shifted into a smile. "She's doing well. Mostly staying close to me, but she's been enjoying playing with Nassir's boy. They're about the same age too, so it makes things easier."

"That's good to hear. At least they can have a semblance of a normal life."

Before they could continue their conversation, another crewman ran up the steps. "Captain!" He was out of breath and trying to deliver his message through ragged gulps of air.

"Breathe, man, breathe."

The crewman took a few deep breaths and finally was able to say what he wanted to. "It's Jack! He's in trouble."

"Trouble? What kind of trouble?"

"He's been kidnapped!"

"Kidnapped?" Edward repeated, astonished. "What happened?"

"Last night he was taken by some men after losing at a game of cards. He couldn't pay, and they took him. He tried to fight them, but they overpowered him."

"Did you follow them? Do you know where they went?"

"Yes, Captain, I followed them to an abandoned house not too far from here."

"Gather a few people together and tell them to grab some weapons."

"Aye, Captain."

"What are you planning to do?" Herbert asked.

"I'll take him back by force," Edward declared.

There weren't many people on the ship at that moment, but they managed to scrape together five, including the crewman who had followed Jack's captors. They all concealed pistols and knives under their clothes. Edward decided to hide a sword as well, sensing that knives might not suffice.

Whoever these men are, they'll know who they're bloody well dealing with.

130

When everyone was ready, the crewman led the way to the abandoned and dilapidated house and around to a side entrance he had found. Edward and his men reached the entrance undetected.

Edward was the first to enter. He pulled out his pistol and held it tight as walked through an opening missing a door, cautious not to make a sound. No one was in the room, but he could hear muffled voices. The rest of them followed and took out their weapons.

They had entered the kitchen. Edward followed the voices to the main entrance. Rotted stairs in the centre led to a second floor and there was one doorway, missing the doors, in each corner. Two led back to the kitchen, and the other two, on the other side of the room, led to the living room. The voices were coming from there. Edward and the rest sneaked over to both openings and waited, listening.

"The boss will make sure he collects what you owe us. We know you have friends. Now where are they?"

There was a long pause and then a loud thud and a groan, like someone being punched.

"Answer the question!" a second man yelled.

"They're with yer mum, keepin' her warm." Jack's voice was low and almost forced with pain, but he managed a laugh.

A crack this time. It sounded like something was broken.

That's it, I'm ending this!

Edward jumped from their hiding place and pointed his pistol at one of the two large men beating Jack near to death. "I think you've done quite enough, mates. I'll be taking back my friend."

Behind Edward two crewmen also brandished their weapons. At the second entrance to the living room, the other three with Edward entered and pointed their weapons at the men.

Jack pulled up his heavy head. His mouth was filled with blood that was dripping on the floor. The two large men backed away. When they were at a safe distance, Edward motioned to a couple of crewmembers to help Jack out of the ropes binding him.

"I wouldn't do that if I were you," a cold voice said from Edward's left.

Ten men with guns and swords out entered the room. Edward immediately turned and pointed the gun at them.

The man who had spoken carried no gun. He was tall—not as tall as Edward, but an imposing figure nonetheless. He was a hardened man with a strong-jawed but ugly face.

"My name is Luke. That man owes me money for a game he played against my boys here. It's not worth dying over, gents. Lower your weapons and we can make a deal."

Edward didn't lower his gun in the slightest. "The one deal I'll agree to is the release of my friend."

"And all I'll settle for is what's owed to me. I think the way forward is clear."

Edward glanced around the room. Edward and his crew were outnumbered two to one. Edward lowered his gun and the other crewmembers followed suit. "How much does he owe?"

"Five hundred piece of eight."

Damn. How much did you bet, Jack? "I'll need time to gather the money."

Luke placed his hand under his chin in thought. "You have one week."

One week? How are we to scrape together that much so quickly? "All right, one week. But, you must promise to keep your thugs away from him. I need Jack alive and well."

"Agreed." The man stepped forward and put out his hand. "Gentlemen make a deal with a handshake."

Edward stepped forward and returned the handshake. "You'd better not break the agreement, or else." Edward stared Luke down and he could almost see the sweat on his face. He turned and went back to Jack. "Jack, how are you?"

"Been better," Jack drawled, blood dripping from his puffy lip.

"Don't worry, we'll be back to pay your debt and bring you back to the *Freedom.*"

Tears fell from Jack's face. "I don't deserve it... You should leave me... I'm not worth it. I failed as a husband. I failed as a father. I couldn't protect them. What do you even need me for? I only play music, and then this happens. Leave me behind..."

Edward shook the man's shoulders. "Jack... shut it." He let the silence linger for a minute in the air as he stared into Jack's bloody red eyes. "Stay strong."

"Aye," Jack sputtered.

Edward motioned to his companions and they backed out while staring down the thugs. "See you in a week, Luke."

Edward and his five men left the house and started walking back to the ship until Henry and Sam ran up to them.

"Edward, we heard what happened. Where's Jack?" Henry asked, glancing about.

"Some thugs are holding Jack ransom because of a bad bet he made," Edward explained.

"Well, what're we waitin' for? Let's get in there and bust some heads!" Sam yelled.

Edward grabbed Sam's arm before he could run off. "We can't. They have twelve armed men, and we can't risk Jack's life. We agreed to pay his debt, and we have a week to gather the money."

Henry ran his fingers through his straight brown hair and let out a sigh. "Edward, we have another problem," he said in his sing-songy Welsh accent. "There's a marine ship approaching. It's an hour away, maybe two at most."

Edward pulled out a spyglass and scanned the horizon until he noticed the ship approaching. *Dad damn it!*

Edward paced up and down the street. The crew watched as he circled around a few times, looking at the ground as if it would provide him with answers. He stopped and shook his head, his wavy black hair swaying back and forth.

"Ready your weapons. We're rescuing Jack now," Edward commanded as he turned away from shore to head back to the house.

"Wait, Ed, I thought you just said you made a deal with them. And aren't we outnumbered?" Henry asked.

"The deal is off. We don't have enough money or enough time to gather it with that marine ship on the way. Force is our only option left. As for the numbers," Edward began, glancing to his meagre regiment, "we'll manage."

"So that's how it's going to be now?" Henry said, anger filling his every word. "Anyone who disagrees with you will die? When did we stop being just *labelled* as pirates and instead *become* them, Ed? I'm no longer seeing the line."

"One of our crew was taken, beaten half to death, and is being ransomed for some coin, and you want to talk about lines and labels?" Edward asked, waving his hands angrily. "If you don't want to join us, very well, but don't act like our hands are clean. I made the same decision when I chose to save you and Frederick from the noose. Our crewmate is in danger, and I'm not about to let one of my men die because I wasn't strong enough to do the right thing. Men died on those islands back there because of me. Not this time."

Edward left Henry standing there, frozen in place. The crew followed Edward after glancing back at Henry.

Edward pulled out his sword and returned to the back entrance of the dilapidated house. The crew joined him as they put their backs against the outside wall. He motioned to two crewmen, then to the left side of the house. They nodded and went around the building, ducking to stay away from the windows. He sent another two around the right then motioned for Sam and the remaining crewman to follow him.

Henry, pistol in hand, came running, half bent, to the back of the house. Edward couldn't voice his thanks, but a look and a nod said more than words could have.

Edward inched closer to the opening, the door long since gone. He could hear voices of the men inside. Two were having a jovial conversation in the kitchen from what he could tell. He turned and peered over the threshold and saw the two, with a third glancing out the windows.

He pulled back and held up three fingers to his companions. After they nodded, he held a finger up to his lips.

He peered over the threshold to see only two men now, the third having moved on. The two talking had moved, and their backs were showing. He crept in. Henry followed behind him. The two tiptoed to the men, standing right behind them.

Edward nodded to Henry, then grabbed the man in front of him, placing his large hands across the man's mouth. Henry did the same. The guards grabbed at the foreign limbs in an attempt to remove them, muffled shock uttered beneath warm palms. Edward slit the man's throat. Blood gushed from the wound and down his arm. He saw movement from the corner of his eye and pulled the dying man close, lifted him off the ground, and stepped back out of sight. Henry followed suit.

The man Edward had noticed coming glanced into the kitchen from the entrance hall. Edward and Henry were up against the kitchen wall, only a foot or two separating them from another enemy. Edward's man was still alive. A muted gurgle erupted, and blood seeped through his fingers. Errant arms and legs still pulled and kicked, but they were more like twitches now. Soon they stopped, and Edward bent down to slide the dead man onto the floor.

His hand was covered in warm blood, and Edward couldn't pry his eyes away from it—the last remnants of life from the first person he'd ever killed.

I had to. I had to. I had to.

Sam knocked Edward on the shoulder, forcing him out of his stupor. Sam nodded to the doorway to the entrance hall, then moved to the other side of the kitchen, to the other doorway. He reached through the doorway and pulled in another victim. He was efficient. His knife went through the skull before the man could utter a word. The only sound was shuffling and then a hard thunk.

"Garry, was that you?" A voice rang out from the far room.

Sam and the crewmate looked at Edward and Henry. Everyone's eyes were wide, save Edward. He pulled out a pistol from his belt and walked into the main room.

With no response, the man who called for his friend walked out of the far room and into the entrance hall. When he noticed Edward, an unfamiliar face, he pulled out his musket. Edward already had his pistol up while walking, and fired before the other man. The noise seemed to shake the empty house. The bullet hit the man's chest, and he fell backwards, clutching his wound and dropping the musket.

Another man ran out of the far room. He had a cutlass in his hands, and in a blink Edward had his sword out again. Another pistol rang out to his left. His eyes were drawn to the source. It was Sam. The man who was about to attack Edward fell to the floor, dead.

Edward nodded his thanks and Sam returned the gesture.

Six men, including the leader, Luke, rushed out from rooms on the second floor, each with a musket or a pistol in hand. Henry pulled Edward toward the far room as the six fired. Bullets rained down, just missing their feet.

Edward and Henry put their backs against the wall of the far room, right next to the doorway. Sam and the other crewmate had made it into the room. Jack was still tied to the chair. Edward nodded to him. He smiled back, but looked anxious.

The sound of footsteps bounded off the stairs and then went silent. Luke and his men moved to the lower level of the entrance. "Edward, I thought we had a deal," Luke called out.

"Circumstances have changed. The deal is off," Edward yelled back. "We're taking our crewmate and leaving."

"What about my money?" Luke yelled back.

Sam cut the bonds that held Jack in place and picked him up to help him walk. He took him back to the wall so that Luke's men couldn't shoot him from the other room.

The crew outside was looking into the far room through the windows. Edward noticed them and motioned for them. They nodded and went back the way they had come.

"You have a choice now," Edward said. "Your money… or your life."

There was a pause before Luke laughed. It was a loud and obnoxious sound, forced even. "As I recall, you have six men with minimal arms. We're stocked, and our pistols are loaded. I return that choice to you. You and the lives of your men, or my money."

Edward turned to his friends. They nodded to him. "There's one thing you have wrong, Luke."

"And what's that?"

"I have more than six men. Now!"

The window at the back of the entrance hall burst open under the butt of a rifle. Luke's men turned to the noise just as Edward's crew kicked the front doors down. Luke's men heard that, too, and reacted to it as well.

The distraction bore fruit. Edward and Henry ran out from the back room. Before Luke's men could choose which way to fire, Edward's crew shot at them from all sides.

When the dust and spent powder cleared, only Luke was still alive. He had taken a bullet in the leg, and he was trying to crawl away from Edward and company. Edward and his men sauntered over to him, and Luke looked up to Edward with fear-filled eyes.

"Your friend's debt is paid. We're square," Luke said, glancing about, moving with his hands and avoiding the gazes of the men in front of him. Eventually, his eyes settled on Edward. "Please, there's no need for more bloodshed. It's over. I won't come after you anymore. I swear it." Edward continued his steady approach, sword in hand, as Luke kept backing away. "Please, don't kill me. Please," Luke pleaded. Edward was not appeased. He grabbed Luke by the chest. "Please, please no…"

Edward shoved the sword through Luke's eye, and the man went limp. He pulled the sword out, let Luke go, and stood up. The sword dripped fresh blood to the ground.

"I had to," Edward whispered.

17. INTO THE STORM

On the ship, the crew's frenzied feet pounded against the deck as they prepared to leave. Those arriving with Edward joined in the frantic activity, and soon they had let loose the sails and left the port without notifying anyone.

Herbert set the course away from the approaching marine ship, and after the wind filled their sails the crew could relax for a moment. Edward himself fell to the deck out of exhaustion and Jack sat down beside him to talk.

"Thank you, Captain. No… Thank you, Edward. You saved my life."

"You're my crewmate, Jack. I'd do the same for any of you."

Tears streamed down Jack's face. "I know, but… seeing everyone there to free me—I just didn't think that would happen. I thought you would have left me, but you didn't. You truly are my family. My new family…" Jack drifted off in thought.

Edward sensed where the man's thoughts were taking him. *Those memories must be painful for him. I'll change the subject.*

"Edward?" Jack cut him off before he could say anything.

"Yes, Jack?"

"I promise you, I won't ever drink again."

Edward nodded, not having the words to reply to Jack's promise. He remembered Jack's words to him the other day. 'All men have uttered those words, but all men return to the drink.' *I hope for your sake, Jack, that isn't true.*

William rushed to the aft deck. "Captain! The marine ship is closing in at top speed." His keen eyes had been, as usual, first to see it.

Edward walked to starboard and took the spyglass from his pocket. As William had said, a ship was approaching under full sail. It was a smaller vessel and a bit faster than the *Freedom*, and it would catch up to them soon. When the ship drew close enough, Edward was able to see the markings on it.

Under normal circumstances this wouldn't cause him any concern, as they had replaced the foresail, but something told him it was bad news. "All hands about face! Hard to port! Head north,

Herbert!" Edward yelled orders as he moved back to the aft deck, his coat lifting in the wind.

Herbert had already changed course; the sharp turn caused some who hadn't yet gotten their sea legs to lose their footing.

"What's wrong, Edward?" Herbert asked. "Don't tell me that ship is…?"

"Aye, it's a marine ship. I don't care if it is smaller than us, we don't have the firepower to fight against it. We're escaping before they can catch us."

"We don't even know if they're chasing after us. There's nothing marking us as enemies."

"I just have a hunch that we should be avoiding that ship. I'll not take the chance they're friendly."

Herbert turned the ship north-east to catch the best of the wind. He yelled to the crew to "Let go and haul," then turned to Edward. "Captain, I didn't mention it before because it wasn't relevant, but there's a storm coming from this direction. There are oxeye clouds on the horizon. If we keep heading this way, the storm will be upon us soon."

"This could be good fortune for us; the marine ship might turn back. How bad will it be?"

"Have you ever seen a typhoon?" Herbert asked.

"No."

"Well, you are about to."

As they approached the storm, the winds rose and soon became violent. Behind them the marine ship drew closer, but Edward was determined to outrun it. The wind lashed at the rigging and sent waves crashing against the side. Rope and sails loosened and whipped with the wind, and the *Freedom* rocked with the waves. Thunder rumbled off in the distance, foreshadowing the true storm yet to come. Despite the ferocity of the storm, the marine ship continued pursuit.

Why do they keep approaching? Edward took another look through the spyglass. Now the ship was closer and he could make out some of the people aboard. *There's something familiar about that ship.* He could see someone standing at the prow with a spyglass pointed at the *Freedom*, mirroring him.

No! It couldn't be! He moved his spyglass to see the name of the enemy ship, and confirmed it to be the H.M.S. *Pearl*, the ship Isaac Smith commanded. He ran to the edge of the aft deck. "All hands to arms! Gunners, man your cannons! Prepare for battle!" How had he found them? For that matter, how had he survived?

Edward turned to Henry. "It's Smith. Isaac Smith."

"What? He chased us here? How did he survive?"

Edward chuckled at the similarity of their thoughts and handed Henry the spyglass.

"He must have heard about Port Royal and then headed in the same direction we did. Or he has the devil's own luck tracking people," Edward said, frustration forcing him to spit out the compliment. "I don't think he'll retreat without a fight."

"Is there no other way?"

"What do you mean?"

"I can't help but think of Robert. These people are just doing their jobs. We shouldn't harm them, of all people. We've done enough killing today, methinks."

"Henry, we're not trying to harm them, we're trying to defend ourselves. They're out to harm us." Edward threw his hands in the air. "What would you have us do? Fall over and die? I know you disagree with my methods, but this is different from those thugs. We must defend ourselves."

Henry thought about it while rubbing his nose. "If you say so."

Edward and Henry grabbed some weapons from the stock barrels. Edward tucked two pistols and a sword into his belt, and carried a musket in his hands. Meanwhile, the crew prepared to fight the heavily armed marine vessel. Cannons were being loaded, guns prepped, and wills steeled.

The marine ship slowly sailed into the sights of the first cannons on Edward's side. Edward ordered his crew to fire. Immediately the marines reciprocated: cannons fired, bullets flew. The sounds of the storm winds, of explosions from black powder and splintered wood, and shouting united in a terrifying cacophony.

Cannons hit *Freedom*'s port side. They smashed into the railing, skimmed across the deck, and off the other side. Wood chips scattered across the ship. Water poured over the side and washed the splinters away. Another cannon hit the side, and another chipped away at the railings. A cannonball hit a crewman and the force of the iron ball ripped his legs clean off.

The water washed him away too.

Edward and Henry stood right among the crew, firing rifles and issuing orders. They had learned, since their last battle at sea, how to reload their muskets. Edward had to resist the compulsion to throw them away for already loaded ones. As he fired a second round he noticed the other ship inching closer to theirs. "Herbert, keep us away from their ship! I don't want them boarding us."

"Yes, Captain!" Herbert shouted over the noise.

From his perch at the helm Edward could see the other crewmembers fighting. He could see John, crouching behind a barrel, reloading his musket. When his weapon was ready, he left his cover, aimed, and fired in quick succession, all in smooth, practiced motions.

William was issuing orders to the gunners at the cannons when a bullet hit one of them in the chest. William took over and fired the cannon himself.

Sam seemed to lack the others' expertise. Either he didn't know how or was too bothered to reload, so he tossed the musket to another crewman to do it. He was firing at a rapid rate, but seemed to be firing blind. Like some others aboard, he needed training.

Anne was in the crow's nest picking off opponents with a new-model rifle she had chosen. She had taken that rifle before any could claim it and kept it in her hammock or on her person at all times. She never missed, and she aimed at the marines' legs or arms, to disable rather than to kill. Whether it was her skill, or the quality of the rifle, Edward did not know, but he suspected a little of both.

The combat went on and on, with neither side willing to withdraw. Herbert's skill, along with the violent waves, kept enough distance between the ships to prevent boarding. The two sides relied on cannons and muskets only. The wind grew in power, causing huge waves to crash against the hull and sending spray over the deck. The ships rode the waves and crashed down into the water, knocking men not used to the sea off their feet almost every time.

The cannons were hitting their mark and sending pieces of both ships flying in every direction. A number of marines, but also several of Edward's men, had fallen from cannon fire or gunshot wounds. *Dammit! We're evenly matched. We need a miracle to get us out of here.*

Then the rain started.

That's not what I had in mind! Edward reloaded his musket and turned to fire. *I have to end this!* He was startled to find himself peering, across the watery chasm between the ships' hulls, down the rifle sight at the one man whose death could end this: Isaac Smith.

He pulled the trigger knowing—feeling—he would hit his mark.

Nothing happened.

What the …? Bullets flashed by him and he ducked for cover. It was then that he noticed something odd: the noise was not as bad as before. The rain and waves and wind were roaring, but the gunfire had lessened. A lot of people were misfiring. *The rain is seeping into the gunpowder.*

Edward took a quick assessment of his crew. Some were lying on the deck with wounds. Some were fighting to keep their guns dry so they could fire. Some were running around keeping the sails and everything else in shape while trying not to be shot.

I can't let my men and my home die like this! Edward ran over to Herbert, who was being held steady by his sister Christina. "We need to flee!" he yelled over the wind. "Any suggestions?"

"None that don't involve suicide!" Herbert yelled back.

Edward gritted his teeth. "Suicide it is! Take us into the storm!"

Herbert's eyes went wide. "Are you insane? We'll all die!"

"I trust you will not let that happen. We only need to be in there long enough to shake them off, then we can escape. Hold for a moment." Edward went to the edge of the aft deck again.

"All hands cease fire!" Those who heard his order repeated it to those who hadn't, until they had all stopped what they were doing. The crew looked at Edward expectantly. "Prepare to fire on my mark! Now, Herbert!"

"Aye aye, Captain." Herbert flung wheel to port to head into the centre of the storm. As the *Freedom* moved, it came close to slamming into the marines' ship.

"Fire!"

At Edward's command, they all unleashed their weapons at once. It was like a wall of fire and iron rammed the other ship and blasted it to hell. The smaller marine vessel narrowly escaped being staved by the *Freedom*, but the damage done was enough. Edward could see Smith rise from the deck of his ship, glancing to his wounded crewmen, the *Freedom*, and the imminent storm. He shouted orders, and they began trimming and furling the sails and slowing down. The ship turned hard to starboard and left the storm.

The marines would be leaving the crew of the *Freedom* alone.

The crew who were able yelled and hooted at their victory. Even Edward had to smile and join in. He raised his hand in triumph as the rain poured down his face. But their joy was short-lived.

The real battle was only beginning.

18. BLACK BART & THE PIRATE COMMANDMENTS

The storm hadn't fully subsided two days later when the *Freedom* ran aground on an uninhabited island in the Caribbean.

No one had detected any sign of land before they hit. The impact was violent and jarring. The majority of the crew were thrown off their feet and many injured. Edward hit his head on a railing and was knocked out. He slipped in and out of consciousness for a few hours.

When the cloud over him lessened, Edward noticed he was in a bed in the crew's cabin. He tried to rise, but a hand stopped him.

"Easy, *mon capitaine*. You took a fall in the crash." Alexandre was right beside him, checking his head.

Anne, still disguised as Jim, was on the other side of him, and she placed a damp cloth on Edward's forehead.

Edward pressed a hand to his head, holding the cloth in place and trying to suppress the throbbing pain. "What's happened to the crew? Is Jack well? He was *already* injured."

"The music man is recovering. The other crew are *démoralisés*. They are lost and angry. I've done what I can for them, but we've lost five to fever and wounds. Four others were missing after the battle and storm."

Edward closed his eyes. Anne placed her hand on his and gripped it, as if trying to impart strength to him. When Alexandre's eyes lingered on the scene, impassive as he was, Anne removed her hand almost as swiftly as she had placed it.

Edward coughed. "We'll have a few words tonight as we bury them. Where did we land?"

Alexandre searched for the words. "Ahh... Herbert?" Edward nodded. "He does not know. And the *nègre* says repairs need to be made before we can set sail."

"I'll have to talk with everyone." Edward stood and started to leave.

"*Mon capitaine?*"

"Yes, Alexandre?"

"*Vêtements.*" Alexandre pointed to Edward's middle.

He followed the finger and noticed he was in his nightwear. "Damn! Where are my clothes?"

Anne laughed as Alexandre pointed to the wall. As Edward pulled the rest of his clothes on, the surgeon and Anne moved on to help the other crewmembers injured in the storm.

Edward dressed, but left his coat behind due to the warmth. After examining the injured crewmen, he went to the top deck and was met by some of the men. They presented mixed looks; it was clear they were glad to see him up and about somewhat uninjured, but their perilous adventures had exhausted them.

He noticed Nassir's son, Ochi, lowering a plank of wood over the side of the ship. Nassir was suspended by a rope on the side, removing and replacing planks from the damaged sections. He still wasn't able to do anything for the gun deck, but it had suffered minimal damage.

"How are the repairs?" Edward asked as he watched.

"Good day Captain! Glad to see you back," Nassir responded in his deep, sonorous voice. He looked around at the side of the ship, pointing with his tool. "She is slow and steady, and would go faster if some others were helping." Nassir grabbed the plank his son had sent down and continued with his work.

"I'll find men to aid you. I'm sure there are some who aren't busy."

Nassir paused, as if he had something else to say, but he thanked Edward and continued working. Edward resumed his walk around the ship. Everyone on board appeared busy, swabbing the deck, fixing the sails, cleaning up in the aftermath of the battle.

He scrutinised the damage to the rails. Some sections were completely torn off, with splinters strewn about on the deck emphasizing the destruction. The fife rails at the bottom of the main mast were damaged as well. Luckily the masts themselves had suffered no harm beyond a few bullet holes.

"Don't worry, girl," he said aloud. "We'll fix you up in no time." He ran his hand affectionately along the railing, but as he did so a sliver of wood embedded itself in his skin. He winced and pulled his hand back. It seemed to him as if the ship were saying it was angry with him for the battle and storm. He pulled the splinter out of his hand. *I'm sorry, there was no other way. I'll try not to let it happen again.*

The first thing he noticed was the pristine water, of such clarity he could see fish swimming along the bottom. The expansive beach turned to grass, followed by palm trees and other foliage on into the centre of the island. The whole area appeared untouched, and in the noonday sun it shone like a tropical paradise.

Some of the crew had disembarked, and Edward noticed several gathered in clusters on the shore. Half of the ship rested on a sandbar, so he climbed down the side on a rope ladder and walked across the shoal toward a group loitering about. After asking them where John and Henry went, he asked them to help Nassir with repairs. The crewmen were reluctant at first, but there was no arguing with Edward's gaze.

He watched them depart, and then set out for the interior of the island. The forest was as beautiful and serene as the beach. Rocky streams wound around towering palms and fruit-bearing trees. The splashing and gurgling of the fresh water was a delicate accompaniment to the calls of bright tropical birds. The shaded path seemed worn, and he wondered whether someone had been there before him. He followed it for about fifteen minutes until he heard a rumbling sound growing louder as he walked. When, in a few more minutes, he emerged into a sunlit clearing, his jaw dropped at what he saw.

It was like a scene from an adventure story. A great plume of water rushed over a mossy forested cliff at least forty feet high and plunged straight down into a circular basin at the bottom. It turned the basin into a pond, lined with fine sand which, combined with the water's depth, made swimming and a dive from the top inviting. And there, lounging about nude in the water, were Henry, William, and a few other crewmembers.

"Oi, Ed!" Henry called out, waving to him. "How are you feeling?"

"I'm well now that I'm here. This place is amazing!"

"I know! It's a paradise. What luck to be brought here after a storm, right?"

"The devil's own," Edward replied as he took in the surroundings.

"Gonna join us, Captain?" one of the other crewmembers asked.

Edward smiled and proceeded to remove his clothes. He scrambled up to the top of the cliff and jumped, making a big splash. The water felt warm on his bare skin. He emerged from underwater and laughed as he made his way over to the others.

"We should bring the whole crew here, there's enough room for everyone." Edward ran his fingers through his wet hair, slicking it back.

"No need to tell them yet. Let's enjoy ourselves. We deserve it."

Edward laughed. "That we do..."

They swam in the lake and everyone had a try at the jump. William declined to participate until Edward forced him to; as ever, William was tense, but when he landed he actually smiled.

They must have been there an hour or more, oblivious to the passage of time. Then John's somewhat plump form burst through the brush and found them merrymaking. He was panting and out of breath.

"Good day, John, care to join us?"

"C-Captain, you must come quick!" John stopped to catch more air.

"What's wrong?"

"A marine vessel and a p-pirate ship have begun fighting on the sea in front of this island."

Edward and the others sprang out of the water and rushed to put on their clothing. They ran back toward their encampment, and as they emerged from the forest of palms they saw exactly what John had described. A marine ship and a pirate ship were fighting an all-out battle offshore. He could see each one's identifying mark atop their masts. For the pirate, it was a man on the left and a skeleton on the right, both holding onto an hourglass between them. For the marines, it was the symbol of the British navy, but Edward let out a sigh when he noticed the name of the marine ship was not the H.M.S. *Pearl*. Their archenemy, Isaac Smith, did not have the clairvoyance to know where the *Freedom* had landed after the storm.

"Wh-what do we do, Captain?" John asked.

Edward watched the ships' cannons firing back and forth. The two vessels appeared evenly matched. "Tell the crew to board the ship. We're going out there to help them." Edward walked over to the *Freedom* as the crew converged on him.

"Who are we helping?" Henry posed.

"Who do you think, Henry? The pirates!" *If they don't win, the marines will attack us. If we help the pirates, they will probably leave us alone.* "Nassir! Nassir!"

The carpenter leaned over the side of the ship. "Yes, Captain?"

"Is she ready to sail?"

Nassir spied the two ships fighting. "As ready as she can be."

"It'll have to do." Edward waved for those watching on shore to come with him. "Everyone board now! Prepare for battle!"

The crew who were still on the *Freedom* lowered ropes and ladders down for the others to climb up, then proceeded to ready the ship to leave right away. The tide had risen, lifting the ship enough so the wind filled their unfurled sails and took them out. The few left back on shore boarded a small rowboat and caught up with the ship.

Edward, on the main deck, grabbed his captain's coat, threw it on, and armed himself. The *Freedom* was in the perfect position to strike against the marine vessel; the two battling ships were moving east with the wind, and the marine ship was nearest shore. Herbert had turned the ship around so they were travelling straight into the marine ship's path. The whole crew moved into position and readied their guns and cannons. The marines only noticed the *Freedom* closing in on them when its cannons let loose at Edward's order. With the continued bombardment from the pirates on their other flank, their ship took heavy damage and rocked back and forth from the impact. Then the second volley from the *Freedom* hit them, and the crew rushed in a frenzy to try to save themselves. They soon realised all they could do was raise the white flag. The battle was over almost before it had begun.

"Cease fire!" cried Edward. "They've surrendered." Everyone stopped firing and watched as the pirates boarded the marine vessel, taking prisoners and weapons from the defeated crew.

"Orders, Captain?"

"Take us back to shore; the other crew can take over now."

"Aye aye."

Herbert steered the ship around in a wide arc so as to circle around the other two ships. As they passed the pirates' vessel, Edward noticed a tall man who appeared to be in his mid-thirties to early forties wearing an outfit similar to his. *He must be the captain.* The man took off his hat and bowed. Edward returned the honour in kind.

The *Freedom* made its way back to shore and landed on the shoal. The crew handed the sails but everyone kept guns and cannons ready to fire at a moment's notice in case the pirates were less than welcoming. They watched as the pirates ransacked the marine vessel. As far as Edward could see, the marines themselves were not harmed, but the pirates took everything they had, including the clothes off their backs. Then they let the marine vessel escape. Stripped of supplies, the marines sailed off to the northeast, back to Jamaica and less threatening territory.

After the marine ship was out of sight, the pirate ship sailed over to the *Freedom*. The closer it came, the more tense Edward's crew became. They knew they had to be ready to open fire at any moment. And, despite the larger size of the *Freedom*, the pirates' sloop, with its larger cannons and more experienced crew, could prove a formidable foe.

Instead of attacking, the ship landed close to theirs, and its captain and many of his crewmen disembarked. Edward decided to follow suit and took along several of his people—who did, however, take the precaution of carrying weapons.

Edward then noticed the extent of the damage the pirate ship had sustained. The *Fortune*—the name was proudly displayed on its side—had many holes caused by cannon fire. The crew who stayed on the ship were already working on repairs and making it seaworthy again.

I guess they wouldn't be able to fight us anyway. We'd probably both end up losing.

Now that Edward was able to see the other captain up close, he noticed how enormous the man was—and how intimidating: seven feet tall, with broad shoulders and massive arms. He was wearing a tight shirt that emphasised his powerful form. His stride was straight and true—never a misstep, never a glance at his feet. He had a strong, clean-shaven jaw. His brown eyes shone with raw determination, and seemed to concentrate the force of his menacing presence.

Edward kept his hand on the sword in his belt. He swallowed hard and began sweating. *He's so huge!*

When the two groups were a hand's breadth apart, the other captain again bowed to Edward. "Salutations, my savior! I am forever in your debt. To whom do my crew and I owe our gratitude?" The man spoke with a slight Welsh accent similar to Henry's.

Edward breathed a sigh of relief. *All right, Edward, you can do this. Just breathe and focus on the captain.* "My name is Edward Thatch." He put out his hand. "And you are?"

The man took his hand. "Bartholomew Roberts."

"Ahhh!" Sam let out a yelp at the man's name and ran up to inspect him. "Black Bart?"

"Oh, my boy, I cannot bear hearing that name. So vile and ungodly a thing. The good Lord blesses my work. I prefer to be called Roberts."

"Is it true you stole gold and jewelry straight from the king of Portugal himself? Out of his own bedchambers?" Sam was smiling from ear to ear.

"Oh you heard about that, did you? It was nothing. We raided his ship and took it; as God had commanded me, I obeyed. Unfortunately, before I returned to my ship, which you see here, I was betrayed by a former comrade. He stole my second ship out from under me. I will hunt him down and he will be judged as the sinner he is! Right, men?" Roberts' crew hollered in affirmation of their captain's words.

"How did you end up here, then?" Edward asked.

"After the scoundrel Walter Kennedy left in my last ship, we went searching for him. We joined a crew sailing a vessel called the *Sea King* and were attacked by the marines you helped us defeat. The *Sea King* fled, and left us to die. We tried to escape and managed to make it here, where providence saved us with your help. Now, please, share with us the story of your arriving here."

"We were chased by some marines through a storm," Edward explained, "and eventually shook them off, but the storm blew us off course and we ended up here. Wherever here is."

"Ah, we are truly like brothers, Edward. These false prophets they call marines can try to burn us, but God is with us. He will not burn his true shepherds." Roberts grabbed Edward and pulled him close, like a chick under his wing.

"Uhh, yes, of course, sir."

"This day delivers us good *Fortune*, and like your ship's namesake, we should celebrate our *Freedom* today. Let us break bread and open the casks! Men, let us celebrate meeting another of God's children! Edward Thatch!" Bartholomew Roberts lifted Edward's hand into the air and both crews cheered and hooted.

God's children?

...

The battle-weary crews had already been more than willing to put off repairing their ships. Now Captain Roberts' words provided them all the excuse they needed. They scrambled to set up small camps all along the shore; they lit fires for cooking, and sat around eating and drinking as they exchanged stories of adventure and pirating.

Roberts had been a pirate for but a year, and already, amongst pirates and marines alike, he was a man to keep an eye on. Sam, in particular, was in awe of the man. Roberts recounted how he had saved a group of his men from being imprisoned. They had been captured on land one day, and to take them back he attacked a local member of the marines, stole his uniform, and went in to rescue them.

"I tell you, men, God was with me that day. The blue marine's uniform was so tight against my breast I thought I would pass out, or at the least be discovered."

The first mate, Hank Abbot, took over for a little of the story. A short man in comparison to Roberts, he looked quick on his feet, and a perfect complement to Roberts. He had light brown hair and thick brows and mustache. Chestnut eyes and a cleft chin made him the picture of a western colonist.

"Anyone in their natural mind would have guessed he didn't belong. His shirt and pantaloons were ripping at the seams, but no one paid him any mind; he waltzed into the prison unopposed like a calf at sundown."

Everyone laughed at the absurdity of it all. "And you have to remember," Bartholomew added, "I was in enemy territory. God may have been with me, but he did not see fit to dry my sweat."

Hank laughed as he continued. "So there the captain is… sweat dripping from his brow, face purple and arms white. He was the like of an apparition walking, but still no one says or does anything. He beats the guard with his bare hands and takes his keys, lets us out—and lo and behold, we find a storehouse of extra clothes for soldiers. I reckon we would have set the place ablaze had we put those uniforms on any faster."

"I tell you," Roberts interjected, "Hank here was shaking in his boots by the end. I wouldn't have been surprised if he had soiled himself."

"But I didn't," Hank assured them, the fire crackling as he continued his side of the story. "And we managed to escape without incident. The next day we set sail like nothing had happened. It was rumored afterward, we heard, that a bear in a blue outfit rampaged in the prison. Frankly, I don't know which should've embarrassed them more: that they had let our captain in looking the way he did, or that they thought he was a bear."

"Ah! The bear again! The crew bestowed upon me the nickname Bartholomew the Bear. I saved them and this is how they treat me!"

Everyone roared with laughter at the thought of Captain Roberts, his burly arms covered with hair, being mistaken for a bear. They laughed, too, in admiration for a man of such intimidating strength who could jest so heartily at his own expense.

And so went the festivities for most of the night. But after a time the seamen, tired from their adventures, battles, and hard work, and sedated by food and drink, fell asleep, many on the ground where they lay. And then it was just Edward and Roberts awake, drunk, and walking around the island singing pirate songs. They walked along the path to the waterfall guided by the light of the moon and there decided to sit down and rest.

As Roberts went to sit, something dropped out of his coat pocket. "Oh, there goes me Bible." Roberts tried to pick it up, but he couldn't reach it. He then tried to reach farther and fell over. Then he shuffled along on his backside over to it, picked it up, and examined it with unfocussed eyes. Edward burst out laughing.

"Hey, Bart. Bear. Bearbart." Edward laughed again at himself as Roberts turned around.

"What?" Roberts crawled over to Edward and leaned his back against a palm tree for support.

"There should be some kind of... commandments... for pirates... no?"

Bartholomew's eyes went wide. "You're... so... smart. Why didn't... why didn't I think of that?"

Roberts was on all fours, his knuckles against the earth. Edward broke into laughter again. "You... you're like a monkey right now. Maybe they should... should call you Monkey Bart."

Roberts appeared serious as he stared at Edward. He watched him until Edward couldn't take it anymore and collapsed into uncontrollable spasms of laughter. Roberts joined in. The two of them continued merrymaking and singing for another hour until Edward fell asleep in front of the waterfall.

...

"Edward! ... Edward! ... *Edward!*"

Edward woke with a pounding headache. Bartholomew Roberts' impressive figure was standing over him.

"Wake up, Edward. We have much to discuss." He pulled Edward up off the sand.

"Day already? Ugh, I can still taste the rum." Edward smacked his tongue against the roof of his mouth to try to rid himself of the poor aftertaste. "What do we need to discuss?"

"The Ten Pirate Commandments."

The what?

Roberts and Edward hiked back to the shoal and discussed his idea while the both of them downed some food and water. It was midday, and the majority of the crew was already up and about, making repairs on their vessels. The wind carried with it the scent of the greenery and the salt water along with the spiced meat and vegetables they were eating.

"When you mentioned commandments for pirates yesterday, it made me think. What if there were ten commandments pirates had to follow? At least, on our own ships. Each man would swear upon the Bible to uphold those commandments, and if he went against them God would strike him down."

Did I really suggest something like that? "I don't know, Roberts. Do you think the men will hold true to it?"

"Of course they will. It's the Bible. Besides, there would be punishments for violators. I have some figured out already."

Edward was drinking from a cup containing a potion provided by Alexandre. It was supposed to help with a night of rum, but all it did was numb his tongue and make him cough profusely from the horrifying taste. *I wish I had some of Jack's bitter coffee right now.* After he was able to speak again, he let Roberts show him what he had so far.

Edward examined the list of commandments, stroking his small black beard as he did so. "Hmmm. On the third one, we should change it so the first mate receives the same shares as the captain and quartermaster."

"Why is that? The first mate ranks below the quartermaster, Edward."

"Oh? I try not to make any decisions without consulting Henry. And what about Hank? Don't you think he deserves a little better?"

"I suppose so." Roberts made the changes on the paper, then handed it back to Edward and he continued to read number four.

No boys and women allowed aboard the ship? That's going to be a problem. "Roberts, I cannot abide by this fourth rule. I already have a child aboard my ship, and we cannot kick him off. His father is my carpenter."

Roberts scratched his chin. "I see. Well, children are a concern during battle; I've had to bury many young ones because of accidents involving black powder. I suppose we can change this to keep them out of battle situations. The problem with women is relations with men, and being kept aboard while offshore. Women have died aboard my ship during battle in the past. God does not like innocent blood to be spilled. Not to mention it is bad luck."

Edward let out the breath he had been holding in. "It's just about the… relations?"

Roberts' head shot up from the page. "Edward, do you have female crewmembers aboard your ship?"

"No! No! I thought the rules should be clear on what was not allowed. So that's number four. Have you thought of more?"

"No, this is all so far. We need six more to make ten commandments."

"Let me have a look. I'll see what I can come up with."

Edward and Roberts worked together, each making suggestions and proposing changes, but after an hour they had created only two more commandments. Then Henry joined them.

"What are you two doing?" Henry sat down on one of the logs they were using as seats.

"Roberts and I are trying to think of ten commandments for a pirate ship. General rules each member should follow. We have six so far, but we're having a spot of trouble with the rest. Here, why don't you take a gander?"

Henry read the page over a few times, trying to decipher the actual text among the corrections and annotations. "It's good so far, but I have a few ideas for the final version."

Edward smiled. "Let's hear what you have."

And so Edward, Roberts, and Henry talked for the next few hours, revising the old, bringing in new, and throwing out what didn't work. In the end they settled upon eleven commandments which they decided to call the "Pirate Commandments," a name allowing them the ability to add as many as seemed necessary. These are the eleven they created:

The Pirate Commandments

I. Every man shall have an equal vote in the affairs of the moment. He shall have an equal title to the fresh provisions or strong liquors at any time seized, and shall use them at pleasure unless a scarcity may make it necessary for the common good that a retrenchment may be voted.

II. Every man shall be given fairly the basic necessities of a list on board, because over and above their proper share they are allowed a shift of clothes. But if they defraud the company to the value of even one piece of eight in plate, jewels, or money, they shall be marooned. If any man robs another he shall have his nose and ears slit, and be put ashore where he shall be sure to encounter hardships.

III. None shall game for money either with dice or cards.

IV. The lights and candles should be put out at eight at night, and if any of the crew desire to drink after that hour they shall sit upon the open deck without lights.

V. Each man shall keep his weapons at all times clean and ready for action.

VI. If any man shall be found seducing any of the opposite sex and carrying her to sea in disguise for the principal act of sexual relations, he shall suffer death. If any man makes a child work for the express purpose of battle, he shall also suffer death.

VII. He that shall desert the ship or his quarters in time of battle shall be punished by death or marooning.

VIII. None shall strike another on board the ship, but every man's quarrel shall be ended on shore by sword or pistol in this manner: At the word of command from the quartermaster, each man being previously placed back to back, shall walk ten paces, turn and fire immediately. If any man does not, the quartermaster shall knock the piece out of his hand. If both miss their aim they shall take to their cutlasses, and he that draws first blood shall be declared the victor.

IX. No man shall talk of breaking apart from the group lest he own a share of £1,000. Every man who shall become a cripple or lose a limb in the service shall have 800 pieces of eight from the common stock and for lesser hurts proportionately.

X. The captain, quartermaster, and first mate shall each receive two shares of booty, the master gunner and boatswain, one and one half shares, all other officers one and one quarter, and private gentlemen of fortune one share each.

XI. The musicians shall have rest on the Sabbath Day by right. On all other days, by favor only.

After they finished, they gathered together their crews and explained the commandments to them. They agreed that any man who did not wish to swear to uphold the commandments could leave at the next shore, and no one would think less of him.

No one took the offer.

One by one, each crewmember swore upon the Bible. The captains swore to act as an adjudicator over disputes, and the senior officers agreed to do so if the captain was involved in the dispute or indisposed.

After the ceremony was over, everyone went back to their duties. Edward's crew still had a lot of work to do on the *Freedom* to make her seaworthy again. After Roberts' crew had finished repairing their ship, they helped work on the *Freedom*.

After the repairs had finished, Edward and Bartholomew stood on the deck of Edward's ship, watching the sun sink to the horizon.

"How do you do it, Roberts? Every day, being chased by marines, hunted by everyone, betrayed by your friends..." Edward looked down at the water lapping against the ship, "killing... Do you enjoy being a captain, being a pirate?"

"Ha! That is like asking a fish if he enjoys water. This pirating business... it calls to me. When the crew and I are up to the waist in gunfire, and cannons, and storms, and treasure... there is no better adventure. This life calls to me as God does." Bartholomew paused, looking Edward in the eyes. "As for the killing, I can see in your eyes you are conflicted. Let me tell you that that is a good thing. God says 'Thou shalt not kill.' However, that did not stop God from commanding the Israelites to wage war against the Midianites. Killing should never be easy, but when it is for a righteous cause, when it is to save the ones you love, then it is just.

"You know, my child, we are not evil. Evil, good, justice, injustice... They are all made by the times, and by those who live in the times. Who is the queen that she can say we are wrong and she right? We do the same thing as she, only in a more surreptitious way. At least we aren't lying about it. And we do not steal more than we need, except by God's will. You want to know the real reason why they oppose us? They're afraid. They fear what we stand for. We're free to do whatever we want and the queen can do nothing about it."

Edward scoffed. "Except kill us."

"Our bodies, Edward. They cannot take away our spirit, or our determination, or our will." Bartholomew took Edward by the shoulders and faced him dead on. "Or our *Freedom*." Those words struck Edward to the core. "In the end, if someone inherits our will, our determination, our spirit, and gains the same *Freedom* we have, they will realise something is wrong in this world... something is wrong in a world that drives men to do the things we have to do to survive. That will is a force greater than any bullet, greater than any government. And that, Edward—that is why they are afraid."

Edward paused to contemplate Bartholomew's words. Chills ran down his back. "Your words fill my heart, but I still have doubts about this life."

"'Tis better being a commander than a common man. And better to be free than suffer in chains." Bartholomew's strong hands squeezed Edward's shoulders gently. "Give it time." And with those final words, Roberts walked back to his own ship to rest for the departure the next day.

Edward stayed, leaning on the stern railing. The fresh smell of the sea and palm trees breezed by him, and he watched the setting sun on the horizon while thinking about Bartholomew's words.

19. THE JUNGLE

The following day, the crews of the *Fortune* and the *Freedom* met one last time for a meal and said their goodbyes to each other. The few days they were together had created a firm bond of friendship, and as a token of gratitude they conferred on Edward half of the loot they had procured from the marines. It included a few items of clothing, marine uniforms, some food to help them reach their next destination, and a decent amount of money and weapons.

"Well, Edward, it appears this be our time of parting. We sail out to do the Lord's work once more. What say you join us on our adventure? You can be a part of my crew," Roberts said with a wink.

Edward laughed. "It's tempting, but we have our own adventures to complete, and I rather enjoy being captain. How about we keep that open for another day?" Edward extended his hand.

Bartholomew gripped it and gave it a firm shake. "When next we meet the seas will tremble before us."

"Aye, that they well."

Roberts turned to Henry and spoke to him in Welsh. Edward couldn't make out what the exchange was about.

"All right, men, back to the ship! We have work to do! There be sinners who need cleansing." Bartholomew and his crew went back to their ship, and Edward's men did the same.

"What did he say to you, Henry?"

"He told me to be brave and protect the crew. I told him I would."

Edward patted Henry on the back as they made their way back to the *Freedom*.

Each crew waved and yelled goodbye to the other as they boarded and prepared the ships, and the noise grew louder as they both took to the sea. Everyone watched as the *Fortune* moved farther away in the opposite direction of *Freedom*, and soon the other ship was out of sight.

"I'm going to miss them," Edward announced to Henry as they looked out at the empty sea.

"Me too, but what do we do now?"

Edward thought it over for a moment. "We still need to solve the riddle to lead us to the next key."

"Do we even know where we are? We landed at that island after being knocked about by the storm. What should our heading be?"

Dammit! I never thought to ask Roberts where we were exactly. "We'll have to head back to a location we are familiar with first."

"No need, Captain," Herbert said over his shoulder. "I found out the location from one of Roberts' crewmen. I figured you would want to sail to the closest island so I set the course right away. We'll arrive in about a week's time. We have enough food to last us until then, and we can restock at the harbour before searching for the islands."

"Well done, Herbert! Keep us steady, my friend."

"Aye aye, Captain!" Herbert replied with a beaming smile.

Over the next week the crew was in high spirits. Not only had they enjoyed the company of other men who weren't trying to kill them, but they seemed to like the idea of the commandments.

To help pass the time, Jack made music, and he even taught others how to play on some of his spare instruments. Another group had pooled their money and bought a pack of cards during their brief stop in Negril before the storm. Since then, the cards were passed around the mess hall each day. Edward allowed the card games as long as no money was being wagered, as required by the commandments.

John spent time tabulating all the items aboard the ship, including the number of cannons and the amount of gunpowder in stock. He calculated how much of everything needed to be in each location and drew up lists on which items could be checked off when purchased in port.

Nassir was still working every day on the figurehead he had promised Edward. It was now about half done. He had started from the bottom, which Edward thought odd, but it was starting to take shape.

Nassir and William had frequent talks when they were alone, or far enough away so no one could hear them. Edward recalled Nassir saying he owed William his life, and found himself wondering what had happened there.

Sam spent his days drinking and being lazy. John had to remind him of the commandments and force him into work several times over the days. He seemed to enjoy practicing swordplay with William and Anne, at least.

The Voyages of Queen Anne's Revenge

Edward had bought a fishing pole at Negril, and he was using it each day there was no wind for the sails. Henry made his own fishing pole and joined Edward. Today they both had their shirts off because of the heat.

"Any bites?" Henry asked as he sat down on the railing beside Edward.

"Not yet."

The sun was strong and beat down on them and their exposed flesh. Having worked indoors most of his life, Edward used to be pale, but with being on the *Freedom* all summer he had gotten some colour. Henry too used to have the typical farmer tan, but now his whole body was darkening from the time out in the sun.

Edward, his black hair in waves down to his shoulders, and Henry, his straight brown hair tied back in a ponytail, sat in silence on the railing of the ship, waiting for some movement in the water. Their bodies, large and muscular, were both like that of stone statues watching the sea lapping against the ship.

But Henry's stone façade soon softened some. His eyes were downcast. "Ed, I want to apologise for the way I acted before. I know your reasons for doing what you did to those thugs in Negril. And, hell! We probably helped that town by doing what we did."

"It took you a week to come around?" Edward laughed and Henry joined him.

"Well, that—and realizing I would have done the same if it was you in there." He took a moment and clenched his fist, deep in thought. When he spoke, his tone was deadly serious. "I want you to know I'll be there when you need me next time."

Edward nodded at his friend's renewed resolve. "I believe I have an answer to your question that day, Henry. The moment we became pirates rather than just being labelled pirates was the moment I took my ship back from Smith. We were naive to think we could live normally while having that label. We have to accept it, all or nothing."

Henry didn't reply as he readied his own fishing rod, but Edward knew he had heard him. Whether he agreed was another matter.

"So Herbert still hasn't figured out the next clue?" Henry cast his line into the water.

"He's still working on it. It has a map on it, so I'm leaving it to him."

Edward felt a tug on his line and pulled back on it. The fish tugged again. He stood up on the railing of the ship and pulled as hard as he could. Henry cheered him on as others in the crew stopped to watch. When the fish broke the surface of the water it thrashed and wriggled against the hook in its mouth. Edward thought it must have been a Bar Jack of at least ten inches. Edward was jumping up and down with the excitement of it all, which was a mistake. He lost his balance, slipped off the railing of the ship, and fell into the water.

"Ed!" Henry yelled.

After a few seconds, Edward emerged from the water.

"Are you well?"

"I am well. Could you lower some rope down?"

When he climbed back on deck—his fishing pole lost to the fish and the sea—everyone patted him on the back and chuckled.

"It's bloody good you can swim, Captain," one of them said.

"You cannot?" The crewman shook his head no. "Who here can swim?" Only two out of the thirty there raised their hands. *Maybe we should teach them. It would be bad if they went overboard.* "I suppose I'm finished fishing for a while. Have fun, Henry."

"Will do, Ed. Let's see if I can avenge our captain, boys." They all cheered Henry on.

Edward had a rag thrown into his face. He pulled it away and Anne was there, smiling. "Impeccable dive, Captain. Good form."

"Har har. Thank you for the towel." Edward dried himself off. "I've seen you and William practicing fighting and swordplay on these off days. What is that strange dance you and him do?" Edward sat down and put his back against the stairs to the aft deck.

Anne joined him. "It is not a dance, but not far from it. It is a fighting art from the East. Would you like to learn it?"

"Well, I'm more interested in the swordplay, but I suppose I could try this too. Sam seems to be more tolerant of William because of it."

"Yes, they are gaining more respect for each other, but their relationship is still rocky, to say the least. If Sam was any better of a fighter, William could end up hurt."

"Well, I'm sure William can handle it, and dish it back out as well."

Anne nodded in agreement as another crewman came by to talk with Edward. "Captain, the surgeon wants to see you."

"What about?"

"I's not sure, Captain. He's doin' some sort of… experiment with grenades."

Edward shook his head immediately. "Oh no, I'm not going down there. Tell him he's on his own." The crewman left and went down to the crew cabin to relay the message.

"Whatever was that reaction for?" Anne asked with a raised brow.

Edward folded his arms. "The last time Alexandre was doing an experiment it was some sort of fire-spitting contraption. It ended up exploding and I almost lost my beard and brows. Unless I need medical attention, I'm staying away that French madman."

Anne had to stifle a laugh.

She has a cute laugh. "Yes, yes, keep laughing," Edward said, pushing her playfully.

Henry turned from his fishing and saw Anne and Edward laughing together. Edward thought he could see a frown on his friend's face before he turned back to his line.

"Captain!" Herbert yelled over the railing. "I've figured it out! Come quick!"

Edward catapulted himself up to the aft deck and ran to Herbert, with Anne not far behind. "You figured out the map? Show me!"

"It took me a while, and some experimenting, but I figured the line 'look at it with eyes clouded by a pirate's home' meant 'clouded by the sea.' I used the reflection of some water and I was able to find the location. We need to sail to Mexico, the northwestern point on the edge of the Caribbean Sea, specifically the Yucatan Peninsula."

Edward examined the map and saw Herbert had marked where they needed to go. "This is astonishing, Herbert. You're a genius. I knew you could find it." Edward gazed at the map, deep in thought. "Why Mexico, why there? There must be some significance," Edward thought aloud.

"I recall hearing a rumor the area is host to a lost Mayan civilisation. It's been left untouched because anyone who travels there never returns. Some think the spirits of the Mayans haunt it."

Edward put his palm to his face and rubbed his eyes. "Either we're caught by traps, or we face ghosts of long-dead civilisations. Oh, Benjamin, when I find you..." Edward left his threat un-uttered. "What do they call that place?"

"The Forest of Burning Hearts."

Edward stared at Herbert in disbelief.

"I swear it to be true," Herbert assured him. "The descendants of the Mayans call it the Forest of Burning Hearts."

"Yea?" Edward replied, dubious. "And where did you learn all this?"

"Being in Port Royal is like being in the centre of the Caribbean. You can hear a lot of stories by being near the port and listening. Whether it's true or not remains to be seen, but knowing is half the battle."

"You say that, but you're not the one who's going into battle. Lay in the course. I'll address the crew."

"Aye, Captain. It will take a few weeks' travel, so I'll take us to a port halfway there to let everyone rest and prepare for the remainder of the journey."

"Understood."

Herbert turned the wheel to port, spinning the ship almost all the way around with the current. The crew's attention went to the helm because of the sudden change in course.

Edward addressed their obvious concern. "We've changed course to our new destination, thanks to Herbert. We now know the location of the next ship key and are headed there right now. As we voted on the last expedition, I thought it appropriate we put this to a vote as well. All those in favor say 'aye.'"

A paltry few responded in favor, with a few stragglers joining in. *What in the Lord's name?* "What's wrong? This key will open another part of the ship, which we'll need to do. Why are you hesitating?"

Fear and doubt filled their eyes. After a moment one man stepped forward. "We all be afraid, Captain. Some of our mates didn't make it back last time, God rest their souls. How do we know that won't happen again?"

"This trial isn't like the others we've faced together, so worry not. I face this trial alone. On the map it said 'Only the captain may enter, and only the captain may leave.'"

This caused more doubtful glances and fear than before. "But Cap'n, you can't! What if you die? You're headed into the unknown, how can we save you from that?"

"I won't die, and I won't need saving," Edward reassured them with a smile. "Now: all those in favor, say 'aye'!"

Many still hesitated, but the majority agreed with their captain. The course was set now.

A few moments later, Henry, John, and William all walked up the steps to the aft deck. "We've got a problem, Ed."

"What is it, Henry? The course has already been decided."

"You're planning to complete this trial alone? It's too dangerous; you have to let some people join you."

"No, I don't. I'm the captain. This is my trial, and my duty. I'll complete it alone."

John stepped forward. He was wringing a cap in his hands. "I agree with Henry. You should t-take others to help you out."

Anne, who had been observing in silence until then, spoke up. "Please listen to us, Edward. We only fear for your safety." She touched his arm almost in pleading.

Edward's hands tightened around the railing. "Must I order you to stand down? I won't have anyone else risking their life for this."

Henry raised his hand to reach out to Edward, but he pulled it back. "Understood, Captain."

...

After a short stop at the Swan Islands, the *Freedom* headed north. Herbert guided the ship along the eastern coastline of the Yucatan Peninsula to find their destination.

Anne forced Edward to start training in both the eastern fighting art and swordsmanship with her and William. His skills improved at a steady pace, though never reaching the level of theirs. He was able to learn only a few proper stances and some simple, effective strikes and counters in the weeks it took to reach their destination.

Anne seemed almost frantic to teach him as much as possible before they arrived. When asked why, she avoided giving a true answer.

"You must learn, so it is as well to be now than later," she said when he asked.

Edward thought there was more to it than that, but wouldn't press the issue.

As the days and nights passed on the journey, the crew learned the name of the forest. More than a few gave Edward passing glances with worry painting their faces. More than once he had to turn down offers of a strong arm for the journey, or reassure other crewmen that he would be all right. For every one who talked with him, there was a group of three or four who had a stake in the proposition, and were disappointed with his answer.

As they followed the coast of the Yucatan, they were guided by the map Benjamin left. The document was surprisingly accurate, so finding the beach they needed to land on wasn't difficult. There was only one spot to land for miles around, unlikely to be found without knowing it was there. Aside from the sandy beach the map pointed to, it was rocky shores or hills as far as the eye could see.

The beach was like any other, albeit small—full of sand and small rocks, and a few crabs scattered about with birds trying to feed on them. The beach went up on an incline to a dark forest of tall trees with intertwined branches and pine needles blocking the light.

As Edward stared into the opening maw of that so-called Forest of Burning Hearts, he felt the tension rise in him. What awaited him was another trial devised by Benjamin Hornigold. If he didn't pass, it could mean death.

Edward steeled himself. *I won't die. Not yet. Not when I've come this far.*

He packed essentials for travelling through the woods: food, spare clothes, rope, camping and travelling gear, compass, sword, two pistols, and of course the map itself.

"Be safe, Edward. Come back alive." Henry put his hand out and Edward grabbed it in return.

"I will."

Anne was standing there, looking at him with steely eyes. Edward smiled in an attempt to reassure her. It was all he could do to show her it was going to be all right.

Edward took one last look at the crew. "If you're going to steal my ship, at least wait until I'm out of sight, yea?" He smiled and they all chuckled. He jumped over the side, grabbed onto the rope ladder, and climbed down to the sandy beach below.

He walked up the beach and into the forest and found a trail, which seemed to be the one located on the map. The forest was dense and the trees stood tall, their thick canopy preventing the sun from reaching him. *It will grow even darker toward nightfall,* he thought. *Herbert estimated I would need about a day and a half to reach the spot marked on the map, so I will have to find a place to set up camp.* As he walked, his nostrils detected a scent both familiar and pleasant. *These trees are the same Caribbean pine the Freedom is made of. Amazing.* For a moment he felt at home. And then he recalled the dreadful name by which this forest was known.

The Forest of Burning Hearts... A sudden chill went down his spine as he took in the sights and sounds of this strange place. From every direction he could hear noises—animal cries, he thought—and as twilight fell, they took on an otherworldly tone. He made a torch out of a stick, a rag, and some oil he had brought. He began to quicken his pace, hoping to find a good place to spend the night before it was too dark to see.

On and on he went into the shady depths of tree roots, bushes and grass, fallen pine, and mushrooms, as the chorus of animal voices echoed louder. He began to feel that the forest was taunting him; he thought he could see shapes moving to the right and left of him, and eyes—terrible yellow eyes piercing through the shadows.

He panicked. *Are those animals? Are they real or am I imagining them? Maybe they're the spirits of the Mayans. Oh God, I'm going to die.* He noticed a large rock in his path, which was almost like a wall in front of him. One of the Caribbean pines was growing atop it, its roots snaking down the rock. The area in front of the rock wall was like a circle of smooth grass with the roots of trees winding their way around. *Perfect!*

Then Edward saw something move, something he knew was real. He ran to the rock and backed up against it as he grabbed one of his pistols. Large, dark shapes began to emerge from the shadows. It was a pack of wolves, seven of them—and they were poised to attack.

"Well, come on, then!" he yelled, but they stared at him, growling. "Very well. I'll take first blood!"

Edward shot at one, wounding it. The sudden loud noise caused the others to lash out. They jumped at him all at once. He dropped his pack, rolled, and threw the flaming torch at one of them. The wolves landed where he had stood not moments before. He pulled out his other pistol and fired it, hitting another wolf. That one fell, but the other five were still on the prowl.

He pulled out his sword and assumed a defensive stance. The wolves circled him. He didn't know which of them would attack next.

There's too many of them! No! Concentrate, Edward. Think about what Anne taught you. "Visualise the enemy in your mind. Breathe deep and do not rely on sight alone. Human instinct is a lost trait among us, but one that is deeply valuable as it uses all the senses. You can use it to sense your opponent's whereabouts and avoid being shot in the back." Now—breathe!

Edward filled his lungs. His blood was on fire, and he became conscious of everything around him, as if his five senses had become one. He saw everything.

He focused on each soft sound made by the wolves. Their paws on the rocks and branches. The panting from their mouths. He could, as it were, see all their movements without sight. One was behind him, limping. Another beside that one was panting and licking its lips. One on his right, waiting. One in front, pacing. And one on the left, snarling, fangs bared.

The wolf to his left jumped at him, the fangs reaching for his throat. He ducked and stabbed the wolf in the chest, rolling with it. Another wolf jumped on top of him. Edward dropped his sword, put his feet against the wolf's belly, and catapulted it against the rock.

He rose to his knees as another wolf ran straight at him; he punched it hard in the snout and it whimpered before slinking into the underbrush. Another pounced at him from the side; he kicked it as hard as he could, breaking its ribs. The second to last jumped on his back and dug its teeth into his shoulder. He grabbed it by the head and whipped it against the rock.

One more! Edward thought to himself as he turned to see it lunging at him.

With no time to counter, Edward shielded himself with his arm. The wolf tore into his flesh with terrible ferocity, boring deep into his skin, down to the nerves. He yelled out in pain.

The animal dug deeper. Edward forced himself to stop screaming and tried to pry the animal's fangs off his arm. No matter how he strained, the wolf didn't release him.

In that moment, when his pain was at its greatest, when he was pulling at the animal's snout, Edward stared into the wolf's eyes. He didn't back down, despite the wolf tearing into his arm. As his gaze, and nails, bore into the wolf, it let him go with a whimper. The rest of the pack, as well, stopped the attack and slinked off into the forest. Before he could contemplate the strangeness of it all, the pain and the loss of blood hit him all at once, and he fainted.

Away from this world, he didn't notice those who had been watching his struggle, and who now gathered around him and lifted his body from the ground. They carried him away to a place where warriors went to face their trials.

20. A SACRIFICE

Edward awoke with a start. Cold sweat was beading down his face, and he felt faint. He didn't recognise his surroundings. He would have expected to awake in the comfort of his ship, or in the jungle. Instead, he found himself in what appeared to be a small grass hut.

He noticed a cloth covering the wound on his forearm. It still hurt to touch, but it wasn't as bad as before and it wasn't bleeding. He raised his head, but he saw no one.

The hut was rectangular, with rounded corners. The floor was of hardened mud or clay, and the roof was made of sheared wood. Several mats rested on the floor, and at one end of the room there was a wooden table with a mortar and pestle, along with materials used for mixing.

Edward was about to stand, but as soon as he removed his blanket he felt a draft.

What in God's name?! I'm naked!

He rushed to cover himself again. He searched, but couldn't see his clothes anywhere. His clothes, his weapons, his pack—all gone. *Whoever brought me here must have taken my things as well, so where are they?* He stood, wrapping the blanket over his nakedness. He couldn't see anyone around through the open door of the hut, so he walked outside.

What met his eyes was a whole village of huts, a civilisation hidden here, deep in the forest. He could see the tall pines beyond the settlement's boundary. He gazed at the scene for a few minutes, and then turned back in the direction of the hut.

What he saw took his breath away.

A large stone pyramid reached above the trees and spanned an area half the size of the village itself. At the four corners of its base were four pillars of intricate design, carved in the form of animals, strange creatures he had never seen before. Steps in the middle of the pyramid went almost to the top. Halfway up the steps there was an opening with a large standing area. Nearby, to the right of the pyramid, was nothing short of a palace, made of intricately carved stone and almost as tall as the pyramid itself. Other buildings, similar in style, were scattered about the vicinity. They did not give the impression of dwellings, but might have served some civic or religious purpose.

Edward stood, awestruck and silent. Then he noticed the village was not deserted: a crowd of people were gathered at the base of the pyramid, and on the opening halfway up a man stood, pointing at something. Edward glanced around, and suddenly it dawned on him. *He's pointing at me!* He noticed others staring at him from the crowd, and some walking toward him, spears in hand. *This cannot be good...* Edward tied the blanket tight around his waist, then turned and ran in the opposite direction. He didn't dare look behind him—it would only slow him down—but he didn't have to see his pursuers to know they intended to catch him. *This is no way to treat a guest!*

He was almost to the edge of the jungle when a figure appeared in front of him holding a spear with its point extended toward Edward, as if in warning. Edward instinctively dropped to his knees and used the momentum to slide on the ground, avoiding the spear and sliding closer to the man. Edward thrust out his hand to grab the weapon, hoping to disarm the attacker. The spear was within reach of his fingertips when, at the last second, it was yanked away.

The man lifted his foot and slammed it down on Edward's face as he was trying to slide past, pinning him to the ground and halting his ill-formed escape attempt.

"You will not escape your fate," the man said, speaking with a deep, accented voice.

He knows English? "Why are you doing this to me? What fate?" He asked, his voice muffled by the foot on his cheek.

"Silence!" the man yelled.

Two other men approached. The three conversed in a language unlike any Edward had ever heard. Then they picked him up off the ground and dragged him back toward the village.

He was now able to see his captor. He was as tall as Edward, about six feet four inches, but even more muscular. He was wearing padded wooden armour over garments of tanned cowhide, loose-fitting to allow great freedom of motion. The entire outfit was ornamented with bones and carved human figures; on its sleeves, feathers of blue, red, and gold were sewn into the leather. On his head was a headdress atop which perched an eagle's skull, and from the front of which long fangs hung down the sides of the man's face. That face was formidable, with a strong jaw and a killer's eyes.

The three men dragged him to the pyramid while the crowd watched and chanted something Edward didn't understand. He tried to pull against them and objected loudly, but he was silenced with a blow to the chest. Only when they reached the base of the pyramid did they let him go. The warrior who'd caught him prodded him with his spear, urging him up the stairs.

As Edward climbed, he looked over his shoulder at the villagers. Their dress appeared bizarre to him. Many were more or less naked, with strange adornments on their bodies; bones pierced their noses and brows, and whitewash covered some faces.

When he reached the standing area halfway up, he saw an elderly man in similar garb as the one who had captured him. But this man was not wearing armour and did not appear to be a warrior. He wore a full cowhide garment, dyed green and red and gold with many feathers attached to it. A multitude of stone figures adorned him, even more than the warrior was wearing. The warrior handed Edward to the elderly man.

"Do you speak English? I didn't know of your village. Please let me leave and I'll not—"

The warrior slapped Edward with the flat of his spear and shook his head, warning him to stop talking. The old man forced Edward to face the crowd and from his vantage point he could see the whole village.

The old man turned to the crowd and addressed them in a booming voice. They stopped chanting and listened. Edward glanced this way and that, trying to see where he might run, but there were warriors everywhere. The one who'd caught him administered a glare as if to drive the very thought of escape from Edward's mind. He was sure he wouldn't be able to fight them all off, and if he caused too much trouble they would kill him on the spot and forego the ceremony.

At the end of the speech, the crowd began chanting again; the man walked to Edward and in one swift motion tore off the blanket covering him. He tried to cover himself with his hands. *Dammit, old man! This is so embarrassing!*

The man handed Edward a cup filled with a strange-smelling liquid.

I suppose I'm to drink this, am I? I guess if I want to stay alive I'll have to do as they say. Everyone watched him as he stood there. Then one of the warriors motioned toward him with his spear, so he drank the potion down in one gulp. It tasted as bad as it smelled, but everyone cheered when Edward handed back the empty cup.

The old Mayan raised Edward's hand into the air, and the crowd cheered again, but Edward wasn't feeling so well. He was already dizzy and tired, and everything was becoming a blur.

The Mayan guided him to a raised platform, then motioned to a pair of warriors. They forced Edward to lie down on the platform—which, given his condition, required very little strength—and tied down his hands and feet with ropes. Edward wanted to struggle, but had trouble even moving a muscle.

Why am I so weak?

When they had finished tying him down, the older man performed a ritual dance with the warrior who'd captured Edward while the villagers made music with drums. The warriors who tied him down cranked wheels on each side of the stone platform, causing it to move towards the pyramid.

Edward pulled his head back as far as he could towards the pyramid and his apparent destination. The platform was heading towards a small alcove, but he couldn't see anything special about the recess in the pyramid. *Why am I moving? What is this contraption?*

The older man had kept dancing and now the younger warrior handed him a torch, which he threw into the alcove of the pyramid, starting a fire.

Ah, I see. I'm to be burned to death. Shite. Edward tried to pull on the ropes, but to no avail.

The platform kept inching towards the flames. The heat felt more intense as he moved closer to his demise. The old man continued his dance to the beat of the drums while the villagers kept chanting. Strangely enough, Edward found the spectacle morbidly captivating.

This must be why they call it the Forest of Burning Hearts.

"Hey!" Edward yelled. The man didn't respond. "Hey! Let me go!" Neither of the dancers paid any attention to him.

The heat was intense to the point of being unbearable. He only had minutes left before he was roasted alive.

"I didn't do anything to you, why are you doing this? I'll give you money, guns, anything you want!" They all ignored him as they continued the ritual.

The top of his head felt like it was burning.

"Let me out of here! You can't do this to me! My crew will avenge me!" His threats garnered no more attention than his pleading.

Mere seconds left.

168

"You'll regret the day you made an enemy of a pirate!" he yelled with all his strength.

The platform, the dance, the drums, the chanting—indeed, the whole ritual—halted. The older man and the warrior wore confusion and shock on their faces. Mutterings in a foreign tongue reached his ears over the crackling of the flames.

They stopped. Thank you, Father.

The older Mayan spoke to the two warriors and they started the wheels again, but this time in reverse. After the platform reached its initial position, they released the ropes binding Edward's hands and feet and helped him up. The old man examined him, turning his head this way and that, forcing open his mouth, checking his muscles. Satisfied, he said something to the warriors and they helped him, still unsteady from the drugged potion, climb down the pyramid steps.

The warrior who had captured Edward stopped them and glared. "You may have saved yourself for now, but you will never pass the tests. I will never consider you a brother." With that he let the others pass.

What was that about? What does he have against me? He looked back at the warrior, who was still glaring at him.

Wait a... Tests?

21. A LEADER

Edward was taken to a hut similar to the one in which he had awoken that morning. When the warriors had left, a young woman handed Edward his clothes. Edward had forgotten his shame, but as soon as he saw his clothes he hurried to cover himself. Laughing at his embarrassment, the woman placed a small cup on a table at one end of the hut, and then left. Edward inspected the cup warily, but it was different from the one he had drunk from atop the pyramid and smelled somewhat normal. He drank the contents and immediately felt a bit better and more alert.

Such strange medicine. I wonder how it works.

The warrior who had captured Edward earlier walked into the hut, still glaring at him. He was angry about something, but Edward couldn't think of what. *If anything, I should be the angry one. They tried to burn me alive!*

"The king requests your presence."

"And if I refuse?"

"We will resume the ceremony."

"Lead the way!" Edward declared. The warrior left the hut and Edward followed close behind. *Maybe if I try to befriend him he might turn around.* "Do you have a name?"

"There will be no talking until you speak with the king."

Well, so much for that.

Edward and the warrior walked through the village, their destination appearing to be the palace nearby the pyramid. People were going about their daily routines, although many stood watching as he passed, jostling each other to catch a glimpse of him. When he smiled and waved to some children, they laughed and ran away.

Edward did not speak as the warrior led him to the king's palace. He stepped up a flight of white and grey limestone stairs into a large, open room. The walls were decorated with murals and a variety of animal skins and weapons—probably displaying the king's own accomplishments—and the floor was inlaid with coloured limestone in patterns that appeared to represent deities or other mythological figures. He could see several doors leading to rooms within the palace on the left and right.

Against the far wall of the room was a raised stone platform supporting a stone throne. The king, the same man who had done the ceremonial dance on the pyramid, was sitting on the throne. Attending him were four warriors kneeling on mats in front of the throne. The warrior who had captured Edward took his place on a mat in front of the king, and a servant placed a mat in the middle of the room for Edward. The servant poured him a cup of water, which he sipped.

After a moment of silence, the king began to speak in the tongue Edward couldn't understand. After he finished, the young warrior who captured him translated. "We are the village counsel. I am the king, Kinchil. This is my son, the war chief, Pukuh."

That young one is the war chief? No wonder I was beaten!

"And these are the village elders: Ixtab, Hanapu, Mulac, and Tohil."

The elders bowed to Edward as their names were mentioned, and he bowed to each in return.

"My name is Edward Thatch," he announced as he bowed to the king.

Pukuh relayed the information without expression. For the moment he seemed to be hiding his hatred of Edward. "You have come here alone to face the trials of the warrior," the king continued. "When you become a warrior, you will become one of us. Then, the trials and the ritual of rebirth will make you a spiritual warrior and a brother to the Mayans."

Pukuh paused, seemingly finished with his prepared speech. Then he added: "You will never pass the tests. I will make sure of it."

The king leaned forward and, frowning, smacked his son's face. Edward had to stifle a smile, but Pukuh did not react. Then the king spoke, and again Pukuh translated.

"First you must make an offering of water to Ah Tabai, the hunter God, and pray for the honour to participate." Pukuh picked up his cup of water, but Edward stopped him.

"Hold, hold a moment! I never agreed to this. Why must I face these trials? I should like these trials rather than be burned alive, but what purpose does it serve?"

Pukuh's eyes flared. "How dare you! It is an honour that one such as you, a weak outsider, should be considered for this! I ought to kill you right—"

Kinchil yelled something fierce at his son, stopping him. They spoke to each other for a moment, and then Kinchil reached in among the multitude of necklaces he was wearing and brought forth an object that startled Edward.

It was a key.

That can't be! Can it...?

The king addressed Edward, Pukuh still translating, while his eyes were captivated by the key. "Many years ago a man came here. He was a brave warrior who could not be bested by any of ours. He fought and ran from us in the jungle for five days until he and I fought on the full moon of the fifth night. We were exhausted, but we fought each other with all our might. We were equals, and neither of us won that day," the king said, a small smile on the corner of his lips. "The king of the time honoured him with trials for his bravery, and he passed them and he became our brother. He called himself a pirate and gave us this key, saying another like him would come one day, and should be accorded the same honour. If he passed the tests, then he would be given this key as a reward."

Benjamin Hornigold! Edward thought back to the man who had taken his money and left him his ship in exchange.

"We have honoured that agreement with you. If you pass, you will gain this key. Does this key hold any significance for you?"

Edward nodded. "I believe it is a key to my ship. I was guided here through a note left in that ship by the previous owner."

"Then you must attempt the trials if you wish to have this key." The king put the key back around his neck, out of sight. "Now, the offering and prayer."

Pukuh picked up the cup again and poured its contents onto the ground in a line. Then he bowed down to the stone, his head almost touching it, and remained in that position. Edward did the same and waited in silence.

To whom should I pray? Their gods? Ours? I care not about either.

After a moment, Pukuh rose, and so Edward sat up as well.

"The first test is one of leadership," said Pukuh, translating the king's words. "You will choose three warriors to accompany you in a hunt. You will guide them and they will act under your orders. You will be hunting a wolf pack that has been attacking our village, and"—Pukuh stared daggers at Edward—"I will be accompanying you."

"You as in *you*, or the old man?" Edward asked, pointing at them in turn.

"You will call him King Kinchil. And no, he will not be joining you." The young warrior clenched his fists. "I will."

· · ·

All the king's warriors were lined up, armed and carrying weapons, for Edward's inspection. The king and the war chief watched as he chose the ones he would bring with him. Beforehand, he was forced to strip and dress in the traditional warrior's garments: a suit of wooden armour and cowhide, and, on his head, a cap in the form of a wolf's head, complete with fur and teeth. It made him appear part man, part wolf. *Well isn't this brilliant. I'm to kill wolves while looking like one.*

Edward walked up and down the line, inspecting each warrior: testing his muscles, examining his eyes, assessing the weapons he carried. *This is foolishness. They all seem capable and in good shape. I'll choose at random.* He stepped back and, without thinking, pointed to three individuals in quick succession.

Pukuh's jaw dropped, and the king laughed.

"What? What is it?"

Pukuh's shock turned to anger and he clenched his teeth. "Nothing. You chose well. We leave immediately. Grab any provisions you may need, and meet at the village entrance."

"Where are my things?"

Pukuh pointed at a nearby hut. "Over there."

Edward gathered a few things, including his compass and some food. But something was missing. *Where's my sword? Dammit!* Edward went back out and made his way to the entrance of the village where the warriors were waiting for him.

"Did you bring my sword or pistols in with my other belongings?"

Pukuh spat on the ground. "That is not a warrior's weapon. We left them where we found you. You will use a spear." He tossed one to Edward.

He caught it easily enough, but eyed the primitive weapon hesitantly. "But I don't know how to use it."

"Then you are not a warrior," Pukuh said. "Will you be a leader and lead, or is that something else you are not capable of doing?"

"I'm going, I'm going." *Now the question is where? Hmm.* "The wolves that attacked me, were they part of the pack threatening your village?"

"Yes. They've attacked people in our village without cause. We used to walk with them side by side, but as of late they have been acting strange. We do not know the reason. We thought a sacrifice would appease the gods, but instead they chose another, lesser way of bringing balance. They are strange beings indeed."

"I'm certainly glad for their decision," Edward said with a smirk. "Since the wolves that ambushed me were part of the pack we're searching for, we'll begin by heading to where I was attacked." The warriors followed Edward, not saying a word.

The Mayans moved with swift and silent feet through the forest. Edward, however, did not. Every time he stepped on a rock or a twig he made a loud noise, and each time he stumbled he cursed. His companions found this intolerable and attempted, with limited success, to instruct him in the proper manner of walking through the underbrush.

Within a few hours they reached the rock where Edward had faced off against the wolf pack. He found the wolf he had killed with his blade. He dropped his spear and bent to grab his cutlass, but before he was able to rise, the business end of another spear was pointed between his eyes.

"Never drop your weapon. The moment you do is the moment you die."

"I do not believe I'd be the only one," said Edward.

Pukuh frowned in confusion—until Edward lowered his eyes, and he followed them down to discover the point of Edward's cutlass almost jammed into the Mayan's ribs. The warrior backed off and lowered his weapon, shock plastering his face and eliciting a smile from Edward.

Pukuh shook his head. "For this trial, swords are forbidden. This is for your warrior rebirth, and you are permitted to use only our weapons."

Edward couldn't be quite sure, but there seemed to be a little more respect in Pukuh's voice than before. "Very well, I'll abide by your rules. But I need my sword when we're done."

"Understood. Now, did you wish to waste time, or do you have purpose in being here?"

"Some of the wolves who attacked me scurried off somewhere. It must have been back to the main pack, so we'll follow their tracks and they'll take us to them."

"You know how to track them?" Pukuh asked.

"No, but that's what I have you for, right? Can you ask the others which of them would be able to track the wolves, please?"

Pukuh did as he was asked and one of the other warriors stepped forward. "All of them can track, but Hukan is the best. He could track a raindrop in a river."

Hukan inspected the fallen wolf and the traces of dried blood on the ground from the wolves wounded in the fight with Edward. He led the group south, following a trail of blood. Soon they found another wolf carcass, and the trail ended.

Hukan conveyed his assessment to the warriors. Pukuh translated. "He says the trail of blood is gone, but the ground is soft around here, so the tracks are easy to follow." Edward nodded to both of them, and they resumed tracking. Hukan examined overturned rocks, broken branches, and bits of animal hair on low vegetation. When Edward thought that the trail was lost, Hukan kept moving as if nothing had changed. Even when the others seemed to have doubts about their direction, he alone proceeded with confidence.

When the day turned to afternoon, they came upon the edge of a low cliff. Small rocks were scattered down its face, all the way to the bottom. It stretched both ways for a good distance. Hukan walked to the verge, then offered his assessment to Pukuh. "Hukan says the wolves went down the face of the cliff. They have worn the ground by their frequent passage. It is not safe for us to climb down, so we will circle around."

"Very well," said Edward, "let's move on." The others turned and walked west, but Edward was fascinated by the scene beyond the cliff edge. Trees as far as the eye could see: a sea of green, shining in the noonday sun. He could hear the sounds of the forest echoing clearly even from that great distance. It was different from the night before—no longer a cry of terror, but a song.

"Come, Edward," Pukuh prodded him.

"Yes."

Edward was turning to leave when a rock beneath him crumbled, and the edge of the cliff collapsed. He lost his footing and began to fall, but Pukuh swiftly reached out and grabbed his hand. Edward held on tight, and for a split second he was safe. But the ground was still unstable, and the cliff edge broke again, taking Pukuh this time.

They both tumbled down the steep cliff to the hard jungle floor, neither of them able to stop the deathly plummet.

The world went black and the two men lost a couple of minutes of their lives to the ether. When he came to, Edward got up off the ground. His head hurt, and he had pains all over. He was sure something was wrong with his back; sharp pain lanced up and down his spine whenever he moved.

Pukuh was holding his leg, so Edward limped over to examine it. The Mayan's left leg was twisted out of place, the bone seemingly broken, but Edward was not sure. The warrior wouldn't be able to walk on it now. He was sweating and it was evident he wanted to yell out in pain, but he only grunted.

A lesser man would be screaming and panicking right now.

The other warriors were peering over the cliff edge and were shouting something down to Edward and Pukuh. Pukuh shouted something back. Then he grabbed his leg and gave it a swift jerk. With a loud crack the leg was immediately back in its proper place.

"What the hell are you doing? That's dangerous!"

"It is the only way," Pukuh said through ragged breaths. "They want to know what to do."

"Tell them to go back to the village to get help, or at least something to help you walk. We'll head east along the cliff face and wait."

"No, you should leave me here, I'll slow you down. I can't walk like this."

"I'm not leaving you behind! You could die out here, and I won't let that happen!"

Pukuh seemed surprised at such a display of concern from Edward, and merely shook his head.

"Tell them," Edward commanded.

Pukuh yelled up Edward's orders and the others made their reply. Edward already knew what they would say, as they were to follow his command. They disappeared from sight, heading back the way they had come.

Edward picked up his and Pukuh's spears and helped his companion to stand, encountering only slight reluctance from the injured warrior. He pulled Pukuh's arm around his own shoulder, and Pukuh used his spear in his free hand to help himself walk.

They followed the cliff, heading east as Edward had suggested. They spoke little, focused on arriving at their destination and avoiding further injury. The sounds of chirping birds and small forest denizens were their only companions. After a few hours of walking, with a little rest at intervals, they reached the end of the cliff. Night had fallen.

They probably arrived at the village and are explaining the situation by now. It'll be dawn before they return. "We should get some sleep. We're going to be here a while," Edward said as he let Pukuh down against a tree.

"Yes," Pukuh agreed as he eased himself down.

Edward also sat down and brought out some of the food he had been sampling through the day. He offered some to Pukuh, who refused it.

The moon shone its pale white light over the dark forest. At the edge of the cliff there were only a few scattered pines; the roots, snaking and gnarled like the fingers of an old man, were sticking out from the ground before plunging deep for nutrients. Various creatures were out and sounding their calls, long and short, loud and soft, screeching and soothing—there was no semblance of order in the jungle of the night.

After a few minutes of relative silence, Pukuh spoke up. "Why did you help me?"

Edward arched his brow. "What do you mean? Why wouldn't I?"

"I haven't been very hospitable to you. You could have left me and saved yourself, but you chose to stay with me. Why?"

Edward thought it over for a moment. "I don't really know why," he said. "I don't carry any ill will towards you. I mean, I could have done without the human sacrifice bit, but what's a few singed hairs between friends?"

"I apologise for that. We have been persecuted before by others of your kind. We protect our jungle and our livelihood any way we can."

So that's why. "Would you have left me behind? You seem to hate outsiders quite a bit."

Pukuh stared off into the dark forest and sat in silence and deep thought for a few minutes.

...

Thirteen Years Ago

"Pukuh!" someone yelled. "Pukuh!"

Pukuh, age thirteen, turned around. He was an athletic youth and, like his father, a great warrior who could best many of the adults already.

"What is it, Jutak? I need to go. My father is calling me."

Jutak was the same age as Pukuh, and just as spirited. A strong, muscular body made him tough for his age. He and Pukuh had been friends and rivals since they were little.

"It is for the test, yes? You take the test to become a true warrior now, right?"

"Yes, and if I am late, I will be scolded."

"Don't forget your promise."

Pukuh walked to the palace. "Do not worry. I will make sure you come with us."

Pukuh ran through the streets of the village to the palace. He went up the limestone steps and into the main chamber. There his father, the war chief, was waiting with the king and the elders. He went to his knees in front of them.

The king, an older man who could no longer speak with ease, sat on the throne with a dignity beyond his failing years. He wore many adornments celebrating his high status and his achievements from over the years.

The war chief, Pukuh's father, spoke for him most of the time. "Pukuh," his father said, his voice resounding throughout the palace, "today you take the test of a leader, the first step in becoming a warrior of this village. You will be participating in a hunt. There are outsiders near the village. You will hunt them down and either capture them for sacrifice, or kill them if they are deemed a threat. This is your decision. Make the offering, pray to the gods for success, and then we will choose four warriors to accompany you. You have our blessing on this hunt for honour."

These were the words of not only his father, but the king. He had their blessing both, and Pukuh's heart swelled with pride. "Yes, my king." He took the cup of water, poured it out on the ground, and prayed to Ah Tabai for success in his hunt.

When he had finished, the king, his father, and the elders all saw him off. The warriors lined up for Pukuh to choose amongst them. It wasn't hard for him to decide whom to take, as he had trained with them his whole life.

However, one person was missing from the group. "Fa— I mean, War Chief? Where is Jutak?"

"He, like you, is not a true warrior yet, and so cannot participate in your test. He will have to have his own someday."

"But I promised him I would take him along!"

"You will have to break that promise, then."

Pukuh crossed his arms in defiance. "You want me to be a leader and make decisions? This is the decision I have made. I would have Jutak with me."

Pukuh's father stared at his son and gave an exasperated sigh. He looked to the king for approval, and the older man gave a nod. "Very well. Do as you wish."

Pukuh's beamed. "Jutak!"

Jutak emerged from one of the nearby huts and ran to his friend. He had armour on and a spear in his hand, ready for battle. He and Pukuh smiled for joy at his being granted the privilege of joining the hunt.

Pukuh chose three others he felt would do well, the best warriors of the village.

After the hunting party had gathered supplies, they set out to track down the outsiders threatening their village. Spears in their hands, they moved with swift and silent feet through the pine forest, crossing streams and rocks and fallen branches. They went on for an hour, until they reached a large, flat, open area of rock and grass, and there they saw a party of white men setting up a camp.

With only four of them in the camp, they did not appear at all formidable. Spectacles adorned their thin faces, and their arms were small and spindly, obviously unused to physical labour. They had strange equipment and notebooks with them.

"Shall we attack now, Pukuh?" Jutak asked. "They are distracted."

"No, we shall wait for the cover of night when they are asleep. For now, we shall keep our distance."

Jutak and the other warriors nodded. They trusted Pukuh and his decisions. They ran back a safe distance and set up their watch.

Jutak was smiling. "Pukuh, are you excited?"

Pukuh laughed. "About what?"

"The beginning of our promise. You become king and I become war chief."

"It has been so long since we made that promise. I cannot believe you still remember."

"Of course I remember. And soon I'll do this test, and we'll both be on the path to fulfilling our dreams."

"Yes, yes. Continue like that all night and we'll leave you behind. Get some sleep." Pukuh pushed his friend and Jutak pushed him back.

"Wake me when we're ready to leave." Jutak turned over and rested his head on a tree root.

Darkness fell, and with it the nocturnal voices of the jungle began to cry out, claiming the night as their own. Some of the group, including Pukuh, kept watch, and some slept to conserve strength. When a few hours had passed, the watchers woke their comrades, and the Mayan warriors stole into the white men's camp, silent as wolves stalking their prey. They found a few tents pitched around a fire which had burned down to its last few embers. The men were asleep; there was no sound save for the animals in the woods.

Pukuh was about to signal an attack, but something made him stop. *Something's not right.*

A loud sound like thunder broke the silence, and a nearby tree broke and splintered as if something had hit it.

Pukuh saw a man with a pistol in his hand walking closer. Five others lined up behind him, all with the same weapons.

"Pukuh! What do we do?"

"Retreat! Run!"

The warriors did not hesitate. They ran from the enemy whose power they did not understand. Had the white men been fewer, he would have attacked, but his warriors were outnumbered.

They ran through the forest, past the trees and rocks and streams, back toward their village and away from the white people and their devices. Pukuh knew they could not pause or risk slowing down, as the thunderous noises kept resounding against the trees. *I was a fool. I should have taken more care. I should have searched harder. Men like that would surely have guards in a dangerous place such as this. I've failed the test.*

A scream from beside Pukuh snapped him back to reality. Jutak was on the ground to the left, holding his leg. Pukuh ran to his aide.

"Leave me! Save yourself, Pukuh!"

"But..." He looked back and the white men were still chasing them. One was reloading his gun and was gaining on them.

"You can't take me with you. It will slow you down."

Pukuh grabbed his friend by the chest and shook him. "What about our promise, Jutak?"

"You have to live for both of us now, Pukuh." Jutak closed his eyes and recited a prayer. Pukuh's eyes were wide with horror. He was caught between the desire to save his friend and the certain knowledge that the attempt would result in both their deaths. *I can still save him! I'll carry him back myself.*

Unfortunately, Jutak made the decision himself. He finished his prayer, took out a small hunting knife, and stabbed himself in the gut. He did not cry out from the pain, but, with his final breath, whispered, "Run!" Then he went limp in Pukuh's arms. Tears streamed down Pukuh's face as he pulled up his hands, covered in the blood of his best friend of thirteen years. He rose to look into the face of the ones who had brought tragedy.

The white man and his guns.

Pukuh didn't remember, but the other warriors claimed he was filled with the spirit of the god that is his namesake. The God of Death, Pukuh, awakened in him. He killed all of the white men himself in a rage. By the end, his body was slick with blood.

Blood of his enemies, his friend, and his own.

...

Present Day

"No," Pukuh said in answer to Edward's question. "I would not leave you..." He turned his gaze back to Edward. "Outsiders have harmed this village before. I did not want that to happen again, but you have shown me you are not like them. Even though you are weak, you are honourable."

Edward wasn't sure what to say. "Thank you, Pukuh... I'm glad I've earned a little bit of your respect."

Pukuh smiled. "Only a little." The two of them sat in silence, staring at the stars. "You remind me of the pirate who came before you," Pukuh said, breaking the silence. "His name was Benjamin. Have you met him?"

As I thought! It was him! "Nearly. He took my money, but left me his ship. I've been chasing down the keys to open it up fully ever since. I can't even use the cannons yet because the cabin is locked. If I find him, he will feel my wrath."

Pukuh laughed for the first time since they met. "That sounds like something he would do. My father said that he was always pulling pranks, something that at his age was seen as strange. He had a youthful state of mind."

"Is he the one who taught you English?"

"Yes. At first I hated him like all white men, but that changed over time. I grew to love him, and he taught me how to speak this language."

"It seems we've both inherited a bit of what he had."

"Yes, it appears that way."

Soon they went to sleep, but they had not slept long when Edward was awakened by Pukuh jabbing him.

"We are not alone," Pukuh whispered.

"Animals?"

Pukuh nodded and pressed his back against the tree. It was all he was able to do in his condition. Edward knew he would have to do any fighting alone. He picked up his spear and readied himself. He could hear the sounds of the jungle closing in: the shrieking of birds, the snapping of branches, the rustling of leaves. Edward couldn't keep track of it all. *Which one do I listen to? Where are they coming from?*

As if hearing his thoughts, Pukuh offered some advice. "Don't listen for what you can hear, listen for what you can't. Close your eyes and distinguish which sounds are from prey running, and which sounds the predators are trying to hide."

Edward followed Pukuh's advice. He closed his eyes and concentrated on the sounds. He could hear the wind rustling through the trees. The birds flew from branches, and then there was silence to his left.

Edward turned, bent his knees, ready to spring, and raised his spear, ready to strike. A wolf jumped out from the bush in front of him. Edward thrust forward, stamping his foot. The spear lodged in the wolf's throat, spilling its blood everywhere. He pulled out the spear as the wolf dropped to the jungle floor. Then, upon their brother's death, more wolves sprang from the brush and circled the men. It was obvious to Edward they were planning to attack Pukuh first; he was injured, and they could tell. They fixed him in their sight, preparing to pounce.

They must think he's the weaker one. Are they ever in for a surprise!

The pair of wolves nearest Pukuh jumped first. Edward turned and stabbed one in the ribs, downing it. Pukuh was able to brace his spear, and the other wolf impaled itself. He dropped the spear and pulled out a knife.

"You can run, you know," Pukuh said to Edward. "I wouldn't be offended."

"You think you can take all the glory yourself? You don't stand a chance with that pitiful knife of yours. I'll pass this test by bringing you back in my arms, like the babe you are."

"Oh, so that is your plan, is it? You are to use me, then?" Pukuh slid himself up the side of the tree to where he was able to manoeuvre a bit better.

"I suppose you could say that. Save the war chief. Be a hero."

"Well, I am not about to be saved by you a second time."

The wolves resumed their attack. One lunged for Pukuh's arm, and he thrust his knife into its skull. Immediately another attacked the same arm, and yet another sprang upon his broken leg. Pukuh cried out in pain and stabbed the one on his arm again and again as Edward slammed his spear into the other's heart.

One wolf jumped on Edward's back and another attacked his injured left arm. As Pukuh gouged the eye of the wolf on Edward's arm, Edward dropped his spear and grabbed the animal on his back, pried its fangs off his shoulder, and threw it at the tree. There was a distinct snap and a whimper as the animal's back broke.

Now only one wolf remained. It had remained aloof, watching the whole contest as if gauging the power of its opponents. It was bigger than the others—and, to judge from its grizzled fur and the scar down its left eye, the alpha male as well. It stood still, watching both men, gazing at the fierce eyes that stared back at it. Their eyes were like its own. They were the eyes of fellow hunters, the eyes of brothers.

The wolf turned and walked away—not out of fear, but out of respect.

Edward watched the wolf until it was out of sight, and then let out the breath he had been holding in. *I don't think the wolf clan will be bothering Pukuh's village any longer.*

Pukuh turned to Edward. "I would say you passed the test."

"Does that mean we're brothers?" Edward said with a grin.

"No."

Edward's smile faded. "Oh…"

"You still have one more test. And I can assure you, it is going to be more difficult than the last."

22. AN UNINVITED GUEST

Toward morning, Pukuh's companions returned and found him and Edward. They brought bandages for their wounds and a wooden crutch to help Pukuh walk back to the village. They were set on hunting down the wolf pack, but Pukuh told them what had happened and presumed that the wolves wouldn't attack again.

That, at least, is what Edward thought he told them, until he saw them burst out laughing at a certain point in the story.

"I'll break your other leg if you're making a joke at my expense."

"Worry not. I told them you screamed like a little boy only once."

They were in good spirits on the journey back to the village, and when they arrived everyone was waiting for them, cheering and crowding around. Edward assumed the attention was for Pukuh, and withdrew, but many villagers approached Edward as well. He didn't understand what they were saying, but some of the older ones cried while holding his hands, undoubtedly thanking him for helping Pukuh. The attention made him blush.

The king soon arrived and embraced his son. He said a few words to disperse the crowd and then invited Pukuh and Edward to accompany him to the palace. This time they sat side by side before the throne. Pukuh recounted, from start to finish and in his own language, the story of the hunt. Edward understood not a word of it, but felt proud nonetheless. Then, as Pukuh finished the tale, all the elders burst into laughter.

Dammit! Again? Edward flashed Pukuh a baleful stare.

Pukuh smiled as he stood and moved to the other side of the room, in front of his father. The king addressed Edward, with Pukuh translating. "You have passed the first test of leadership. Your decision to send for help, as well as your decision to stay with the war chief, has brought you honour and made you a leader in the eyes of the gods. Tonight there will be a feast in honour of your defeat of the wolf clan."

Edward bowed deeply. "You honour me too much. I'm afraid I couldn't have made it out alive without your war chief either."

Pukuh translated, and the elders returned Edward's bow. Their respect for him was evident.

But then a commotion rose outside. A warrior soon ran in and relayed a message, whereupon everyone rushed out of the palace.

"What is it? What's happening?" asked Edward, as he and Pukuh hurried out.

"There's another white person coming into the village, and he is on the attack. I hope he is not one of your friends, because he's about to be killed."

"I should hope not! I told them all to stay at the ship." Edward ran out of the palace and down the stone steps, hurrying to the village gate, where he could see someone fighting with the warriors. *Dad damn it! That* is *one of my crew! I have to stop that fool before someone dies.*

Outside the village perimeter, one warrior was lying on the ground, and inside two warriors circled the crewman, one at the front and one at the back. They both thrust their spears, aiming at his legs and chest. The crewman jumped, did a flip, and caught the spears in midair. Then he spun around and thrust one spear into each warrior's leg.

Edward's jaw dropped at the incredible sight.

The crewman stood up, and that was when Edward noticed that his hat had fallen off in the last attack, and he could see the red hair of Anne Bonney.

Anne saw Edward and her face lit up. She began to run to him as he ran to her. Before they were even close, all the warriors in the village rushed upon her at once, forming a circle, their spears pointed and ready.

"Stop!" Edward yelled. "Don't kill her!" he pleaded as he ran.

They didn't attack, but they didn't lower their weapons either. Anne did not let her guard down, but even she knew when she was beaten. Edward forced his way through the tight circle, pushed their weapons aside, and grabbed Anne close, trying to protect her. He again told the warriors to stop as Pukuh stepped forward on his crutches to intervene.

"Please, Pukuh, tell them to stop. This is my friend."

Pukuh did as he was asked, and the warriors put their weapons away but kept them at their sides. This "friend" had taken out three of their warriors with ease.

Edward let Anne go when he was sure no one else would attack, but he still shielded her.

"Why did she come and harm my people? Someone could have been killed, Edward!"

"I know, Pukuh, and I'm sorry. I tried to tell everyone to stay on the ship, but some are a little too free-spirited, it seems." Edward glanced back at Anne. She averted her gaze as she scratched her freckled nose. "I'm sure you have some warriors who are the same, correct?"

Pukuh thought it over for a moment and then nodded. "Yes, I suppose you are right. My men shouldn't have attacked her without my orders."

"Well… I was the one who attacked first." Anne stepped forward and made a quick bow. "My name is Anne. I'm sorry; the thought of Edward in danger drove my hasty actions. I thought that I could let him alone, but when he was gone for a few days, I feared the worst and needed to find him."

Pukuh considered Anne for a moment, and then he turned and told the warriors and villagers gathered around something. All the men smiled, and the women pouted in jealousy.

Oh, what did he say now? Edward palmed his face in frustration, wondering what clever humiliation Pukuh had brought down upon him this time.

"Come," Pukuh directed. "We return to the palace to discuss what to do next." As they all walked, Pukuh explained the situation to the elders while Edward and Anne followed at a slight distance and talked privately.

"So you came because you thought I was in danger?"

"I did not think it would take so long, these tests. I feared the worst."

"I hope you at least told William you were coming here." Anne was silent. "You told someone, right?"

Anne's ears went red like her hair, and she averted her gaze. "I left a note… with John."

Edward shook his head, exasperated. "Let's hope for your sake no one else decides to defy orders and try to find me. There's a feast tonight, and I should like to attend instead of handling more of my crew."

"A feast? Why?"

"Well, the tests mentioned on the map were tests of leadership issued by the people in this village. The previous owner of the *Freedom* gave a key to the current king. I finished the first test, so they're having a feast. If I pass the next, we get the key."

"What was the test?"

"We had to find a wolf pack that had been harming the village."

"Is that how you received those wounds?" Anne asked, pointing to his arm. "You aren't hurt, are you?"

"It only aches most of the time," Edward said with a smirk. "The test is also why I'm wearing this guise." Edward motioned to his warrior outfit.

"I was hoping you would explain."

Edward chuckled. "I suppose I look rather silly, do I?"

"Yes, yes you do," Anne said with a sly grin.

Anne and Edward entered the king's palace and sat down. Once again, the king spoke and Pukuh translated. "You have the prowess of a warrior, Anne. Many of my own could not equal your skill. That is extraordinary in a woman."

"I assume you do not train women?" Anne asked.

"It is rare, but not unheard of if one shows the desire," he replied. "You wish to stay during Edward's next test?"

"If you would but grant me the honour." Anne gave a humble bow.

"You are granted permission, but if you are to attend the feast tonight you must follow our rules. This goes for both of you." Edward and Anne nodded in agreement. "You will dress in the festival clothes of our tribe. Edward will dress in garb appropriate to a warrior, and Anne will be clad in the formal dress of our women. Is this acceptable?" Again they nodded. "There is one more condition. Edward must learn a warrior dance, and Anne must help prepare the food with the women."

"A dance!" Edward exclaimed, but caught himself and whispered to Anne, "A dance? I..."

"We agree to the terms."

Edward frowned at Anne. "I have to dance? I *can't* dance!"

"I am sure you'll do well enough. Besides, *I* intend to enjoy it." Anne grinned.

The king continued: "With that settled, you may take your time and explore the village before we have to start preparing. Enjoy tonight's feast, for tomorrow your second trial begins."

After bowing to the village elders and the king, Edward and Anne set about wandering around the village. Everywhere people were walking and talking, the doors of their huts were open and welcoming, and everyone came and went as they pleased. Children playing in the streets ran up to the white-skinned strangers. The girls seemed enamored with Anne's beautiful red hair, while the boys wanted to touch Edward's beard.

They visited the other stone structures in the village Edward had noticed when he first arrived. They were smaller than the palace and the pyramid, but no less picturesque. Anne guessed they were all made of limestone, and had some kind of religious significance.

"These could relate to specific times of the year," she offered. She pointed to a statue in the centre of the room of a man holding his hands, palms up, in front of him. "Maybe when the light hits the hands it means something."

"We'll have to ask Pukuh about it at the feast."

By the time they had finished studying the temples, Pukuh had come for Edward, and a woman for Anne. They took them to do their chores before the festival, and to dress them. Anne gathered fresh vegetables and helped prepare the palace for the feast, and Edward spent the rest of the afternoon practicing a traditional dance of the Maya.

As it happened, he needed every bit of that time.

Why do I have to do this nonsense? Edward thought for the fifth time since starting. He would make it halfway through the dance before making a mistake, and then they had to start all over. Pukuh and the other warriors teaching him the dance would be joining him in the performance, so they could tolerate no mistakes.

"If you make a mistake you shame our village," Pukuh's deep accented voice warned for the fifth time.

"I know. I'm trying."

"Once again…"

When the time for the feast arrived, Edward appeared in an outfit donated by one of the warriors. It was a tight fit for his large size, but it showed off his muscles well. The men all wore the colours red, gold, blue, and purple, arranged in a specific pattern. Pukuh explained that the colours were traditional and specific to their tribe, and if he were to see another tribe's colours he could tell where they were from. Edward thought them a nice change from the bland colours he was used to wearing.

The feast was held in the centre of the palace. A long, low table was set with all kinds of food, mostly vegetables and fruit, with a little meat. Surrounding the table was a soft mat, and pillows were scattered everywhere for people to lie on.

The king was there with his wife, relaxing at the head of the table, waiting for everyone else to arrive. Edward and the rest of the men entered first and sat down. He sat to the left of the king, Pukuh to the right. The warrior next to Edward had been instructed to keep a seat open beside him.

The women walking in caught Edward's attention, and what he saw made his mouth stand open like a sail caught by the wind.

Anne was dressed in the fashion of the Mayans. Her outer garment was loose-fitting and went down to her ankles; it was tied at the waist and had a slit up each side, revealing colourful trousers beneath. The colours were red, blue, pink, and purple in a star pattern with gold trim and flowers stitched to the bodice around the neckline.

But it was not her clothing that made Edward's jaw drop.

Anne's hair was loose at the back, with her long red curls flowing down past her shoulders. Two long strands of hair fell from behind her ears down her chest, each bound with gold ribbon, and thin braids looped around from her forehead to the back, where more gold ribbon bound them together.

She's stunning.

Anne walked up to Edward, but he was rendered speechless. Everyone sat down as he stared at her. It took him a moment to realise he was still standing, and then he swiftly sat down with Anne beside him.

The king stood and recited a prayer, which Pukuh would later tell Edward was to their rain god, thanking him for their bountiful blessings. After that, the warriors performed their dance. This particular dance was another part of the ritual of thanking the rain god, intended to help bring rains and end droughts. *Obviously*, thought Edward, *the gods don't always require human sacrifice.*

But he still felt like a fool. *I think I'd rather be sacrificed than experience this embarrassment. And in front of Anne, no less!* He tried to watch her face as he was dancing around a fire. She was smiling; not laughing or smirking, but smiling.

He only stumbled a little, and no one seemed even to notice, for which he was grateful. After it was done, everyone at the feast cheered and praised the dancing warriors as they seated themselves. It was time to eat.

Everyone talked and ate together at once, and there was much laughter. The king and his queen were not in any special seat and sat as equals amongst the guests.

Anne leaned over to Edward. "This is so nice," she whispered as she glanced about. "And so unlike the dinners at..." She looked at Edward and her smile faded. "Never mind," she said as she straightened herself and filled a wooden plate with food.

Edward cocked his brow, but she didn't notice and he decided to let her be. He turned to Pukuh. "So what is tomorrow's test?" he asked.

Pukuh put his food down and then went quiet. "You will find out tomorrow."

It can't be any worse than what we've already been through. Edward decided to leave it at that. "Can you tell us more about the temples we saw?"

"Ah, those are for the winter and summer... what's the word? Solstice! When the sun is at the correct angle, it will shine on the hand of the sun god."

They talked and ate throughout the night. As the end of the feast neared, a strange, sweet drink was served. It was fermented and, while it was full of fruits, it was as strong as rum. Edward and Anne had only a little—Edward, because he knew he needed to be alert for tomorrow, and Anne, because it was her custom to drink sparingly. After a few small servings, however, Edward could tell she was more relaxed.

"My mother wants to know when you two met," Pukuh said.

Edward took the lead. "We met on the ship. I was in a port looking for some men to join my crew and she boarded. She dressed as a man because women are considered bad luck aboard ships."

Anne continued. "He later found me out. I still conceal my identity from most aboard the *Freedom*, but there are a few with whom I can be myself."

Pukuh relayed the story to his mother. She was a beautiful woman. She wore her hair in braids, and was dressed in garb similar to Anne but more ornamental, decorated with what looked like real gold. Her mannerisms and demeanor bespoke her royal status.

"When were you two wed?" Pukuh asked, sipping his drink nonchalantly.

Edward and Anne both registered mild shock on their faces and then sat up straight. "We're not married," they said together.

"We have only just met," Anne asserted.

"We barely know each other. Only a few months now," Edward added.

They glanced back and forth at one another and around the room. Everyone was smiling at their shyness.

"Yes, yes, I understand," Pukuh reassured them before he translated for his mother.

After a moment of discomfort, other questions followed, and Edward and Anne soon relaxed again. Many asked them about the ship, how it was to live on it, what they did there, and what it meant to be a pirate.

"I suppose I've never really thought about it," Edward said. "I've always learned a pirate was someone who killed anyone without mercy and took whatever they wanted from hard-working citizens. Now, though, in our situation, I can see it in a different light. We don't have to follow any rules that we do not wish to, and we can travel wherever and do whatever we please. It's freedom, like the name of our ship."

Pukuh, being the primary one who understood English, was momentarily speechless in contemplation of the words. He stared at Edward until someone snapped him out of it and asked him to translate.

After a long night of celebration, people retired to their homes. The guests thanked the king and queen before departing, and many of them hugged Anne and Edward as they left.

"So, where will we be staying tonight?" Edward asked Pukuh.

"We have prepared a place for you in the palace. Come, I will show you the chambers we have for guests."

Edward and Anne bowed to the king and his wife, thanking them for their hospitality, and then left with Pukuh for the eastern section of the palace. Passing through the large limestone arches, he took them to a medium-sized room equipped with everything they would need. It held a bed consisting of a cotton mat and a dozen pillows, a divider for privacy, and a separate section for bathing, with a limestone tub and a fire to heat the water. The room even had a mirror on a wooden stand in one corner.

"So is this for Anne or for me?" Edward asked.

Pukuh scratched his head. "It's for both of you."

"Both of us? But... but there's only one bed!" Edward stammered in embarrassment.

"Yes. You do not want to share it? Aren't you two... how do you say it in your language? Special friends?"

"Ah! N-no! You've got it all wrong! We're not s-special friends, or anything!"

Pukuh smiled and patted Edward on the back. "I'm sure it will not be a problem for one night. The woman has already made her decision." Pukuh motioned to the bed.

Anne was already lying in the dozen pillows, curled up and fast asleep. Edward turned back to Pukuh with a look of defeat on his face. "Very well. I guess you win. Have a good night, Pukuh."

"You as well, Edward. You'll need it for tomorrow," Pukuh said cryptically, and walked out.

Edward let down a dark cotton sheet which acted as a curtain for the opening to their room. He took off his shirt and walked over to the pillow-strewn bed. A few blankets made of thick cotton lay in a heap on one side. He covered Anne with one blanket, and then set up a few pillows on the opposite end for himself.

"Thank you," said a voice from beneath the pillows.

Edward glanced over to her. "So you are awake. I thought it was odd for you to fall asleep so soon."

"It was easier that way."

Edward mumbled in agreement as he made his bed and lay in it. A comfortable silence descended between them. They could hear the hum and click of bugs and birds from outside, and a cool breeze blew over them from a window.

"I never had a chance to mention it, but do you know you scared me when you first showed up?"

Anne turned around to face Edward. "Scared?" she asked.

"I was afraid, and a little angry," he said with a chuckle. "I didn't know what they would do to you. I know you're strong, and I know you can beat anyone you face, but I was still scared. I didn't want anything to happen to you."

Anne blushed. "I'm sorry… I was scared too. That's why I had to come." Anne placed her hand over his and looked deep into his dark eyes. "How do you feel now?" Anne sidled closer to him.

"How do I feel now?" Edward shifted and they were closer still.

Anne moved herself even closer to Edward. "Yes, now."

Her red hair was lying out on the pillows and flowing over her shoulders. Her beautiful green eyes were gazing back at him. Those eyes were like the ocean, and they, too, called to him. He gripped her hand while keeping his eyes fixed on her, and then he leaned in and kissed her.

"Does that answer your question?"

Anne flashed a coy smile. "I thought I told you not to kiss me without my permission."

Edward smiled. "Sorry. It slipped my mind."

Anne kissed him back for a brief, sensual moment. "We should sleep. You supposedly have a big day tomorrow." Then she turned over and pulled her blanket over her. Edward thought he saw her wipe a tear from her eye.

"Good night," Anne whispered.

"Good night," Edward replied. Thoughts of home, and the woman he'd left behind, were far from his mind.

...

Edward woke to a cold wind blowing on him and the golden sun rising on the horizon. Instead of soft pillows and a warm bed, he was lying on cold limestone. Instead of a ceiling above him he saw open sky.

Where am I?

He arose, and immediately felt the surface on which he had lain start to shift with his movement. Shock and fear moved his feet to keep his balance, and the surface became level again. He stood on a large, square slab of limestone, and, to judge from the landscape, it was somehow perched high in the air. It was not one solid piece of stone, but a multitude of large stones held together by something. A spear lay at his feet, and when he turned he saw Pukuh standing on the other side of the square, his own spear in hand.

"This is the second test. Prepare yourself." Pukuh ran to Edward. His eyes were fierce, as they had been when the two of them fought the wolves.

He was ready to kill, and ready to die.

23. A WARRIOR

Pukuh attacked with incredible speed. It took everything Edward had to dodge his spear, a task complicated by the ground shifting under their feet as they moved. The platform tilted precariously and Edward could feel his footing start to slip. He ran to the other side and the stone platform leveled out.

"What are you doing, Pukuh?! Are you trying to kill me?"

"This is the second test. You must defeat me in mortal combat."

"That's absurd! Why must we fight? What does this have to do with being a leader? I cannot believe Benjamin would participate in this test."

"This is the same test he and my father had when they were younger. The location has changed, but the fight was the same. He happened upon our village by accident, and my father, then the war chief, fought him to protect the village. Now we duel here, twelve years later. The test of a warrior."

"Where are we?"

"This is on top of the pyramid. This stone slab will not fall, but if you fall off it you will die. Now, take your weapon and fight me!" Pukuh kicked the spear over and Edward picked it up.

Very well, if it's a fight he wants I'll give it to him!

He gave the spear a swipe in the air and prepared a defensive stance.

"Defense will not work here, Edward!" Pukuh ran at him again in a bull rush, swifter than a wolf with blood on its lips.

Edward sidestepped and slipped behind Pukuh, trying to hit him with his elbow. Pukuh dropped and tripped him. Edward had to use both hands and feet so he wouldn't fall off the slab. Pukuh seemed secure and sure of his balance.

How is he doing that? And with a broken leg, no less!

"Rise, Edward."

Edward pushed himself to his feet and readied himself.

Pukuh's right. I can't win this by being defensive. If I start running around, I'll likely fall. He looked over the side of the pyramid.

"What is wrong, Edward? Afraid of heights?"

Edward took a closer look at Pukuh. His legs were trembling despite his stability, and he was pouring sweat.

It's amazing he's able to move like that, but there's no way he's fully recovered yet. Maybe I can force him to surrender.

Edward inched forward and used the back end of his spear as a blunt weapon. He kept jabbing at Pukuh's torso and pushing him back. Pukuh dodged the blows or deflected them. When he had had enough and countered, Edward went in to strike his leg. It was a clean shot right on the broken area.

Pukuh suppressed a scream of pain and then slammed his own spear into Edward's arm on the same spot where he had been bitten by the wolves. The nerve endings were raw, and the strike was hard, opening the wound even deeper. Edward also suppressed a yell.

Dammit! Bastard!

"Do not think I am the only one injured here, Edward." Both men were short of breath and sweating.

"Edward!" he heard someone yell from behind him.

It was Anne. She was on the roof of the palace. He had been too concentrated on surviving to notice earlier, but many villagers, including the king, were gathered there to watch. The warriors on the roof had taken a bow from her hands and were trying to restrain her, but they were having difficulty.

No! I don't know what they'll do to her if she tries to interfere! "Anne! Stop!"

"Edward!" she yelled as she fought against the many trying to hold her down. "Let me go!"

"Anne, please stop!"

She finally stopped struggling, her eyes still fixed on him in worry.

"I'll be fine," he told her. "I promise."

The warriors let her go. She pursed her lips and nodded to him through heavy breaths. The king laid his hand on her shoulder and stared into her eyes for a brief moment before motioning for the fight to continue.

Edward turned around and Pukuh rushed him again. He tumbled out of the way. Pukuh back-flipped to the opposite end of the slab, slamming his weight down onto it. Edward's side shot up into the air, sending him flying.

It was immediately clear to Edward that he was going to fall past the edge of the fighting grounds to his death. He caught a glimpse of Pukuh's face; its expression was one of great sadness.

No! We'll pass this test together! No one dies today!

Just as he went over the edge, Edward thrust his spear into the crack between two of the stones. It wedged in far enough to allow him to hang off the spear shaft, and his weight pulled his side of the slab down and caused Pukuh's side to shoot up.

Edward was able to hang on, but he couldn't climb at that angle. He could only wait for Pukuh to fall back down onto the other end, which would level the stone and allow Edward a chance to climb back up.

Pukuh landed, but slipped on his broken leg and rolled down the slab towards Edward, unable to stop or right himself. He was sliding across the stone like rainwater, and within moments he fell off the end of the slab next to Edward.

No!

Edward reached out and grabbed Pukuh's hand just before he fell out of reach. The collective gasp of the onlookers on the palace roof could be heard all the way across the intervening space. Their war chief's life was now hanging by a thread.

But it wasn't over yet.

Edward was hanging onto the spear with his injured arm. He had put too much strain on it, and the pain was ripping into him. He was desperate to hold tight, but his hand was starting to slip. The fight to hold on was sending waves of pain through his arm and his whole body. His fingers wanted to release from the struggle, and his hand was giving way.

Not today. We will not die today!

He screamed, a scream less of pain than of determination. He swung Pukuh up and onto the limestone arena. Pukuh was able to secure a foothold this time and scrambled to the other side to level out the square. Once it was stable, Edward released the spear and climbed back up. Covered with sweat and gasping for air, he stood up and faced the spectators.

"I refuse to fight!" he declared.

"Fight or die, Edward! Those are the only choices!" Pukuh said with equal force, as he clutched his shaking legs.

Edward turned to Pukuh, but yelled so everyone could hear. "No! There is always a choice. We are allies. Killing each other only weakens us," he said. "If these are supposed to be tests of both leadership and fighting skills, then the two must go hand in hand. As a fighter I have already shown my prowess against the wolves. Now, as a leader, I will not continue this fight." He turned to the king, Pukuh's father. "I know you can understand me, King, and I know you made the same decision years ago when you faced

Benjamin. Fighting is only good when you have something to protect. Benjamin wasn't your enemy, and your son is not mine." Edward threw his spear down off the edge of the arena, and the noise of it clattering on the stone below resounded like a clap of thunder punctuating Edward's words. "I will not fight."

The villagers were speechless. In a way, Edward had committed treason. No one knew what the king was about to do.

"You are quite right, my boy," the king announced in perfect English with an accent not unlike Edward's own. "Benjamin came to me in peace, and I was too much of a fool to see it. He took the same stance you have taken, and I spared him before striking the final blow. By being prepared to die, he made me change my ways. He would not bring harm where no harm was due. When we parted, I vowed never to speak his language—*your* language—again, until his successor arrived." The king had a wide grin plastered on his face. "I congratulate you. You have passed the test."

Edward bowed to the king and smiled to Anne. She beamed with pride and hooted along with the villagers in celebration of his victory. He turned to Pukuh and bowed to him, as well, before joining him in the centre of the arena.

"Congratulations, brother." Pukuh held out his hand.

Edward grabbed Pukuh's forearm. "Brother." Edward brought him close in a quick embrace, which he returned. There was a moment of silence before Edward looked around the platform. "Uh..." he said with a dumbfounded expression, "how do we get down?"

With their fight finished, a warrior opened a hole through a loose piece of limestone, allowing the two brothers passage out. Pukuh and Edward were able to climb down the hole to stone steps at the back of the pyramid, which was how they had brought him up in the first place.

They immediately went to the palace, where the king announced that they would perform the ritual of rebirth for Edward. He extended the invitation to Anne as well, and she accepted joyfully. The rite would be performed at a dome-shaped structure called a temazcal, north of the village, which, Pukuh explained, was made of stones from a nearby volcano. There the participants would cleanse themselves for an hour after the battle, and Edward and Anne would be reborn as Mayan warriors.

When they all arrived at the site, the king prayed in front of the temazcal—Pukuh later told Edward he was asking the gods to allow them to enter it. He also summoned the guardian spirits of life, earth, and fire to assist in the rebirth.

When the prayer was finished, they entered through a small doorway. The interior was spacious and warm. In the centre was a stone pit, where a low fire burned beneath a bowl of stones and herbs wafting a delicious scent of mint into the room. Circling the pit were rings of stone at different levels like an amphitheatre on which the participants would sit.

After everyone was seated, the king, who also acted as the village shaman during rituals, poured water from a carved stone vessel onto the rocks. Fragrant steam filled the room. Speaking in his native tongue while his son translated, he told stories of the gods and of the path of a warrior. His words were passionate and lively, and Edward and Anne were eager listeners. At the end, he told those present to release all worries to the temazcal with a warrior's shout. All joined as brothers and sisters in a great shout of liberation, which was heard all the way to the village.

When Edward and Anne least expected it, the king poured cold water on them to finish the ceremony. The two of them yelped at the unexpected shock of cold, and everyone laughed and gathered around them. As they all embraced, the king prayed to keep their new brother and sister safe as they walked the warrior's path—the path of Ah Pukuh, the God of Death.

Edward and Anne left the ceremony feeling refreshed and rejuvenated.

On the walk back, Edward recalled the trials he had been through, and the last one his crew had faced. He had seen so much, and gained new friends, but he couldn't help but think of the future, and the rest of the keys they needed to find.

"Let's pack our things, Anne. We must return to the ship."

"You are leaving so soon?" Pukuh exclaimed. "We were to have another feast."

"I'm sorry, Pukuh, but we can't. We finished what we came to do, and my crew is waiting for us. It's already been four days. They're probably restless with worry, missing two crewmembers. I hope you understand."

"I do. We will gather some supplies for you to take back. We shall await you at the village centre."

They walked back together, but when they reached the village, the warriors and Pukuh headed one way and the king accompanied Edward and Anne to the palace. They climbed the steps side by side, without distinction of rank, as equals, friends, and brothers.

"I am truly glad you arrived, Edward. It is like seeing Benjamin in his youth once more."

"What was he like?" Edward asked as they ascended the stairs.

"He was a brave warrior, and he loved everyone he met. Anyone whom he called a comrade or a friend was like family to him. To anyone who tried to harm a member of that family he showed no mercy. He told tales of his adventures, which paled in comparison to those I experienced with him. I imagine he became quite the pirate, as you will one day."

"Maybe that's why he made these tests," Edward reflected. "To make a crew like the one he had himself. Through the trials, we grow stronger." Edward gazed at his hands—scarred, but stronger than they had been a few months ago. "Or maybe it's just a fool's game."

The king laughed. "Perhaps both, young one. He enjoyed playing games, but they always seemed to have a deeper purpose."

Edward and Anne returned to their room and packed what they had brought with them. They then left the palace and headed to the centre of the village where everyone was waiting.

Nearly the entire village had turned out to greet and say goodbye to them. As they passed among the people, many hugged or shook their hands, and shoved food and clothing into their packs, as if they were family. Children ran up to touch Edward's beard or Anne's hair one last time, and Edward picked up one of the boys and carried him on his shoulder as he walked through the crowd.

It's astonishing how kind they are. I hope we can return someday.

They reached the front of the village, where Pukuh was waiting for them with all the warriors as well as the king and queen. Piled on the ground was a large stock of food tied up in bundles, as well as a few stone weapons, spears, and daggers.

"It pains us to see you leave so quickly, my friends. Is there anything I can do to persuade you to stay longer?" the king asked.

"I wish I could, but we need to depart before the crew starts to worry, which I'm afraid they are already doing. Someday we will return, and then you will meet my whole crew, and we shall have a great feast."

The king chuckled. "I long for the day." Edward and Anne both hugged the king and queen, thanking them again for their hospitality.

Edward turned to Pukuh. "Well, brother, I guess we'll meet again in a few years?"

"With your permission, I would like to join you for a time."

"What? But you're the war chief, aren't you? You can't abandon your responsibilities, can you?"

"Please, Edward. We have no need of a war chief who doesn't know the ways of war," he said with a grin. "I would join you for training, so I might better myself for my village. Besides, there are many capable warriors here to protect my home while I am away. Of course, the decision is yours to make, as you are the captain."

Edward could see the man was quite serious. He even had a bag packed. Edward looked to the king for approval. "Is this all right with you? He's not only your son, but your greatest warrior."

"I'm afraid Pukuh is following the tradition I created twelve years ago. I did the same as he wants to do. As then, you may choose to take him or leave him."

They're all prepared for it. It would be nice to have him aboard. We'll have another fighter with us.

"Very well. Who am I to break with tradition?" Edward smiled, looking at the beaming faces of Pukuh and his father. "I'll allow you to join, but remember one thing: I'm the captain. If you're my crewmate then my word is law. Aboard my ship, I am king." Edward held out his hand.

"Understood, Captain." Pukuh grasped Edward's hand, sealing the bond.

The king placed his hands on top of theirs. "In this," he proclaimed for all to hear, "the pact created twelve years ago between Benjamin and me is renewed, unweakened by the passage of time. This is an honour to our village and to our people." The king lifted their hands in the air, and the people began to cheer and shout. Then he reached into his cluster of necklaces, brought out the key which Edward had now won the right to possess, and handed it to him. Edward accepted it with a bow of gratitude to the king, and then placed it around his own neck.

Edward, Anne, and Pukuh departed to the sound of the villagers cheering and shouting wishes for their good fortune. Edward listened to the echoes of that sound with a mixture of gratitude, joy, and sadness as it faded behind them and was swallowed up in the deep silence of the pines.

For a time, as they trekked through the forest, they did not violate that silence. A while later Edward spoke.

"I hope you're prepared for this, Pukuh. Have you ever been on a ship? Did your father tell you about what pirates do?"

"My father has told me at length of the adventures he had with Benjamin. I know full well what I am becoming, and I know it is an experience that will benefit me."

"As long as you are aware."

They had walked for a few hours when they reached the spot where Edward had fought the wolves for the first time, and Edward found his sword still near the body of the wolf he had killed with it. His pistol still lay on the smooth rock he had slept on. He went and picked up both weapons.

"My father told me those things that spit fire and rocks are not as accurate as a good bow," said Pukuh.

"Yes, but they're powerful, and on a ship when you're being boarded they can be quite handy."

"I'll stick with my spear."

They resumed walking, but Edward stopped short. "Oh, yes… Anne, you should probably change."

"What?" Anne asked, her brow cocked.

"It dawned on me that you're still wearing women's clothes. I know we aren't there yet, but you need to be accustomed to being a man again."

"Oh, perhaps you're right." She folded her arms as they kept staring at her. "Do you plan to keep watching while I change? Get going! I'll catch up."

"Yes, ma'am!" Edward said as he and Pukuh hurried away.

Pukuh was smiling. "Are all your women like that?"

"No, she's one of a kind."

24. THE REVELATION

Once more disguised as a man, Anne hastened to catch up with the other two. When darkness fell, they stopped and set up camp and a fire to stave off the cold. Pukuh had brought along a few bedrolls, so all three of them were able to sleep in relative comfort.

Pukuh eyed the darkness just outside their firelight. "We should not all sleep. The forest is dangerous at night."

"Who wants to take first?" Edward asked.

"I shall," Anne offered as she set up her bedroll.

Edward gazed at her in her masculine attire, a far cry from her appearance at the village. *She looked so striking in that dress. I hope she didn't throw it away.*

"I shall go after," said Pukuh. "Edward, you will take the last."

"Very well. If anything goes wrong, wake us all up. Don't try to do anything stupid."

With everyone in agreement, Edward and Pukuh crawled into their beds, but their sleep was short-lived.

Anne woke them a few hours into her watch. "I hear noises in all directions. I think we are being surrounded."

The men moved with caution as they tried to rise without a sound. Pukuh threw Edward a spear and he caught it deftly. They could hear the noises now, too. Anne produced two daggers, one in each hand.

The sounds were coming closer. Whoever or whatever it was either wasn't good at hiding, or wanted to be heard. Branches gave way with a violent snap, night birds flew away, bushes rattled.

On every side of them wolves appeared. There must have been at least twenty of them altogether.

"There're too many of them, there's no way we can kill them all," Edward said with gritted teeth.

"With that attitude, you might as well offer your throat to them as a gift," Anne said. "We shall make it out of here, Ed. We just have to work together."

"She is right. Let us put our backs together so they cannot divide us."

They did as Pukuh suggested and made themselves as one. Each had weapons raised, ready to strike when the wolves attacked.

But the wolves did not attack. They didn't even growl. They stood in silence, watching.

"What are they waiting for?" asked Anne.

"I don't know." Edward tried to discern exactly what they were doing.

There was no escape—the wolves far outnumbered them—yet nothing happened. Then Edward noticed one of the animals moving towards them. It was the leader of the pack, the old wolf who had walked away from their last encounter. It was large and strong, and Edward could tell by its deliberate approach this animal had a lot of pride.

He's not attacking. He knows if he comes closer I could strike him down. Why is he continuing? He could have jumped at me by now.

The wolf stopped, lay down on the ground, and gazed steadily at Edward. He put his weapon in one hand and bent down.

"What are you doing, Edward?" Anne exclaimed.

"Trust me." He put his empty hand towards the wolf's mouth, so close the wolf could have bitten off his fingers with ease. Instead, it licked them. Edward moved closer and the wolf rose. He patted it on the head and scratched behind its ear. "It's all right, they aren't here to fight. I think they're here to protect us."

Anne and Pukuh watched in amazement as Edward knelt beside the alpha male. It was being completely submissive to him.

"Pukuh, I think we have been invited into their pack. Or I'm now seen as their leader."

Anne looked astonished by Edward's command of the wild animals.

Pukuh glanced at the other wolves with a furrowed brow. "Are you sure they are docile?"

"They haven't attacked us even though we've lowered our guard. Is that not proof enough? Now we can all rest."

At a gentle push from Edward, the wolf stood up and went back to the rest of the pack. Some of the wolves then dispersed to form an outer circle of sentries, and some stayed close in as bodyguards.

Pukuh peered about. "I think we should still take turns with the watch."

Edward agreed and told Pukuh to wake him when he was to take over, then lay down in his bedroll and made himself comfortable. Anne was still standing and staring at him.

"Anne…"

"Huh… What?" she answered in a daze.

"You can sleep now."

"Oh… yes. Good night," Anne mumbled as she crawled into her bedroll. She lay awake for some time, staring into the darkness, the possible dangers far from her mind.

How did he do that?

Anne kept asking herself that question, but she could find no answer.

...

The wolves had kept up their watch for Edward and his companions. As the morning light began to penetrate the forest canopy, Edward saw the alpha male walking to greet him. He pulled out the last bit of dried meat he had and, after taking a little for himself, gave the rest to the wolf. Then, with a wave of his arm, he sent the pack back into the depths of the woods.

Edward woke the others, and they packed up their things and prepared to walk once more. They would be home aboard the *Freedom* within a few hours.

"I still cannot believe it."

"Can't believe what, Anne?"

"You commanded a wolf as if it were a simple house pet. It's… unprecedented."

"I guess it was kind of odd. But Pukuh and I showed them our strength a couple of times already. That one with the scar too. I guess he felt, since I bested his pack, he should join the stronger one. Right, Pukuh?"

"Wolves are honourable spirits; they would not take the killing of their pack lightly. It would make sense that either he would kill you or join you for protection."

"See?"

"I suppose that makes sense," Anne said, but Edward could tell that she was still skeptical.

They walked down the path once more after eating a little to keep up their strength. The jungle was bright despite the dense canopy, and the sounds seemed less ominous than when Edward had first entered. It was a pleasant walk all the way to the ship.

They emerged back at the small hill and sandy dock where they had landed. "There she is, Pukuh. The *Freedom*. Isn't she beautiful?"

"It is as I remember," he said as he walked down the slope.

"Not quite the same. This time it's a new crew and we'll be able to make our own adventures. Come, Anne—I mean, Jim! Let's board. Pukuh, you have to remember to call Anne Jim. No one can know she's a woman. It'll cause trouble."

"I understand, brother. I will keep the secret."

The crew noticed them approaching and they all gathered along the side of the ship. Some let down a rope ladder, while the rest of them cheered and shouted greetings. Edward and Anne returned the greetings and climbed up to the deck. Pukuh was close behind them.

Henry was waiting on deck. "Welcome back, Captain. Was it a success?"

Edward smiled as he took the key from around his neck. He lifted it into the air and everyone cheered once again. "I'd say it was a success. We also have a new crewmember. He's a native of the village where I stayed."

Henry looked over Edward's shoulder at the newcomer. Pukuh was greeting everyone as Anne introduced him. "Are you sure he'll be a good fit aboard the ship? What can he do?"

"He's a warrior, so I imagine we'll have to train him in how to work on a ship, but I don't think there'll be any problems. He's strong; even now he has a broken leg, yet you would never be able to tell. I'll tell you all about what happened later. For now, let's find out what this key opens."

Henry grabbed Edward's arm before he could leave. "What about Jim?"

"What about Jim?"

"He disobeyed a direct order. Aren't you going to punish him?"

"He went out of concern for me; I can't fault him for that. I wouldn't punish anyone who did that," Edward said, folding his arms. "It was dangerous, but it turned out all right in the end. Come, let's go."

Henry folded his arms and frowned as he watched Edward head aft.

Edward first went to the aft cabin and tried the key, but it didn't open. Next he went to the cannon deck. He put the key in and turned it, and the lock opened with a click. Edward smiled. He pushed open the door and walked in.

The spacious room was clean and well kept, and the smell of Caribbean pine almost stung the nose. On the port and starboard sides each were fifteen twenty-two-pound cannons, lined up and ready to deploy. Beside each one there were large cannonballs stored for immediate use. On either end of the deck, as well as in the middle where the main mast came down through, were storage areas with more cannonballs and black powder. At the stern of the room was another door, but it had a lock on it as well.

If this follows the pattern of other frigates, that would be the captain's cabin, though the bow end still remains a mystery.

Everyone rushed in and examined the cannons, admiring their beauty. They appeared brand new, never used. Everyone was excited, especially the gunners who, because of insufficient cannons, had to rotate shifts during battle. Now they would all be able to fight at once.

With these, we now have fifty-three cannons aboard the ship. We'll be a lot more dangerous in battle.

"What're these things?" A crewman examined the cannons' firing mechanism with a confused look.

"What is it?" Edward asked.

"These cannons 'ere 'ave some sort o' string on 'em that moves this." The crewman demonstrated the mechanism on top of the cannon.

It was like a flintlock on a gun, but it was attached to the cannon and stuck when the string was pulled. Edward had never seen anything like it.

"It's to fire the cannons, I suppose. Quite the clever addition," Edward said as he stroked his beard. "This will make it safer for you, I imagine?"

The crewmate examined the cannon again, and then nodded. "Yes, Captain. We'll be more accurate, too."

"Good, that's what I like to hear."

"Captain?" A crewman was standing on the other side of the mast, pointing at something.

Edward walked over. He already had a fair suspicion of what he would find, and he was right: another piece of paper, with instructions for obtaining the next key. Edward squinted and frowned as he examined it.

This is just gibberish!

It was a set of letters, but they didn't spell anything or make any apparent sense. Edward turned the paper over.

Finally, real words!

"In the centre of the Navassa Island the decoder for the cipher can be found."

Apparently they would have to sail to this Navassa island to find out what the script on the other side of the note meant. Edward thought Herbert might know where to find it.

Edward was headed for the stairs when he was stopped by Henry. "Ed! Come quick! We have trouble!"

"What kind of trouble?"

"British Navy trouble."

Damn! "All hands, prepare for battle!" He yelled as he emerged from the lower deck.

"Here," Henry said, handing Edward a spyglass. "You know more of ships than I do. Can you tell what class it is?"

Edward peered down the spyglass at the approaching ship. It had three masts, with a forecastle and quarterdeck at the bow and stern respectively. "I think it's a fifth-class frigate, same as us. I guess it's a bit of providence we now have as many guns, if not more."

The crew were frantic to get ready for battle: gathering weapons, preparing the first wave of cannons, checking and rechecking everything just in case. William, Henry, Herbert, Pukuh, and Edward were the only ones not rushing about. In perhaps ten minutes they would be in battle, but they needed a clear plan.

"You think it's Smith again?" Henry asked.

"He's been at us for six months now so he's probably the only one who would travel this far to catch us."

"But how did he find out where we were headed? How can he be so good at tracking us?"

"I haven't a clue." Anne once said they called him "The Hound" in the marines. *Maybe he can smell us? No, that's foolishness.*

"He's one lucky bastard, that's for sure."

"William, can you suggest any strategies for the battle?"

William had been listening the whole time, but was waiting for orders before offering an opinion. "Just one: Hit them with everything, and then do it again."

"I like that plan." William nodded. "All right. Herbert, we'll be counting on your skills here. Are you up to it?"

"I won't let you down, Captain."

"Good. Everyone to arms! Prepare broadside volley!"

Edward went to a gun hold and grabbed two pistols, a sword, and a few daggers. Everyone hid behind barrels or railings for cover from the rain of bullets soon to be upon them. Edward's gaze turned to the opposite end of the ship, where he saw Anne, watching him, holding a pistol in one hand and a dagger in the other. She nodded to him and he smiled back.

Pukuh appeared beside Edward. "So I guess I am to learn the hard way how to be a pirate?"

Edward considered him for a moment, and then said, "I want you to stay below deck."

"What? Why?"

"You're in no shape to fight. I won't have you dying in the first battle of your career."

"And what about you?" Pukuh grabbed Edward's wounded arm. He winced and brushed him off.

"Don't do that, dammit! Look, I'm saying this as your brother. Don't make me say it as your captain. I can still fight with this, but you can't move well with your leg broken."

"Very well. I will stay out of battle—for you, brother."

"Thank you." Edward knew the Mayan's pride was hurt, but he couldn't have him die under his care. He wouldn't be able to look Pukuh's father in the eye if that happened.

The navy ship was approaching at a steady pace with the wind, bobbing up and down on the waves. On the side of the ship was the name H.M.S. *Pearl*. On the bow stood a man dressed in a blue navy uniform with several medals of commendation on the breast and shoulders. Edward could see him through the spyglass. There could be no mistake.

It was Smith.

Herbert concentrated on the approaching ship, gauging its distance as it sailed closer and closer. "Not yet," he whispered under his breath. "Not yet… Almost there… No… Now! Fire starboard!" he yelled.

All the gunmen on the top deck simultaneously dropped their linstocks into the cannons and let loose a barrage on the other ship. At the same time, a crewman relayed the signal to those on the gun deck and they pulled on their strings in quick succession, one after another, setting off a continuous sweep of explosive fire from stem to stern.

The *Pearl* countered immediately, and cannonballs shot towards the *Freedom* at lightning speed. They ripped through the hull, shattering boards, sending pieces of wood flying everywhere. Some crewmembers were struck by the wood; one man died from a stray shard in the eye, and another had his legs shredded by a cannonball.

"Fire at will!" Edward yelled. The crew raised their rifles and muskets and began to fire. The screams of men and the loud bangs of guns filled the air. The blowing of the wind and the calls of the gulls were swallowed completely by the terrible sounds of combat. In the minds and senses of all present, only the battle existed.

After the ships passed each other, Herbert went hard to port to turn the *Freedom* around, tacking into the wind as he did so.

"Transport the wounded below deck quickly!" Edward yelled. He reloaded his rifle and ducked behind cover. The salt air filled his nostrils with the smell of blood and burning black powder and danger. The smell invigorated him, but also sickened him. His thoughts were flying this way and that, never focusing on one thing for long.

We have a fore cabin filled with cannons. We'll be heading straight for the Pearl soon. We can attack them twice!

"Gunners in the fore cabin! I want those cannons set to launch in one minute!" Edward was running up the stairs to the quarterdeck while some rushed in to do as he commanded. "Herbert, I want you to head straight for them. We'll fire a volley at their bow."

"Aye aye, Captain."

"When we are as close as possible I'll yell the order to fire, and then I want you to swerve the ship so we can fire a port-side volley." Edward went to the railing overlooking the lower deck to watch the approaching ship.

"Captain?" Herbert asked.

"Wait for it."

The ship came closer.

"Captain…" Herbert's voice was more urgent.

"Not yet… Now! Fire forecastle!" he yelled, and a crewman relayed the order.

But Edward had waited too long. Two of the shots missed, and the ones that hit did little damage as they glanced off the curved wood of the *Pearl*'s hull.

Bollocks!

To compound the misfortune, Edward's hesitation had resulted in the *Freedom* turning aside too late. Instead of making a close pass, the two hulls scraped together, damaging both, and brought the ships to a standstill. The marines threw grappling hooks over to pull the two vessels together and lock their movements.

Edward yelled, "Fire port!" and a volley of cannonballs bombarded the *Pearl* as they were preparing to board the *Freedom*. The navy gunners retaliated in kind.

The close blast of cannons erupted in the middle of the two ships. Wood and smoke shot up from between them. The force rumbled across the ships like an earthquake.

A gangplank was dropped and secured across the gap between the ships by the marines. Edward pulled out two of his pistols and ran to the stairs as marines began to cross the gangplank to his ship. Fifteen ran over, then twenty, and all had pistols and swords drawn, ready to meet their sworn enemies—ready to die, if need be.

"Kill any who try to board!" Edward yelled. "Have at 'em, men!"

The two groups clashed above the gap between the ships. Swords rang out and the blast of guns and cannons echoed like cracks of lightning in the middle of a hurricane.

Two marines swung on rigging ropes and landed next to the stairs. They both ran at Edward, their swords ready to slice him open. He backed up and shot the two of them at point-blank range. Their blood and brains splattered against the deck.

Edward felt sick, and not just from the carnage. He felt pain growing in his left arm; his exertion had opened the wound, and it was bleeding again. The loss of blood and the sway of the ship nauseated him. As he stared at the dead bodies of the two marines lying in front of him, the face of Robert Maynard flashed into his mind—Robert, his old friend, who wanted to join these men in battle against him, a pirate.

He retched on the deck.

Edward shook his head violently.

Keep yourself together, man! Your crew depends on you. They're the enemy, that's all they are. They're not Robert.

He pulled out his sword.

Ignore the pain! Ignore the nausea! Keep fighting!

His eyes scanned the main deck. The two crews were fighting with each other in a writhing mass of bodies. Amongst the barrels, the masts, and the ropes, they clashed with swords and shot pistols. Edward could see William fighting, but he seemed to be disabling his opponents, not killing them. He could see Sam laughing and smashing in skulls and slitting throats, completely at home in the anarchy. Edward also saw Henry fist-fighting and taking on more than he could handle, as usual. Then John came to his rescue, killing one marine by firing his rifle and another with his bayonet. Here, in battle, he seemed a different person, his eyes filled with determination and the cold detachment of one used to death and killing.

Then Edward saw the man he was searching for: Captain Isaac Smith.

There he is. He's the one who caused all this, and the one who can end it.

At that very moment Smith cut one of Edward's crew down.

"That's enough, Smith! It's me you're after, is it not?"

Smith smiled. "Well if it isn't young Edward Thatch the supposed non-pirate. You look a touch pale. Don't tell me you're seasick."

"Hardly!" Edward jumped on the railing and ran down it, sword drawn. He jumped off and aimed a vicious cut at Smith, causing him to back off. Edward kept up the assault and slashed at the man relentlessly, but each stroke met Smith's blade.

"Is that all you can muster after all this time apart? I expected more!" Then Smith went on the offensive.

Each strike was more accurate and more deadly than the last. Edward put up his blade to try to parry, jumped this way and that, and almost had to run to avoid being hit. The difference in skill was as clear as a spyglass.

I have to distract him.

"Who taught you how to fight, Smith? Your mother?"

"No, my father." He kept attacking Edward, but with the talking he was a little slower. "Your crew looks a little more capable this time around, and a full set of cannons to boot. Stolen, no doubt. Pirate scum!"

"It's a rather humorous story. I'd be glad to tell it if your men weren't dying around your feet." Edward laughed and Smith's eyes wandered around.

Perfect!

He slashed at Smith and grazed his arm. Smith sidestepped and countered, hitting Edward in his injured arm. He screamed out in pain and tried to run as he held his arm close, but Smith was right behind him.

Edward ran around the mast pole, only to run into another marine. The man knocked him down and Edward fell flat on his back. The marine jumped on top of him, his sword coming down to Edward's throat. Edward grabbed the marine's hand, stopping the sword inches from his neck, but dropping his own sword in the process.

The marine grinned wickedly and pushed his free hand on top of his sword hand, trying to drive the blade down and ending Edward on the spot. Edward made a desperate grab for his last pistol from his belt, but the marine seized his arm. He fought to aim the pistol, struggling clumsily with the marine for control of the weapon.

The sword blade was centimeters from Edward's neck, and his injured arm was having trouble blocking it for much longer. With all his strength he forced the pistol closer and closer to the marine's face. Soon the marine's sword began to cut into Edward's flesh; the blade was trembling from the strain of Edward trying to push it back, and he knew he wouldn't be able to hold it off much longer. He pulled his knee up and hit the marine in the groin with all his might. The man coughed in pain and his strength seemed to wane, giving Edward the break he needed. He pulled the pistol up to the marine's chin and fired.

The shot of gunpowder burned Edward's ear, and his head rang and everything became a blur. The dead marine lay on top of him, blood pouring from his neck. He pushed the man off him and rose to his feet, gripping some rigging to help himself up. The ringing disoriented him and the edges of his vision were turning black. He saw Smith standing in front of him, now holding a sword in each hand. He was saying something, but Edward heard nothing.

Smith went in for the kill, his blades crossing over his head and swiping down in a vicious arc.

Then someone ran between them and stopped Smith in his tracks. Edward could barely hear the ting of blades clashing.

Who is that? Anne!

Edward shook his head and the ringing and dizziness began to subside. Slowly his hearing returned. He was able to hear all the terrible noises, and Anne's shocking words that instantly made them all stop.

"In the name of Anne Sophia Stewart, princess of Denmark, princess of Norway, and daughter to Queen Anne of England, I command you to stop this attack!"

25. THE PRINCESS AND THE PIRATES

The words fell as a command. The revelation stunned those close by into silence. As others noticed the sudden stop in violence, they too joined and the words were passed to everyone in turn. Weapons were lowered, and the silence was all the heavier for all the tumult just preceding it. None knew what to do or what to think, only that they had to stop whatever they were doing.

Anne removed her hat and let out her red hair before presenting to the astonished Captain Isaac Smith a necklace holding a signet ring.

Smith stood, unable to move or speak, shock and disbelief plastered on his face. After a moment, with all eyes on him and on Anne, he dropped his swords and knelt down.

"We are at your command, Your Royal Highness."

The rest of the marine crew followed suit and dropped to their knees. The crew of the *Freedom* watched in disbelief and awe the scene unfolding before them.

Anne's the princess?

Some of the pirates moved to start the attack again. "All hands cease fire!" Edward commanded, which the crew reluctantly obeyed. Most were still confused—including Edward himself.

She can't be the princess. This must be some kind of trick. She must look like her. I'll... I'll play along with it, until we can sort this mess out.

"You and your men are to leave this ship and return to England," Anne commanded.

Smith's gaze shifted to Edward, then back to Anne. "But, Your Highness..."

"I issued you orders, Captain. Any action not involving steps to put those orders into effect will be considered an act of treason." She stepped forward and lifted Smith's chin with her finger. "You would not think to commit treason, would you, Captain?" Anne's demeanor and accent had taken on a menacing and cold perfection that was sharper than any knife.

Edward watched her in amazement. *She's really acting the part.*

"No, Your Highness. I will follow your orders immediately." Smith stood up, saluted, and walked away. "Men, we leave."

The crew of the *Pearl* still gawked at Anne, utterly stunned.

213

She stood with her hands on her hips, her hair blowing in the wind, and she was looking down on them with the cold, haughty eyes of a princess, eyes boring into them more than any words could. They all rose to their feet and walked back to their own ship. Anne dismissed Smith, who followed his crew. They rushed to remove the grappling hooks tying the ships together and soon were sailing off to the east.

After the *Pearl* had left, Edward walked up behind Anne.

"That was bloody brilliant, Anne! Where did you learn to act like that?" Edward turned her around to face him. To his surprise, she was on the verge of tears, and shaking with anger.

"I cast my lot with pirates, and this is how it turns out," she whispered. "I guess I can never run from my past, can I, Ed?"

"What are you talking about, Anne? It was all an act, wasn't it?" Edward noticed she was wearing the ring now. He pulled her hand up and looked at it. He realised with a shock what it was: a signet ring bearing an engraving of three feathers encircled by a crown, below which were the words, *Ich Dien*, "I serve." That ring was bestowed upon the heir apparent to the throne of England. The queen had no sons, and all her other children had died at an early age. It being in her possession meant Anne was the heiress presumptive to the throne of England.

"It can't be true!"

"I am sorry, Ed. I am sorry!" Anne ran to the fore cabin, with William close on her heels.

Edward's crew gathered around him, bewildered and seeking direction.

"Is she really the princess?" "What are we to do with her?" "Wasn't that Jim?" "What do we do now?"

"Everyone, stop! Clean up or something. Have Alexandre examine the wounded. Get the ship out of here!" Edward pushed through them to the fore cabin.

Anne was sitting in a corner, her back to the door. William stood near her, sword in hand. Anne's head was almost lying on her knees, slumped, defeated. The sight broke Edward's image of her even more than the revelation had done, and something like sadness pulled at him to see her in such a state.

"Leave us," he ordered William. William didn't move, but tightened his grip on his sword.

What does he think he's doing? Is he going to fight me?

"It will be all right, William," Anne said without looking at him. "I'll be fine."

William bowed, though her back was turned, and left. On his way out he glared at Edward, as if to say, "If you dare hurt her, I'll kill you." Edward simply nodded as he left.

"So what you said wasn't a lie? You are the princess, truly?"

"Yes, Edward. It became harder and harder to reveal to you who I was, and I imagined if I did you would make me leave. I knew you would not hurt me, but I did not wish to leave. I still do not wish to leave." Anne turned around to face him. She was crying.

Edward went to her, kneeled down, and embraced her. "Anne, it doesn't matter who you or your family were. Now you're a part of this family."

"You... you mean I can stay? I can stay with you?"

"Yes, of course."

Edward's calm acceptance made Anne cry all the harder. They held each other for what seemed like hours: she in his arms, letting out her emotions, and he comforting her.

"At least now your posh accent makes more sense," Edward said with a chuckle.

Anne laughed and wiped her eyes. Edward was happy he could at least see her smile again.

Noises from outside the cabin had grown louder as the seconds passed, and Edward could ignore it no longer. "I'm sorry, Anne. I have to check on what's happening." Edward walked over and opened the door to the main deck.

The whole crew was standing outside, with William in front of the door, blocking access with his sword. The men were making a great commotion, yelling and screaming.

"What is this nonsense? Stop this at once!" yelled Edward.

The majority ceased their commotion, but one crewman, Frank, decided to be the voice of the mass. "We have with us now a golden opportunity. The princess of England is aboard our ship. With her we can demand a ransom from the queen in exchange for her safety."

"You're a fool if you think your plan will work."

"You can't see the potential in this plan, Captain? We would be richer than any pirates alive. What do you say, boys?"

The crew cheered and yelled.

"Silence!"

Everyone immediately became quiet as Edward stared them down. "What would you do then, hmm? When we've gotten the money and given them the princess, you think they will go lightly on you? You think they will let you walk away? They'll chase us to the ends of the earth to make an example of us. It would be no different if you asked for a pardon in exchange. The mere thought that the marines were at your mercy would need to be purged from everyone's minds. Once the bargaining chip is handed over, they don't have to hold to any agreement."

Frank faltered but for a moment. "Then she should leave. She's a danger to us all. Not only is she bad luck, but those marines will chase us down to retrieve her anyway." Once again the crew shouted their agreement.

Edward walked into the crowd. "This is one of our crew you're talking about. We've been together for the past six months. You've cleaned together, you've eaten together, you've laughed together, and you've fought together. She is a part of our family now. Would you willingly cast aside your own brother, your own sister, your own son or daughter, just for some coin, or because you're afraid? If you aren't willing to die for the people you stand next to, then maybe you shouldn't be on this ship. I want each of you to think long and hard on this, because if you aren't willing to die for your family aboard this ship, then you don't deserve to be here. When we land at the next port, make up your mind and then leave if you want to. As for me, I am allowing Anne to stay here as long as she likes."

"Aren't we going to vote on this? According to the commandments we have that right."

Edward grimaced at the man who spoke up. "According to the commandments, you have the right to vote on the affairs of the moment. Affairs of the moment are where we are heading, division of shares, and other business which does not involve who *I* choose to have aboard *my* ship! Another commandment states that to leave the ship you need one thousand pounds, though I am disregarding it for those of you who wish to depart due to this. Would any like to object to my fairness today?"

No one could challenge Edward. No one who looked into his eyes could want to. The crew saw in them an implacable authority that had grown, in the months they had served under his command, to equal the authority of his legendary father.

Edward waved his hand in dismissal. "Now back to work. We're heading back to the Swan Islands. Herbert, take us south."

"Aye, sir."

The crew shuffled off and went back to work. They were not feeling their usual enthusiasm; men shot sidelong glances at each other, probably wondering how many would stay and how many would leave when they reached the next port—wondering which of their brothers would be willing to die for them, and which would let them die for profit.

As Edward stood watching the crew resume their tasks, Henry walked up to him.

"We need to talk."

"Things are a little hectic right now, Henry. I don't have the time. I... oh, my head!" Edward felt a sudden stabbing pain, and brought his hand to his forehead. His vision blurred, and the earlier dizziness returned in force.

"Ed, are you all right? Ed? Edward!"

But Edward was already beyond words, and fell to the deck, unconscious.

...

Edward drifted in and out of consciousness over the next few hours. He had been taken to his bed near the stairs in the crew's quarters. When he finally woke up, he pulled himself upright and noticed Anne nearby, watching him, and William off in the distance.

"Welcome back," she said with a sad smile.

"What happened?"

"You passed out yesterday on deck."

"Ah! Yesterday? I've been asleep for a day?"

"You were injured during the battle and lost a lot of blood. Alexandre took care of you. I wanted to be here when you awoke, so I have been changing your bandages and feeding you water."

"Thank you, Anne."

Anne twisted her mouth and looked down. "I... I should be the one to thank you. You defended me."

"You're special to me. I defended you because of that. I'd do the same for everyone in the crew."

"Hmm..." Anne's eyes narrowed.

"What?"

"You say I am special, and yet you would defend everyone in the crew. That's not very special now is it?"

Edward began sweating. "Well, you're a different kind of special. I'd say you are more special."

Edward rested his hand on Anne's. She gripped it tight. They both smiled as they held hands.

"So... so how's the crew been while I've been out cold?"

"They are well. There have been some arguments. It is obvious what they are about." Anne released Edward's hand and looked off, dejected.

"It matters not; those people will be able to leave soon. They shouldn't be a part of this crew anyway if they're going to act like that. What else has been happening?"

"The crew is worried for you, but they will not draw near to me. Mostly because William glares at them so much. And Henry still wishes to speak with you. He wants to have a meeting with all the senior officers."

Edward frowned. "I should like to get it over with now." He started to rise, but Anne stopped him.

"Alexandre said you shouldn't be walking so soon. You need to have something to eat and then some rest to let your body recover. I shall bring the others here."

"No… no wait!"

Anne ignored him and walked away and up to the top deck, with William following close behind.

She's strong. Stronger than me. As soon as this is all over and things are back to the normal way they were, she'll bounce back.

Edward lay there, waiting patiently for them to return.

Henry came down the stairs with John, William, and Anne close behind, and they all walked down to the end where Edward was waiting. Anne said some words under her breath to William and she started to leave.

"Wait, Anne, don't leave. You're a part of this discussion as well."

Anne turned around and glanced at Edward, and then at Henry.

Henry shook his head. "Ed, I don't think she should be involved in this."

"Whatever you have to say I'm sure you can say in front of her."

Henry sighed. "Who am I to go against the captain's orders?" Anne sat in a hammock on the other side of Edward while Henry and John sat down in chairs.

"So what is this about, Henry?"

Henry let out a sigh. "I think Anne should leave."

Edward was shocked at the bluntness of his statement. "Explain yourself, Henry, but know this: Anne stays as long as she wants. I'll not change my mind."

"I had a feeling you'd say that. She'll be a danger to us at some point. Maybe not now, but down the road it will cause trouble for us."

"I already told you, I know they will chase us. I'm willing to fight to keep our crew safe and whole."

"Whole save for the bullets in them," Henry replied with a scoff. "If you would take a moment to separate your feelings from your common sense, you would realise the risk is too great. The reason why you want to keep her around is you fancy her."

Edward clenched his fists. "That's not true. I would do that for any aboard the *Freedom*, no matter how great the danger."

Henry turned his gaze to John. "John, you've been with us from the beginning. What's your assessment of the situation? What do you think our rival Smith will do once he returns to England?"

John jumped from his seat with a start. Beads of sweat began to form on his forehead. "W-well…" He glanced back and forth before clearing his throat. "S-Smith doesn't like to lose. He'll no doubt call on the navy for help, possibly even the qu-queen herself." Anne shuddered at the mention of that title. "Th-they'll bring the full might of the British navy down on us. When they find us, we'll be tried as enemies of the state. And found guilty, of course. No matter if the p-princess claims otherwise." John looked at Anne. "Sorry." Anne shook her head to try to alleviate his guilt.

"And you, William? What do you think?" Henry asked.

William looked at everyone in turn and then finally at Anne. He hesitated until she nodded approval. "I believe John's assessment to be correct. My apologies, Your Highness."

The tension rose as silence settled on the room. Everyone waited on Edward. He was the captain. No matter what was said, he was the final authority.

I can't just tell them this is my order and they have to follow it. Henry's anger will build if I don't do something.

"Henry, what would you do if I were being attacked?"

Henry cocked his brow. "Huh? What kind of a question is that?"

"It's relevant. What would you do if I were in trouble?"

"Ah! I see what you're doing. Well, I would save you, obviously. And I know you'll say because of that, we should save Anne."

"Yes, I am. What if I had thought saving you from the gallows was too great a risk?"

Henry's face registered shock. He obviously hadn't drawn that connection. He certainly had to remember how, at the time, he'd said that Edward should have left him to die.

Edward continued. "I didn't think about the risk. All I cared about was saving you. I think you would have done the same, because we're brothers. Besides, you knew from the beginning we would be chased by the marines because of being pirates. How does this change anything?"

"Don't sidestep the issue, Edward. You are right that you saved me, but you decided to save me after you heard I was captured. Right now we're talking about our future safety. She's a liability, and you're a fool if you think otherwise. Smith is one thing; the entire British navy after us is another." Henry's penetrating gaze was equal to Edward's.

Edward turned away from Henry and muttered something under his breath. As he talked his voice kept rising in volume. "I am captain of this ship. If Anne wants to stay, then she stays. If you aren't willing to accept that, then I make you the same offer I did back when I offered Herbert a position. If it's such a problem to you, you can leave. Our dream was freedom, and I don't see how you can abide by denying someone else that dream."

"Tch," Henry spat. "I'm not leaving. But don't expect me to risk my life for her. When the inevitable happens, I'll be there to save your arse like usual, and then I'll say I told you so." Henry left with a scathing glance at Anne, his feet stomping loudly until he reached the top deck.

John was next. "I pr-promised your father I would be by your side when you needed it. I won't break that promise."

Edward nodded to John and he also left.

William shrugged. "I will protect the princess, no matter the cost. I have made mistakes in the past, and I do not intend to repeat them. If she wishes to stay, I cannot go against that, but I won't leave either."

Anne nodded to William, and he went back to the other side of the ship to keep guard of the stairs. It was only Anne and Edward now.

"I am sorry, Edward. I did not mean to cause a fight between you and Henry," she said, her eyes downcast. "Maybe I should leave… They are right. I am putting everyone in jeopardy."

"It doesn't matter. Henry will come around eventually. Besides, I want you to stay. Making you leave goes against what this ship stands for. Making you leave against what I stand for."

"*Freedom*, huh?" Anne said, staring at the floorboards. She seemed almost nostalgic about something. "Thank you, Edward." She smiled a little. "Ed."

Edward smiled and held her hand again.

···

As the days progressed, many in the crew became more vocal about their opinions. The debates intensified, and if not for the presence of

Edward and the other senior officers, fistfights would have broken out. The crew was split between those who would stay and those who would leave.

They had to be reminded several times of the fact that if they had a quarrel it would have to be decided by a duel.

Anne was feeling isolated. Some who supported her as a crewmate were walking on eggshells around her with no real reason. They saw her as the princess now, not as a common pirate. That attitude was better than those who were outright against her, but still.

The only thing keeping Anne's detractors from taking her captive was the other half of the crew willing to protect her.

"So, William, I guess I had the wrong idea about you," Edward commented one day.

"Explain your meaning."

"I thought you were infatuated with Anne, and that's why you wanted to protect her, but I suppose that's incorrect. If I had to guess, by the way you avoid any marine's gaze, and by how well-mannered and highly trained you are, I'd say you... must be..."

William responded with a blank stare.

"An indentured servant!" Edward smiled. "Am I right?"

"No."

"What? I was wrong? Then what are you? Ex-marine?"

"Yes." William never lost his blank expression, but Edward thought he could see a twinge of anger.

"Ah! That makes sense. You're still loyal to the monarchy. Will you turn me in to the authorities?"

"I have not decided."

Edward's jaw dropped, but William's expression was as still as stone. "Haven't decided? Should I consider myself lucky?"

"I have my reasons to stay away from the marines. You saved my life, and the princess likes you, but if it comes down to her or you, I won't hesitate to bring you down. You seem to be different from most pirates, though, so I haven't decided what I'll do yet."

"Thank you... I think."

William went almost nose to nose with Edward and, despite the latter's height advantage, seemed to look down at him. "Know this: you walk a fine line here. The moment you think of crossing it is the moment I take matters into my own hands."

Edward returned the look in kind. "I understand."

William nodded and walked away.

Later that day, Edward had a talk with Herbert, as the matter of having women aboard concerned him as well. "Herbert, I think after the crew is allowed to leave we should tell everyone about your sister."

"Aye, I thought it might come to that."

"Is Christina comfortable with it?"

"I already told her about the possibility, and in truth she would enjoy it quite a bit if she could stop pretending to be a boy." He smiled. "I cut her hair short the day before we set out, and she cried so much I thought we would drown before I finished. I'm sure she'll want to grow it out again."

Edward laughed. "Soon she will be able to."

The next day Edward had a brief talk with almost everyone in the crew. He asked each man to express his opinions and feelings freely. Some were vocally against Anne staying, and said so much with very harsh words.

"That bitch has no place on a pirate ship." "She's a woman and a princess; it's likely the gods have cursed us." "I can't stay on a ship with a woman!"

Edward tried to reason with the crewmen who had decided to leave, but their hate and superstition blinded them to his words. Those vocal against Anne had made their decision and Edward could not change that.

Some crewmen were still undecided, so Edward presented them with the same thoughts he'd left with Henry. He talked about the name of the *Freedom* and what he believed it meant to be aboard it.

Edward even had a chance to talk with Alexandre when he was receiving a checkup. "And how do you feel about having a woman on board, Alexandre?"

"Nothing has changed, *Capitaine*. I've always know Jim was a woman."

"What? How?"

"I believe I have shown you my *pouvoirs de déduction*? I noticed things."

"Hmm… I suppose that makes sense. I remember you could tell Henry had broken his nose simply by looking at him. So, you're fine with Anne being aboard?"

"*Oui*. I never had an issue with women aboard ships. Anne is also a princess. This makes things… interesting. I will enjoy watching the events unfold."

"I don't know whether that's a good or bad thing, but I'm glad you'll stay with us."

Edward then approached Jack.

Jack rubbed his chin in thought. "Well, I knew about the superstition concerning women on a ship, but I didn't realise people took it so seriously."

"Neither did I. So, will you be comfortable staying?"

"Why, of course. I don't mind her being aboard. And, if I remember correctly, she always enjoyed my violin. I like those who appreciate fine music."

"Well, I'm glad you're staying. The days would be even duller without you."

"I'll do my best to lighten the mood, Captain."

And then Sam.

"A woman on a pirate ship! What were ya thinking, Captain? And she's the bloody princess! This is a bloody big mess." Sam ran his fingers through his straight black hair in frustration.

"She's been quite useful. She did save our lives in that last battle by revealing her identity."

"Heaps and mounds that does us when we'll be drinkin' salt water all the way to Davy Jones' locker."

"So you're to leave as well?"

"I be stayin'."

Edward arched an eyebrow. "But you said…"

"Aye, I know what I said. If I was afraid o' danger, I would'a left a long time ago. I'll hafta get used to it, is all."

Edward laughed. "That's good to hear." He turned to leave.

"Captain?" Edward turned back. "I know ya care fer her, so I 'ave a little advice. Don't let anyone near her 'less you trust 'em. Not everyone aboard here is like you."

Edward responded with a stern look and a nod.

I know, Sam. I'll protect her.

Within a week of Edward's talking with the crew, the mood aboard ship seemed to shift, with less bickering and more willingness to adapt to the new situation. But many still wanted nothing to do with the woman and the trouble she would bring, and they weren't afraid to make their feelings known.

The *Freedom* was heading back to the Swan Islands, the same place they had stopped on their way to finding the last key. Edward addressed the crew once more as they neared port.

"Those of you leaving today will have all weapons confiscated. You will receive as much compensation as we can afford for your work, but the weapons remain. If you've already made your decision to leave, bring your belongings to the main deck to be inspected."

There was a small outcry among those intending to leave. They didn't want to be searched and to have their arms taken away.

"These are the terms. Abide by them, or be thrown off with nothing."

At that they all stopped complaining and reluctantly gathered their things to leave. In total about fifty people were leaving the ship, almost a fourth of the crew. *That's better by half than I'd expected. We'll still need to replace them, but at least we won't be a skeleton crew.*

"Now, search them."

The remaining crewmembers were reluctant to follow this command, but with a stern glance from Edward they obeyed. Nearly a third of those leaving were found to have concealed weapons among their possessions. By the time the search was complete, the ship was pulling into port.

Their former crewmates disembarked in silence. Those men had made their choice, and would never again set foot on the deck of the *Freedom*. Edward wished them well and provided them as much as he could spare from the common stock for their work to that point.

"Anyone else?" Edward asked when the last one left the ship. No one spoke. "Good. Turn the ship around. We're leaving."

"We're not going to stay, Captain?" Herbert asked.

"No. Head southwest until we're out of sight of the islands. We'll decide our next destination soon. We don't want them to know where we're headed. They could harbour some ill will towards us."

"Aye, Captain."

Edward turned his gaze out to sea once again. The salt air filled his nostrils—that sweet smell that brought the nostalgia of his youth. He let out a long sigh as he stared into the emerald waters.

Father, I know I can't be a fisherman like you. But if you were here, would you be proud of me?

"So, where are we headed now, Ed?" Henry brought Edward back from his reverie.

"I don't know. We need some new crewmembers. Pirates, of course. Where do you think we should go?"

Henry shrugged. "You expect me to know?"

"Herbert, do you have any ideas?"

"Well, there is one place I know of. I haven't heard much about it recently, but it's close by. The Cayman Islands. The Grand Cayman, specifically."

"All right, we'll try there first. Set sail for the Grand Cayman!"

26. THE SMELL OF BLOOD

The voyage to the Grand Cayman wasn't a particularly long one, but to Edward the weeks felt like months. They were especially monotonous, with the crew finding little to do, and the heat being so oppressive. The sun was rising earlier and setting later each day, and on deck there wasn't much shelter from its glare.

Edward held a thick, twisted strand of rope in his large hands as he and some others helped trim and tie down the sails. He had already spent time moving some barrels out of storage up to the top deck and others back down into storage, and, before that, doing general maintenance with Nassir and his son. He was always eager to learn every bit of what it was to be a sailor, and that meant he had to have his hand in everything going on aboard ship. During these long days on the empty sea, his only wish was to keep busy, however exhausting the work.

How did my dad do this every day? Edward thought as he fanned himself on the top deck. Seeking relief after working the sails, he lay in their shadow, shirtless, exposing the skin of his muscular chest to the warm breeze.

"You aren't much of an imposing presence right now," a sweet feminine voice rang from outside his vision. Edward sat up to see the only possible owner of that voice. She handed him a cup of water and sat down beside him.

"Thank you. It's tough to be captain-like with this heat. The air is so heavy today." He took the water and downed it in one gulp, then gazed at her, sitting next to him.

She was wearing a loose shirt that exposed her arms, and her trousers were rolled up almost to her knees. Edward couldn't help but stare at her bare legs and shoulders. Her soft skin with a healthy colour from the sun and freckles here and there caught his eyes and wouldn't let go. He could feel his heart starting to beat louder and faster in his ears.

"What's wrong, Edward? Is there something on me?" Anne asked as she checked herself.

"Uhh, no... No! Sorry, I was thinking about how you don't seem exhausted from all this work."

"I learned a lot of Oriental disciplines in my training. Many of them talk about controlling everything in your body using your mind. They say some of the more learned among them, masters who have trained all their lives, are able to break rocks with their bare hands and stand on burning coals without injuring themselves. Some say they can even evade bullets through concentration."

"Are you saying you aren't exhausted because you keep telling yourself you aren't?" Edward arched his brow in disbelief.

"Essentially," was all Anne gave.

"How is that possible?"

Anne thought about it for a moment. "The body has built-in limiters to protect us, but it's all in the mind. If you can break those limits, with your conscious or unconscious mind, you pass from the realm of normal human ability. If you tell yourself you can do something so often that you believe it with all your heart, it is bound to change what you can actually accomplish."

"And so that's how you can keep going without tiring? You tell yourself you can?"

"At its simplest, yes, but otherwise it can happen naturally in extreme circumstances. It also helps that I am used to exerting myself."

"Have you been able to do other things that way? Like dodging bullets or something?" Edward laughed even as he said it, skeptical of the whole thing. To a simple fisherman's son, this was like a penny-book fantasy.

Anne didn't seem to hear him. Her eyes were staring straight ahead, wide and glazed over as if she were lost in a daydream, remembering.

...

The smells of sulfuric gunpowder and coppery blood mixed with the salty air, filled her nostrils, and made her gag. She knew she would never become accustomed to it, but it was different this time.

This time the she had killed the man that lay in a pool of his own blood. She felt sick. Anne had never taken a life, and though he was a pirate, he was nonetheless a human being.

It was not so easy for her to justify.

"You'll pay for that, bitch!"

"We're gonna have our way with ye before we get a ransom coin."

"You'll pay with yer body and yer blood."

The crew was closing in on her. She had only a sword left with which to defend herself. The captain made his way to her through the crowd, brandishing his own sword. His tall, imposing figure made him look more beast than man, and his rage-filled eyes pierced her like those of a hawk upon its prey.

Calico Jack was what the marines called him, after the cotton print clothes he habitually wore. He was known by another name, as well: Mad Jack, the most wanted pirate in the Caribbean.

"Stand down, little queen. Don't make me cut your arms off."

She did not back down. She wasn't naive; she knew what they were saying, and what they would do. She would rather die, rather kill herself then and there, than let them have their way.

She attacked the giant in front of her. He swatted her away like a fly. She could taste blood in her mouth, but she kept attacking. She fought until she could no longer lift the sword in her hand, and then she fought some more.

When she was on the verge of collapse, and her world was starting to turn black, she could see the twisted faces of the pirates before her—their yellow, rotten teeth, scarred faces, greasy matted hair, hunched backs, jeering, lewd smiles, demonic eyes—and she could feel them closing in on her weary body with hideous intent.

No, I will not let it end like this!

She forced her eyes open and, summoning a strength and speed she didn't know she still had, lunged at the captain with her sword, cut his face from his right eye down to his mouth, then leapt high and kicked him in the chest. She cut down everyone in her path, all the way to the edge of the ship.

Everything around her felt slow, or she was moving faster than anyone or anything else. She could see the bullets they fired flying past her; it was almost as if she could reach out and pluck them right out of the air…

...

"Anne? *Anne!*" Edward shouted, waking Anne from her thoughts. "Anne, are you well?"

Edward was clutching her arm, shaking her. His eyes were wide with concern.

"I am well, Edward. I apologize, I seem to have been lost in thought. What was your question?"

Is she truly well? Edward stared at Anne, prompting her to repeat that she was in good health. "How are you able to do something like that? It seems impossible."

Anne provided herself one last shake to clear her head. "Well, part of it is training, and part of it is instinct. Recall what I mentioned before? Instinct is something lost to humans because we have become lazy. If you train yourself so that when you fight you attack without thought, then instinct can aid you. It might even be possible to control its more unbelievable manifestations. I can help train you, too."

Edward sighed. Any thought of work exhausted him even more. He lay back down on the warm wood of the deck. "Maybe some other day," he said, making it sound more like "That will never happen."

"That was not an offer! We start tomorrow." Anne left no room for dissent. She was smiling a beautiful smile, making any feeble objection float away like mist.

She got up to leave, but Edward stopped her. "Speaking of training, talk with William. When we gain some new crewmembers I want to have everyone learn from you two. We need to become more organised, and better at fighting as a group. That last fight should have been an even match, but we'd have been dead in the water if not for you," he said with a nod in her direction. "And, on the topic of water, we should train everyone to swim as well."

Anne had her mouth half open as if she wanted to say something. After a second, she turned from his gaze.

"Now I know something is wrong. Why are you hesitant? You never had a problem training the crew before." Edward stood up.

"… Now that everyone knows who I am, they are fearful even to be near me. You may have turned them away from trying to ransom me, but I remain a woman in their eyes," she said as she casted her eyes downward. "Either they are afraid to hurt me, or they think it unlucky to be around me." Edward had rarely seen her so dejected.

First, her real family, and now this one. How am I to show everyone they may treat her the same as anyone else aboard?

Edward scratched his head in frustration, and then it hit him. "I think I'll take you up on that training, but let's do it right now." Edward walked down the poop deck stairs.

"But… I thought you were exhausted?"

Edward turned and smiled. "Not too exhausted to beat you."

Anne looked taken aback at first, but she caught onto what he was doing. "Oh is that so? We shall see about that, Thatch."

She smiled and followed him down to the main deck, where they sparred with each other, holding nothing back, for the whole crew to see.

...

It was the third day of travel, and the second since Edward had resumed his training with Anne. Each day she became more aggressive to help with his reflexes, but it was taking its toll on his body.

If this kept up, Edward would have to see Alexandre. He'd prefer to avoid that; he didn't want to feel as if he was risking his life each time he sought medical attention.

Now Edward was resting on the foredeck. The sun wasn't as strong today, the clouds letting through just enough of its rays to provide subtle warmth. He listened to the faint sounds of Jack's music and the ocean lapping against the boat. The salty, humid air made his wavy black hair sway like the folds of a sail.

I quite enjoy this. It's a pirate's life for me, I suppose? Edward chuckled to himself at the thought.

"This is a strange thing, the sea," a deep, accented voice said from behind him, and Edward turned to see Pukuh approaching, spear in hand. He was a sight to behold: bone piercings, wooden armour and leather undergarment, animal feathers, and tattoos all over his body—a mere glimpse of him could elicit fear. He needed some normal clothes, Edward decided.

"Good day, Pukuh," Edward said. "What do you mean?"

"I would often look upon the sea as a child, thinking back on the adventures my father told me he had with Benjamin," Pukuh replied, gazing out at the endless blue surrounding them. "It has a strange pull to it, don't you think?"

Edward knew what Pukuh was talking about; he could feel it, but he couldn't help thinking his feeling was different. "I've always wanted to be on the sea, but I didn't choose the life of a pirate. I was forced into it."

"Benjamin claimed many were, and I imagine the same is true today. My father told me Benjamin had chosen the life for the excitement, and for that he is stranger than any other."

229

"What was he like?" Edward asked, curious about the one who had, however inadvertently, bequeathed him the life he found himself living.

"I only truly know what my father has told me," Pukuh replied. "When he left with my father I actually hated him because he was an outsider and took my father from me." Pukuh chuckled, a wisp of nostalgia in his eyes. "When my father returned, stronger than ever and with so many adventures to share that filled his face with joy, I could not fault the man that brought this about. My father said Benjamin was an odd man who didn't listen to any conventional wisdom, choosing instead to suit whatever fancy called to him at the time. He was dangerous, a warrior without peer, and an inspiration to his crew. He was not afraid of anything, and inspired fear in his enemies. My father admired him as well, which I always found odd: a king admiring a pirate." They both laughed.

"I suppose that is a bit odd."

"Yes, I thought the same until I met you."

"Until you met me? Why?"

Pukuh leaned his back against the railing. He looked to the many crewmembers tying ropes and running about, some talking and others working. "You may not have chosen this life at first, but you are like Benjamin: you do not fear it. You could have run, you could have tried to escape from the other ship a few days ago, but you didn't. It was the same with the wolves. You stood your ground, almost pushed for the fight, even. You chose the warrior's path at all times."

"But I had to. I couldn't have done anything to escape."

"Maybe so with the wolves, but not with the marines. You had the same size ship, yet you only thought of fighting. And as I understood the story from the other crewmembers, you chose it from the beginning as well. When you thought you would lose your treasure, you fought instinctively to protect it. You aren't afraid to spill blood—or lose it. A true warrior and a true pirate." Pukuh patted Edward on the shoulder and then got up and walked away.

Edward opened his mouth to make an objection, but as he thought it over he realised Pukuh was right. At each turn, he could have run away from this life, disappeared, and become a sailor at some other port, his dream fulfilled. Instead, he'd chosen at all times to fight.

Does that mean I really did choose this life? The life of adventure and constant bloodshed? Edward's heart raced at the thought, and the possibility began to scare him.

...

Edward descended into the lower decks, limping on one leg and breathing staggered breaths. As he entered the crew's quarters, he saw Alexandre at work in one corner. The small desk at which he sat, made for him by Nassir, was bolted to the side of the ship. Edward could see numerous objects on and around it: medical equipment such as gauze, needles and thread, various knives, and other things he didn't recognise, scattered sheets of paper, covered with scratches and scribbles, weighted down by miscellaneous items including a gun, and more contraptions, small and large, that he knew better than to ask about.

He moved halfway into the room before he stopped.

Maybe if I leave I'll be able to let it heal on its own, he doesn't need to see it. No, no, it's fine.

Edward wanted nothing more than to turn around and escape the possibility of more pain, but a familiar, French-accented voice from the dimly lit corner stopped him.

"Your leg is dislocated and you have several bruised ribs," Alexandre said matter-of-factly from his seat, his eyes still focused on papers. "Fighting with Anne again?"

"Yes, you're right. I don't suppose you'll tell me how you knew without even looking up?" Edward dragged himself to a chair beside the desk and sat down. The smell of sulphur and black powder pervaded the air, mixed with ether and other odd scents. *How can he work in this?*

"The timing of your step was off, indicating a limp. You wouldn't be walking on it if it were broken, so dislocated. Your breath is ragged, and you coughed when breathing in, so bruised ribs. Looking at you makes it all too easy."

"You're as stunning as ever, Alexandre, and I see your English is better every time we talk."

"Yes, well, I have had my practice. Come, sit down." Alexandre got up and motioned to a chair on the other side of the table.

Edward sat down and Alexandre examined his leg further, twisting it this way and that. "Lost again?"

"Oh, yes."

"It shows, *mon ami*. You two have been practicing more often of late." He quickly pulled on Edward's leg, snapping it back into place for him.

"Ah! Blimey Frenchman!" Edward yelled, but the pain was gone in a moment. "Thank you. And yes, we have been. The more I work with her, the easier it is for the crew to accept her."

"Noble. I noticed, despite your riveting speech, their hesitancy about having a woman aboard. Not to mention the queen's daughter. Your fighting her as if nothing were out of the ordinary would of course make some hesitation dissipate. Now lift your *maillot*."

"Lift my what?"

Alexandre sighed. "Shirt, lift your shirt, man. I learned from you *rosbifs*. The least you could do is learn a little French."

Edward lifted his shirt and apologised.

Alexandre examined the bruises on his chest, eliciting winces from his patient. "I will apply some ointment. It will help with the bruising on the outside and cool the inside."

"Thank you." Alexandre went back to his desk, opened a couple of drawers, and took out some herbs, which he threw together into a mortar and ground with a pestle. "So where did you learn medicine?"

"Why the sudden interest?" Alexandre stopped for a moment and added a clear liquid that foamed on contact.

"I realised how little I know about you. Our first meeting was rather rushed, if you recall."

"*Oui*, I remember," Alexandre replied. "I have been all over the world, the old world and the new, learning from many, and gathering much practice. This," he said, pointing to the mortar, "I learned from a shaman in the north of Asia. It uses oil from a local plant and leaves that is applied like a... *coller?*"

Stick? A sticky ointment? "A paste?"

"*Oui*, a paste. Now, lift your shirt again." As soon as Edward did so, Alexandre applied the white substance over his ribs, producing more winces until he was finished. Alexandre put gauze over it and a wrap to keep it in place. "There, *tout fini*."

This feels so odd. It's tingling and cold, but the bruises don't hurt anymore. "That's amazing. I don't even feel it anymore. Thanks, Alexandre!"

"You are welcome," he replied, returning to his desk. He grabbed a different ointment in a stone jar, which Edward was already familiar with, and walked back to him.

The Voyages of Queen Anne's Revenge

Edward pulled up his left shirt arm, revealing the red mess, which used to be an even uglier red mess, of a scar. It was healing, slowly, and if not for Alexandre and the treatment he'd received from the Mayans, he probably wouldn't have an arm at all now.

"I told you before not to spar while you are healing, but you won't listen to me no matter what I say, will you?"

"I should say... no." Edward laughed as Alexandre finished applying the ointment.

"So how is Pukuh's leg?"

"It was not broken, simply a bad sprain and dislocation which he set himself with you present, I understand, so it has already healed."

"Well, at least one of us is all better. Thanks again, Alexandre." Edward rose to leave.

"Ah yes, here." Alexandre picked up and handed Edward a pistol.

It was modified and had something different in the barrel from the pistols Edward was used to. "What's this?"

"If I can't stop your practice fighting, I can try to stop the real thing. When we met, I was testing this pistol. This is the completed version," he said, motioning towards the pistol. "It has rifling and uses custom bullets. They take a long time to make, but they are more accurate and have longer range than regular pistols. You'll need only one bullet to kill, if you take proper aim."

"I could definitely use this. Can you make me a matching one?"

"*Certainement*. But, as I said, it will take time."

"I should like to know as soon as it is ready, if you please." Edward started to leave, but stopped himself. "Alexandre, why did you join us? And, for that matter, after being through all these battles, why have you stayed? You know the risks, and this obviously isn't the usual ship to be on if you want to explore the world."

"It is the same as I mentioned at our meeting. I want excitement. This world is dull, but you've proven to be more than adequate entertainment. I shall enjoy seeing your descent."

Descent? "What do you mean?"

"You are a pirate, but so far you've only had to defend yourself and attack those who attack you, or whom you consider evil already. Soon, you may run out of people you can steal supplies from. You will need to go on the offence to survive. At that time, I will be able to see an answer to a question that's been puzzling me."

Edward stared deep into Alexandre's eyes. The blank stare did not wholly conceal an unsettling glint of excitement. He believed he knew what Alexandre's question was, and he knew he didn't want to acknowledge it. But—despite it making him sick to his stomach—he had to ask.

"What question?"

Alexandre smiled, and Edward cringed as the smiling mouth asked, "Do you enjoy the smell of blood?"

Edward spun around and left without another word, terrified by the man who knew so much from just observing. That he was able to know exactly what Edward wanted to know was amazing; that he was excited to know the answer to the question was horrifying.

What made Edward sick to his stomach was that some part of him was excited too.

27. THE BODDEN TOWN BANDITS

"We are close to the island now, Captain. I hope it's still the safe haven for pirates I've heard it is. You remember what happened when you thought Port Royal was safe?" Herbert turned himself around in his wheelchair. The creak and clank of the wooden joints made the wheelchair seem likely to break, but it stood fast, as it had for years.

"How could I forget?" *Henry almost died because of Frederick. No, not Frederick, rest his soul. The magistrate was at fault, but I don't want anything like that happening again.* "We can't take any chances this time. The more discreet we are the better."

"That's well and good," Henry said as he walked up the steps to the foredeck, "but how do we remain discreet when we need at least twenty-five, maybe forty, crewmembers?"

"So few? I thought we lost more."

"Yes, well, a lot of those who left were freeloaders, and while we were at sea John had plenty of time to reassess how many we need aboard. Operating with a skeleton crew has shown us we can work with less."

"See, Henry? It all works out in the end." Edward smiled.

"You don't have to tell me, I'm with you."

"You have to agree all's well that ends well, eh, chap?" Edward said as he smacked his friend's back.

"Edward, I'm agreeing with you. Yes, it's good they left."

"Be as contrary as you want, some good came out of this mess." Henry wiped his face. "I hate you."

"Aww, love you too, mate." Edward punched Henry in the arm.

Herbert, watching this exchange, just shook his head, but Edward noticed a smirk on his face.

After Edward and Henry had finished laughing at their own foolishness, Edward realised for the first time the oddity of seeing Herbert on the foredeck. "Herbert, why aren't you at the helm?"

"Christina's taking over for a bit. She wants to feel useful aboard the ship, and I've been teaching her a little of how to read the sky and manage a ship of this size."

Edward frowned. *It will be dangerous for her if she's on deck when a battle breaks out.* "If she's going to be on deck then she would do well to learn how to defend herself. She won't be forced to fight, as per the commandments, but she should at least be prepared so she can stay alive. Either she learns to fight as well, or she stays below deck."

"Understood, Captain. I'll let her know her choices." Herbert turned and climbed back down to the main deck with his chair in tow, his massive arms straining with the effort.

"What are you thinking?" Henry asked, his anger apparent.

"What's your meaning?" Edward replied casually.

"Having her trained to fight?" Henry's eyes were fierce and he gripped Edward's arm. "Are you mad?"

"What of it? If Christina is to be above deck working, then she has to be prepared to fight, even if it's mentally."

"She's a fifteen-year-old girl, Edward!" Henry yelled, which caused everyone on the foredeck to stop and stare, hoping to watch the expected argument. Edward gave them stern looks and they went back to work. Then he leaned close to Henry and talked in a harsh whisper.

"Don't you ever talk back to me on deck. You've done it before, but it has to stop. This is my ship, and I'm the captain. If you have an objection to the way I do things, then we can discuss it in private. We don't need dissention in the ranks. Are we clear?"

"Clear as the wide sky." Henry turned to leave. "Captain."

Edward watched him walk away, and then noticed some were still staring. "Back to work!" he barked. They all rushed to obey his order the second time. Then Edward went to the front of the deck and gazed out at the open sea. He stood there brooding for a while, until his anger wore off and was replaced by melancholy.

...

The next day Edward was at the helm with Herbert. On the distant horizon a land mass was taking shape. It was the first of the Cayman Islands, and it was a welcome sight to a weary crew.

"So where are we landing?" Edward asked Herbert.

"We will be landing in Bodden Town, but that's not the official name."

Edward raised his brow. "Not the official name? Why?"

"Well, the islands around here are owned by the British, but because they're such convenient stops for transients they've been settled mainly by thugs and rogues. The government doesn't like to officially acknowledge its ownership of the land, and so hasn't bothered to name any of the settlements."

"So why is it called Bodden Town?"

"Because of the Bodden family."

"And why is it named after them?"

Herbert almost seemed to be tiptoeing around the subject. "It's because… they own the town."

Edward palmed his face and his voice took grew agitated. "How can they own the town?"

"Outsiders call them the Bodden Town Bandits, but it's worse than it sounds. The family controls the trade and all the activities on the island through force. They have an extensive network throughout, and have their hands in everything. It's quite the lucrative business, I hear."

"And how does the family feel about people who encroach on their territory?"

"As long as it's business, it's fine, but you have to defer to them first. If you don't, then… well…"

"Herbert?" Edward prodded.

"You're silenced."

Edward sighed. "Don't you think we would have been better served had we been told this before we arrived? This makes things difficult." Edward stroked his short black beard, deep in thought.

Herbert waited for orders, but they never came. "Do… do you want me to change course?"

"No, no. Stay steady, this doesn't change our plans. We simply have to be even more careful."

Edward was still brooding and stroking his beard when John walked up to the aft deck to check on things.

"John! Perfect timing. Come here."

"Yes, Captain?"

"I want you to tell everyone who's been tasked with finding potential crewmembers to keep a watchful eye, even amongst the rogues. Tell them to seek out individuals, no one in groups. This town seems particularly lawless."

"Understood, Captain," John said as he went about his task.

"I should like it if we can have some peace while here. We've had enough trouble of late as it is. I'm going to find Nassir to talk over the *Freedom*'s needed repairs. Keep her steady," Edward ordered Herbert.

"Aye, Captain."

Edward walked down to the main deck. People were running this way and that, some carrying rope or barrels of wine, some swabbing the deck, and others practicing swordplay or checking weapons. Some saluted or called out to him as he passed, and he greeted them in return.

He located Nassir on the gun deck, checking the sideboards while his son watched from nearby. He had a puzzled look on his face, as if something was not quite right.

"What's the problem?" Edward asked as he approached.

Nassir and his boy Ochi acknowledged Edward's presence, and then Nassir went back to the sideboards. His deep, rumbling voice sounded troubled. "There is no problem, but that is the problem."

Edward cocked his brow. "You are speaking in riddles."

"Yes, that is exactly what this is." Nassir was rubbing his hand over the pine boards. "There is no damage in this area of the ship."

"None? What about the battle we just had?"

"Yes, there is recent damage, but not from before. Nothing old."

"But... I remember you saying it was damaged. Back when we met Bartholomew Roberts. You said you couldn't repair it for some reason."

"Yes, it was the same reason I didn't want to try breaking open the locked sections: This ship was built like no other ship I've seen and I didn't want to risk permanent damage by cutting into the wood from the outside. Now that I can see it from the inside, however, I can tell that the damage in this area is new. The old damage would have shown signs of rot, but there is none."

"Hmm, that is odd..." Edward scratched his head and thought about it for a moment. "Perhaps we were merely lucky it didn't rot. We should take it as a blessing."

"Perhaps," Nassir repeated, still doubtful.

After another moment to ponder, Edward moved on. "I wished to speak with you regarding the repairs. How bad was the damage, and how long will it take to fix?"

"The battle was not long, and so the repairs will not take long, provided we have sufficient supplies and manpower."

"Confer with John for and supplies any provisions you may need. I should like to see the repairs completed as quick as possible. We may not be here long."

"Aye, Captain," Nassir said as he bowed.

Edward patted a smiling Ochi on the head and nodded to Nassir as he left. *Quite the head-scratcher indeed. But I have more important things to worry about.*

...

The *Freedom* eased into the harbour as the crew raised the sails and readied the lines to secure it. Edward watched the preparations, issuing orders as needed. He wore his full outfit—tricorn hat, black coat, breeches, and tall boots. He appeared older than his years, with his black beard now being rather large, and his maturity evident in his command. He addressed the crew, telling them to stay out of trouble and keep a low profile—the less trouble they made, the longer they could stay—but otherwise to enjoy their leisure time.

Edward asked Anne and Henry to join him for a drink at the local tavern before they set to work on recruiting. It had been a while since Edward was able to relax, and he meant to as soon as possible.

The crew put out a gangplank, and Edward was first to disembark, with Anne and Henry close behind. He sauntered down to the harbour with some of his crew following after. Those on the ship threw rope down and those on the pier lashed it to pegs, securing the ship, while Edward was met by the harbourmaster.

"Name?"

"Edward Thatch."

"Business?"

"My business is my own. If it is a matter of coin, then my quartermaster John will oblige you. Now if you'll excuse me, I'll be on my way." He went around the man and strode off, with Henry and Anne following him.

The harbourmaster ran up in front of him again. "Stop. Stop, I say!" The man placed his hand over Edward's broad chest. "The brothers Malcolm and Neil Bodden request the presence of all... prominent travelers such as you. My associate will guide you to their house." He pointed to a young Negro in a servant's suit.

"My apologies, but you can tell the Brothers Bodden I refuse. I do not know them and so I have no business with them. You can tell them if they want to speak with me then they can come see me themselves."

The harbourmaster was left speechless and flustered. He motioned to the other man, who nodded and ran off.

"Do you think that was wise, Edward?" Anne asked as they started walking down the harbour towards town again.

She was wearing a simple, leather jacket over a loose white tunic, tight-fitting trousers, and comfortable boots. Her hair was tied in a ponytail in the back and loose in the front. Now that she was known to be a woman it afforded her a more comfortable choice of apparel. Edward stared at her, dumbfounded.

"Edward?"

He coughed and raised his eyes. "I told them the truth. I have no business with the men. We've just arrived and I wish to relax. They can't expect people to do business the moment they arrive. I mean, look at this place!"

Past the harbour there was a sandy beach with the salty sea lapping against it with each oncoming wave. In the distance, palm trees and green grass holding loose coconuts and various flowers went as far as the eye could see, swaying in the wind like sails.

Straight from the stone steps Edward, Anne, and Henry had walked up, there was a local market with vendors hawking fresh fish, produce, and other local delicacies stretching far to the left and right on the cobblestone roads. The smells were heavenly and a welcome respite from the old biscuits, dried meat, and soft cheese they were used to at sea.

In front of them the main street went all the way to the end of the small town. Strewn about the street there were patches of green and palms growing from them, left untouched from the making of the road. It gave a feeling of earthiness and brightness to the dark stones.

Some of the houses and businesses going up the street were made of wood from the local palm trees, or thicker imported woods of lighter colour. All the houses in the town were one or two stories high, and none unkempt or in disrepair. The setting sun bestowed a magical hue of gold and the place felt like a painting come to life.

"It doesn't feel like the locals are too fond of visitors," Henry said as he peered this way and that.

As they walked along the streets, they became aware of people standing in doorways and at windows, watching them. Whether it was direct and blatant staring, or more subtle glances, the whole town seemed curious about, or suspicious of, the newcomers. Men with cigars blew great puffs of smoke from their mouths. Others held newspapers that covered their mouths but left their eyes showing. Still others stole glimpses from behind decks of playing cards. All but the children playing in the streets eyed them with one thought.

They all stared at the three strangers, expecting trouble.

"What of it?" Edward scoffed.

Though the air was thick with tension and the town eerily quiet, Edward wasn't fazed. He sauntered down the main street with his back straight, his coat flapping in the wind, his face expressionless as stone. He walked until he found the first bar, and went inside.

A gang of toughs, full of bravado, potentially even some pirates, were stationed in the seats as if they had them on permanent reserve. Everyone in the bar was laughing and drinking, but when Edward, Anne, and Henry walked in, they all stopped. They owned the place, and the young man standing tall amongst the veterans was like an insult to them. No one moved, but their eyes followed the newcomers.

Edward went to the bar and sat down on a stool. "Rum, please." Seeming pleased by his choice, the rest of the patrons went back to their carousing.

On the outside Edward was calm, but he knew if they all fought, he and his companions would lose. He was the one who had warned the crew to tread lightly. He had to be an example for them.

Henry sat and ordered rum, like Edward, and just as Anne was about to sit down, someone smacked her on the behind. "Be a good wench and fetch me a beer!" an overweight man in a dirty tunic yelled, provoking the laughter of his friends.

Anne's face flushed red and hot—not with embarrassment, but with rage. "Stay calm, Anne," Henry warned.

"I am calm." Anne's words sifted through grinding teeth and she sat down with a hard plop on the stool.

But the man mistook her flush and decided to push his luck further. "Aw, come now lass, don't be cold. Let me buy ye a drink and you and I can head to the back and I'll show you the pleasure a real man can provide."

Anne let out a long breath, then turned to the thug. "No, thank you." The perfect pronunciation—so out of place where they were—made her stand out even more, which further goaded the thug.

"Oh, ho, we have a prissy little bint here, don't we?" the fat man said, eliciting laughter from those in his entourage. He grabbed Anne's arm. "Come on, lass, don't knock it 'till ye touch it."

Edward was silent through the whole incident, but he downed his rum in one gulp, rose to his feet, spun around, and smashed the glass on the fat man's head. The man fell to the ground, screaming and bloody. The more he tried to grab at the glass in his eyes, the worse he made it. His friends jumped up, as did everyone else in the bar.

The only things keeping them all at bay were Edward's cold stare and his stature. At six feet four inches, he was taller than any man there, and his second in command, Henry, was almost as tall and just as powerfully built.

"So much for not making trouble, eh Ed?"

"I suppose I can't control my temper like you can, Henry." They both raised their fists to prepare for the twenty-some men, and a few women, about to pounce on them. Anne stood between the two of them and prepared herself as well, nodding to each of them to signal she was ready.

But just as pandemonium was about to break loose, two average-looking men sauntered through the door, followed by several well-armed men of more intimidating build. They were twins, dressed in matching outfits of the finest silk, and Edward could easily guess who they were by their superior air and lack of weapons. At the sight of them, the whole room fell silent.

"The Brothers Bodden!" Edward announced.

The brothers assessed the scene before them. "Any trouble here with our newcomers, boys?" asked one of them in a faded Scottish accent.

Everyone went back into their seats and to their drinking, quiet now.

"Good," the other brother said in similar accent.

The fat man was still writhing on the floor, his companions trying to silence him. He motioned to the table and one of the men under the Boddens' employ went over and shot the poor fellow in the head, silencing him for good.

"You must be Edward. We heard from our associate you would only come if we invited you ourselves." His brother continued, "Well, here we are. We have business to discuss. You will come with us."

"And if I refuse?"

The Bodden Brothers' men instinctively pulled out their pistols and surrounded the three pirates. The brothers chuckled. "You wouldn't want to do that," one of them said. They smiled at each other and walked out the door.

Their thugs prodded Edward and the rest to follow, and they all left the bar, heading up the main street. The local residents stared at them but gave their procession a wide berth. When they reached the end of the long, sloping cobblestone road, they arrived at a large metal gate in a tall, thick stone wall. The gate opened onto a stone path leading to a large whitewashed house.

Like the gate, the house was made of fine materials and a higher quality design than the other houses and businesses in town; it was built of imported wood, and had two stories and several rooms. On a balcony some women were sitting at a table sipping tea, tended by Negro slaves. The whole estate might have been a high-class inn or a manor house for a wealthy family back in England.

Edward, Henry, and Anne were led up the path and into the house. The interior was even more extravagant than the exterior had suggested. They were taken through a large ballroom up to the second floor, and ushered into a study.

The walls of the room were lined with shelves holding numerous books, weapons and relics, including a Scottish coat of arms. At the back was a large wooden table with several papers strewn about where all of them sat down.

"Now that you are on this island," the brother seated on the left began, "it is best we explain the rules to you."

"Brother, manners!" chided the brother on the right. "Introductions first, business after."

"Yes, yes, it always slips my mind. I am Malcolm Bodden, and this is my brother Neil. We know the captain is Edward Thatch; our boy told us that much. Who are the beauty and the beast with you?"

"What do you say, beauty, beast? Care to give your names?" Edward asked.

"No," Anne and Henry said in unison with the same nonchalant attitude.

Edward shrugged at the brothers' questioning look.

Malcolm, on the left, started again. "No matter. Now, the rules. Things are a little different here in our town—and I do mean ours, because we own it. Any and all business is to be done through us, or our associates."

Neil picked up after Malcolm. "Don't trouble yourselves about fights or anything of that nature. We realise that the heavy supply of booze we bring in daily, as well as the... groups we attract, are responsible. There's really nothing that can be done. Simply enjoy yourselves."

Malcolm piped in. "And don't die in the process." The two brothers laughed at their own joke, but Edward, Anne, and Henry didn't see the humour. "So, fellows, do you have any business you hope to accomplish here?"

Edward thought about it for a second. "As you put it, we're here to enjoy ourselves and not die in the process, of course—but then, that's a full-time business. Your men seem to have rather itchy trigger fingers. Should I be worried?" Edward stared the two down as he leaned back in his chair.

The tension was evident on the brothers' faces, but they tried to laugh it off. "Perish the thought! Our men would never seek to harm our guests." Malcolm said. "… Unless you cause us trouble—or don't relinquish our share."

"Your share?" Henry asked.

"Yes, we were about to discuss that. If you plan on selling anything…"

"Spices, clothes, slaves," Neil interjected.

Malcolm smiled. "The usual for your types… All that is taxed by us."

This was Anne's territory. "How much?"

"Twenty percent," Malcolm stated.

"That is ludicrous!" Anne almost jumped up out of her seat, but Edward restrained her.

When Anne had calmed herself, Edward spoke with the brothers. "We understand the rules now. Is there anything else, or can I and my friends resume drinking and causing a ruckus in your town?"

The brothers laughed again. "Yes, our men will escort you out. Enjoy the town, and remember: we're watching, always."

Edward, Anne, and Henry left without another word, and were soon on the main street, heading to the ship.

28. THE PRINCE & THE PAUPER

Pukuh watched as Anne, Edward, and Henry all left the ship to explore the town. The thought of being on solid land once more enticed him, and so he made his way to the gangplank.

"Uhh, Master Mayan, sir?" a voice from behind said tentatively.

He turned to see who it was. "You are the one they call John, yes?"

"Yes."

"You may call me Pukuh."

"Yes, of course. Do you plan on travelling into town like… that?" He gestured to Pukuh's clothing.

"What is wrong with my warrior clothing?"

Some other crewmembers who were listening laughed, as if he were a fool for even asking.

"W-well, there's nothing wrong with it, but you might attract unwanted attention from the locals, is all."

Pukuh made a spitting sound. "Let the white people stare. I have no shame in wearing what I have earned from the gods." He turned and crossed the gangplank.

Pukuh looked back and noticed John praying, possibly to those same gods, that he wouldn't get into, or cause, trouble.

Pukuh's first stop was the local market stationed right above the harbour. A straight street led up the hill, all the way through town, and he could see Edward and the other two walking up it. On the left and right was the market street with many people littering the small available area. The noonday sun was shining down on him, and several people were buying and selling and walking around.

The street was lined with stalls. Fruit, vegetables—both local and exotic—fresh fish and fishing equipment, and even weapons and ammunition could be bought there. Almost everything imaginable was for sale.

Pukuh stood out like a beached whale with his nut-brown skin, bone piercings, tattoos, and leather warrior's outfit decorated with eagle feathers. The locals, in their conventional tunics and trousers, stared at the strange sight, and some of the women actually cowered at his approach. But Pukuh was indifferent—even oblivious—to the attention.

The market fascinated him. Examining some of the local produce, he saw foods he had never seen before. There was a brown, ball-like thing that sounded as if it had liquid in it when he shook it, as well as a hard round fruit with stripes of alternating light and dark green. They didn't seem too appetizing to him. He noticed some apples and took one, and began to munch on it as he walked.

"Oi, you have to pay for that!"

Pukuh turned back to the vendor. "Pay? I have no cacao beans on me."

"Cacao beans?" The man raised his brow and had a confused look in his eyes. "This is no trade. I'm talking about this." The vendor pulled out a coin from his pocket and showed it to Pukuh.

"Ah yes, my father mentioned something like this." Pukuh pulled a purse from off his belt. He opened it and tossed a gold coin to the vendor. "That should suffice, I hope?"

The vendor's eyes bulged at the sight of the gold, as did those of others close by. "Yes, yes, that's quite enough!" He laughed, and Pukuh turned to leave. "Wait, hold a moment. I can't let you go just like that." He filled a bag with apples and some other fruits and handed it to Pukuh.

"Thank you," he said, taking the bag.

After that, everyone around tried to sell things to him, scrambling to find their best wares and foods to present to him. He declined them all politely, but he was becoming annoyed, so he went off down a side street leading away from the market.

"I didn't realise those shiny coins were so valued," he remarked aloud.

"Hey stranger, you want to have a good time?"

Pukuh turned his gaze to the voice. The owner was a woman standing in front of a white house of several floors with a red door. A few other women were standing close by. They all wore ordinary clothing, but were showing off their legs and shoulders.

He walked over to the woman who had spoken. "Mmm, you look different," she purred. "You have money?"

Pukuh showed her the gold coin. "What does this mean: 'good time'?"

"Why don't you come in and I'll show you?" She grabbed his hand and pulled him in through the door.

After about ten minutes, he hurriedly came back out. He didn't say a word to them as they pursued him, yelling profanities. Back out on the streets, he shook his head. *What kind of a world is this that forces women to do that for trade?*

He continued a short distance down the street and noticed an establishment with several people inside, talking and drinking. The swinging doors creaked as he entered through them, and immediately all eyes were on him. Pukuh sat down at the bar and flashed a gold coin.

"I would like a drink."

The barman wasn't fazed by Pukuh's odd appearance, but several customers took notice. The barman noticed their curiosity, and then said to him, "We don't serve your kind here. This is a civilised establishment, and I don't want any trouble."

"I am not here to make trouble. I wish to have a drink. My father told me there is something called a beer I must try."

"I already told you I'll not serve you." He leaned in and whispered to Pukuh, "You'd best leave now before my regulars do something."

Pukuh glanced around the bar and noticed everyone still watching him. He scoffed and left the bar without another word. A few of the patrons followed right behind him.

"Hey, foreigner!" a man yelled.

Pukuh turned to see three ragged, ill-smelling, thuggish-looking men approaching. "What is it? I have no business with you common white men."

"Common white men?" They surrounded Pukuh. "Who do you think you are? You look like a savage, but the gold you carry says otherwise. I suggest you give it to us before we take it."

Pukuh assessed the situation. There were three of them—a short man in front, a fat man on the right, and a muscular man on the left. He was surrounded. Not very good odds, were he someone else.

Pukuh jumped high and kicked the short man in front, sending him flying backwards. Pukuh fell to the ground, but swiftly pushed himself back up. The other two men grabbed the Mayan warrior as soon as he stood. He slammed his fist into the elbow of the fat man on the right. The bone broke with a muted snap, and he let go with a scream. The muscular man on the left punched him in the jaw. He rolled with it and kicked the man in the groin. The brute doubled over, clutching his manhood.

The short man in front had recovered quickly from the kick and attacked him with a knife. His bag of fruit still in hand, Pukuh grabbed it in both hands, swung back, and smashed the hard fruit into the man's chin. The bag hit him with so much force he nearly flipped in the air before falling to the ground with a thud.

The fat man, still cradling his broken arm protectively, pulled out a gun with his other hand. Pukuh jumped and rolled to the side as the sound of thunder roared and the bullet flew past his face. The man's eyes went wide as his last attempt at defense was thwarted. Pukuh dashed to the fat man with the spent gun. All in one motion, he picked the fat man up by the neck, lifted him off the ground, and slammed him back to the stone.

With two of his assailants unconscious and one still doubled over in pain, the fight was over. Pukuh had a bead of sweat rolling down his forehead, which he promptly wiped from his brow. Recalling Edward's words to stay out of trouble, he grabbed what was left of his bag of fruit, went back to the main street, and walked back to the *Freedom*.

As Pukuh approached the ship, he saw a few crewmen swabbing the deck, and a few others cleaning barnacles off the hull.

"Is the one called John still on the vessel?" Pukuh asked

The closest crewman laughed when he noticed Pukuh's garb. "He be below decks."

Pukuh nodded to the crewman and headed down the stairs to the crew cabin, where, amongst the swinging hammocks, he found John cleaning the floor.

"John?"

John jumped at the sound and then stood up. "Y-yes?"

"I would like a change of clothes."

29. WHAT MATTERS MOST

"Edward, what are we to do? The brothers have a monopoly on everything. I imagine they will want compensation if we start trying to recruit people. And what about the tax?" Anne spoke in a whisper as they walked down the street.

"We don't have to worry about the tax," Henry interjected. "We've nothing to sell. As for the recruitment, we didn't mention it and we know nothing of their rules concerning it. Ed, you should have told them about it."

"No, Henry. This way, our plans remain secret, and if they do find out, we can feign ignorance."

"What's your plan, then?" Henry asked.

"Unfortunately, I don't have any ideas yet, so I'd like the two of you to search the town, find our men, and tell them not to ask anyone about joining until I give further notice."

Anne stopped Edward before he could leave. "Where are you going?" she asked.

"I should like to see what John and the others have to suggest. Return to the ship when you're done."

They watched Edward walk away towards the ship, lost in thought.

"Is he always like this?" Anne asked.

"As long as I've known him. When he makes up his mind, there's usually no changing it. He's less quiet and shy than he used to be, but still the same Edward. When his father disappeared, I couldn't stand to see him crying, so I started talking and playing with him. We fight a lot, but we've stayed friends."

Anne kept gazing at Edward's back as he disappeared into the distance.

"I want to apologise for what I said to you before, back after Edward kissed you," stated Henry, "and also for my wanting you off the ship. I've come to realise you aren't like I thought." Henry made her face him directly. "But remember this: If he's harmed because of you, you'll never have my forgiveness." Anne nodded and Henry walked away. She opened her mouth to say something, but didn't follow through. "I'll handle the left side of town," he said. "You handle the right. Meet you back at the ship." He waved as he went into the nearest bar.

Anne stood there. She couldn't see Edward any longer, but she could see the ship down the slope. She clutched the ring between her breasts and thought about the terror coming for them, wondering whether she would have the strength to protect him when the time came.

···

"So, any suggestions?"

The few members of the *Freedom* left on the ship all sat at the table in the mess hall. Alexandre, John, William, and Sam all listened, not saying a word. Edward waited.

"Nothing at all?"

"I have *une* question."

"Yes, Alexandre?"

"Why am I here?"

Edward glared at him. "You're here because I'm your captain and I asked you to be here. I need ideas on how to solve our problem."

Alexandre slumped forward in his seat and sighed. He wanted to make it evident he wasn't excited by any of this.

"What if we brought people to the ship?" William suggested.

"That's what we's trying to do, mate," Sam mocked. "You have anything more to add?"

William gave Sam a stern look. "I mean, bring them based on a common interest. Such as drinking or a game of cards. Then we have the whole ship to talk in without unwanted listeners."

"How will we know which people work for the B-Bodden Brothers? Anyone in town could be under their employ." John was sweating, as usual. He wiped it from his forehead and kept himself small, which was hard for such a big man.

"You have a point. How are we to distinguish friend from foe in this town?"

"Not like we can jus' walk up to the blokes and ask 'em outright," Sam chuckled.

"It's a risk we'll have to take. We can always tell the Boddens that their people asked to join us."

Alexandre groaned.

"Something to share, Alex?"

"You are inviting your own downfall if you think that will work."

"Then what do you propose we do?"

"Sit, *mon ami*. I have a plan which, I believe, even lesser minds such as yourselves will be capable of carrying out."

Edward sat down. "This had better be good."

"Never fear. It will be."

...

William walked into the room they had reserved in the small, two-story inn on the main street. "Is everyone in place?" Edward asked when he entered.

"Yes, Captain. Our keenest eyes are in place and ready to keep watch on all the entrances."

"I still do not understand why we are here," Anne complained. "You did not explain it properly."

"We're going to watch the comings and goings at the Boddens' villa. Whoever leaves the villa will be followed to see where they frequent, and to find out who are their usual contacts. We'll take a week to do this in shifts, while the rest of the crew does upkeep on the ship. As soon as we know who's with the Boddens, if they try to mix in with anyone we bring aboard we'll be able to kick them out."

"I wish to follow people rather than stay here. I don't believe I could stay awake during this," Anne said, stifling a yawn.

"No, Anne. William's going to do that. You're with me tonight. We'll sleep in shifts." Edward watched the door of the villa intently. "Oh, there's someone leaving! William, get down there quick!"

"Yes, Captain!" he said, as he went out and down the stairs.

Anne plopped herself on the bed. "Edward, this will be such a bore," she said with much pouting. "My talents are being wasted here; I am much better at tracking. What is the purpose of it anyway? There are other places we can pick up crewmembers, other towns on the Grand Cayman, other islands in the Caymans even. Why this town?"

"We landed here first, and we need to repair the *Freedom*. Besides, it's a nice break for the crew, and they need it."

Anne stared at Edward as he gazed on the Bodden house and the gate before it. "There is more to it than that, Edward Thatch, I am sure of it. I just do not know what it is."

"Whatever do you mean? I have given you the reason, what more do you wish to hear?"

"Very well, I merely hope this does not come to blows. I don't think that would be the nice break the crew would want or need. I do not wish anyone to be harmed." Anne placed her hand over Edward's. "I do not wish *you* to be harmed."

"I won't be harmed. No one will. These brothers aren't the fighting type." Edward noticed someone entering the Boddens' so he made note of their appearance.

"Let us hope you're right. They are not so different from us. They are bandits—and we are pirates." Saying the word made her smile for a brief second, but the smile was quickly replaced by a frown. "Does it ever get easier?"

Edward looked at Anne and let the question hang in the air. "No…" He turned back to the villa. "It never gets easier."

...

The days and nights were long for everyone that week. Waiting and watching wasn't natural to a rough gang of seamen, and they were restless. Jack was keeping the cleaning crew happy with songs, ballads, and tall tales. John had bought Pukuh a regular set of clothes for seafaring. Pukuh brooded about it in silence, as was his way, and it was plain to all he hated wearing it.

Edward and Anne were feeling the effects of long hours spent sitting in chairs throughout the day. Having each other's company helped; they were able to talk and laugh and tell stories during the night, and they took turns sleeping during the day.

"So what is it like, being a princess?" Edward asked one evening.

"Humph. It is not so glamorous as one would think. Many gatherings with people of high class, all of them namby-pamby nobility who had not done a decent day's work in their lives. Not my type of people."

"Judging by the company you're mixed with now, that much is evident."

Anne laughed, but it sounded more cynical than happy. "My fondest memories are not of being with my mother, but with the Bettys in the kitchen. Either I was helping them prepare a meal, or talking with them. After a while, they treated me like a normal person instead of someone who would off their heads at the slightest misstep."

"So what is your mother like? You don't talk much about her."

Anne hesitated for a moment. Edward felt she would still prefer to avoid the subject. "She is a strong woman who has lost a lot. I am the one child that has survived to adulthood, and because of that she was too protective of me. She is highly intelligent, and a strong commander; she takes an active role in war and in politics. When her mother once told her the queen does not have much power, she retorted, 'But I will.' She has a defiant attitude towards anyone who opposes her, and does not hesitate to do whatever is necessary, no matter how dire the situation."

"She sounds a lot like—"

"Do not *dare* finish that sentence!" Anne almost screamed as she turned in her chair to face Edward. "I am nothing like her." Anne set her gaze back to the street and continued her watch in silence. Edward thought to apologise, but decided against saying anything. For a few hours an awkward silence pervaded the room, and when normal conversation resumed, her royal status was not brought up again.

The other watchers at the inns were too preoccupied with memorizing faces and tailing the bodies attached to them to think about anything else. Exhausted and irritable, they longed for the week to end so they could rest again. Their brains were so full of faces and descriptions that even their dreams were invaded by floating heads and words.

While those in the inns were watching people, William and the others were gathering information. They acquired a list of the names of known associates of the Boddens. It was extensive, containing over two hundred souls. It included informants, toughs, and those running businesses owned by the Boddens, any or all of whom might be feeding the brothers information or helping with their dirty work.

And all of whom needed to be avoided.

After completing their reconnaissance, the senior members of the crew met back on the *Freedom* to discuss their findings.

"Every one of these businesses is controlled by the Boddens by one means or another," William reported to Edward. "Either they own it outright, own it under the table, or exact a fee for a permit to continue operating. The ones that pay a fee aren't exactly loyal to the Boddens, so the brothers employ several informants who seek to fill their purses by frequenting the bars and businesses in search of new tidbits of information. Those are the ones we want to avoid," he said, glancing around the table to ensure his words were heard. "Then there are the cutthroats who do the Boddens' dirty work. They collect the fees from the businessmen and frequent the bars the rest of the time. Some of them will probably end up mixed with the crowd we bring in. We don't have to worry if one or two see what we're doing; they have not the intelligence to tell the brothers what they've seen, especially if they are burdened with enough spirits."

Edward thanked William. "It will be a lot easier, knowing who we're dealing with."

"You are welcome," said Alexandre, stressing each syllable and smiling at Edward, who ignored him.

"Good work, everyone. Rest up, for tomorrow the town won't have the chance to sleep with our revelry!" The group responded with yawns and low hoots and groans. Edward laughed. *They'll be better tomorrow. You've lost, Bodden Brothers, wait and see!*

Throughout the following day, Sam and the other crewmembers brought in many people from all around town for an afternoon and night of booze, singing, dancing, and games. Edward appointed guards from among the crew and positioned them at the docks to stop anyone from coming aboard, or even near, the ship if one of the regular crew wasn't with them. The crew who had watched the Boddens' home spotted their men and swiftly booted them from the ship as well, keeping prying eyes away.

As night drew closer, the party grew more raucous, and some fought and caused trouble. Edward and Henry kicked out any who became too violent. The senior members aboard the *Freedom* also talked with some of the potential recruits, and by nightfall they had managed to enlist twenty men.

The day had been a success. But the night destroyed it all.

Accompanied by fifty of their strongest men armed to the teeth, the Bodden Brothers themselves broke through the barricade of guards and forced their way onto the *Freedom*. Everyone aboard stopped what they were doing and stared at the intruders. No one moved.

"This gathering is over." "Clear out and go home."

The two of them had issued their orders, and in an instant most of the people from the village obeyed. It didn't matter that they were on a ship with almost four times as many hands. They were, simply, afraid.

It should be me whom they fear more.

"You are beginning to become a nuisance, Edward Thatch," said Malcolm. "We think you should leave," Neil added.

"And what is this all about?" Edward stalked straight over to them. Several of the bodyguards pointed blades and guns in his face, but he paid them no heed. He stared daggers at the brothers and they backed up instinctively, despite the guards.

"You have two days." "Finish your business and be gone, or else."

They rushed down the gangplank and headed back into town, leaving their threats lingering in the air.

...

Edward slammed his fist on the table in frustration. Everyone in the mess hall jumped at the sudden display of anger.

"Damn those Bodden Brothers! We can't bloody well do anything without them interfering!"

"Don't become angry over it," Henry suggested. "There's nothing that can be done."

"Nothing? Nothing!" he replied through gritted teeth. "Are you suggesting we give up?"

"We're not giving up. We tried our best. We can stay and run a fool's errand, or leave and seek help elsewhere. We've survived this long without the necessary crewmembers. We can last a little longer."

Edward paced the mess hall. The senior members as well as several of the other crewmembers were sitting and watching. No one said a word, but their faces said everything: concern, frustration, defeat.

"How many stayed of those we gained?"

"O-only five, Captain," John said.

Edward paced some more and wiped his face. "Five! Five out of twenty. That's not good enough. We need crewmembers."

"And why do we need to recruit them here, Captain?"

"Because, Henry, it *has* to be here."

"But why?" Henry stood to face Edward.

"Because they're taking away our freedom!" Edward yelled.

Everyone within earshot of Edward's voice was listening intently.

"All our lives we've been pushed, we've been beaten, and we've been told what to do, Henry. Even you," he said, pointing at his friend.

"What are you talking about?"

"I'm talking about this world, Henry," he replied with a flourish of his arms. "They all want us to follow their rules and do what they say. They have from the very beginning. Your parents wanted you to keep on being a farmer and take over the business. They hated me and our talk of being fishermen because it wasn't their plan. They didn't care about your freedom, and they would have been ruling your life even after they died. That's not the way I want to live.

"When I finally accepted this ship as my own, and I took that first step towards freedom, it was a feeling I hadn't experienced before. And you know what? Because we're here today, and this is happening to us, I know why I fought that marine captain, Smith, right from the beginning: because he too threatened my freedom.

"I make you a promise today, Henry: I will never let anyone take my freedom away. When I lose my freedom it will be on my own terms, in death or otherwise."

When Edward had finished speaking, a hush fell in the ship. The whole crew was staring at him as if stunned. Anne had a soft smile on her lips. Henry distractedly ran his fingers through his hair. Any doubts surrounding their staying filtered into the ether.

"Very well, Ed. You win. We can't let them do this to us. But what are we to do? The Boddens own this town. How are we to do anything about that?"

"I don't know."

Henry rolled his eyes and heaved an exasperated sigh. Edward sat in thought for a moment. He looked at all those gathered in the mess hall, gazing at him, their leader, the man whom they would follow almost without question, each of them battle-hardened warriors, pirates, and sailors unified together in a terrible force to be reckoned with.

"Henry, you said the Boddens own this town, right?"

"Yea, I did."

"Then to hell with it. We're pirates. Let's steal it from them."

30. FREEDOM VS. THE FAMILY

"Everyone with me? To arms, men! It's time to take this town for ourselves!" Edward pumped his fist in the air, and those gathered in the mess hall cheered. Henry and Anne looked shocked.

"Ed, this is madness. Shouldn't we think this over a bit more?" Anne asked.

"There's nothing more to think about. We have enough people to take over their little mansion by force. I'm surprised no one else has done it already."

Henry shook his head. "I guess nothing we can say will stop you?"

"No."

Henry shrugged his shoulders to Anne. Following Edward, they all went up the stairs to the main deck. It felt like an army, with the clatter of so many boots on wood. *Edward's* army.

Edward went to the fore cabin and reached into his arsenal. He took two cutlasses, two pistols, a third pistol which Alexandre had made for him, and a musket. He also saw a weapon he had never seen before.

"What is this monstrosity?" he asked of no one in particular.

"That... is a blunderbuss," Anne replied as she grabbed a sword and the rifle she loved so much. "It fires lead shot. It is excellent in small quarters."

"That's mine!" Henry claimed as he grabbed the blunderbuss from Edward's hands. "I think you have enough weapons."

Edward tried to reach for it again. "You can never have enough weapons. Give it back. I want it!"

"Enough, children. We are on a mission, remember?" Anne said.

"Very well. You can have the blunderbuss, Henry, but I get it next time."

"Deal," Henry said as he chuckled with his new toy in hand.

Edward went back out as men poured into the fore cabin to grab their armaments. He went to the helm and found Herbert right where he wanted him.

"What's happening, Captain? Why does it look as if everyone is preparing for war?"

"Because we are. We're going to attack the Boddens and take this town for ourselves." Before Herbert could ask any more questions, Edward gave him a set of instructions to carry out after the crew left the ship.

Herbert smiled. "You can count on me, Captain."

"Good to hear it."

Edward turned to the crew on the main deck. Some who had not been with the group in the mess hall were wondering what was happening. He explained the plan, and then chose just over one hundred people to take with him, leaving about sixty on board to guard the ship and to carry out the orders he had entrusted to Herbert.

Nassir and Jack stayed behind to take care of the children and guide the remainder aboard the *Freedom*. William was to guard Anne, and Sam was… well, he was going to be Sam. Pukuh changed back into his warrior's clothing and had his spear and daggers ready. He also brought along a bow and arrows. Alexandre asked to join as well, and brought a pistol, along with his medical supplies, in a small leather bag.

Once everyone was prepared, Edward issued some final instructions and led the group out. They marched up the main street, all one hundred and some of them, armed to the teeth. This time, bystanders looked at them not with suspicion or contempt, but with fear. They sensed what was about to happen. The cigar smokers, the newspaper readers, the card players—all retreated to their homes and shut their doors and windows. Some ran away, and some even ran to the Boddens' home.

By the time the company reached the top of the hill, the town was virtually deserted. When they walked up to the mansion's iron gate, Edward stood in front, Anne and Henry at his sides, and raised his fist in the air to signal his crew to stop.

Guards with muskets and rifles appeared on the balconies of the house's second floor. The Bodden Brothers strolled out the front door and stopped, staying far away from the gate.

"What are you doing, Thatch?" "This doesn't seem like a friendly visit."

"It's not. I'll give you one chance, brothers. Surrender and I promise to be lenient with you."

They both looked at each other and burst out laughing. "You can't touch us." "You'll never make it past the gates." "Boys." They nodded to their guards, who aimed their muskets at Edward and his crew.

"Men." Edward signaled his crew.

They walked off to the sides, leaving the street outside the gate empty except for the figure of Edward. The Boddens were confused at what they were seeing. Edward turned, pumped his fist in the air, and walked off to the side with the others.

After a few seconds, thunder sounded from the shore. The Boddens' eyes grew wide as they realised what was happening, and they ran back inside the house.

Metal crashed against metal as the iron gate was smashed off the stone wall by cannonballs. It flew back, almost hitting the house, and fell to the ground with a grating crash, the cannonballs embedded between its beams.

"Attack!" Edward yelled.

He pulled out his musket and fired at one of the guards on the second floor of the mansion. The bullet hit the guard in the chest and he tumbled over the balcony to the floor below. Edward ran to the stone wall which had held the gate and put his back up against it.

His crew fired at the guards on the balcony before they realised what was happening. Only a few managed to survive the onslaught.

Anne and Henry joined Edward at the stone wall. Guards were pouring out the front door and the side of the building. The crew divided into those who would stay outside and those who were to invade the house.

Edward, Anne, Henry, and William were among the invaders. Pukuh, Sam, and John were in the defense group.

Edward nodded to his group and then went out past the wall as he drew two pistols. The guards hiding behind pillars at the entrance popped out and fired upon Edward. He ducked and rolled out of the way as Henry and Anne fired their guns at the two guards, taking them down.

Edward rose when two guards ran around the corner. He fired his pistols at them. He hit one in the arm, and the other went back behind cover. He ran to the door and drew one of his cutlasses.

"We need to head inside. Anne, Henry, William, you're with me. The rest of you split between the left and right and head in the back way. Ten of you, with us!" They all rushed to follow his instructions. "Blunderbuss, would you do the honours?"

"Gladly!" Henry said with a smile.

Edward went up to the door and kicked it down. Five guards were lying in wait for them. Henry fired the blunderbuss in the middle of them all, then dropped to the ground. Two of the guards fell and three jumped out of the way. William and Anne headed inside and took them out with their pistols.

The rest of Edward's group headed inside to finish off the rest of the Boddens' guards. Outside on the main street, the thugs loyal to the Boddens made their stand. There were twenty of them so far, and more were coming by the minute.

"So, savage, what say we clean these streets?" Sam offered to Pukuh.

"If you can keep up with me, white man, I will award you a gold piece," Pukuh replied, his deep accent contrasting with Sam's cockney.

Sam laughed. "You're on."

Pukuh, barefoot and wearing his own clothing of leather and feathers, ran to the men gathering on the streets, spear in hand. Those who saw their death approaching fired at the Mayan. He jumped and rolled out of the way.

Sam took out a rifle and shot it at the men on his side of the street. He hit one of the rogues in the chest, dropping him. He pulled out twin pistols and ran to catch up with Pukuh. The thugs focused on Sam now, pointing their muskets and shooting at him. He ducked into a side street for cover.

John, still at the end of the main street, loaded his rifle and fired it at the crowds, downing one man with a shot through the head. He reloaded while Sam and Pukuh did the dirty, close-quarters work.

Pukuh stabbed a man through the heart, then jumped into the air and kicked another in the face. A third man pulled a gun on him and fired at close range, but Pukuh pulled another man in front and used him as a shield.

Sam, having expended his ammunition, drew his cutlass and held it in two hands like a club, but it was no club. They came at him like moths to a flame, and he laughed, in a frenzy, as he hacked and chopped.

Inside the house, William had a bullet in his shoulder from protecting Anne, but insisted he could keep going. Henry was down with a bullet in his leg. Several others were injured and in need of medical attention.

"Where are the Boddens? We've searched everywhere," Edward said between deep breaths.

"I saw someone go into a secret door over there," Henry announced, pointing to the wall beneath the stairs leading to the second floor.

"Sit still and put this in your mouth," Alexandre ordered Henry as he gave him a piece of wood to bite down on. He began removing a bullet lodged in his leg.

Edward went to the place Henry had pointed out. It was a small oval alcove with a three-pronged candelabrum on a shelf with some books. He examined the alcove, but couldn't find anything like a door.

"I have seen something like this before. There are doors like this in Buckingham Palace," Anne said as she walked past Edward.

She put her thumb to her teeth as she considered what to do. She grabbed hold of the candelabrum and tried to pull on the sides, but nothing happened. Then she pulled back the spines of the books one by one. On the third one there was a sound like a lock opening, and then a hidden door in the alcove opened from the right to the left. Inside was a staircase leading down.

"Excellent work, Anne! Everyone loaded and ready?" Those who were fit to join him nodded. "We're finishing this."

Edward had a musket in his hands, ready to fire, as he went down the stairs. It was a long, winding corridor with candles lit in small alcoves along the sides. It went down a fair distance and it took the group a few minutes to reach the bottom, but they didn't meet any resistance along the way.

At the bottom, another corridor branched off to the right. Edward had everyone stop as he inched around the corner. Immediately he was met with rifle fire. He jumped back and the bullets missed him, hitting the wall.

"All your guards above are either dead or too injured to fight, brothers," Edward yelled. "Come out peacefully and we can end this." No answer. He whispered to one of his crew, "You have a grenade on you?" The crewman replied by pulling out four, and Edward took two for himself. "Good. On my mark, we throw them, then rush in." The crewman acknowledged his understanding as they lit the long fuses of the grenades. When the fuses had burned to within an inch of the end, Edward nodded and they both threw them down the hallway and into the other room.

"Grenade!" one of the Boddens' men yelled. Rapid stamping of feet and thuds were heard, followed by four distinct explosions.

"Now!" Edward yelled. He went around the corner and down the short hallway.

Smoke filled the small room. Edward shot a nearby thug in the neck. He fell to the ground, convulsing and clutching his bleeding throat. To his left, the guards were coughing from the smoke and trying to gather their wits about them. The rest of Edward's men, including Anne, killed the remainder of the guards amidst the confusion.

When the dust cleared, Edward was able to see the whole room. It was square and not much higher than their heads. There were boxes and bags filled with sand which the Boddens' thugs had used for cover, but they were now broken and torn from the grenades. At the end of the room there was a large iron door with no visible mechanism for opening it.

Near the door was a large copper cone with a copper tube leading up to the ceiling and through the stone wall surrounding the iron door. *I wonder what this does.* Edward tapped on the cone with his knuckles, causing a tone to travel through the tube.

He heard a voice through the strange device. "Who is this?" "Is that you, George?" "Are they dead?"

Edward recognised the voices of the Boddens through the device. He replied, "No, this is Edward Thatch. You've lost, now surrender so we can end this."

It took a few minutes before one of the brothers talked again. "All right, we surrender. We're opening the door now."

Edward smiled at his comrades. The iron door swung open a crack, but then stopped. He walked over and opened it up more.

The door had barely opened halfway when Edward found himself staring down the barrel of a cannon.

On instinct he pulled back, and the cannon fired, the sound of thunder deafening everybody. The cannonball hit the door and ricocheted into the room, but it embedded itself in the far wall without injuring anyone.

When the ringing in his ears had receded somewhat, Edward pulled out his cutlasses. The cannonball had opened the door wide, and one of his crew had thrown a grenade inside. The thing exploded and filled the inner room with dust.

Edward ran in, and was met with two small cannons, manned by the brothers. Edward saw one of the brother's hands lowering a linstock towards the cannon.

Edward's body reacted, knowing what to do long before he could form the words in his mind. He turned his body to the side and fell backwards. The sound of the cannon erupted and an iron ball shot out towards him. He could feel the force of the ball on his stomach as it passed inches away from him, tearing at his insides like a dozen punches.

The Voyages of Queen Anne's Revenge

The other brother lowered the linstock into the cannon. Edward was still falling as the second cannonball passed over his chest this time. The speeding ball, like a giant bullet, transferred its power through the air and hit Edward in the chest. The cannonball passed over him and hit the iron door, ricocheting off and into the square room.

Edward landed on the ground on his back, and then got up with unsteady feet. He noticed his hand was trembling and his stomach and chest ached with pain and pressure. He shook his head and turned his attention to the brothers, who sat motionless beside their smoking cannons, paralysed with astonishment. He strolled over to the brothers and put one blade to each throat. "This battle is over!"

31. THE CROSSED SWORDS FLAG

The first thing Edward did was take the Boddens upstairs to stop the fighting outside. After the Boddens sent their men away, Edward's crew stayed and guarded the home.

Edward, with his newly taken authority, told the Boddens how they were to run the town from now on. He would allow the brothers to keep managing their business, but he was to have a cut of the profits.

They would first lower the rates at which they taxed the citizens. The town was to become a safe haven for pirates, but protecting the local businesses was to be the brothers' job and that's what would allow them to tax. Edward didn't want the brothers administering false protection and using extortion like they had before. They would also have a full militia paid and trained so that something like what Edward just did wouldn't happen again.

They were also to keep records of everything taxed and traded, and confer twenty-five percent of their earnings to Edward.

"If I examine the numbers and find something doesn't add up, you'll find yourself sleeping with Davy Jones, understood?"

"Yes, sir," the brothers said in unison.

With that business finished, Edward released the brothers so they could start repairing their home and carry out their orders. He and the rest of the crew, aside from a few left to guard the mansion, headed back to the *Freedom* for further instructions.

Edward and Anne helped Henry limp back to the Freedom. They had found something to bandage the gunshot wound in his leg with, but it wouldn't fully heal for some time.

"Are you sure you can trust them to keep their word?" Henry asked.

Anne gave a short derisive laugh. "Did you see their eyes? They are too afraid of us now."

"I don't think they'll betray me," Edward replied. "I'll send letters every once in a while to remind them who their boss is."

Over the next week, the crew of the *Freedom* helped fix the gate on the Boddens' property and tended to the wounded. The crew kept order in the town until the guards still alive were healed.

Edward also gathered new people for the crew over the week, which wasn't hard given their impressive display. Men flocked to the *Freedom* by the dozen after they took over the town.

Edward introduced the new recruits to the ship's officers, laid out for them the rules for living and working aboard the ship, and had them speak to John, who compiled a list of their skills and prior experience so they could each be assigned suitable work. He then explained the pirate commandments to them and had them sworn in, as the others had been.

Edward wanted to speak with Henry about their next course of action, namely sailing to Navassa Island and continuing with the journey to unlock the next section of the ship. But before they could even begin to talk a voice interrupted them.

"You folks are mighty strong. It be a fool's game challenging the Boddens like ye did, but ye won."

Edward turned to see an older gentleman standing there, leaning on the port-side railing. "Oh? Then why did you join us fools, old man?"

"Because after I saw your power, I knew you could help me out. And by that I mean we can help each other."

Edward walked over and leaned on the railing. The man had salt-and-pepper hair and beard, and eyes like an old trickster. His cheeks and stomach were full, like they had once been taut and muscular, but were now sagging, perhaps from nothing more than laziness.

"And what, pray tell, does a man like you need help with?"

The old man flitted his eyes this way and that suspiciously. "Perhaps we should discuss this in private."

They took the old man to the fore cabin and emptied it of everyone else. The three of them sat down at a table placed there for meetings, and the man, who went by the name Bill Hastings, related his tale.

"So you and your friend had a dispute over how to spend some gold, and now you want our help to retrieve it before he does?"

"That is correct."

"And how much gold is it?"

"One thousand Spanish doubloons of the finest quality."

Edward looked at Henry for a moment, and then both of them howled with laughter. Bill was shocked and became flustered. When the laughing didn't seem close to stopping, he finally became angry.

"What do you find so amusing in this? We're talking about gold here! You take me for a fool?"

Soon the laughing stopped and Edward wiped a tear from his eye. "No, it is quite the opposite, sir. It would be you who would take us for fools if we were to believe your story. What is it? We sail to the place where the treasure is and your group attacks us and steals our ship? Or maybe there is—"

A gold piece, round but irregular, fell into Edward's lap before he could finish his sentence. It had inscriptions and pictures on it showing that it had been minted, if poorly. He examined it to make sure it was real.

"Where did you find this?" Edward asked as he passed the coin to Henry, who inspected it as well.

"I told you, it's part of the one thousand me and my companion had. We lived similar lives to yours, and that was our last payday. The details don't matter, the only thing that matters is I can show you where it is, and I'll let you have ten percent."

Edward yawned in apparent disinterest. He strolled over to Bill. "Hmm… Even if I did believe your tale, I wouldn't settle for such a meagre share. Without us you have nothing." He walked past him and headed for the stairs.

"Fifteen," Bill said without turning around.

"Thirty," Edward replied.

Bill spun around. "That's extortion! There's no way you're getting thirty for my life's work!"

Edward shrugged. "We're pirates. And remember, we are protecting you and stealing from your friend too."

Bill gritted his teeth and clenched his fists. "Twenty! Without me you've nothing either."

Edward paused for a moment, walked back over to Bill and put out his hand. "Twenty it is then." Bill stood up and they shook on it together, sealing the bond. "Now, where do we need to go?"

Bill smiled. "First we need to head to my home and retrieve the first part of the map. It's in George Town a few hours west of here." Bill started to leave, but Edward stopped him.

"First part of the map?" Edward asked.

"Yes. I have one part, and my friend has the other. We'll secure mine, and then we'll grab my friend's. And—oh yes: I don't want my friend to think ill of me, so would you kindly pretend you have me hostage?"

"Pretend to take you hostage! Sir, you are trying my patience. Maybe I really will take you hostage."

"Oh, pish posh and a bottle of hops," Bill said with a wave of his hand. "This is easy, you boys'll do fine." And without another word, Bill turned and left.

Edward sighed and rubbed his eyes in frustration, to which Henry shrugged. "You brought this on yourself. You never had to accept the deal." Henry and Edward went back to the main deck.

"Yes, well a lot of good your advice will do me now. You were silent the whole time."

"Well, silence must be golden, because I'm the one with the doubloon." Henry held up the coin between his fingers.

"Give me that." Edward held out his palm.

"What, this?" Henry taunted with a grin.

"It's mine."

"This little coin? No, you must mean this peso." Henry threw him a copper piece.

Edward's gaze went from the copper, then back at Henry, his eyes full of contempt. Henry twirled the gold coin, smiled again, and ran off before he could try to grab it. He let him go, and went instead to Herbert.

"Herbert, we have a new heading. George Town, on the west side of the Grand Cayman. You know of it?"

"Aye, Captain, I know of it."

"Keep her steady then."

Henry walked up the stairs to the stern, still holding the gold piece, talking to no one in particular. "Well I guess I'll deliver this to John to deposit, since our friend hasn't claimed it."

"Keep it." Bill joined them at the stern deck. "Consider it a token of good faith." Henry nodded to Bill and headed to the main deck to seek out John.

"Very well then," Edward said. "I merely hope that faith isn't misplaced."

"Oh, it isn't, Captain. Worry not. We'll all be better off. You'll see."

It took them less than half a day to reach their destination. They disembarked at George Town and Bill led Edward, Henry, and William, all of them armed at Bill's behest, along a path leading through open fields to his house beyond the edge of town. The three asked Bill why he was at Bodden Town to seek help with his venture, and he replied: "I came because I heard the rum was good, and that pirates frequented the place. But mostly because of the rum."

Edward and Henry were growing less impressed with the man the more they learned about him.

When William was told the story of how they came to be on this journey, his response was on par with his usual: indifference. This time, however, there was a hint of disbelief. Edward told Henry later that he thought they were called idiots despite no words being uttered.

"Yes, well, if William was saying that, he does have a point. Everywhere we go things end badly for us. We search for the keys and we all risk our lives. We search for crewmembers and we fight bandits at their game and ours. I wouldn't be surprised if other pirates show up, we fight, and then don't gain anything in recompense."

"You exaggerate. It won't end like that. If anything, our fortunes are due for reversal and this will be the greatest payday we've ever had."

"We will see," Henry said, clear doubt in his tone.

"Here it is," Bill announced as they approached the small, two-story, wooden house where he lived alone. They could tell immediately that the door had been broken in.

"Everyone quiet," Edward whispered as he drew his Alexandre-made pistol.

The others drew their weapons as they approached the door, Edward and Bill on the left, Henry and William on the right. On the silent count of three, William kicked open the door, and they all rushed in, guns pointed and ready to shoot at... nothing.

There were plenty signs of a break-in. Tables and chairs were flipped and strewn about, objects were broken, books were torn and thrown to the floor, every cupboard and storage space was emptied.

"Are any valuables missing?" William asked.

"Not that I can see. There's money left on the nightstand." Bill pointed to his bed in the corner and a wooden stand beside it. "A trifling amount, truly, but still there. Why?"

"Because they were here for something specific," William said.

Something specific? "The map!" No sooner did the words leave Edward's mouth than Bill rushed up the stairs to the second floor.

In a spot near the middle of the room, a few loose floorboards concealed a small sunken compartment. Bill had kept it covered by a carpet, which was now rolled back, the floorboards pried up, and the compartment was empty.

"It's gone." Bill's voice was dead and his face drained of colour.

"Dammit!" Edward kicked a nearby chair, breaking it. "Now what?"

Bill trudged down the stairs and sat on the bottom step. "What can we do? My friend Theodore must have been here. Maybe he even had people helping him." He shook his head in frustration. "But it doesn't matter. We have no way to reach the treasure now."

"You two have an excellent friendship, I must say," said Edward, "both plotting to steal the other's share at the same time!"

"We're a regular pair," he said, his eyes fixed on the floorboards.

"Can't you remember anything from the map? Even the starting point would give us something."

"What use will that be? We won't know where to head once we arrive."

"If Theodore is there then we can follow his tracks, or the tracks of whoever was with him."

The glint returned to Bill's eyes and he jumped up. "You're right! If we leave now we can still catch them!" He ran out the door, and the others raced to catch up with him, their vigour renewed and their minds filled with the hope of treasure.

They were, for the moment, incapable of imagining the danger awaiting them.

...

The island they sought was northeast of the Grand Cayman by a half day's travel. Bill remembered the riddle he had written on his half of the map: "Nor'east of seven mile the treasured island lies." He seemed very proud to have thought of it himself.

"That's too easy," Herbert said when he overheard it. "You live in George Town, and Seven Mile Beach is directly north of it—that riddle isn't likely to fool anybody."

Bill was offended. "Well... not everyone can read a map like you can."

Herbert rolled his eyes before setting the course.

After a half day's travel, the crewman on the crow's nest yelled "Land ho!" and everyone's gazes turned eagerly toward the bow.

Edward, along with many of the crew, moved to the prow to view the island through a spyglass. Anne joined him and leaned over the side of the ship, her red hair swaying in the wind as she tried to catch a glimpse of the island.

"What do you see, Ed?"

"Not much. The whole island is covered in a thick forest, and from this distance it's hard to judge its size. Other than that... Wait, I think I can see a ship."

"Where? Let me see!" Edward handed the spyglass to Anne. A ship was indeed anchored at the island, but it was too far to make out its size or its flag. "I wonder who they are." She handed the spyglass back to Edward, smiling from ear to ear.

"You seem happy."

"Oh! I suppose I'm simply excited." Anne walked back to the main deck.

"All right, everyone! Back to work. This ship won't sail itself. Prepare for battle! We don't know if that ship is friend or foe." Edward followed Anne. "Why are you excited? It may be dangerous."

"I suppose it is as you said back in the mess a few days ago. I feel free now more than ever. I do not have to hide, I have nothing to fear, and I can live my life the way I want. And it is all thanks to you, Edward." Anne leaned up to Edward and kissed him on the cheek, causing everyone around them to stop and stare and whisper things like: "The princess and the captain?" "Anne kissed 'im!" "Lucky bloke!"

Edward grew red in the face and yelled to them all to get back to work. But the warmth of the kiss, and the feelings it evoked, lingered. He couldn't focus on the task at hand until a shout brought him out of his thoughts.

"Cap'n! You should see this!" one crewmember yelled.

"What is it? Is the other ship shoving off?"

"No! Look at the flag, Cap'n!"

Edward took the spyglass out again and stared at the ship. He could see its flag flapping in the wind; he had already guessed it would be a pirate flag, and his suspicions were now confirmed. It had a large skull, but instead of crossed bones below the skull it was crossed cutlasses.

Henry stood beside Edward amidst the commotion, and he had a smug smile on his face. "Don't you even start!" Edward said.

"I'm one for three," Henry said.

Edward scratched his beard. Had Henry's prediction been right? Would they have to fight these blackguards and gain nothing out of it?

"This means nothing," Edward said firmly, then turned to the crewman who had called him over. "So, what of it?"

"Cap'n, that's the flag of John Rackham, Calico Jack, the ruler of the Caribbean Sea."

Edward's jaw dropped at the mention of that name. His focus shifted to the helm, to Herbert, who had joined Edward's crew to avenge himself upon this very man.

Are you to take your revenge today, Herbert? Is it within your power to accomplish?

More worryingly, is it within mine?

Edward did not know the answer, but he had a feeling he would soon learn it.

32. THE HUNTER AND THE HUNTED

"Captain, I want to go ashore! No, I *must* go ashore!" Herbert demanded.

"You realise it will be dangerous," Edward warned.

"I don't care. I've been waiting years for this. If I can't face him now, then I can't face him ever."

"You could die."

"I'm willing to take that risk. And I'll do this whether you let me or not!"

That's a good answer, Herbert. How can I refuse such conviction? "Very well, but you stay in the middle of the group—and if there is a fight, no one is going to be able to protect you. Understand?"

"I won't need to be protected," Herbert replied with a sinister look in his eyes.

Edward turned to the deck and addressed the crew. "All hands prepare to engage the enemy! We'll show them what it means to be real pirates!" The crew roared in approval.

Anne motioned for Edward to come over, and then led him to the forecastle at the furthest point on the ship away from Herbert. "I do not want you doing this, Edward."

"What? Why not?"

"Some have already mentioned it, I am sure, but this man is Calico Jack. He is dangerous. It is better to stay away from him."

Her words were curt and perfunctory, as if she was reading the newspaper, but her mannerisms told a different story. She had her arms wrapped around herself almost like she was protecting herself from a cold breeze. Edward saw in her eyes something he had never seen before, something he never thought he would see: fear. The sight almost made him rethink his decision.

But he couldn't.

"My apologies, Anne, but I've made a promise to Herbert. I can't back down now. Besides, we'll watch each other's backs, right? We have nothing to fear in that case."

Anne gave him a smile, but he could tell it was forced.

I'll have to show her there's nothing to fear. Calico Jack is a man, and all men bleed.

Edward guided the crew to land the ship on the beach, and half of them went to shore to fight the enemy. As he ran with them to confront the group of pirates on the sandy ground, Calico Jack's men didn't pay he or his crew any heed despite the noise. It took Edward a moment to realise why.

They were drunk, the lot of them.

The only men of Calico's crew sober were those on the ship itself. They were desperate in trying to rouse their comrades to awareness, but it was no use. The enemy fired one shot with the cannon, which missed by a heavy margin.

They surrendered themselves to Edward and his crew immediately after.

Edward and the crew on the beach gathered the enemy crew together and bound their hands with rope. "And this, gentlemen, is why we don't drink while on duty." Those in the landing party laughed as Edward turned to the group of captives. "Who's in charge here?" After a few seconds of silence, one of them raised his bound hands. Edward stared in surprise at the intoxicated man sitting on the ground, went over to him, and knelt down. "Where are your senior officers?"

The man smelled of the strong stuff, and his eyes were unfocussed. He seemed unsteady even sitting down, and before he spoke he hiccupped. "Nah, all de senior occifers went inta the bush. We was supposed ta be protectin' tha ship, but..." He raised his hands, motioning to the scene before him, and then burst into a fit of laughter.

"Which way did they go?" Edward asked. But it was no use, the man was too far gone. Edward grabbed his cheeks in a vice grip and shook him a little. "Which way did they go?"

"Itsh a secwet," he slurred, and started laughing again.

Edward released his grip on the man and he almost fell over. *I need to talk with someone who isn't tanked.*

The sound of shifting sand and the creaking of wood came up behind Edward as Herbert wheeled himself up beside the captain and the drunken man. "Maybe this will loosen everyone else's tongues," he said as he shoved a pistol into the man's temple and fired. Blood sprayed everywhere, and the man fell dead onto the sand.

"Herbert, what the hell are you doing!" Edward grabbed the pistol out of Herbert's hand, but it was already spent.

Immediately one of the other captives stood up. "I'll tell you where they went! Please don't kill me!"

"I'm getting results," Herbert growled, wheeling himself over to the man who had spoken.

"They went into the jungle. If you head straight in for about five minutes, you'll see a path. We arrived an hour ago, so you should be able to catch up if you hurry."

Edward shook his head. *No point in arguing over dead enemies.* "Well, this is it!" said Edward. "You ready to kill this Calico Jack?"

"It's not him," Herbert replied as they moved away from the men tied up.

Edward stopped. "What do you mean, not him?"

"It's Gold Division Commander Gregory Dunn's ship."

"Gold Division? What's that? Who's Gregory Dunn?"

"There's gold trim on the ship's flag. It denotes the Gold Division of Rackham's pirate crew, for which Gregory Dunn is the commander. I noticed it as soon as we landed. It's all right. Golden Arm Dunn will do for today." Herbert wheeled up to the edge of the jungle and peered in.

"Why do they call him Golden Arm?"

"I'm not exactly sure, but I believe it's because he's in charge of acquisitions and manages the monetary side of John's operation. They say he's a coward, and leads a bunch of them too, but they're good fighters in a pinch. I wouldn't take them lightly, Captain. This is one of Calico Jack's men, after all."

"Worry not; I won't do anything rash, like you." Edward folded his arms and glared at Herbert, but knew he wouldn't back down—not this time, not over this. "I'll gather some others to join us. You wait here."

Edward went back to the members of his crew guarding the enemy pirates and told them to search them for any weapons, or anything that could be used as one. He then went back to the ship and gathered together the senior officers and some of the better fighters to take along with him and Herbert. Half of the crew would stay behind to watch the ship and the hostages.

Pukuh, William, John, Anne, and Henry took the chosen fighters down to the entrance of the forest and waited. Edward gave some final instructions to Jack, who would be left in charge while they were away.

"Keep an eye on Dunn's men. We don't want them trying anything while we're gone," he said to Jack. "Make sure no one drinks. I don't want what happened to the other crew to happen to us." He laughed along with Jack, and then whispered: "And keep an eye on Christina. Without Herbert here to protect her, I fear for her safety. Maybe bring Nassir up here with her, all right?"

"You can count on me, Captain. I've been taking the combat lessons along with everyone else, so I'll use force if I have to."

Edward thought he could hear Jack say "I won't fail this time," under his breath, but he couldn't be sure so he ignored it. "Good man. I'm counting on you."

"It's good to hear Herbert has a chance to avenge those who wronged him." Jack gazed at Herbert on the beach. He was pushing himself up the sand to the entrance of the forest.

Edward could see in Jack's eyes a determined focus which he'd never seen before. He felt there was more to it than him simply being happy for another crewmate's revenge. There seemed to be hope buried deep down in those eyes.

"It's not going to be so easy. We got lucky. This is the first step, really; the hard part comes next." Edward patted Jack on the shoulder. He felt like saying more, prying a bit more, but he couldn't. He had a job to do. "Take care, Jack."

"Take care, Captain."

Edward went back down to the beach, and the group he had told to wait had gathered at the edge of the jungle. Pukuh, William, John, Anne, and Henry were all there, along with about fifty other crewmembers, all decked out with weapons.

Pukuh was wearing his traditional warrior's garb: eagle-skull headdress, feathers down to the wrist, bones across his chest. Edward smiled. "I recall you saying there were two types of warrior classes you could be a part of, yes? Jaguar and Eagle? Why did you choose the Eagle?"

"Because my father was a nobleman and he was also an Eagle warrior," Pukuh explained. "And because the eagle is freer than the jaguar. It can soar the skies to its heart's content, as you sail the sea."

Edward felt a twinge of embarrassment. His paean to freedom had been making the rounds since that day in the mess. "I understand the appeal in that," he said. Then he turned to the rest of the group. "Everyone ready? Keep a sharp eye as we move through the brush. The rest of that crew is out there somewhere."

Edward took the front, accompanied by Anne, Henry, and Bill. John and William were close behind, followed by the rest of the company, with Herbert and Pukuh guarding the rear. A few minutes into the jungle they found a well-trodden path wide enough for three or four to walk abreast.

"Bill, it seems like these pirates were the ones who ransacked your home and took the other section of the map. That means either you and your friend think very much alike, or that he's in danger."

"I know." Bill looked solemn. It was a blow to him.

As they walked, they could hear the sounds of the jungle on all sides. The hooting of birds, the chattering of monkeys, and the rustling of the trees in the wind blended with the breaking of twigs and branches from the footsteps of the crew.

Since his time spent in the Mayan woods, Edward had been trying to enhance his hearing, but had a difficult time. It was not so easy here as it had been then. Eventually, he gave up trying.

They're at least an hour ahead of us. I shouldn't have to worry right now.

"Look, Ed!" Anne said, pointing to a patch of mud.

Edward made a motion to stop everyone and then he knelt to examine the mark. It was a boot print. "Tracks." He looked ahead and saw they followed the path for as far as he could see.

"Now we know they were headed this way. If we keep following, then we won't need a map. Can you tell how many there are?"

Anne searched for other prints, as well as trampled vegetation and broken twigs and branches along the trail. "I can't tell exactly, of course, but it appears to be at least as many as we have here, if not more. They were travelling at a leisurely pace. We can catch up if we pick up our pace."

"Hmm, more than us won't be a problem if they're cowards, as Herbert claims."

"It will be a problem if they ambush us," Henry warned.

"Very well. Let's split the group. John, William, each of you take fifteen men and go out one hundred paces from us on either side. Keep pace with us as best you can. We'll stay on the path, and if we get a scare we'll send a signal to attack."

"What will that be?" William asked.

"I don't know... How about the sound of an eagle?"

"I've never heard the sound of an eagle," one man said. A few others confirmed that they hadn't, either.

"Truly? You have never heard an eagle? Well, it matters not. If you hear a screeching sound over and over, come running to help us."

"I think we should at least hear the sound of an eagle before we plan on using it." They all nodded in agreement.

Edward sighed. "Pukuh?"

Pukuh put his hands together and made a series of high-pitched noises in quick succession.

"But that sounds like everything else in the forest!" "I'll not be able to hear that!" "Pick something else!"

"Enough! How about I just yell 'help'? Will you be able to hear that?"

"That's much better." "I like that." "I feel safer now."

"Is everyone satisfied?" They all nodded. "Good. Now back to the task at hand. If they want to ambush, they'll do it from the jungle, so we can outflank them. When you hear us yell for help, come back to the path and attack the enemy pirates. Now get going."

"Edward, have you had any formal education?" Anne asked as they started walking again.

"What kind of formal education?"

"Military."

"Oh, no. But my father did serve in the Nine Years' War. He taught me how to play chess and different things like that. It must be from that."

"Your father must have been a very smart man. I am sorry that he has passed."

"What are you talking about? My father is alive!" Edward snarled, glaring at her. Those hate-filled eyes had never before been directed at her, and she began sweating. "I... I am sorry, Edward. I thought... Henry said..."

"Calm down, Edward," Henry interjected. "I'm the one who told her he disappeared. It was a natural assumption after all these years."

Edward stared down both of them, and then walked away in a huff.

"Sorry about that, Anne," said Henry. "I should have told you. His father was all he had when he was younger. Edward won't accept his death. He's not mad at you, but just give him some time."

Anne's thoughts were elsewhere. "All right," she mumbled, as everyone continued walking except her. She stood there, the vision of those eyes piercing her to the core. So many emotions rushed over her in that moment. *But why do I feel it so much? Is it because it was directed at me? Am I simply more sensitive to it?*

Pukuh touched her arm. "We must keep moving."

She came out of her daze. "Yes." She started walking again.

"You are close to him?"

Anne regarded Pukuh for a moment. "Yes, I suppose I am."

"Then it is clear you would be affected by his stare. It was one of emotion rather than intimidation. The large one, Henry, was not affected because he's seen it and felt it before."

Anne nodded at the logic. "You are right. How do you know of this power he has?"

"In your tongue we call it the Eagle Eye, the eye of the hunter. Something only a rare few possess, it is in many legends we tell. My father has seen it in one man, besides Edward."

"Who was that?"

"Benjamin Hornigold, the previous owner of the ship *Freedom.*"

Anne was even more shocked than before, if possible. She stopped once again, and Pukuh with her. "*Freedom* was Benjamin Hornigold's ship?"

"Yes. My father travelled with Benjamin for a short time when I was a child. Do you know this man?"

Anne was rendered speechless. *Everyone who knows anything about pirates from ten years ago knows that name! I thought the name* Freedom *was just a coincidence... What star was Edward born under that he would be the next to inherit the Golden Horn's ship?*

"Miss Princess?"

"No... No. I am not familiar with him."

Pukuh eyed Anne curiously, but didn't press the issue.

They ran to catch up with the group and kept walking together. Anne stayed at the back with Pukuh the rest of the way. They kept a good pace, following the obvious tracks left by the enemy pirates. They kept walking for a half hour until the tracks abruptly ended.

Edward knelt down. "They must have travelled into the woods after this point."

Henry glanced about. "Everything's gone quiet. What happened to all the animals?"

Before anyone realised what the lack of sound might mean, the enemy crew jumped out from behind bushes and trees. The surprise caught everyone off guard, not the least of them Edward. He took a sucker punch square in the jaw, thrown by the captain of the other crew, and went flying. His brain was so rattled by the force of the blow that he couldn't think straight.

What hit me? It felt more like a sack of rocks than a fist.

He got to his knees, then picked himself up off the ground and saw the Gold Division Commander of Calico Jack's pirate crew, Gregory Dunn, stalking toward him. It was then that he knew the real reason for the man's nickname, The Golden Arm.

Dunn's right hand, from the balled fist to below the elbow, was covered in solid gold. The upper arm appeared more muscular than its left counterpart, no doubt because of the added weight and extra use. The elbow looked raw and damaged from the perpetual shifting of the hard metal on the skin.

How is that even possible?

Dunn had a smile on his face. Edward gritted his teeth and brought himself to his full towering height. He called for help, and soon the sound of reinforcements could be heard in the distance.

Edward drew his twin swords. *Let's see how you are on even ground!* Edward focused on the enemy in front of him. No one else mattered to him. His head, though ringing with pain, was clear.

Dunn pulled out his own sword and put up his right arm as a guard. Edward attacked, but Dunn blocked one stroke after another, either with his golden right arm or the cutlass in his left hand. Every few times Edward attacked, Dunn countered, but he was able to parry the sword and Dunn's fist out of the way. At first Dunn was far from hitting him, but then the sword strokes became subtly more accurate. Then the golden punches nicked his side. Both the enemy's sword and arm kept inching closer to Edward.

He's reading me! I have to become unpredictable.

Edward began to call upon his training in hand-to-hand combat and varied his stance, stepping in and then pivoting on the balls of his feet. He combined his twin blades into one for a slice, and then separated them to jab at Dunn in different areas at once.

He seemed to be gaining the advantage when a pounding weight slammed into his gut. It was the golden arm. It seemed to appear out of thin air, and it hit him harder than anything he had ever experienced. He fought the urge to double over, but was overcome with the pain. He coughed as air and spit forced its way out and he began collapsing forward. As he fell, Dunn punched his jaw again, and Edward went reeling onto the jungle floor.

Dunn went behind Edward and forced him to stand by pulling the blade of the cutlass across his throat. Then he yelled to the crowd still fighting: "If you don't want your captain to die, cease fighting." The words soon broke through the tumult and everyone stopped what they were doing. "Good. Now drop your weapons. Boys, surround them."

Dammit! If I weren't so weak, this wouldn't have happened. Edward was quick to blame himself, but as he looked at his crew it appeared they, too, were on the verge of defeat. Despite his strategy of outflanking them, Dunn's crew, with their numbers and training, were winning against Edward's mostly inexperienced troupe.

Anne watched on in horror. Her eyes met Edward's, and all he could do was stare back at them.

I'm sorry, Anne. You were right. But I'll find a way out of this.

"Kill them!" ordered Dunn.

"No, wait! Stop!" Edward yelled with outstretched hand. "We have the rest of your crew at the beach! If we don't return, they die!"

Dunn paused. "Very well. Boys, stay your weapons. Where do you suggest we go from here, Captain? We seem to be on even footing—at least as far as captives are concerned." He laughed at the implied insult to Edward's fighting abilities.

I can't believe I'm so weak, and he's that strong. It was as if he were toying with me.

Edward thought quickly. "Let's work together. We'll find the treasure and split it in half. There will be more than enough for us both."

Dunn mulled it over for a moment before ducking behind Edward. The sound of a rifle shattered the quiet of the jungle. A bullet sped past Edward, so close he felt air tremble as it passed his ear.

"Who fired that?" Dunn yelled. "Who's fool enough to risk his captain's life?"

Edward knew who it was even before he was found. The enemy crew closed in on Herbert at the rear of the crowd, took the pistol out of his hands, and pushed his wheelchair toward Dunn.

"And who are you, that you would try to kill me in that state?" He cackled. "You're a fool to think you can hit anyone with a pistol at that range. You can't even walk. How did you expect to run away?"

"I would never run—unlike you, you little coward! I'll kill you!" Herbert grabbed a knife out of one of the pirates' belts and tried to throw it at Dunn, but Dunn's mates stopped him. They took him out of the wheelchair and tossed it aside, breaking it. They threw him on the ground and pinned down his arms, one of them stepping on his neck.

"Feisty one, do you know who I am? I'm one of Calico Jack's generals! You don't even know who you're dealing with, do you?"

"I know who I'm dealing with!" Herbert mustered all the strength of voice he could with the boot on his throat. "You don't remember me, but I remember you. You were a coward back then too. Always running around, wiping the boots of your master. You've moved up in the ranks, but trash is still trash."

Dunn cocked his brow as he re-examined Herbert. After a moment his eyes opened wide. "Oh, ho! I remember you now!" Dunn guffawed. It was high-pitched and grating in Edward's ears. "You're the little boy who became a cripple after the accident with the powder. That was so many years ago now. Captain had high hopes for you. Too bad he doesn't accept cripples in his crew and tossed you aside. If I'm trash, then what does that make you?" Dunn cackled again as Herbert struggled to free himself. "Now... no one makes fun of me and lives to tell the tale. Men, exact punishment! I'm a touch occupied over here. Make it slow and painful." His crew nodded and kicked Herbert while he was on the ground.

"Stop. Stop, I say!" cried Edward. "You can have the gold, all of it! Leave my crew alive and I'll even help you bring it back to your ship."

Dunn let the beating continue for a little bit longer, and then told the crewmen to stop. "We have a deal." He let Edward go and stepped away.

"Edward, what are you doing?" Bill whispered forcefully.

"Would you rather have your treasure, Bill, or your life?"

"My treasure!"

Edward sighed. Dunn told the three who had beaten Herbert to join him. Herbert was bloody and already bruising. Edward went up and knelt next to him. He took out a handkerchief, wiped the blood from his face, and turned his head to the ground to allow his lungs to clear.

"How... could you... Captain?" Herbert said through ragged breaths and coughs full of blood. "You promised you would help me with my revenge."

Edward couldn't look into Herbert's eyes, those sad eyes filled with bloodied tears. "I know, Herbert. I'm sorry. I have more to think about than your revenge right now. The lives of the crew, including yours, are on the line. I'm sorry." Edward rose and walked away.

"You promised me! You traitor! You betrayed me like Rackham!" The tears streamed down his face as he yelled, his voice strained with pain.

Dunn spat on the ground. "Shut him up."

Edward lunged with lightning speed and grabbed the Golden Arm's shoulder in a vice grip. Edward's anger flared and he felt as if it could crush the smaller man's bones in an instant. Dunn's crew pulled their guns and swords on him, but he didn't care. His eyes saw only the enemy before him. Dunn waved his men off. "Never mind, leave him alone."

Edward released his grip, and then he, Dunn, and three of Dunn's crew set off down the path toward the treasure. Edward could hear the cries of Herbert as he walked deeper into the jungle. His heart sank deeper and deeper as the sound faded away.

33. THE PREDATOR AND THE PREY

Dunn took the lead, followed by one of his crew, then came Edward, and then the other two men in the rear with guns trained on their captive. Dunn held the top and bottom halves of the map together, puzzling over the strange instructions. He settled on a direction and the group set out.

This jungle was a stark difference from the one Edward had been in on the Yucatan. Instead of the tall pines, there were palms of all sizes. Thin trunks stuck out of the green grass at odd angles and led to long and wide leaves of the fullest green, with coconuts just beneath them. The ones on the tree were mostly green, and many brown ones were littering the grass beneath.

The sounds were similar, but also very different, from the Mayan jungle. He could hear the sway of the palm leaves brushing against each other in the breeze. He also heard different bird calls he didn't recognise, and the screech of lizards as they crawled up the trees.

The odd group of travelers walked down a natural path of grass or muddy sand left undisturbed save for the tracks they were leaving behind.

"So how did your arm become golden, anyway?" Edward asked bluntly.

Dunn's men stopped short, stared at Edward in alarm, and backed away from him. Dunn turned around and punched Edward in the gut. "That's how. Now shut it and keep walking."

The crew pushed Edward forward even as he clutched his stomach. *That right arm of his is a nuisance.* "Touchy subject, I guess. What does the map say?"

"Didn't I tell you to shut it?"

"Very well, I won't talk. Just trying to make this less of a bore."

Edward kept walking the path with his enemy, being pushed and prodded all the way despite his willingness. He thought back on the look Herbert had worn before he left with Dunn. Those eyes pierced him deep in his heart. Edward furrowed his brows at the enemy captain in front of him. *I'll find a way.*

They walked through the jungle until the path ended and stopped at a rift in the earth. The gorge went as far as they could

283

see, east to west, through the whole island. In the gorge, they could see water running over jagged rocks at the bottom. On the other side, the island and the forest continued on, but there was no path. The rift was too large to jump across, and they couldn't walk over the jagged rocks.

"Oi, Blackbeard! We need us a bridge. Grab that log over there and lay it across."

Blackbeard? Is that supposed to be an insult? Edward stroked his beard as his gaze turned to the log. He saw it, moss-covered and slick-looking; it didn't seem strong enough to support a normal-sized person, let alone Edward. "You expect to cross that?"

"No, I expect *you* to cross it. There's a tall tree you can tie some rope to so we can swing across."

Edward grabbed the log in both hands and lifted one end. He shifted and swiveled it around until it was right by the edge and let it drop to the other side. He inched to the edge of the gorge. It had to be at least fifty feet to the bottom, and the rocks below looked sharp enough to kill.

Edward felt a slight pressure of something hard in his back. It was Dunn, prodding with his golden arm and holding a pistol in his other hand. "Move."

"Will you provide me the rope, or do you expect me to procure that on the other side as well?"

Dunn put his pistol away. He grabbed the rope from one of his crew and then shoved it at Edward. "Here, now make haste. You know what's on the line."

"Yes, better than you." For Edward the treasure no longer held any real worth, except as the means of procuring the safety of his crew.

Edward stepped up on the log, positioning himself sideways with his feet pointed outward, and shuffled along it inch by inch, keeping his eyes on the far end. A gust of wind blew in his face and threw him off balance, but he managed to right himself.

"Faster! We're losing daylight!"

Edward turned his head to look at Dunn. "I should like it if you'd stop distracting me. That would help me go faster." He turned his head back, but glanced down at the rushing water by accident. He couldn't take his eyes off it. The wind blew in his face again, he lost his balance, and this time he wasn't able to regain it. He slipped off the log, and the others gasped. His body scraped along the mossy bark as he fell. Then, at the last instant, he thrust out his arm and wrapped it around the trunk.

Dangling in the air, he took a deep breath, hoisted himself up, threw his other arm around the log, and pulled himself back up on top of it. This time, instead of standing up, he shimmied across on his stomach.

When he reached the other side, he paused to catch his breath, stood up, and searched for a place to tie the rope. He saw a tree close to the edge of the gorge that appeared sturdy enough to hold it. He climbed the trunk and secured the rope near the top before climbing down and throwing it across.

One at a time, Dunn and his men swung across the chasm to the other side, while Edward was told to wait far enough away so he couldn't do anything to them. Last to cross was Dunn, who did it with one hand, refusing any help. The other men took down the rope while he studied the map again, holding both pieces in his one good hand. He kept looking at the map in confusion, turning it this way and that for a good few minutes before putting it away in frustration.

"Do you need help?" Edward offered.

"No, I've got it under control!"

They followed Dunn northeastward through the jungle. With no path, they had to hack their way through thick vines, bushes, and leaves blocking their way. The five walked for about twenty paces, then changed direction, going forty paces north, forty southwest, and ten south, at which point they emerged from the jungle at a spot somehow familiar.

It was a gorge like the last one, except the water at the bottom of it flowed in the opposite direction. Edward took one glance at the gorge and then smiled to himself.

"This is the same spot where we were before," he stated.

"Are you saying I can't read a map? This is where we were supposed to go!"

"Easy," Edward said in an attempt to calm Dunn. "Look over there. It's the log we used." He pointed to the undeniable proof in front of them.

They all walked over and confirmed it to be true. They had gone in a loop. The question was whether or not this was intended by the instructions. *I don't think Bill or his friend is clever enough to come up with something like that.* "Let me see the map."

"What? You think we're headed the wrong way? I followed it perfectly."

"Then you won't mind me checking it to make sure. If you're right, then I'll admit it and we'll continue."

Dunn seemed to relax his guard, and handed Edward the map. He needed but a moment to solve the riddle, but he read it a few times to make sure, because it seemed too simple to be true.

The Golden Arm must not be good at puzzles, this is so simple. I guess I have to hand it to Bill and his friend. They were able to stump someone.

"Follow me."

Dunn folded his arms and snorted, but followed Edward back into the jungle. They went through the thick brush again, but this time their route was different: forty paces north, twenty northeast, and forty east, at the end of which they reached a wall of rock.

"Here we are. Now we have to climb over this and we'll find a path. It says so right here at the last part. Some of the numbers were there to throw us off."

Dunn still had his arms folded, but he accepted what Edward said without objection. "What are you waiting for? Climb up and tie some rope for us."

Edward sighed and began climbing. This part was a little easier than the last; there were plenty of crevices for his hands and feet, and no slippery moss to deal with. He went at a slow pace, making sure not to release a good position before testing the next. He reached the top before long and secured the rope to a boulder so the others could climb up.

Once again they climbed one by one until Dunn was left by himself. He could only pull himself with one arm, and stubbornly tried several times, but he didn't know the proper way to do it.

Eventually Edward yelled down to him. "Either tie it around your waist, or wrap your legs around it and use your right arm pressed against your chest to pull yourself up." The Golden Arm swallowed his pride and did as Edward suggested. He put the rope between his legs, pulled himself up with his good hand, and then pulled it tight to his chest with the right so he wouldn't fall as he went higher.

Dunn finally reached the top, though at a snail's pace, and Edward put his hand out to help once again, but Dunn knocked his hand away. "You take me for a fool, Blackbeard? Get him away from me." The other crewmembers pulled Edward back, and then one helped their captain up from the ledge. When he was safe, they let Edward go.

As Edward had predicted, a path was right in front of them. They all set off down it, but this time Dunn walked beside Edward. The familiar sounds of the jungle returned, but Edward thought he heard an odd rustling behind them and turned around.

"What is it?" Dunn asked.

Edward observed the thick forest for a moment, but he couldn't see anything or hear anything more. "Nothing... Just my imagination, I suppose."

The minutes rushed by with the exertion of walking, but Edward grew tired of the silence. Despite being men of similar background and from the same crew, there was not much rapport between them.

"So what happened between Herbert and John, anyway?"

Edward was a little surprised Dunn didn't berate him or punch him. "He must have told you his side already. What good will telling the same story do?"

"I've not heard his side of the story," Edward explained.

There was a short pause before Dunn spoke again. "He and I were never on the best of terms, even back then. I was in my teens, and Herbert, being the younger, received special treatment from the captain. He took a shine to Herbert because he could see potential in the boy. No matter what I did, he was always praised. He was always the favorite." Dunn's voice had an edge of pent-up irritation.

So Dunn was envious.

"After the accident, the captain didn't want to have a cripple aboard and so he was left at Port Royal. Then it was my chance to shine. I worked harder than ever, and without competition I came to where you see now," he said, tapping his chest with his golden arm. "I'm part of the greatest pirate crew in the world today. You rookies won't ever understand without seeing it firsthand. I can't even hold a candle to the captain's flame. If you thought I was strong, then you don't even know what strength is. You and your crew are weak," Dunn scolded.

He's right, we are weak. We need to be stronger if we're to face what's coming. I need to be stronger.

Edward heard the rustling noise again, but once again when he turned to look he saw nothing and heard no other noises. *I know I heard something this time, I'm not going mad. I should be on guard.*

As they kept walking the path, Edward glanced behind and to the sides in search of the source of the mysterious sound. After walking for another twenty minutes, they reached the end of the path, and nothing they saw seemed to indicate what they should do next. After a moment of perplexity, Dunn pulled out the pieces of the map again.

"What does it say to do next?" Edward asked.

"It says to look up." They stared at each other for a second, and then both looked up into the green canopy above them, having no idea what to expect.

High up, hanging by a rope from a tree, was a large wooden and metal chest. Its sides adorned with elaborate carvings of fine craftsmanship, there was no denying it was an object of worth, and no doubt to any that this was what they had come to find. The two of them smiled, and Dunn pushed Edward toward the tree from which the chest was suspended, motioning for him to climb. "Go on then, get me my treasure!"

Edward pulled the Golden Arm close to him. "You remember our promise, Gregory? I give you this gold, and my crew and I—*all* of them—leave safely."

"I'm a man of my word, Blackbeard. Just keep your cripple away from the captain—and me, of course."

Dunn handed Edward a knife. Edward didn't say a word or make a motion of agreement. He turned and walked to the tree.

That is something I will not do, Dunn. I already made one promise.

He climbed with caution, almost to the top, and it made the tree bend down with his weight. He took it slow, inching forward toward the rope holding the chest.

Those on the ground tried to goad Edward into moving faster, but he continued forward at his own pace. Finally he was able to place one hand on the rope while supporting himself with his legs wrapped around the tree trunk.

How did they put this up here in the first place?

Hanging in that precarious position, he used the knife to saw through the heavy rope, but the fibers were not easy to cut. The chest began to sway. Edward put his weight into the cutting down to the final thread, and with one last slice the chest fell to the jungle floor. Edward had to drop the knife and grab onto the tree, which sprang back when relieved of its burden.

The chest opened on impact. Hundreds of coins spilled out and covered the ground with bright flashes of gold. Despite the exuberant response of hoots, hollers, and pats on the back between Dunn's crew, they didn't presume to touch any of the gold. Their commander, however, almost dove into it; he grabbed fistfuls of the doubloons and let them run through his fingers like a parched man finding clean water.

He soon shook himself out of his manic obsession, however, ordering his men to gather up the coins and put them back in the chest as he turned to see Edward descending from the tree. And as soon as he touched the ground, Dunn pulled out his pistol.

"Not a step closer, Blackbeard!"

"What... What is this? We had a deal, Dunn! The gold in exchange for my crew and me. You mean to dishonour our arrangement?"

"Oh, I intend to honour it, but do you? I see the lust in your eyes. You were waiting for this moment to take our lives and steal the chest for yourself were you not?" he asked, though in his eyes no answer would change his mind. "It ends here. You won't take my gold, as I'll take your life."

"You're mad! You're blinded with..." Edward stopped. He was hearing the strange noise again, but this time it was in two places—and after a split second two huge forms burst from the bush and canopy.

A gargantuan jaguar leaped out from behind the trees, landed on one of Dunn's men, and crushed his head in its powerful jaws. At the same time, what appeared to be a giant eagle swooped down and struck at Dunn's head. He swerved and jumped back just in time to avoid the strike, but his pistol was broken by the beak of the animal. It was no beak, however, nor was the eagle truly a bird.

Pukuh had jumped from a tree, attacking with his spear. In his warrior's dress, he was like an animal in motion, striking fear into the hearts of those around him. Of equal fear-inducing fortitude was the jaguar. With yellow fur and black spots like a leopard, it had two large fangs on the top and bottom rows of its large mouth. It must have been at least three hundred pounds of pure muscle. Dunn's group didn't know of which to be more afraid: the real jaguar or the man-eagle. As for Pukuh, he was focused on the jaguar, and the jaguar on him. They each knew where the true threat lay; the others were just prey.

Pukuh pulled out another spear he had strapped behind him and tossed it to Edward. He pulled his own spear from the ground, crouched down low, and stared at the jaguar, which returned his gaze as they began to circle each other. Edward grabbed his spear off the ground and circled in the opposite direction, also facing the beast, which growled and hissed at them as they sought to corner it.

"Just like old times, eh, Pukuh?"

"Yes, but this beast is not tamed so easily. It must be killed, or we must leave its territory."

"Right." Edward gripped the spear tighter and crouched lower, imitating Pukuh.

"We'll leave this in your hands!" yelled Gregory 'Golden Arm' Dunn.

Edward turned his head to see Dunn and his two remaining crewmembers carrying away the chest full of gold. They had seen an opportunity to escape, and they were taking it.

"You damn cowards!" Edward yelled back.

"Look out, Captain!"

Edward turned back in time to see the fangs of the jaguar closing in on him. He turned his spear sideways, dug his feet in, and pushed its shaft against the animal's front paws. The animal kept trying to force its way forward on its hind legs, snapping at Edward's face and trying to free his claws. It took everything Edward had to hold on to his spear as they struggled and pushed each other back and forth.

"Keep him still!" Pukuh said as he tried to strike at the jaguar— but he hit only air, or almost nicked Edward.

"I can't!" Edward growled.

He pulled in a deep breath and pushed the jaguar forward and off him at an angle. He arched the spear and slashed the animal across the chest as he forced it off him. After the jaguar fell it rolled back to its feet in an instant, unfazed. The cut had been too shallow.

This time it sprang at Pukuh, swiping and striking. He jumped and rolled out of the way, the jaguar missing him by inches. The pressure was intense, and Pukuh barely kept up. Edward tried to jump into the fray again and managed to lure the jaguar away from Pukuh.

Sweat rolled down Edward's and Pukuh's faces and their breathing became heavy. The exertion of keeping the jaguar off them was taking its toll. "I don't know how long I'll last like this, Pukuh."

"We can win, brother! Follow my lead."

Pukuh ran to the right of the jaguar, leaving Edward to the left. He thrust his spear out, inching closer to the animal but not striking. Edward followed suit, and the beast wasn't able to follow both. It backed up from them and tried to claw at the spears, but missed. It kept backing up until it hit a stand of trees. With nowhere to move, it was just where Pukuh wanted it.

"Now!" he yelled.

Edward thrust his spear forward with full intent to kill. The jaguar leapt upwards and dodged the blow. Pukuh then followed with blinding speed and stabbed the creature in the neck. Blood seeped from the open wound in huge spurts, and after some futile pawing at Pukuh's spear, the huge beast fell limp with a bitter groan.

Edward and Pukuh both collapsed on the ground, physically and mentally exhausted. Nearby lay the body of the slain member of Dunn's crew, a stark reminder of how close they had come to death.

"We seem to have trouble with wild animals, you and I," Edward said.

"Yes, I suppose they feel threatened by other wild animals encroaching on their territory."

Edward laughed. They sat there for a minute until Edward thought back on Calico Jack's pirate crew. He stood and brushed the dirt off him. Then he noticed something shiny near the mauled man's body. He walked over, lifted the body, and beneath it found ten golden doubloons.

"What is it?" Pukuh asked as he peered over Edward's shoulder.

"A taste of what we can have." Edward picked up the gold pieces and pocketed them. "We need to head back. There'll be a battle once Dunn reaches the shore."

"Yes, he is unpredictable. Also, the cripple seems to want to kill him. It will complicate things. Do you have a plan?"

"No, but I'll find a way to end this today. For Herbert."

34. HONOURING THE DEAL

Edward and Pukuh ran back along the jungle path as quick as their tired legs would carry them, dodging brush and jumping over logs, trying to catch up to Dunn. "They won't be able to travel fast with the chest in tow. Do you have any guns with you?"

Pukuh scoffed as he ducked under a branch. "No, those are not a warrior's weapons. A coward's, maybe."

Edward laughed. *I should have expected that.*

They soon reached the cliff, but the rope had vanished. Edward started to climb down the ledge, but Pukuh stopped him. "This way is faster," he declared before jumping to a tree a few feet away. Like a monkey he jumped from tree branch to tree branch, finally grabbing a low angled palm and letting himself gracefully down to the ground.

There's no way I can do that.

Pukuh, as if reading Edward's mind, reassured him. "You will make it. Come down."

"No, thanks, I'd rather not break my arm."

Edward, knowing he could not compare in agility with the Mayan, went back to the ledge and clambered down. When he reached the bottom, Pukuh was grinning coolly at him.

"What? I would have died attempting that, and you know it."

"Whatever you say, Captain."

As they continued on the path, they had to slow down, as the fight with the jaguar had taken its toll on Edward. He was breathing in heaves and sweating through his shirt. They hurried on beyond the path and into the bush again until they reached the gorge with the rapids at the bottom. Edward stopped running and sat down to catch his breath. He couldn't see the log they had used before.

"They must have broken the log to stop us."

"They will fail. Come, I'll show you how I crossed."

Pukuh led Edward along the edge until they reached a tree leaning far out over the gorge. He pointed to a thick vine suspended between the tree and another on the other side.

Looks safe enough.

Pukuh climbed up first, followed by Edward. They both suspended themselves on the vine, climbing out over the chasm, holding on with their legs and arms. As they went farther, the vine sagged more and more.

"Uhh, is it supposed to do that?"

"No… Perhaps hurrying will do us good."

They moved faster, but that seemed to make things worse. Edward looked back to where they got on the vine, and what he saw made his thoughts turn grim. The vine was starting to thin and appeared about to snap.

Before Edward could warn his friend, it broke and they fell. Luckily they were holding the part of the vine still attached to the tree on the far side of the gorge. They held on tight and swung forward, landing safely, if roughly, on the other side of the gap.

Edward stood up and dusted himself off. "Why is it every time we're together I always end up in mortal danger?"

"You chose the life of a pirate, and I am the one who puts you in danger?"

"Good point. Let's keep going."

Edward and Pukuh continued the chase until they reached the spot from which Edward had set out with Dunn to find the treasure. He and Pukuh found no one there. They concluded that when Dunn returned he took them back down to the shore. Pukuh could see their footprints heading back, and Edward could see the still-fresh bloodstains on the path where Herbert had been beaten. His wheelchair was gone as well, which hopefully meant he was still alive.

Herbert, I promised you revenge, and I hope I can deliver on that promise.

"The tracks are still fresh. We might be able to reach the shore at the same time they do."

Edward nodded, and they took off running. They went on for half an hour before the path ended, never catching sight of their quarry. Edward slowed down as they reached the edge of the forest.

"I don't hear sounds of fighting. That means either we're just in time or too late."

The forest ended abruptly, and there were several bushes and fanning leaves before the sandy beach. Edward and Pukuh hid behind some of the bushes. Now they could see both crews on the sand of the beach, each with their captives in tow. Jack appeared to be conversing with Dunn in the centre of the beach, trying to negotiate a mutual release. Of Edward's crew, about eighty were on the ship, some of them pointing rifles and cannons at Dunn's crew, ninety were on shore guarding the hostages, and the other group of fifty were still held by Dunn. Edward's crew outnumbered Dunn's by fifty; they could take them in a fair fight, but under the circumstances couldn't risk harm to Edward's senior officers.

"Pukuh, I want you to sneak aboard the *Freedom*. I'll remain on shore to distract them and try to bring the rest of the crew on our side. I want you to tell the gunners to fire when I give the signal. No one is aboard their ship and they aren't ready to depart. We can win if we play our cards right."

"What is this 'playing of cards' you talk of?" Pukuh asked.

"It... it's an expression. It means... when two people are playing a game with..." Edward shook his head. "I'll tell you later, we don't have time. Go give my orders to the crew and everything will work out."

"Yes, brother." Pukuh went farther down the shore, closer to where the *Freedom* was anchored.

Edward waited until Pukuh was gone and then came out of hiding.

"Already started without me, Dunn? Shame on you. Not only are you a coward but you have no manners."

"You! How did you survive?" Dunn asked, his brows furrowed.

The Golden Arm was at least as shocked as everyone else. Elated cries of "Captain!" and "Edward!" reached him from all sides. Henry and Anne wore bright smiles of relief.

"The report of my demise by our pirate friend here was somewhat premature. As you can see, I am perfectly safe. I can take over here, Jack, thank you. Keep everyone on their toes, eh?" Edward said as he glanced toward the ship.

Jack nodded and grinned before he went back to the crew guarding the tied-up pirates. Jack whispered some words to them.

"You bastard, how did you win against that jaguar? And where is your dark friend?"

"I won because I fought. You lost because you ran. My friend died because of that animal." Edward gritted his teeth to give the appearance of anger over his lost crewmate.

"And you say *I* lost? Ha! I'm still alive."

Not for long if I can help it.

"If you want to keep living I suggest you let my crew go. We had a deal, remember?"

"That hinged on the fact of me gaining the gold, but do you see a treasure chest here? No. I have four dead crewmen and nothing to show for it."

The Voyages of Queen Anne's Revenge

"You lost the gold on the way back?" Edward arched his brow, trying to remember if he'd noticed it along the way back, but he knew the answer. "That's what you get for your greed, but our agreement was met. I led you to the gold and gave it to you. What happened after is your fault."

"I've lost four crewmen, including the one you killed here on the beach, and you've lost one. I think it's fair that we take three of yours in compensation."

"Look behind me, Dunn, and then behind you," Edward said, pointing for emphasis. "I have more armed crewmen than you, and the ones from your crew are tied up while mine are simply unarmed." Edward grabbed Dunn by the chest and pulled him in close. "You start fighting now and you'll be the one who dies. I suggest you take the offer I gave you before and we can all leave safely." He released Dunn, pushing him away.

Beads of sweat ran down Gregory Dunn's forehead, leaving streaks on his dust-covered face. "Yes, maybe it would be best to keep to our arrangement. We'll let all the hostages go and then head back to our ships."

Edward nodded, and both of them turned and told their crews to free the captives, who then moved to rejoin their own crews. They exchanged hostile glances that threatened a fight, but Edward's stern eye curbed any thoughts of attacking. John wheeled Herbert past Edward in his half-broken wheelchair. Herbert kept staring at the ground, dejected and looking the worse for his wounds.

With the crews back in their proper places, Edward and Dunn nodded and walked away from one another, their business concluded. But Edward was not finished with the Golden Arm. He motioned for one man to toss him a sword, and then gave the crew on the ship the signal to fire with a swipe of his hand.

"Attack!" he roared.

A loud blast of cannon fire broke through the silence, followed by several more. The cannonballs hit the beach with thunderous impact, shooting sand into the air, then rolled along the ground, crushing and maiming several of Dunn's men. Edward's crew rushed over to the enemy as the cannon blasts stopped, and the sounds of a ground battle soon replaced the thunder of the cannons. Swords clanged, guns blazed, and screams echoed along the beach.

Through the commotion Edward sought his prey. This time he would win against him, and Herbert would have his revenge. He cut through the others in his way, and soon found Dunn shooting a pistol and taking out a cutlass, his back turned. Edward came up behind him and attacked, but Dunn saw it out of the corner of his eye and dodged.

"You call me the coward and yet you attack us while our backs are turned?"

"No different from you, ambushing us in the jungle. Call me an opportunist."

Their swords clanged together with mortal intent. Dunn was serious this time, but Edward had learned from their previous fight. After the battle with the jaguar, he faced a foe that was all too human, and all too predictable.

"I guess this means our arrangement is broken and we won't spare your crew," Dunn said through rapid breaths.

"I think you have it backwards, Gregory. My crew will leave here today, as will I. At no point did I agree *I* would spare *you* in our arrangement."

Edward slashed and thrust at Dunn, but couldn't reach him no matter how he tried. Dunn used his golden arm deftly, blocking and parrying Edward's sword.

That arm is mine!

Dunn went to punch Edward with his golden arm, and Edward grabbed it, pulling him forward. He flipped Dunn to the ground, jumped on his back, and wrapped his legs around Dunn's neck and arm, making him drop his cutlass. Edward pulled the golden arm back, placed his sword at its elbow, and thrust the blade down with all his strength.

Dunn screamed out in pain as Edward dug the blade in deeper. Blood spurted from the gash and washed over the sword, Edward's hand, his trousers, and the sand. He kept pressing into the elbow as Dunn tried to escape from the vice grip he was in. Edward rose to his feet, stepped on Dunn's chest, and pulled the arm with all his strength.

Others heard the screams and watched in terror as the golden arm was being torn off. Blood splashed everywhere as Edward's muscular arms pulled hard. The whole time he wore a smile on his face that kept all, his own crew included, far away from the centre of the horror.

The din of battle died off and the sounds of Gregory Dunn screaming and the crunch of shattering bones replaced it. With one final pop Edward ripped the golden arm from Dunn's body, then raised it above his head as a symbol of their victory.

His crew yelled and cheered with excitement, and the other enemy pirates surrendered and dropped their weapons. Their commander was defeated. The Golden Arm was no longer.

Dunn's crew surrendered without further fighting. Edward's crew gathered them all together on the shore between the ships. Dunn himself was becoming weaker and weaker from loss of blood. Edward propped him up on his knees and he sat there, listlessly swaying in the wind, waiting for the end.

"Herbert! Where are you?" Edward yelled.

Herbert wheeled himself to the front of the crowd and over to Edward and Gregory Dunn. "Here, Captain."

"I'm sorry about before, I…"

Herbert cut Edward off. "No, Captain, I'm the one who should apologise. I know you were thinking of our safety first and foremost. I'm sorry for what I said."

Edward gave a small, sad smile and squeezed Herbert's shoulder. "Well, here's the chance for the first step in your revenge." Edward claimed a pistol from a crewmember, which he then handed to Herbert. "This is your job."

Herbert took the pistol and Edward backed away. Herbert moved closer to Gregory Dunn, the Gold Division Commander of the Calico Jack Pirates. He took aim.

Dunn laughed weakly. "So this is it, then? Killed by the cripple John loved?"

"Shut up! You don't know anything! He doesn't love anyone. He's a pirate! He used me, and when my usefulness ran out, he discarded me. It would have been the same for anyone."

Dunn laughed again. "It's you who don't know anything, boy. You were like a son to him, and I was the tool. All of us still are… He doesn't care about us, but you he did. Now, though, if you pull the trigger"—and he nodded toward Edward—"*he'll* be the one who pays. You don't know the hell you'll wake by taking out your petty resentments on Mad Jack. You'll all die for this! You'll all pay for angering the King of the Caribbean. You'll—"

Herbert pulled the trigger. Gregory Dunn jerked and he fell to the sand, dead. The Gold Division Commander was no longer, and the first step in Herbert's revenge was complete.

Edward passed Herbert and stood next to the corpse, facing Dunn's crew and addressing them. "Return to your captain and tell him what happened today. Tell him we killed his Golden Arm because he crossed us. Tell him we're coming for him, and that there's a new King of the Caribbean."

Everyone within hearing of his voice stood watching Edward in awed silence. Then someone called out: "What do we call the new king?"

Edward looked down at the corpse of Dunn, then raised his head high and scanned the eyes of the vast company, friend and foe alike, gathered on the beach.

"My name is Edward Thatch, but you can call me Blackbeard."

35. THE ARM SWORD

After their victory, Edward sent a few crewmates back to the trail to search for the gold Dunn lost on his way back to shore, but they returned empty-handed. There was no sign of the chest or the remaining gold pieces.

Edward thought he knew what happened. It had probably been dropped into the gorge. With the rapids and jagged rocks at the bottom, there was no way they could check. The treasure was likely lost to them. Edward sighed.

As compensation, Edward's crew ransacked Dunn's ship for supplies and anything that could be sold. Cannons and gunpowder, spices and food, as well as a good supply of clothes and weapons—all were taken. They left enough for the other crew to survive on, but no weapons were spared. They even found a few hundred pieces of eight in the captain's quarters.

A few members of Gregory Dunn's crew were willing to swear allegiance to Edward in exchange for freedom. Among them was Bill's friend who had also vied for the treasure, Theodore Hammersmith by name, who had a tale to tell.

"And so Bill, when I couldn't find you, I went to these men for help. They said they would help me, but they overheard me talking about treasure and gold and so they kidnapped me instead to find the treasure. They tortured me something fierce, but I never told them nothing. Why, you might as well call me Stone Lips."

Bill had a look of teary admiration on his face.

"Oh? So how did they find Bill's home and his half of the map if you were so tight-lipped?" Edward asked.

Theodore, better known as Ted, had a confused expression for a moment, and then burst into feigned tears. "Oh, they tortured me night and day, Bill, night and day." Edward sighed and covered his face. "I may have let slip that a map was in your home. Oh, but you must forgive me my momentary weakness, Bill; I'm so sorry. But see what fortune has brought us! Someone has delivered us a knight in shining armour to save us from the cruel oppression of Gregory Dunn. How did you ever meet such a man?"

"I met him while on… a business trip. I returned home to my house robbed and the map gone, so I thought the worst. I immediately asked them to help me, and through memory I navigated them to the island. It was a good bit of providence I was able to put together what had happened to you. I knew you were in some peril and had to be saved. I'm glad Edward was here to help, or else we might not have found you." They hugged each other in an obvious display.

These two...

"It's such a shame. All our hard work gone like that."

"I know, but at least we have our lives." It was obvious both of them were upset and holding back their anger.

Edward reached into his pocket and pulled out the ten doubloons he'd found. "Dunn dropped these in his haste."

Bill and Ted reached out at the same time to snatch the gold from Edward, who pulled his hand out of reach.

"Hold out your hands. Both of you."

They smiled falsely to each other as they opened their hands. Edward placed four gold pieces in each of their hands, and left two in his own. He lifted it for both of them to see.

"Twenty percent," he explained, to avoid a dispute arising. *I wouldn't want to shatter the stories these boys told. That would just be a shame.* "This is my cut for helping you both."

Once again, Bill and Ted smiled to each other in the most insincere way Edward had ever seen. "Well, I suppose that's only fair," Ted said.

"Yes, only fair," Bill agreed.

Edward went back to the ship and handed John the two pieces of gold. Henry noticed and went to talk with him.

"So I guess that's our twenty percent?"

Edward chuckled. "No, we actually have three. Remember?"

Henry smiled when he realised what happened. "So I guess in the end you got what you wanted in the first place—thirty percent."

Edward had a devious smile. "Not only that, but we have the Golden Arm's arm. If it's made of solid gold, we'll be rich!"

"I can't say I enjoy the thought of having a dead man's arm, nor using it for profit, but I suppose it's better than attacking innocents."

"I'll drink to that."

With their business finished and Edward's ship filled with people and supplies, they shoved off the island and headed back to the Grand Cayman. The return trip took a little longer than the way there. Night fell three quarters of the way through and so they decided to hoist the sails and let the crew have some rest.

Edward awoke in the middle of the night, the dream shaking him awake him as it was prone to do, and decided to take a walk. Lighting the lantern near his bedside, he gazed upon his crew packed tightly into the hammocks around the cabin, all sleeping soundly. He thought back to when he had first received the *Freedom*, to how he couldn't think of it as his home, no matter what, despite his desire for a ship. Now, amidst the sweet smells and those familiar wooden floorboards and the crew, he couldn't think of a place he'd rather be.

He went up to the main deck and noticed Herbert gazing at the full moon. He looked solemn, almost reflective.

"So?" Edward said as he joined Herbert at the railing on the port side.

"So?"

"How's the wheelchair? I saw it was damaged during the ambush."

"Nassir fixed it. There wasn't too much damage."

The wind was blowing and the sails flapped with each gust. The ropes swayed and the masts creaked. It was a beautiful night, and the moon's light reflected on the rippling waves.

"How do you feel, now that you've taken the life of one of Calico Jack's crew? You don't seem very happy."

"I am. At least, I think I am. I don't know how to describe this feeling. Satisfaction? Contentment? I feel like I've taken the first step in the journey I started eight years ago. You've made it a reality for me, Captain. And for that I'm grateful."

"You're welcome. But you have to remember that your life is more important to me than revenge. If a situation like that comes up again, I may end up doing something you don't like."

Herbert shook his head in shame. "I know. I was so filled with rage I couldn't see what you were trying to do. I've had time to think, and I know it won't happen again. I know now you'll fulfill your side of the agreement, and I'll keep mine as well. I have to be patient and wait for it."

"So what will happen when it's all said and done? Will you leave the crew? Live a peaceful life with your sister?"

Herbert looked confused. "No, Captain. I'm with you to the end. You've brought me this far, and it would shame me to leave you when you've helped me with my goal. I'll help you achieve your goal as well."

"My goal?"

"Yes. Don't you have a goal in mind? Why did you become a pirate?"

Edward thought about it for a time and then smiled. "I want to always be free."

Herbert smiled along with him, and then took another look at the large silver moon off in the distance. "I'd like that too."

...

As the sun broke over the horizon, they landed at the Grand Cayman once more. Bill and Ted left the *Freedom* together. They went off to drink and spend their new gold pieces.

The crew unloaded some of what they procured from the other ship and sold it at a good profit. They resupplied the ship with enough food and other necessities and then headed back to Bodden Town to sell the rest.

"Why Bodden Town?" Anne asked Edward.

"Merchandise we sell in Bodden Town will be taxed, and that tax will come back to us bit by bit. We'll be making more this way in the end. It's just good business."

Anne smiled a knowing smile and nodded in approval.

Having landed in Bodden Town, Edward headed straight to the Bodden Brothers' home. He took a few of the crew with him; it had been a few days since the fight and the agreement, and he wanted to make a strong impression. He also brought John as he would be best to check over the ledgers and make sure the brothers had everything in order.

The newly repaired gates were opened for him, and the brothers were swift to greet him. They hunched over in unconscious submission to him.

"Mr. Thatch! What brings you back so soon?" asked Neil.

"Had we expected you we would have prepared a meal," Malcolm added.

Edward walked straight to them. "No need for pleasantries, brothers. I returned to make certain our arrangements were being carried out, and to sell some supplies we've acquired."

"We'll make sure you receive the best price for the goods."

"We'll send someone down to organise the sale right now." Malcolm waved to one of the servants, who hurried down to the harbour immediately.

"Now as for the other matter, please step inside. We've drawn up some ledgers, which you can inspect. This way, please."

Edward nodded and followed them into the opulent house. They went into the second-floor study and examined all the pertinent records. Edward's name was at the top of the list of partners alongside the brothers'. Twenty-five percent was accorded to Edward and the rest shared between the brothers, as he had stipulated. Already he had amassed a good amount of coin.

John, after taking a bit of time to check everything in the ledger, nodded in approval, confirming everything was in order.

"The town is growing at a rapid pace, especially when you factor in all the merchant and pirate ships visiting the harbour," Neil said.

"It's becoming a popular trade spot. Before you arrived, we were working on plans to expand the housing supply to accommodate more permanent residents," Malcolm added.

"I'm surprised you haven't done so already. Have you started construction yet?" Edward asked.

"No, Mr. Thatch, not yet," Neil said.

"Good. I want you to make the houses small. Keep them cheap to maintain and live in. Cater to pirates and lower-class citizens. Spread the word to the surrounding islands and towns that Bodden Town is the place to be for profit and avoiding the authorities. Do that, and in less than a year, you should have twice as many people here."

The Boddens smiled at the prospect. They liked the idea. "It will be done, Mr. Thatch."

"Now, is there anything else you need?"

"Yes, I'm in search of an appraiser. I have some gold I want melted and minted."

"If it's an appraisal you need..." Neil started.

"...we would be happy to provide that service," Malcolm finished.

Edward turned and took a large bag from one of his crew. It was slick with blood at the bottom. He reached inside and took out the arm of Gregory Dunn.

The brothers' jaws fell open and they stared at the severed limb in shocked silence for several seconds.

"Where... did you..."

"...find that... thing?"

"I took it from a man who crossed me. I wanted to see what I could sell it for. What do you think?"

Edward handed the arm to the two brothers and they reluctantly took it. They examined it by weight first, with each of them lifting it and giving it a gentle toss in the air.

"This is solid metal."

"Solid?" Edward questioned with a raised brow.

Neil nodded. "Though how it was fused to his arm is beyond our reckoning."

They cleared their worktable and pulled out some tools for a more thorough examination. They used a magnifying glass to examine the whole arm, and paid particular attention to the spot where metal ended and flesh began.

"This is an alloy, not pure gold, if it's even gold at all."

"It's much too strong. You say you fought the man?"

"Did you hit the arm with your sword at all?"

"Yes, several times I struck it with my blade."

The brothers turned to each other, then back to Edward. "Come look at this." Edward joined the brothers on their side of the desk. "Do you see any spots here where you hit it with your blade?"

Edward examined the whole arm up and down several times but couldn't find a chip, a scrape, or any damage at all for that matter. *Dunn used the arm as a shield. He must have had the arm for years and practiced with it all the time. How is it there's no damage showing at all?* "That's impossible," he mumbled.

"Yes, but it is clearly true."

"This metal is like no other we've ever seen. You could quite possibly sell this for a fortune."

Edward stroked his beard as he examined the golden arm once more. "I have a better idea."

...

For the next two months, the *Freedom* remained moored at Bodden Town, where the crew was set to working on two projects: the cleaning of the ship, which had been neglected during the hunt for the treasure, and the building of new housing in the town, under the direction of Nassir.

Many of the builders were, at first, opposed to a Negro leading them, and Edward would have given them a talking-to, but Nassir stopped him. Nassir showed them his skills as a carpenter and his capacity for hard work, and, by his example, turned them around on his own. In the end, in spite of some continued grumbling, they were all working side by side with him and the rest of the crew.

Edward finished making arrangements with the Boddens concerning how funds would be distributed and what they should do next for the town. They started sending out messenger ships to let other islands know of the wealth in Bodden Town, and they soon saw the results as more and more ships appeared in the harbour.

Edward had the best swordsmith in Bodden Town create a cutlass out of the metal from Gregory Dunn's arm. It took the whole two months of their stay, and cost a good amount of coin; the swordsmith had never worked with a material of such hardness and strength. When finished, it was the finest piece of art Edward, and many aboard the *Freedom*, had ever seen. The hilt had a hand guard made of silver and steel, ornamented with an eagle design, and the shining, golden blade was of such quality that it took on an edge sharp enough to cut clean through six inches of solid oak as if it were paper.

"So the Golden Arm lives on still. It's rather fitting we should be in possession of this after we killed him."

"I imagine we'll have more to remind us of victory over Calico Jack later," Herbert said to Edward as he piloted the ship out of the harbour. "His commanders are... unique, to say the least. They all have their quirks and oddities."

"Oh, such as?"

"There's the Silver Division Commander, Lance 'Silver Eyes' Nhil. He works as a scout for John."

"Let me guess, his nickname is for his eyesight?"

"Yes, they say he has supernatural eyesight and is an excellent marksman. Before he was a pirate, he took part in competitions around the world and tested rifles for several arms manufacturers. He's the best there is. He's also said to be an unflinching optimist. No matter how bleak things are, he and his crew never lose their morale. That's won them a lot of battles."

Edward chuckled. "And is there a Copper Division Commander?"

"Yes, Grace 'Copper Legs' O'Malley. She kept her name, but she's actually married to John Rackham. She's the messenger and judge in the pirate crew. If the other divisions get out of line then she takes swift action to deliver punishment. She also has a pair of greaves and boots made of copper, apparently of her own invention. I'm not sure what they do, but I can imagine it's something dangerous if she's named for them."

"Both of them will chase after us now that we've taken out one of their commanders. I'll be relying on your knowledge to help me take them down, Herbert. We're in this together."

"I know Captain, and I thank you. I'll give you my best in anything you need. Where to next?"

"Next? Next we're off to Navassa Island. There's a key we've been neglecting."

"Aye aye, Captain. Next stop: Navassa Island."

36. THE PAST AND THE RELAPSE

Five Years Ago

Rachel felt the cool morning breeze on her face and pulled a strand of her long chestnut hair behind her ear as she watched the sun rising. No matter how often she had seen the day begin, the beauty of that golden-red ball inching over the edge of the world never ceased to enchant her.

"Good day, wife," a man said as he walked up behind Rachel and wrapped his arms around her.

"Good day, Husband," she said, holding her husband Jack's arms close to her. The aroma of coffee sitting on a nearby table mixed with the scents of the cool breeze and morning dew. Rachel closed her eyes as she leaned back into his chest. "I could get used to this."

Jack laughed as he rested his head gently on top of hers. "Every morning I come out here, and every morning you say that. I would think you would be used to it by now."

She smiled. "That's the thing about dreams, love. You never get used to them."

"Well, if this is a dream, let's pray we never awaken."

They stood there, wrapped in each other's warmth, taking sips of the coffee together. They watched from their back porch as the sun rose over the horizon. They listened to the birds singing from their treetop perches, and the faint sounds of the sea.

"Are the kids still asleep?" asked Jack.

"Yes. They won't be up for another few hours." Rachel turned and gazed into his eyes. Jack knew what they both wanted at this moment. With his arm around her shoulders, he led her indoors.

They came back out when the children woke up. Rachel made breakfast as Jack prepared to leave for work. Their two children, Maximilian, ten, and Jessica, nine, sat at the table.

"Good morning, Father. Good morning, Mother," they both said.

"Good morning, children."

"What did you two dream about last night?" Jack asked, as he always did.

Maximilian spoke up first, excited. "I was at sea, and this big monster whale broke the boat in half!"

Jack lifted the young man in his arms. "Whoa! And what did you do then?"

"I… I bopped him in the 'ead and told him to stop."

"You sure showed him," he said with a chuckle. "Jessica, what about you?"

"I dreamed I was a lion, and then I went 'roar' and all the other animals were scared."

"That sure is a scary roar. Why don't you do that again? I don't think Mother heard it."

Jessica did her best imitation of a lion roaring as Jack and Rachel smiled. Jack loved these hours before his workday began, when he could relax with his family. Living a modest but comfortable life in his little house, in the small village of Hastings, he was truly happy for the first time in his life.

After playing with the children some more, Jack finished off his breakfast and set out. He held classes teaching others how to play, read, and write music. He enjoyed the work, and on this day the time went by like it was nothing.

"And so that will conclude today's lesson. Katie, remember to practice those chords I showed you for next time, and all of you remember to study the sheet music tonight. Whoever can name and play all the notes will receive a treat." Jack packed his things, including his violin, into his bag. He said goodbye to his students and to their parents who picked them up.

On his way home, Jack gazed at the setting sun in the distance. It was late. He could see the various shops and offices down the dirt road, the passing horses and carriages, the men and women dressed for their daily business, the children still playing in the streets. He smiled as he headed back to his home where his wife and children would be waiting.

Their one-story home with the fence and apple tree in front was as he had left it. The leafy branches and green grass swayed in the wind and sent to him the sweet smell of spring. He approached the steps of his house—and then he noticed something odd. Muddy footprints led up the steps and into the house.

Hmm, I wonder if Rachel had guests.

Jack walked up the steps, opened the door and stepped inside. Silence greeted him. "Rachel?" he said into the dark room.

A violent blow struck his temple as the butt of a musket was rammed into his head. Jack fell to the floor unconscious.

A while later he awoke, tied to a chair, his head pounding.

A man was sitting across the table from him, flanked by three others dressed in uniforms all too familiar. They were marines of the royal navy. But the man before him was familiar to Jack for another reason.

"George? What is the meaning of this?"

George Rooke, aged thirty, was an impressive figure with dark eyes and slick black hair, clean-shaven and strong-jawed, with the toned body of a marine official who kept himself in excellent condition. He wore white gloves with his black uniform and was immaculately clean in every way, as if he had an aversion to dirtiness.

When Jack had known him, he was a recruit in the marines, but now he wore the badges of a rear admiral. It had been ten years since they'd last met.

"The meaning? The meaning! Don't play dumb, Jack. You knew this day was inevitable. You couldn't run away with my bride-to-be and think I wouldn't track you down, could you?" He picked up a glass of water and drank from it. "And children too! So cute for bastards who shouldn't have been born."

Jack's eyes grew wide with fear. "What have you done with them?"

"Nothing... yet. We couldn't start until the whole family was here, now could we?"

George motioned to one of the marines. They went into one of the rooms and brought out the children. Jack could see Rachel tied up there as well. She let out a muffled scream when she saw him.

"Rachel!"

The marine who had hit him with the gun stock put a gag in his mouth as he tried desperately to break from his bonds. His children were brought to the side of the table. They, too, were bound and gagged.

"Such precious little ones. Do they know how you stole my betrothed, the woman I loved, from me? By all rights, they shouldn't exist. They are an abomination." George Rooke pulled a knife from his belt. "I do so hate to have blood and filth on me." He turned to one of his men and held out the weapon. "Kill them."

Jack tried to scream and pulled at the ropes binding him.

The man in the white tunic and brown trousers took the blade from Rooke.

Jack bit at the cloth until his mouth bled.

The man smiled as he walked to Maximilian, Jack's son.

Jack pulled on the rope as it dug into his flesh.

The man placed the blade along the boy's neck as the young one cried out.

Tears flowed from Jack's eyes as he put up his futile struggle.

In one swift stroke, it was done. He did the same to Jessica, and soon a pool of blood formed beneath them and spread over the floorboards. Jack screamed out in pain through the gag, hoping to God this was a fever dream.

But the nightmare was only beginning.

George had a smile on his face, watching the tears flow from Jack's eyes as he stared at the dead bodies of his children.

"Now, Jack. Jack, pay attention, I'm talking here." The man who had gagged Jack forced him to look at George. "That's better. Now we have a problem because, you see, my man Lucas here has a certain... shall we say... medical condition. Whenever he sees blood, an uncontrollable fever grips his loins. I'm not about to let him release his frustrations on me, and neither are the other men here, so there's only one option left." He turned to Lucas, who was breathing in heaves, the knife still in his hands. "No need to restrain yourself, Lucas. There's a woman back there more than willing to take your cock for a ride. She's already whored herself out to Jack here for the past ten years. Be sure to finish her off when you're done."

Lucas walked into the back room.

Jack screamed in fury and pulled at the ropes binding him. He could see Rachel backing up as Lucas closed the door behind him. Her screams could be heard even through her gag.

When it was all over, Lucas returned and Jack could see a red pool beneath Rachel's lifeless body.

He had struggled so much he was worn out. His eyes and wrists were red, and he was sagging in the chair. George rose from his seat, smiling, and his men freed Jack from his bonds. George walked to the door and opened it.

"Good day, Jack."

George Rooke went out the front door as his men emptied bottles of lantern oil around the room, then threw lit lanterns down, setting the house on fire. They left, their work done.

Jack crawled to his children as everything burned around him. He grabbed each of them in his arms and pulled them close. Their bodies were listless and limp, their former energy lost. He wept and cradled them as fire lapped at their precious memories.

Jack's life, one that he had built up through love over more than ten years, was destroyed in one night.

...

Present Day

One night, on the way to Navassa Island, when the moon was shining, Edward went for a walk on the main deck. Approaching the stern, he heard a familiar sound, and he found Jack Christian, drunk and singing a sad lullaby. Jack had not kept his promise.

"Jack."

Jack turned around and smiled from ear to ear. His hair was disheveled and it seemed as if he hadn't shaved in weeks, and his eyes were red from tears. He held a bottle in his hand and the stench off him was strong. He was unsteady on his feet and swaying from the drink.

"Cap'n! Join me for a drink!"

Edward slapped Jack hard, knocking him to the ground.

"Whut was that fer? That hurt, you bastard!" he yelled and tried to stand, but ended up merely flopping around. "I'll get you in a minute."

"Stop fooling around, Jack. What about the promise you made?"

"Whut about it?"

"You promised to stop drinking, yet here you are with a drink in your hand," he said with a wave towards the bottle. "Give me the bottle." Edward put his hand out, but Jack drew back. He pulled it close to his face and sipped at it while he watched Edward from the corners of his half-opened eyes. Edward reached for it again and again, but Jack kept pulling it away. Edward ended up fighting him for the bottle, and he won, but received a few kicks and punches for his trouble.

Jack was thrashing this way and that after Edward took the bottle. "Give it back!" he screamed.

"No," Edward replied.

Tears rolled down Jack's face. "I need it. It hurts, Cap'n. It hurts too much. I can't take it."

"You're stronger than this, Jack. You don't need it."

"No! I do need it! Give it *back*!" Jack wailed, stretching out his hand. He kept repeating it again and again. His voice went from a yell to a whisper as Jack clutched Edward's leg, begging him for the bottle.

It was a pitiable sight, and Edward couldn't take it. He wasn't strong enough to deny his friend his vice when he was like this, no matter what happened to him.

His bottle back in his hands, Jack smiled as he downed half its contents and started singing again. Edward walked away, his head bowed in shame, tears stinging his eyes.

I need to be stronger.

37. THE THIRD ISLAND

It took a week and a half to arrive at Navassa Island, and the crew sang sea shanties with Jack and trained with William and Anne to relieve the boredom of an otherwise uneventful journey. The new crewmembers consisted of pirates from other crews, some seamen from fishing boats, and former merchantmen who knew their way around a ship. They soon learned this was a different type of crew, and they could expect to see a lot of combat.

William showed them how to use muskets and other flintlocks; they learned how to load, how to aim, the proper time to use each weapon, how and when to take cover, and how to follow orders. Anne taught them hand-to-hand fighting and the use of close-quarters weapons. Many navy officers used longswords, but Anne taught with the cutlass, a smaller blade that was more practical in the confined space of a ship.

One day, when there was no wind and travel was at a standstill, almost the whole crew was able to have dinner together. They broke out the best foodstuffs: salted meat, cheese, and biscuits were the mainstay, but since they had just left Bodden Town, they had some unspoiled fruit and vegetables as well. With Edward's permission, they drank light rum and water. The mess hall became quite animated, with everyone telling jokes, eating, and playing games. Some played cards and others arm-wrestled, while the crew working in the galley brought out food at varying intervals.

Edward was sitting with Henry and John. Anne joined them. "It certainly is lively now, is it not?" she said, smiling.

"Yes, I was just saying how we've gained quite the crew," Edward agreed.

They all observed the merrymakers. Pukuh was having a drink with Sam, hesitantly trying rum for the first time. Ochi, Nassir's boy, was with Christina, Herbert's sister, and a few of the men. They were showing her tricks with coins and cards, and she laughed at the magic on display. William was even having a little to drink with Nassir, Alexandre, and Herbert, who sat at a table together, eating and swapping stories.

"I would not want to be anywhere else," Anne said.

"Hear, hear!" Henry raised his glass and the rest of them joined.

Anne leaned toward Edward as they talked and placed her hand on his under the table.

The festivities continued well into the night. A bond was formed over that meal, a sense of belonging—of family, even—which affected even the new members, and remained strong as they reached Navassa Island.

The island was small and uninhabited. Rocky shallows prevented the ship from landing near shore.

"If we sail any closer we're liable to run aground, Captain."

"This is well enough. We'll take a longboat ashore. William, you're with me. Henry, are you coming?"

"I suppose I shall."

The three, joined by a couple of other crewmembers, jumped into one of the dinghies, lowered themselves into the water, and rowed to the rocky shore.

The island was small and quite plain, with gentle rolling hills covered only in grass and scrub. From the top of the first rise one could see the other side of the island without need of a spyglass.

"So what are we searching for?" Henry asked.

"There's supposed to be something that will help decode the gibberish of the last clue left by Benjamin. It's supposed to be in the centre of the island."

They all walked to what seemed to be the right place, but there was nothing to be seen. They searched the ground, combing through the grass, but to no avail. No paper with a cipher, no secret code, nothing.

"Was it already taken?" asked Henry.

William answered immediately. "This island doesn't see any activity. The location would be a prime spot for traders, but the rocky shore means it is bypassed. The probability of it being taken is slim at best."

Henry turned to Edward. "You said it was in the centre of the island, right? What if it's buried?"

"That would make sense." Edward directed a couple of the men to return to the ship to retrieve some shovels.

"Captain, I found something," William said.

Edward went over to William. He was pointing to a patch of grass. "What is it?"

"The grass in this area is patchy and there are rocks upturned, as if it was dug up. If we dig here we may find what we are looking for."

"Good job, William. I knew those keen eyes would come in handy." Edward patted William on the back.

When the men returned with the spades, they dug in the spot William had pointed out. They made a wide circle to cover plenty of ground, and they took shifts—necessary, because they only had two shovels. As Edward was taking his break, he heard someone yell from the hole.

"Ed, I found something!"

Edward ran back to the hole and Henry tossed up a triangular stone to him. On each of its three sides there were inscriptions. Edward helped Henry and another crewmember out of the hole.

"What's on it?" Henry asked, wiping sweat off his brow.

"I'm not sure, but this must translate the message on the paper we found. It's covered in dirt, so let's head back to the ship and we can clean it off and examine it." Edward tried to sound calm, but he was excited and eager to find out what the message was going to be.

On the boat ride back, Edward washed the stone with ocean water, revealing that the inscriptions consisted of letters of the alphabet. On each of the stone's three sides were two sets of letters, one to the left and one to the right. To the left was a section of the alphabet with the letters in alphabetical order: A-I on the first side of the stone, J-R on the second side, and S-Z on the third. To the right, however, was a seemingly random ordering of the same letters of the alphabet.

It must mean the left side is what was on the paper, and the right is the true meaning. Brilliant! With this we'll be on our way in no time!

While rowing back to the ship, all Edward could think of was what they would find at the next island, and what part of the *Freedom* would be opened when they found the key.

Back at the ship, ropes were lowered to them, they secured the longboat, and the ship's crew pulled them up. Edward immediately jumped off and went to the crew's quarters where he kept the paper left by Benjamin Hornigold.

Having procured some parchment, a quill, and a bottle of ink, he went to the mess hall. Several of the other crewmembers who saw his urgency followed him, curious to see what he had found. He started from the beginning and copied down the translation on the parchment. But, as he went along, his excitement turned to confusion, and then to anger.

Gibberish and more gibberish! It doesn't solve anything!

The frustration of finding clues that meant nothing, and of pursuing wild goose chases to find still more nothing, was building inside Edward. He gripped the stone triangle in both hands. He was shaking with rage.

"Uhh, Captain?" one of the crewmembers called.

Edward shot to his feet and hurled the stone triangle at the wall. Fuming and breathing through flared nostrils, he turned to the gathered crew and shouted, "Back to work!"

Everyone saw the look in his eyes, and the mess hall emptied quicker than if someone had pulled a gun. William, Henry, and Anne remained.

"There was no need for that, Edward," Anne said as she walked over to him.

"Yes, there was! That damned Benjamin is taunting us with his riddles and tricks! He creates these trials, which are supposed to test us, and it ends up killing some of our crew and injuring others. And he treats it as some game!"

Henry chimed in. "Yes, and you've been playing the game up till now. You were excited up to the point where it wasn't going your way. If you don't like it, then why even participate? We have the important areas unlocked, why not quit now while we're ahead?"

"We can't quit!"

"Why not?"

"Because it's still his ship!"

Henry looked confused. "What do you mean, it's still his ship?"

"He sold the ship to me knowing full well we would have to do this. He sold us part of the ship and it was as if he said 'It's up to you to find the rest.' He still owns the parts of the ship we haven't unlocked, and until we do it's not really my ship." Edward had calmed down and was no longer shouting. "This ship is still his, and if we truly want to own it, if we truly want to have our *Freedom*, then we have to play the game." He let out a sigh. "I was just a little frustrated. But I'm not giving up. I will beat his game, and this ship will be mine."

"Take a few breaths, and we'll try to figure this out together." Anne stroked his cheek in a soothing manner.

Edward closed his eyes, nuzzled into Anne's hand and gave it a kiss. "It's all well and good, I'm fine now. I'll grab the stone and we'll see if there's some trick to it."

Edward turned to where he'd thrown the stone triangle, and saw William there, bent over, examining it. He had two pieces in his hands.

Two? Oh no...

"Is it broken?" he asked, as he knelt down next to William.

"Not quite. It appears this was meant to be broken apart."

Edward's mouth fell open and he cocked his brow, so William handed him the pieces to examine. In the centre of one there was a triangular hole, and on the other a peg of the same shape meant to keep them together. He could see an inscription of numbers on each of the sides of the triangle. The side with A-I had the number 3, J-R had 1, and S-Z had 2.

Wait a minute!

315

Edward dashed over to the table, where Anne and Henry were reading the gibberish on the paper.

There are three paragraphs. The numbers must correspond to the paragraphs. What about the other half of the stone?

Edward inspected it.

They have numbers 1-3 as well.

Edward examined the paper again. He kept repeating the word "three" over and over in his head.

"That's it!"

"What's it?" Henry asked.

"The three faces of this stone triangle have 1, 2, and 3 on them respectively. There are two sides to it, and both sides have the numbers on them. There are three paragraphs we need to decode, and each paragraph has three lines. The left side of the triangle relates to the three paragraphs, and the right side to the three lines for each paragraph. We have to arrange the two sides of the triangle to correspond with the paragraph and the line."

"How are we to rearrange them?" Henry asked.

Edward showed them the broken stone and smiled. "If I hadn't gotten angry we wouldn't have found this out. All's well that ends well, eh chaps?"

Henry and Anne both chuckled and shook their heads. They all sat down and worked at the paper. Now that they knew what to do with it, translating it didn't take very long. The message was short and plain. It contained instructions to find the next island, with no more riddles.

South of Jamaica,
East of Providencia,
Northwest of Barranquilla.

The Lone Island
Holds the next
In the line of keys.

One entrance, one exit
Two corridors of tests
Two enter, two leave.

"That's fairly straightforward, wouldn't you say?"

"I believe so, Henry. I'm still curious what the two entering and two leaving part means," Edward said, stroking his beard.

"It could be people. Maybe this is a trial for the captain and first mate?"

"That makes sense, similar to how the first trial was for the whole crew. This will test the leaders of the crew themselves," Anne added.

Edward nodded. "Yes, but it doesn't necessarily have to be the captain and the first mate. In the second trial it was very specific in that it was for the captain only. Why wouldn't Benjamin do the same here if that was the case?"

"Well, we can figure that out later. For now, let's sail to the island," Henry said, putting an end to the debate.

"Right. I'll fill in Herbert."

Edward and the others dispersed and went back to work. Herbert set the course south-southwest to their destination. He used the three positions from the clues to triangulate and give an approximate location of the island. After a quick stop for more supplies they headed for the island.

The journey took a couple of days, uneventful except for the hot weather and a particularly bad storm along the way which, thanks to Herbert, they rode out without serious trouble. But on the morning of the third day they sailed into a sudden mist, which Herbert thought odd.

"This shouldn't be here. There's been no change in the air, and it's a hot day, not humid, so any fog should evaporate. Strange," he said with a furrowed brow.

"Hmm," Edward mumbled as he stroked his beard. "Eyes forward! There's strangeness afoot!" All hands aboard kept sharp eyes on every inch of the water. The fog wasn't thick, but caution seemed warranted. The wind was slight and the ship slow. No sound broke the eerie quiet other than the rocking of the waves and the seamen going about their business.

A crewman's voice came from the crow's nest. "Captain, off the stern! A ship!"

Edward turned and pulled out his spyglass. Sure enough, a ship was trailing behind them, a grey shape just visible through the mist. Edward studied it through the glass, recognised it by its shape, and cursed under his breath.

How does he keep finding us? Damn him to Davy Jones' locker!

"What kind of ship?" Herbert asked.

"Frigate. It's an old friend who would love nothing better than to have me in irons. Run us to the wind, Herbert. Maybe this mist will help us lose him."

"Aye, Captain," Herbert said as he moved the ship farther to starboard.

"Let all the sails fly, gentlemen! Make this ship live up to its name!"

They went much quicker with the wind full in the sails. Edward turned to take another look at the ship behind them. It was gaining on them still. The fifth-rate frigate named the H.M.S. *Pearl* moved like a vessel of a lighter class. It knew these waters, and, like the commander on board, shot straight to its target.

The minutes passed like hours as it drew closer and closer. Then the mist broke, and Edward could see, dead ahead, the island that was their goal.

"There, Herbert! Head around the island!" Edward went to the edge of the deck. "Get ready to fight, you scallywags!"

The island was not quite an island. More of a small mountain, it had high rocky cliffs covered by moss, grass, and a few trees here and there. It did not appear habitable, nor was there a spot to land on.

The *Pearl* was gaining on them as they tried to round the island. Herbert had the *Freedom* hugging the shore as close as possible to the mountainous island while avoiding the rocks. The *Pearl* was closing in on the port side of the ship, and it wasn't long before a familiar sound erupted from it.

Cannonballs flew toward the *Freedom* one after the other. Some hit the water, others the cliffs, sending chunks of rock hurtling towards the crew. A few hit the ship, causing damage and injuring crewmen in their wake.

"Return fire!" Edward yelled.

The cannons on the top level erupted almost all at once, and those on the lower followed soon after. The *Freedom*'s volley did more damage than the *Pearl*'s had, making holes and breaking railings. The *Pearl* had the clear advantage, however. Anything shot was bound to hit the island, if not the ship itself, and the falling rocks were the most dangerous and unpredictable part of the attack.

Sweat beaded on Edward's face as he searched for some way out of their vulnerable situation. He noticed a sort of inlet to starboard, an opening to the island, big enough for a ship to enter. "Herbert! Into the island!" Herbert nodded as he threw the wheel to starboard. The sudden shift in direction knocked some of the less experienced seafarers off balance. Edward held to the railing with one hand and grabbed Herbert's chair with the other to keep it from rolling or tipping.

The *Pearl* followed soon after, and because it was already pointed in the right direction, it ended up right beside the *Freedom*. The two ships were almost close enough to be able to board.

And then something strange happened.

As they entered the inlet, a strong current took both ships and began pulling them forward, limiting their maneuverability, and forcing them into the island's interior, side by side. Overhead a rocky ceiling covered them as they moved into the hollow of the island itself.

Neither ship took this surprising turn of events as adequate reason to hold fire. The cannons never stopped, and rifles began firing as well. Edward could see Smith staring across at him with a satisfied expression.

Bastard. You chase us across half the Caribbean and think it will be easy for you? I'll show you the terror of a Thatch!

"Captain, eyes forward!" Herbert yelled.

Edward's glance shot to the prow. Ahead of them loomed a huge rock, splitting the tunnel in half and permitting the passage of only one ship on either side. Edward knew the division of the tunnel would increase the speed of the current, and once a ship went in, there could be no turning back.

So this is what's meant by "two enter and two leave!" Two ships, not two people. This is a trial for the crew. Or is it crews?

"Captain, what do you want me to do?"

"We have to go through on the right side. There's no other way. There's no room for two ships, so the *Pearl* will have to take the left."

No sooner had Edward spoken than he noticed, seemingly oblivious to the looming threat, the *Pearl* drawing even closer to the *Freedom*.

That fool! He intends to kill us all! Well, then, if he wants to play that game, we'll play.

Edward grabbed the wheel from Herbert. He pulled the wheel to the port side, aiming the *Freedom*'s prow at the *Pearl*. The two ships were in a dead heat with each other, but still far enough away that no one dared to board for a direct assault.

Edward stared down Smith as both ships headed towards the rocky pass in front of them. Neither crew cared to carry on the battle now. They were focused only on their imminent destruction and on the two men who appeared ready to lead them to it.

All Edward and Smith cared about now was the game.

The two of them were an even match. Neither backed down from the other's challenge. The ships moved ever closer to the rocky divider. The crews were running around and frantically yelling.

Closer.

Sweat beaded on Edward's forehead.

Closer.

A few more seconds. Closer.

The H.M.S. *Pearl* turned hard to port, and out of harm's way, which made Smith turn away and yell at whoever changed the course. Edward flung the wheel to the starboard side.

Freedom turned at a forty-five-degree angle to the oncoming wall. The current pushed them further into the cavern of the island. The ship's momentum slowed as it shifted with the current, but the wall was imminent. The crew collectively held their breath, or clenched their teeth, waiting for the collision.

The current pulled *Freedom* forward just as it touched the wall. The grating noise of scraping wood on rock rumbled over the rushing of the current. The noise lingered until the current righted the ship and took her fully in its grasp.

"You could have killed us!" Herbert yelled.

"It was a gamble, and I won. Otherwise we both would have died for certain. There's only room for one ship in each tunnel, and if this is anything like the first trial, we'll need him to complete his side to escape here."

Herbert sighed. "So what happens now?"

"One entrance, one exit. Two corridors of tests. Two enter, two leave," Edward recited. "We'll meet up with them again at the end of this island's gauntlet. We both entered and will face the tests, but only one of us will leave here alive."

38. A SHIP OUT OF WATER

The current took them deeper and deeper into the tunnel at an alarming speed. Herbert was throwing the wheel this way and that to avoid smashing against the rocks, as the frequency of twists and turns increased.

"How is this possible?" Edward yelled as he grabbed the railing at the next bend.

"The inside of this island seems to be pulling in wind somehow. It's filling the sails and causing the water to flow," Herbert replied.

"Furl the sails!" Edward yelled to the crew in response.

"It's either that or something supernatural, like that mist," Herbert yelled over the frantic voices of the crew, who were rushing this way and that to pull up the sails and secure the rigging.

Something's certainly not natural about all this... Benjamin's work, no doubt.

Even after pulling up the sails, the ship was still speeding through the tunnel inside the island. Edward focused on the path ahead of them. The ship was heading straight towards a sharp ninety-degree turn in the rock tunnel.

"Herbert, we're going to crash! What do we do?"

There was a moment's pause from the navigator. "I don't know!"

Edward panicked. *What do we do? What do we do?* The craggy wall of doom was inching closer with each second.

Alexandre appeared from the main deck. His eyes were wider than Edward had ever seen them. "Herbert, turn the ship on my command. Captain, have every crewmember grab grenades and throw them into the water off the port side at the same time."

Edward stared at him. "What will that do?"

"Do not ask questions. Trust me!"

Seeing Alexandre's determined expression, Edward turned to the main deck. "All hands grab grenades and stand at the port side deck!" The crew looked at him the way he had at Alexandre a few seconds before.

"Don't stare at me like a bunch of gits! Get movin'!"

The crew scurried like lizards across the deck to where the grenades were cached in sealed boxes. Some crewmembers brought their fellows up from the lower deck, and everyone took grenades, as instructed.

Edward had the gunners position themselves in front of those holding grenades. Each gunner had a linstock in his hand, ready to light the fuses of the grenades. When everyone was ready, Alexandre yelled to Edward to start. "Light those grenades, everyone! Go! Go! Go!" Everyone pushed the fuses to the linstocks and waited for the next command.

The ship turned and its port broadside was now facing the wall of the tunnel. It was still being carried by the current, and if they did nothing it would smash into the wall.

"Now! Throw those grenades!" Edward yelled as he threw his at the wall ahead of him. It bounced and fell into the water along with dozens of others. Mere seconds remained before the ship would smash into a wall of rock.

"Hit the deck!" Edward yelled as he jumped away from the side rail to the floor of the ship.

Everyone followed suit. A thunderous explosion and a crash of waves erupted from the port side. Edward thought that the ship had smashed against the rocks, but the underwater explosion of dozens of grenades had sent up huge waves between the ship and rock wall. The waves slowed the ship and cushioned the impact enough for them to survive.

After the explosion, everyone rose to their feet as the current continued to carry the ship deeper into the island, although slower than before. Edward assessed the damage. There were some bruises and scrapes, but nothing serious. He went over to Alexandre, who was still with Herbert at the helm.

"How did you know that would happen? And for that matter, how did they stay lit in the water?"

"As I have told you, *mon ami*, I observe, and therefore I see what others do not. It was a simple deduction. As for the underwater trick, I did a little experiment with the fuses. I used several different chemical treatments to make them work while underwater. This was the field test."

"This was a test? You're mad!"

Alexandre shrugged. "*C'est la vie.*" He and Edward paused after his remark, and then they both laughed.

Herbert kept his eyes on the tunnel ahead, and shouted: "All hands brace yourselves!"

Edward's and Alexandre's heads spun around toward Herbert, then toward the bow. They grabbed the railing when they saw, dead ahead, the water was gone from their path. The *Freedom* was about to slide over a small gap which the rushing water was falling into, and onto stone. Some grabbed safety lines while others wrapped their arms around the railings or other sections of the ship. Then they could no longer hear or feel the rush of water around the ship's hull. The ship moved past the water and slid onto the smooth stone path with the speed of the current. At the end of the slide they passed from the small, cramped tunnel into an open room.

The room was a large, square cavern within the island. The walls were covered with patches of moss, and water dripped down from cracks and stalactites. There was no flowing water in the vicinity and no visible exit.

When the ship stopped sliding forward, it tipped to the side, but stopped on the angle of its keel. Some supplies and weapons on deck slid off and fell to the rocky ground below, but no one went with them. After a little getting used to the tilt, it was possible to walk. Edward looked back to where they had come from. He could see the rocky ramp that had brought them into the room. He noticed that the floor of the cavern was perfectly smooth.

"Thanks to the way *Freedom*'s keel is shaped, and that smooth surface," said Herbert, "there's probably only minor damage to her." Herbert's sister was now wheeling him on the deck; the tilt of the ship would make wheeling himself too dangerous. "If our keel broke we'd be dead even if we got out of here. But then, leaving does appear to be a problem."

"Yes, it does. I can't see an exit, can you?" Edward asked. Herbert and his sister both shook their heads. "We should check everywhere around here to make sure. There might be something hidden that can't be seen from here."

Edward took John, Nassir and his son Ochi, Anne, and several other crewmen with him, and climbed down the side of the ship by rope. Edward, Nassir, and Ochi inspected the keel for damage. Once satisfied it would be all right, they began looking around.

The cavern was almost a perfect square, with a floor too smooth and walls too straight to be natural. The ceiling, however, had craggy rocks and stalactites hanging from it. In the corners were large mounds of piled-up rocks, perhaps debris from the process of smoothing the floor and walls.

Edward noticed above the corner where he was standing, on the ceiling, there were large rocks shaped like a semicircle with a hollow middle. Each corner had a similar rock formation, located far above the mound of rocky debris on the floor.

"What do you make of those, John?" he asked, pointing at the ceiling. "Do you think that's an unusual rock formation?"

"They certainly seem man-made, Captain."

Anne was kneeling on the ground, inspecting the rocks in the front right corner. "Ed! Come look at this! Here, in between the rocks, you can see something at the back."

Edward knelt down beside Anne and peered into the spot she was looking at. He could see something at the back made of wood. "What is it?"

"Let's find out, shall we?" Anne said, starting to move some of the rocks away.

Edward and some mates joined in and began removing the piled-up rocks and putting them aside. As they worked, the other crewmembers cleared the other corners. When they removed the topmost layers of debris, they found the same apparatus in each of the four corners. There was a large hollow wooden cylinder fashioned around a rock sticking out of the wall. On the end of the wooden circle there were four holes that could hold something in them. At both ends were metal grooves and stoppers, meant to stop the wooden part from being spun in a certain direction.

The process of clearing the rocks was sweaty, tiring work, and the air in the cavern was muggy. "I wonder what those are for," Edward asked, mopping his forehead, catching his breath, and grateful to be sitting down at last.

"They look like they can spin around," said Anne, also perspiring but not the least bit breathless. Edward couldn't help but admire her beauty even then. "They could be pulleys for use with ropes, but the purpose of that down here eludes me."

No sooner did the words leave Anne's lips than a great rumbling noise rose through the floor. Everyone sprang up, startled. The noise grew louder as the room shook violently. Cracks began to appear on the walls, and the shaking became so strong the crew could not keep their footing.

The wall in front of the ship began to crack and crumble near the ceiling, and fell three quarters of the way down before an abrupt stop. On the walls to the left and right, chunks of rock fell off, revealing four hidden compartments. Finally the shaking stopped, and everyone was able to rise from the ground. Edward, after reassuring himself no one was hurt, asked those on the ship what lay beyond the newly formed opening.

"It be water, Captain, and another tunnel. That be our way out," one crewman relayed back.

The problem is moving our ship up there. Whatever is in those compartments in the side walls must be the key.

Edward went over to one of the compartments and was able to see four iron poles and an incredibly long and thick bundle of rope. He picked up one of the iron poles to examine it. Before he could get a good look at it, the pole slipped out of his fingers and fell to the ground. With the impact, an explosion erupted inside the pole. It sounded like a gunshot and caused the pole to fly across the room, almost hitting a few people on the way.

"What in God's name was that? Everyone be careful with those iron poles!" Edward admonished. "They're dangerous." None sought to argue with his brief assessment.

Edward left the other poles alone for the time being and examined the rope. The rope was in a neat, untangled coil, but it was much too long and thick to be of any use to them on the ship. It was the same for the other three compartments that opened.

He picked up and examined one of the poles with caution. On one side, several holes went along the length of the pole with small plugs in them. Inside the holes he found black powder. Peering down the length he thought he could see flint attached to a long strand of rope.

That's what caused the explosion. It must work the same way as the cannons on the Freedom. Pull the rope and it moves the flint and ignites the black powder. How does this tie in? We have strange iron poles, the huge rope, and a system of pulleys—but what to pull? I suppose we can pull the ship, but how, and where?

Edward looked up to the loops of rock on the ceiling.

Maybe...

He turned to the crew. "Let's bring this to the ship, I want to try something."

While the crew worked to haul the rope on board, Edward went below decks and returned with a large iron javelin from the *Freedom*'s short-lived whaling days. He tied the rope to it and attempted to hurl it up into the hole in the ceiling.

He pulled back his large muscular arm, spread and bent his legs to maximise his potential strength, then released the javelin with all his might, almost falling with his great heave of a follow-through.

It fell far short of its mark.

Sam chuckled. "And you're supposed to be the smart one?"

Edward frowned. "It was worth a try. Do you have any bright ideas of how to get the rope into those holes?"

Sam just shrugged, and after a few moments of perplexity all round, John came forward. "One thing your father used to do was have a cannon shoot a javelin towards a hard-to-kill target. That was why he preferred metal to wood: it was sturdier."

"Let's try that then. Someone set up the cannon." Edward pulled the rope with the javelin back onboard. The rest of the crew packed gunpowder into a cannon of suitable size, and Edward pushed the javelin deep inside, packing it tighter. Once it was ready, he had one of the gunners aim it at the hole. The cannon fired and the javelin shot straight and true—for the most part—right to the mark, and then the rope fell to the floor as the crew on the ship held onto the other end.

"This will work. I want four teams down on the ground to tie that rope to the pulleys in the corners. Cannoneers, get the javelins from below deck, and repeat this procedure for the other three holes with the other rope we found in the compartments. Everyone else, start removing everything you can from the ship. We need to have the ship as light as possible."

Herbert raised his brow. "What are you planning?"

"We have to lift the ship into the air to move it over that wall. We'll use the pulleys to do it."

Herbert shook his head. "I hope you know what you're doing."

The crew who manned the cannons were able to shoot the javelins through the four rock semicircles in the ceiling after a few tries. Once the rope was lowered to the floor of the cavern, the crew on the ground tied them to the four pulleys.

The rest of the crew went about removing anything not tied down to the ship. A multitude of hands and enough rope allowed them to clear the ship within an hour. The hardest part was the cannons, which required several people to handle, and if they weren't careful, it could damage the ship during transport. They decided to leave the cannons on the gun deck and only remove those on the main deck and foredeck cabin.

Once everything was unloaded, the crew took the end of the rope not tied to the pulleys and snaked it through the gun deck of the ship. They made sure to weave it in and out of the port and starboard holes, which were used for the cannons, to help disperse the weight. Then they tied the rope together around the mast pole to secure it all.

"Do you think it will hold?"

Herbert scanned it over. "I don't know. The rope seems strong enough, and the weight should disperse enough now that we've removed all the cargo. If it doesn't hold, the keel is sure to break this time."

"Well, I don't see a better way. It's the only thing we can do."

The teams on the floor inserted the iron poles into the holes on the side of the pulley, and left a supply of gunpowder near each. When turned, the iron poles locked into place. Edward's theory was that if all the poles were fired at once the force would cause the cranks to spin, and move the ship up. When everything was set, Edward gave the order and the rope triggers were all pulled at once.

The simultaneous explosion of the poles sent out massive flares as they went red from the heat, and the force of it propelled the cranks forward and the ship upwards. The rope went taut and the wood creaked and groaned across the ship. Edward and the crew gritted their teeth in suspense. The ship moved up, slowly but surely, and within a few seconds stopped and hung suspended in the air. The crew let out a collective breath.

Edward instructed the four groups to fill each pole once more with the gunpowder. They had to repeat the process three more times before the ship was well above the rock wall they had to cross. The top mast was a hundred feet below the ceiling when Edward called the crew to a stop.

The whole crew was staring at their ship, their home, hanging in the air, moments away from ruin. One misstep, one hitch, and it would be destroyed. The attitude was somber, but they couldn't dwell on what ifs. Now was a time of action.

We've come this far. Now how do we move it into the water?

Everyone looked around for a clue as to what to do next. Edward was staring at the ship, and he noticed it was swaying slightly from the move upwards.

Hmm. That could work.

He turned to Herbert. "Herbert, from what you saw of the water, was there a current?"

"No, Captain."

"Good. Everyone, listen up! We need to move the ship into the water. To do that, we'll need excellent timing—and luck. What I need is to have everyone grab the rope from each of the pulleys, and start pulling on it. Those in the back of the room will be trying to pull the ship back in unison, and those in front pull the ship towards the water in unison. Hopefully we can get the ship to start rocking back and forth. Then, when we have enough of a swing, we'll release the pulleys and the ship should move into the water."

The crew eyed him like he was mad.

Edward sighed. "Does anyone else have a better idea?"

No one spoke up, so Edward began implementing his plan. He used hand signals to indicate to the two groups when to pull. At first the ship moved only slightly, but the more the men pulled the more the movement became a rocking motion.

As they continued, Edward could see the ship getting closer and closer to passing over the rock wall and then the water. Farther and farther it went over the line dividing the rooms. The stress of the situation transferred to the crew; the ever-looming threat of their home being in constant danger and the weight of the ship in their hands made their sweat hit the smooth stone ground like rain.

The ship moved back as far as it could, almost hitting the back wall, and Edward knew this was the moment. When it went past the halfway point of the room, he yelled "Now!" to release the pulleys.

The crew heard the order, and they hit the release mechanism at the perfect moment.

Save one.

The release mechanism on the front left pulley jammed, and the ship buckled to the side as it moved forward and down. If the rope wasn't released soon, the ship would smash against the wall.

The ship was falling. Edward's ship, Edward's *Freedom*, his home, his crew's home. It was going to crash, and he could only watch as it did.

No!

Edward pulled his golden blade from its sheath. He planted his feet and reared his arm back. His arm, long and muscular, tightened and bulged as he drew all his strength into it. He threw the blade at the rope. It spun in the air almost like a top, the golden blur flashing in the torchlight.

The crew watched on in horror, every second passing with a thousand grim thoughts on top of a thousand others, making it seem to last for hours.

Edward let out a howl like a lion's battle cry, his eyes fixed on the sword.

The blade hit the rope, slicing through it like butter. The ship fell with a thunderous crash, and from both sides great waves surged up and soaked some of the crew. When the water cleared, the crew could see that the *Freedom* was in the water, and mostly unharmed.

Everyone cheered and released the tension they held within. Some grabbed drinks, others hugged their mates, and still others yelled and fired pistols into the air.

Edward went to Anne, pulled her close, and kissed her with unrivalled passion. He had his arms wrapped around her waist and nearly lifted her off the ground. After a split second of obligatory shock and outrage, she reciprocated with abandon, pulled him tighter, and kept her mouth pressed to his. The room grew silent, and, hearing the sudden hush, Edward and Anne turned their heads to see everyone staring at them, whereupon the whole crew burst into cheers and laughter once more. They were all in high spirits, and for a little while all thoughts of being trapped inside an island with a formidable enemy left them.

When the celebrating was done, the crew threw grappling hooks to the ship and boarded again. They brought aboard the cargo and iron poles, as Edward had an idea for making use of them. It took them another hour or so to have everything back to normal again.

"All right, everyone, now that we're all back on the ship we need to move on. We have a job to do, and there's one more trial to go before we have to face off against Smith. When that's over, then we can celebrate." The crew all crowded close to their captain, nodding their approval. "Now, let's move it! We have a battle to win!"

39. A CAPTAIN'S RESOLVE

They had to use oars to move the ship forward, as no wind was breezing through. It was similar to the first tunnel, but without a deadly current threatening them at every turn.

"I much prefer this relaxin' ride," Sam said.

Edward frowned. "Keep your wits about you; we don't know what tricks Benjamin might still have in store for us."

"Right," he said, as he glanced warily from side to side. "If you don't mind me askin',' Captain, who is this Benjamin ya be talkin' about?"

"He's the one who sold me this ship. The truth of the matter is, I don't remember him. I was drunk at the time. I must have showed him where I had my life savings, and then he left me this piecemeal ship."

"Sounds like this ship is only jus' beginning its adventure." Sam smiled and then laughed. He never seemed to be afraid of anything.

Looking at him, Edward thought it odd for the man to be a pirate. He was only a few years older than Edward himself. Edward knew how he himself was turned to this life, but not how Sam came to the same fortune—or misfortune, depending on outlook.

"Now I'll ask you a question. How did you become a pirate?"

Sam's blithe exuberance changed to thoughtfulness as he took a moment to consider the question. "I jus' always been. I never put thought to it, but I wanted to do something different, so I joined your fishin' group. Then, with all that's happened, I figured I 'ad no choice in the matter. Stayin with ye seemed like a good way to be entertained, and I haven' been disappointed yet."

"You've been a pirate all your life?"

"Fer as long as I can remember. I had powder or a cutlass in my hands since I wus a boy. Is all I know me whole life."

"How many people have you killed?"

Sam scratched his head. "Must be at least a hundred or so."

Edward couldn't help but feel somewhat sad for one who had lived this life since childhood. He would never have had a chance to play, to have friends as Edward had. He may not even have known his parents. Yet when Edward imagined himself having grown up as

330

Sam did, he felt a strange excitement. He preferred to ignore that feeling.

"We only kill to survive here. If we can take a ship without killing anyone, we'll do so."

"Sometime you 'ave to show a little blood before they understand the consequences." Sam smiled and his eyes glinted.

"True."

Herbert called down from the helm. "Captain, you should take a look at this. Straight over the bow."

Edward turned his attention to the front, where the tunnel opened up into a massive dome-shaped room, with about two-thirds cut off at the left by a flat rock wall. In front of the *Freedom* there was a tall wooden barrier and a wall of rocks blocking the view of what lay beyond. "Let her swim!" Edward commanded. The crew stopped rowing and pulled in the oars. The ship floated forward until it hit the wooden barrier and bounced back a bit.

The rocks on either side of the barrier were large and round, with steps carved into them leading to a pedestal on the top of each. Edward felt safe in assuming that these rocks would show them how to open the wooden barrier, and much to the surprise of his crew, he stripped down to his trousers and dove off the starboard side into the cavern's icy water. He swam to the rock, climbed the slippery steps to the summit, and found, as he had expected, the next puzzle in Benjamin's game.

On the pedestal he saw a horizontal wheel with pegs all around it, almost like a ship's wheel, making a sort of circular tabletop. The points of a compass were painted around its edges, and a small wooden ship sat in the centre. There was also a metallic arrow pointing due north.

From his high vantage point, Edward could see past the wooden wall blocking his ship. A short distance beyond the wall he saw a miniature ship that looked like the *Freedom* sitting motionless in the water. It had full sails, and even miniature cannons and crew. It was surrounded on all sides by random sets of curved wooden barriers. The barriers were all over the water and seemed to make a maze, but it was disjointed. Some parts appeared to define a path, but it didn't have enough continuity anywhere to suggest a true maze. Near the centre, all the wooden barriers were absent.

That central area is probably where we need to send the model ship, but how to do it? I could jump into the water and move the ship myself, but that would be too easy. There must be something preventing us from doing just that.

Edward looked across the wooden wall to the other rock on the opposite side. On the top of it was a wooden pole sticking out of the rock, which he guessed to be the lever of a switch.

"Someone bring Herbert here with a few other crewmembers," he yelled back to the ship, "and get a couple of crewmen over to that other rock."

Herbert leapt overboard and proved himself a powerful swimmer. Nassir followed and helped Herbert up the steps to where Edward was, and Sam joined them. Two others stationed themselves at the second rock and awaited orders.

"I think what needs to happen," Herbert said, pointing to the replica ship, "is that boat over there needs to be moved to the middle of the maze for the barrier to be removed."

"I figured that much out myself," Edward said, to which Herbert responded with a look of irritation.

"So let's move it then!" Sam said, making to dive into the water past the rock.

"No, wait!" Edward grabbed him by the trousers, holding him almost suspended in the air.

The surface of the water roiled and broke, and crocodiles leaped out at Sam one after another. Their powerful jaws snapped at the tasty flesh about to offer itself to them. Edward pulled Sam back and threw him onto the wheel. Sam was wide-eyed and breathing heavily. The crocs were waiting and watching with only their cold beady eyes above the water.

Well, I guess we know why we can't move it ourselves.

"By the devil's beard, that was close! Thanks, Cap'n. Ye saved me life."

"Don't mention it. I knew it would have been too easy if we could do that," he said. "I wish to find out what that switch does before anything else." Edward motioned to the group on the other side to flip the switch, and together they pushed and pulled the large wooden pole as far as it would move.

When they flipped the switch, the fragmented walls of the maze sank into the water and another set of walls of equal incoherence replaced them.

It must be that both sets together are the full maze. This will make things tedious.

Edward reached out to turn the wheel and see what it would do, but before he could start it, the ground began to shake and rumble. He and the others grabbed the wheel to steady themselves. He searched for the cause of the quaking, and what he saw made his heart leap into his throat: the rock walls of the channel *Freedom* floated in were starting to close, and they would soon crush the ship and anyone aboard. Edward shot his gaze to the other rock. "Turn it back, quick!" The crew complied, and the maze shifted back, but the walls threatening the *Freedom* kept moving.

"Dammit! Move the wheel! We need to find out what it does."

As they turned the wheel, the crew on the ship was going mad. People were shouting and running. Some jumped off and into the water, trying to swim to safety on the spherical rocks. Others tried to contain the panic and calm the others, but to no avail.

"Get yourselves together, men!" Edward yelled, his voice echoing off the walls. "You are members of my crew, and I will not tolerate such weakness! Put the ship broadside and fire the cannons at the wooden barrier to break it. Now get back on that ship and get to work!"

With a clear task to accomplish, and reassured by the words of their leader, the crew calmed down. The crew onboard help those who'd jumped off back aboard, and then placed oars into the water. Using the oars, they turned the ship so its broadside was facing the wooden barrier. They loaded the cannons and fired, trying to break the wooden barrier apart. The gunners kept firing again and again, but the large iron balls only made dents in the thick wood.

Edward gauged how fast the walls were closing in. They had ten minutes at best. "How's the miniature ship?" Edward asked.

"The wheel moves the red arrow of the compass on the table and opens up panels in the ceiling of the dome to let wind in," Herbert said as he pointed above. Beams of light shone in at different spots along the rock face of the dome. "This wind fills the sails on the miniature ship and allows it to move through the maze. Wherever the red needle of the compass is pointing is where the wind will blow."

Edward looked at the wheel and the compass once again, and took notice of the needle and the location of the holes in the ceiling. He nodded in silent agreement with what Herbert said.

"After we flipped the switch," Herbert continued, "a wooden box opened up at the centre of the maze. That's where we need to put the ship, I imagine. The problem is that at this angle it's hard to see the full maze. Not to mention only half the maze is showing at a time."

Herbert commanded the direction of the wheel, dictating the way the red arrow of the compass moved and in turn the direction the wind was blowing. They also had to switch back and forth between one setting of the maze and the other depending on what they needed to see.

The cannon fire was doing nothing to break the barrier, and the walls were closing in on the *Freedom* with each passing second. It was taking too long to complete the trial. Edward shouted: "Cease fire! Turn the ship back around! The walls are too close!"

The crew stopped the cannons and rowed the boat back to its original position. They only had a few minutes left before the walls would reach the ship and start to crush it. Fear was beginning to sculpt the lines of Edward's face. He watched as the miniature ship reached another dead end.

Dammit! We won't make it in time!

He turned back to the *Freedom*. "Throw me some grenades!"

The crew threw him grenade after grenade until he had six, and then a linstock for lighting them. He lit the grenades and threw them all in the water. They exploded a moment later with a thunderous boom and a splash of water. Edward drew his golden sword and, when the explosion subsided, put the blade between his teeth and dove in. He swam with the current made from the wind, peering this way and that, but the murky water made it impossible to see anything. The water chilled him to the bone; every stroke sent pain through him.

There was a flash to the left, an open jaw, and razor sharp teeth. Edward gripped the sword in his hand and thrust it deep. His arm was slow in the water, but the blade went through the croc like it was paper. Blood filled the water.

He had to come up for air. He splashed around, taking deep breaths. The crew was yelling to him; the rock walls were still edging closer and closer. He turned back.

He was at the edge of the maze. "Edward! To the right!" someone yelled, but it was too late.

The jaw snapped shut on Edward's stomach, and his whole side was engulfed in pain worse than the icy cold. He was losing blood and the creature wasn't letting go. He could see the croc's companions closing in faster, excited by the blood.

Edward stabbed the bold one right between the eyes. He swam and grabbed onto the nearest barrier of the maze and pulled himself up. The dead body of the crocodile still hung off his side. He pried the jaw open and threw the body back into the water. The other crocs savagely ate the dead one as soon as it fell.

Edward could see the hungry eyes of hundreds of them teeming in the water. The pain in his side throbbed. He hoisted himself up onto one of the walls of the maze, then leaped from wall to wall to avoid the creatures. The crocs followed him out of the water, snapping and making a terrible hissing noise from their open jaws as they swam toward him.

Edward was paying so much attention to where he was he didn't look where he was headed. He was closer to the ship, but now he didn't have anywhere else to jump. The water was too murky to see where the submerged wood was, and the hissing beasts were closing in on him.

"Flip the switch!" he yelled.

Slowly the other sections of the maze rose as Edward was lowered into the water. The crocodiles moved even quicker than before. He leapt to the raised sections, trying to put distance between himself and the bloodthirsty animals.

He stopped at the model ship now located in a dead end of the maze. He put the sword in its sheath at his side and picked up the ship off the water's surface with both hands. It was heavy and awkward in his wet hands. It was also hard for him to see where he was jumping now. Sweat and saltwater poured down his cold face. He kept up his pace, moving closer and closer to the centre of the maze. He called on the crew to pull the switch twice more as he jumped from wall to wall. The crocodiles were gaining on him.

And the walls were still closing in on the *Freedom*.

Edward was at the point where he could no longer move forward. The centre of the maze was right in front of him, and uncountable pairs of hungry eyes were right behind him. He jumped into the water with the ship still in hand and kicked his legs as quick as they would go. The crocodiles slipped past the wooden barriers, closing in on him at the centre. He reached the centre and pushed the ship into the wooden box.

Another wall closed on the wooden box and the whole thing lowered into the water, maze and all. Anything blocking him from the crocs also departed into the deep. The eyes closed in on him from all sides. He pulled out his sword, took a deep breath, and let himself sink.

Come on, then!

The crocs were only feet away from Edward when hundreds of iron balls began to fall into the water like rain. The multitude of bullets pelted the crocodiles around him, causing the water to turn red. Edward surfaced to see the crew alive and well, firing rifles on the beasts. They fought with all their determination to keep their captain, their friend, their brother, alive.

In mere moments, all the crocs were dead.

After it was done, Edward swam over and climbed up a rope ladder let down for him. "Thank you everyone, you saved my..."

Anne stopped him before he could finish. She placed her hands over his mouth. "It is we who owe you thanks, Ed. You saved our lives; we were merely returning the favor. We are family. How could we do any less?" She looked at the crew and they nodded in agreement with smiles on their faces.

Edward closed his eyes and smiled as well.

They turned the ship around and picked up Herbert and the others. The rock walls once threatening the *Freedom* had closed completely, and the wooden barrier was open like a gate, parted down the middle. When Edward asked what had happened when he put the ship in the box, they told him how the wooden barrier opened and allowed them to paddle out. As they headed to save him, the wall on the left side of the dome had fallen, but revealed another wall just like it.

I think I know what's happening. "Crew, listen up!" They all gathered around him. "On the other side of that wall is our enemy, Isaac Smith. He's chased us all across the Caribbean for the past ten months and more, and he thinks he's got the better of us. I know we have the hardier crew, the superior ship, and the greater heart. We can win against him and end his terrorising of us today!" The crew roared approval. "And whatever happens, I want you all to know that you are the best crew anyone could ask for, and the best family a man could have." He smiled and put his hand out, palm down. "To *Freedom* and family!" Everyone reached out to put their hands on top of his, or on the shoulder of another crewmember.

"To *Freedom*... To family!" they repeated, as they lifted their hands into the air. To some of them, those words meant more to them than all the jewels, all the gold, all the treasure in the world.

They certainly did to Edward.

Now, as they all stood together on the deck of the *Freedom*, the earth began to shake and rumble once again, the second rock wall fell into the watery depths inside the island, and the H.M.S. *Pearl* stood revealed. The enemy ship turned towards them.

"All hands prepare for battle! It ends here!"

40. NO REGRETS

The *Pearl* and the *Freedom* approached one another. Their battle would soon begin. In the dome of the island, it felt as if they were the only two ships in the world, caught in an eternal battle in the centre of the earth: one representing justice and order, the other freedom and anarchy.

There could be only one victor.

Edward rushed to don the clothes of a captain: his tricorn hat, leather long jacket with white tunic beneath, black pantaloons, and leather boots. Fitting himself for battle, he tucked four pistols into his trousers and strapped two cutlasses to his sides, one of them the priceless weapon forged from the Golden Arm. In his hands he held a rifle, and to his back he strapped another in case he didn't have enough time to reload.

Having completed his preparations, he noticed Henry heading below deck.

"Henry, what are you doing?"

Henry stopped and turned to face Edward. He looked tired and worn, his eyes baggy and his brows sagging.

Henry let out a small sigh as he ran his fingers through his hair. "I cannot participate in this battle. I tried to fight them last time, but I can't kill these people, Edward. Every time I do, I see Robert's face."

"But… these marines aren't Robert," Edward pleaded. "I've said it before: he would understand."

"Would he? Would he really?" Henry snapped back, the fire returning in his eyes. "You think he would understand us killing marines? People like him? You think he would understand us stealing? You think he would understand us becoming pirates?"

"Henry…" Edward called, reaching out towards his friend.

"No, Edward!" Henry said, pushing away Edward's hand. "Robert wouldn't understand that. I'm fine when it's people like the Boddens, or those thugs that kidnapped Jack. I understand that and have learned to deal with it. But not this," he said, slowly shaking his head and closing his eyes. "Every time I try, I feel sick inside. Whatever comes, I'll see you at the end of this battle. I hope you don't lose yourself, Edward."

Henry turned and descended the stairs, and Edward watched him leave. Edward gripped his rifle tighter and turned to the oncoming ship.

The ships drew abreast of each other.

"Fire!" Edward yelled. The crews on both ships let loose their cannons and guns. The smell of gunpowder filled the subterranean dome. The two ships circled each other as they fought. Cannonballs smashed through wood; splinters flew everywhere. Both ships had about the same number of crew, the same number of cannons, and the same strength. They were too evenly matched, and it was clear to Edward that neither could gain an advantage. He turned to the aft deck.

"Take us in close, Herbert!" Herbert nodded and flung the wheel to the side. "All hands prepare to board! We're taking the fight to them!"

The ship pitched hard to starboard and they pulled in the oars, letting the ship's momentum carry it. The marines saw this and duplicated the maneuver. Edward climbed up the main mast and grabbed a rope. Others did likewise at the different levels on each mast, waiting for the two ships to come closer together. When they were close enough to board, Edward yelled "To victory!" and swung off the mast to the other ship.

He landed in the middle of the main deck with a thunderous crash and a fierce grin that kept everyone at bay. Fear was evident in their eyes, and they thought twice about approaching.

Their hesitation would cost them.

Before anyone could make a move toward him, Edward pulled out and fired two of his pistols at the same time. Then, in one swift motion, he threw them away, spun around, and drew and fired another two. He had shot four marines in less than five seconds. Rising to his full height, he pulled out his two cutlasses.

The marines attacked him at once with their swords. Within moments, Edward noticed one person lagging. He weaved through the other marines' swords and slammed his shoulder into the weak link, pushing through the circle of death. With the other crewmembers boarding as well, the marines couldn't all focus on Edward. With several marines' attention moving to his crew, he found himself with more manageable numbers.

The sounds and smells of battle filled the dome. The two ships stood hull to hull, now locked together by hooks. Hundreds of men fought on the dual battleground.

At the foredeck of the *Freedom*, Anne and William were fighting several men, but neither side was attacking with weapons. The marines because they knew who Anne was, and William and Anne because they didn't want to harm marines.

William stood in front of Anne. Two of the marines went for his arms to disable him, but William kicked the first one in the chest, then grabbed the second one's arm and twisted it back. A third attacked him with the butt of a rifle. He threw the second man into him, knocking them both over.

Anne kicked a marine in the temple, knocking him unconscious. Another jumped her, pinning her down. She rolled with him and flipped him overboard. A third tried to lock her arms when she stood up. Anne twisted around, took the marine's arms with her and threw him into a group, knocking them all over.

"I don't know how long we can keep this up, Your Highness," William panted.

"We'll do it as long as it takes; I do not want their blood on my hands," she replied.

John, on the poop deck of the *Freedom*, fired his rifle at a marine trying to swing across from the other ship. The bullet hit the marine in the arm, and he released his rope and fell into the water. Another jumped over in front of John and charged. He thrust his bayonet deep into the man's chest. Yet another man jumped at his back when he wasn't paying attention. Nassir appeared out of nowhere and bashed the man on the head with a large block of wood.

"Thank you, Nassir!" John said.

"Do not mention it," Nassir replied with a quick smile.

One man jumped on Nassir's back and put him in a choke hold. He elbowed the man's chest, causing him to fall to the deck, clutching his ribs. Nassir swung with the large block of pine and hit the man in the face, knocking him out.

Back on the *Pearl*, Sam and a group from the *Freedom* were making their way across the stern. Sam swung his cutlass like a club at the first marine he saw and hit him in the neck, dropping him instantly. He fought without sparing a thought for technique or finesse, swinging wildly at anyone in the path of his blade. A marine attacked him from behind, and Sam spun and backhanded the man on the cheek, laughing like a hyena.

Pukuh was on the *Freedom*, spear in hand, dispatching men left and right as a paragon of an Eagle Warrior. One man lunged at him with a sword. He sidestepped and hit the man's nose with his elbow, breaking it. Another man attacked from the left. He thrust his spear into his chest. One more pointed a pistol at him and fired. He jumped into the air, flipped, and kicked the man in the face, landing on top of him. Those who faced Pukuh had fear in their eyes, some for the first time ever.

Edward, on the *Pearl*, was now confronted by two large men, each with swords as big as they were.

"Those don't seem standard issue, fellows." Edward made sure to keep his distance.

"We call 'em the whale killers," the one on the left said.

"We used to be sailors, but found the game was too easy," the other said.

"Well, it seems we have something in common. The name's Edward, but you can call me Blackbeard."

The one on the left spoke up again. "Catchy. I'm Donald, and this is me brother James."

James gave a slight bow. "Now that introductions have been concluded, let us have at it, shall we?"

The one called James lifted the huge whale killer over his head with both hands and threw it down at Edward, who jumped out of the way just in time for the blade to smash a hole into the deck of the ship. The wood cracked and splinters flew up as if a cannonball had ripped through it. Others in the marine crew saw the brothers fighting and gave them as wide a berth as possible.

And then a clear voice resounded over the din of battle.

"Stand down, men. That one's mine."

Isaac Smith walked down the stairs from the aft deck. There was blood on his sword, and a cut on his cheek. One of Edward's crew swung down on a rope and dropped in front of him. Smith kicked him in the face, sending him to the deck, unconscious. "So you call yourself Blackbeard now?"

"It's grown on me. Come to try to capture me again?"

"We're not here for you, Thatch. We came for the princess."

"I don't think she wants to leave with you, Smith."

"We'll see how much of a choice she has once you and your crew are dead."

"I'd like to see how you manage that."

Smith, sword already in hand, went to meet Edward. He raised his blade and swung it straight down. Edward used his two cutlasses to block it, but this allowed Smith to get in close and knee him in the stomach. He bent over in pain, and Smith uppercut him with his elbow, sending him staggering back.

The Voyages of Queen Anne's Revenge

Edward raised his head to see a blade being thrust straight at his eye. Instinct took over and he moved his head to the side and out of the way. The strokes of Smith's blade thrust and slashed at him in rapid succession, each blow aimed at his vital organs with surgical precision. He had to use everything in him to avoid the blade: his swords to parry, his legs to jump out of the way, and the weaving and bobbing of his body to dodge. He noticed the blade Smith was using was long, and as they moved it was difficult for Smith to maneuver in tight quarters. Edward led the captain around the mast, avoiding the strikes the whole way. He climbed backwards up the stairs, and left an opening for Smith to attack on purpose.

Smith struck downward; Edward smiled and moved out of the way, and the blade went past him and bit into the wood of the ship. Smith struggled to pull it out but could not. Edward laughed and kicked the captain in the chest, sending him flying backward down the stairs. Smith flipped and fell onto the main deck, and Edward leapt down the stairs to finish him off. But Smith was quick to regain his wits and took a pistol from the belt of a fallen comrade.

Edward was running towards him, both cutlasses forward. Smith aimed his pistol at Edward. It could have been over in an instant for either of them.

"Hey, Smith!" a man yelled from the other ship.

Smith turned to see Henry jumping through the air, heading straight for him. It was too late to react. Henry had a rifle in his hand, but he held it like a club. He swung the rifle hard and the butt of it hit Smith across the cheek and nose. His nose broke on impact and he fell to the deck once more.

Edward went behind him and put his golden cutlass to Smith's throat. "Marines, stand down!" he yelled. "If you don't want a headless captain, stop fighting!" He bent over and whispered to Smith: "This remind you of something, *Captain*?" He emphasised the last word, making Smith grit his teeth in anger.

The marines all looked at their captain, with Edward's sword one whisker away from fulfilling his promise, and Henry with a rifle pointed at Smith's gut for backup. They stopped, as commanded, and threw their weapons down.

It was over.

The pirates gathered the marines in the centre of the ship and bound them. Smith was put in with the group as well.

"Please don't kill my crew. You can take my head if you want, but leave my crew out of this. They were following orders."

"And why should I listen to you? You wouldn't listen to us in the beginning, and now here we are." He put the blade to Smith's neck once more, making him wince at its sharpness. "I'm not going to kill you, despite how you wronged me. Nor will I kill anyone else. We're done here." He turned to the *Freedom*. "John, tell Alexandre to bring over medicine and other supplies."

"Aye aye, Captain."

Edward turned his attention to Henry as the threat died down. "You saved my life, Henry," Edward said.

Henry clenched his jaw and looked away from Edward for a moment. "I'm sorry," he finally croaked. "I thought only of myself when you were all putting your lives on the line... I forgot what was most important."

Edward went up to his friend and smacked his shoulder. "I forgive you, old friend. I forget sometimes, too."

Edward and Henry clasped hands. The crew yelled loudly in triumph. This was the victory they had been wanting and waiting for.

Anne walked over to Edward, but he could tell by the restrained smile on her face something was wrong.

"What is it, Anne? We won."

"I know. I cannot help but think this is not the end. They were after me, Ed, and this will not stop them. They will keep chasing us."

"And we'll beat them each time they do," he replied, gripping her shoulder before pulling her into an embrace. "Come, let's go back to our ship and leave this cave."

Anne nodded and they walked together back over to the *Freedom*.

Edward consulted Herbert about how to leave the island. Herbert pointed to a square hole in the dome that appeared big enough for a ship to fit through. Light was pouring in through it, but water was flowing in from it as well.

The only issue was that the hole was two hundred feet up the dome.

"Hmm... That water is flowing towards us from the ocean, but the exit is up too high. We might be able to climb up, but we'll never leave with the *Freedom* as is. What do you think, Herbert?"

"I don't know how to get the *Freedom* up there. It doesn't seem possible. I examined the room as we were battling and I wasn't able to see any switches or tricks usually accompanying these trials," Herbert surmised. "And heading back isn't an option... We could wait for the water coming from the exit to fill this interior area, but at the rate it's falling we would run out of food before that happened."

"This is quite the predicament." Edward contemplated the dilemma for a bit when a thought occurred to him. "We're forgetting something. The key for the ship! Where is it?"

Edward could see nothing that might be holding a key—no pedestal, no out-of-reach niche that might be holding a chest. He looked at the openings in the ceiling, and then a glint of light struck his eye. In the centre of the dome a key was suspended in the air on a long chain. Edward climbed the rope ladder to the crow's nest, and then up the rest of the main mast. He guided Herbert in moving the ship until the key was within reach. He grasped the key and it pulled free.

The next step in the game was complete, and soon the whole ship would be his.

From his high perch, Edward noticed something else. The openings in the ceiling which had provided the wind to move the miniature ship through the maze were on both sides of the dome; the side where the H.M.S. *Pearl* had been waiting had similar openings to theirs. Edward recalled that manipulating the openings had caused slight changes in the wind inside, and to the flow of the water.

I wonder...

Edward climbed down and went to the starboard side. The crew was guarding the marines, and Alexandre and the military doctor were tending their wounds.

"Smith, did you have to solve a puzzle using a wheel to create wind and currents?"

"Yes, we had to navigate through a maze made of stone walls almost as tall as our ship," he said. "We had to relay orders to those manning the wheel to change the wind's direction. Why do you ask?"

"Because that is how we leave here."

Smith smiled. "Oh, aren't you the clever one."

Mock me all you want. We won.

"Have you puzzled out how to leave?" Herbert asked over the railing.

"I have an idea, but first I want to find out what this key leads to."

Edward went to the nearest locked door, to the stern cabin. He put the key in, it turned, and he opened the door and stepped inside. What he saw astonished him.

The stern cabin's decorations were opulent, to say the least. A large chandelier hung from the ceiling, and a red carpet covered the centre of the floor. At the sides were shelves built into the ship itself, filled with a great variety of books protected by glass. From the rarest fiction to all manner of nautical books and maps, it was a treasure in and of itself. The wood-panelled walls were perforated here and there by small windows to admit light and allow sight to the outside. Installed around the whole room were oil lamps of the finest quality, along with decorations of pistols and swords. In the middle of the room was a large, wooden, oval table with several chairs around it. On the far end of the table there was an ornate, high-backed chair with red upholstery trimmed in gold. It was, no doubt, the captain's chair for meetings.

He found the next clue for the game on the table in front of the captain's chair. It was in the form of a letter sealed with an imprint of a golden hunting horn. Edward didn't open it, but instead slipped it into his pocket. He left the cabin, locked the door behind him, and went to talk to Herbert.

Edward's idea for their escape involved the use of the wheels atop the pedestals. He placed several crewmembers at each, and had them set the compasses to point north so the wind was blowing towards the exit. As soon as the compasses faced north, something large clicked and the wheels fell into the rock and disappeared. More rock at all heights on the walls receded and water began gushing in from above. The water was coming in from the ocean and filling the interior of the island at a rapid rate.

"Everyone back on the ship!" Edward yelled, but the crew needed no convincing to rush back to the *Freedom*.

The crew glanced left and right, staring warily at the water pouring in, but after the shock subsided, their faces were brimming with joy. The water flowed into every crevice of the island and caused the ships to rise with it.

Herbert was astonished. "Whoever created this is brilliant! The placement of the openings is perfect."

"How could someone construct such a thing?" Edward exclaimed.

Herbert could not help bursting into laughter. "It would have taken years."

Edward, Herbert, and the crew gazed at the spectacle in front of them in awe. The water began causing eddies and a chaotic flow of the current, and Herbert came back to his senses.

He ordered men to furl the sails, and others to man oars, then yelled for the crew on the *Pearl* to do the same. For an hour, he masterfully directed the crews in shifting the ships away from the waterfalls, and circling the centre of the island, where the waves and current was the most stable. Through skill, and a little luck, the two ships avoided smashing into each other or the rock walls of the island's belly.

When it was over, the currents subsided, and the water had reached its peak. The exit was now level with the water *Freedom* and *Pearl* were floating in.

"Let's go!" Edward commanded.

Herbert ordered the crew to lower the sails of *Freedom* and *Pearl*, and the wind inside the island pushed the ships into the tunnel exit.

Anne came up to the deck with Edward and Herbert, and gave Edward a kiss. Anne and Edward held hands and gazed into each other's eyes as they passed through the short tunnel, exiting the island once and for all and entering the light of the world once again.

They didn't even notice the terror around them until it was too late.

"Captain. We have a problem," Herbert said.

"What is it?" Edward asked, but there was no reply. He followed Herbert's astonished gaze and thought he was seeing a mirage. Ships were at various distances from the island, ringing the horizon. Edward ran to the main deck, with Anne following on his heels. His mouth opened wide with shock as sweat poured down his face.

There had to be over a hundred ships approaching from every direction. Edward took out a spyglass and examined the flags. They were royal navy ships of varying classes and armament.

"This can't be happening," Edward whispered.

Before Edward could even think of a plan, four ships of equal size, all of them larger than the *Freedom*, surrounded the pirates. They flew the flags of the three divisions of the navy, White, Red, and Blue. The fourth ship was flying the general flag of the navy, the flags of the naval divisions, the flag of Denmark, and finally the British flag at the top.

Before anyone even realised it, four men jumped onto the starboard side of the *Freedom*, one of them in the lead, the others close behind. All of them wore ornate uniforms with an abundance of medals on their chests and insignias of rank on their shoulders.

At the rear, on the leader's left, was a well-built man wearing a white suit and white gloves. Clean-shaven and immaculately groomed, with slicked-back black hair, a strong chin and pleasing features, he would be considered handsome by many. He projected an air of something like smugness, or perhaps disgust, to the pirates in front of him. He held his gloved hands in front of him, palms out, as if disdaining to soil them through contact with the world or even his own clothes. He was the youngest of the four, but his perfect poise suggested a dangerous power like a coiled snake ready to strike at a moment's notice.

He was Sir George Rooke, the Admiral of the White.

The man in the middle was elderly and rather frail-looking, with grey hair, a full grey beard, and a furrowed face. He wore a deep red suit with more decorated medals than those of his fellows, and carried a cane of ornate design. His carriage belied his fragile look: he held his gaunt body erect, took in everything with a glance—nothing escaped the wrinkled slits of his eyes—and was quick in his reactions, almost to the point of precognition.

He was Sir Cloudesley Shovell, the Admiral of the Red.

The man on the right, clad in deep blue, was both tall and rotund in the excess, suggesting a greater-than-normal appetite. He had a round face with several rolls under his chin, and a large moustache curled up across his cheeks. He wore a bulky powdered wig reaching down to his shoulders. In one hand he had a chicken leg, from which he ate heartily as he glanced about with nonchalance bordering on malaise.

He was Sir Strafford Fairborne, the Admiral of the Blue.

In front of these three was a man dressed in black and gold. He, of all of them, was the least to be trifled with. Clean-shaven but for a well-trimmed goatee, with chiseled features and a superbly formed body emphasised by his fitted uniform, his extraordinary physical power was unmistakable. But his eyes were the key to him: in them a lion lay in wait, too self-possessed to search for prey, but ready to move with infallible precision and speed should it appear. His whole bearing seemed to create, in whatever setting he might find himself, a still point of invulnerable calm—and, for those with reason to fear, of danger.

The man was Prince George of Denmark and Norway, Duke of Chamberland, Lord High Admiral, husband to Queen Anne.

Edward knew who these men were by the ranks on their shoulders, even though he did not know their names. There was no mistaking the four most powerful men in England, and no mistaking the fact that Edward Thatch now had absolutely no way to escape. The *Freedom* had been defeated before its captain and crew even realised the situation they were in.

"Father!" Anne stood immobile, rooted to the deck in shock.

Prince George ignored his daughter and stared straight at Edward. "I trust you know why we are here?"

Edward stood to his full height. "Aye," he replied. "What will happen to my crew?"

"If you cooperate with us, you will all have a trial in Great Britain. If you make things difficult, you can guess what will happen."

Edward's eyes darted left and right in a last desperate search for a way out, but it was futile. Four battleships surrounded the two smaller ships, the *Freedom* and the H.M.S. *Pearl*, and beyond them lay over a hundred warships in the distance.

"Father, please let them go. I joined them willingly. They did not kidnap me," Anne explained.

"They are pirates, my dear, sweet Anne. In what world would we ever let them go now? They will be tried, and the world will see justice served to the criminals who kidnapped you. Then life will move on. Now come with us."

"Let's negotiate something here!" Edward said. "I'm sure we can make a compromise that would benefit everyone."

Prince George responded with a dry laugh, but before he could say anything, one of Edward's crew spoke up. "I can't let you do that, Captain." It was Jack. He had a rifle in his hands and was pointing it at George Rooke, Admiral of the White. "I cannot allow this man to live."

"Jack! Put the weapon down, you fool! Do you not see the situation we are in?"

"I understand, Captain, but that man…" He stared at Rooke with an intensity of malice none could understand save him. "That man…" He couldn't utter the reason for his hatred, but everyone could see that he was trembling and on the verge of tears. "He's a dead man!" he yelled, and fired.

In the instant the gun went off, George Rooke disappeared from sight. The bullet went past where he had stood and hit the side of the *Freedom*. Immediately Rooke was in front of Jack. His eyes went wide with shock, and then he gritted his teeth in anger as he thrust the rifle's bayonet forward. Rooke sidestepped and kicked the gun out of his hands, sending them up into the air with the force. Rooke delivered another kick to his face which sent him flying to the mast where he hit it with a thud. He fell to the deck unconscious.

The *Freedom*'s men pulled their weapons on the admiral. The other admirals all pulled out their weapons.

"Stand down!" Edward yelled. For Edward's crew, his words carried a force not to be resisted, and all of them immediately put their weapons away.

Edward turned back to Prince George and knelt down on the deck. He prostrated himself before the powers of the British navy, bowing his head before them.

"I beg of you, please allow my crew to leave alive. For this favor, I offer myself to you."

Prince George looked beyond his daughter to the tall, proud man begging for the lives of the crew he loved.

"And why should we release them and take only you? Who are you that your life can substitute for all of theirs?"

Edward looked up to the man before him, his eyes speaking the resolve in his heart. "I am Edward Thatch, the dread pirate Blackbeard, and I am the captain of the ship known as *Freedom*. Surely I alone could serve as warning to other pirates that dare cross the British Navy?" he questioned. "Consider this the last wish of a dying man."

"Well said." The prince turned to George Rooke. "Rooke, stand down. This fight is over."

Rooke nodded. Holding his gloved hands fastidiously in front of him, he went back to the side of the other admirals.

"Edward Thatch… Blackbeard," Prince George declared for all to hear, "I hereby arrest you for the kidnapping of Princess Anne Sophia Stewart, daughter of the Queen of England. You will be imprisoned, tried, and put to death as the mastermind behind the kidnapping. The ship will be confiscated and the crew released—save one." He looked at William.

William hung his head in shame as he walked up beside Edward. Edward turned to him, but William shook his head. He would go willingly.

"Father, please!" Anne begged, but her words and tears went unheeded.

Prince George waved for one of the ships to come around. The battleship drew up beside the *Freedom*, and the crew placed gangplanks between them. Several marines came over and, at Prince George's instructions, bound Edward and William in irons.

"May I have a few words with my crew?"

"Of course. Men." Prince George motioned to his men and they backed off.

Edward turned to his crew. He saw the confused and stricken looks on their faces. Some had been there since the beginning, all the months at sea, through all the battles and trials. Others, though their time aboard was short, knew they had experienced the greatest adventure of their lives. They all looked at him standing there, ready to die, and felt an unbearable sadness.

Edward gazed upon them all—from Alexandre, tending to Jack, yet looking up to him, to Pukuh, the stoic warrior who understood more than any other his resolve.

"Ed, there must be some other way!" Henry pleaded.

"Sorry, Henry, but there isn't. This is all we can do. Use this freedom the prince is giving you to live full lives. Don't do anything stupid while I'm gone." Edward smiled for the last time to his crew. "Goodbye."

And with that he turned and walked away.

He heard voices crying his name and his title behind him as he walked toward the gangplank. Tears fell from the eyes of many on that ship as they watched their captain, the man who had brought them together and fought for them to the very end, go to his death.

Anne stood beside the gangplank. Her eyes had never left Edward's face. He walked over to her. The marines put up their guard, but Prince George motioned for them to stop. "I won't have another chance to say this to you, Anne, so I'll say it now." Edward leaned in and whispered something into her ear, and then walked across the gangplank to the marine battleship.

Anne's eyes widened and she stood, stunned and motionless. Her father moved close to her and spoke softly. "Do not let him see your tears, my dear. Do not make him regret his decision this day." Then he led her across the gangplank.

The naval crew took Edward to the stairs leading down to the brig of the battleship. "Take care of my *Freedom* for me," he said to Prince George. The prince nodded as they took Edward below. He went down into darkness.

The final words Edward had whispered to Anne lingered in her mind and heart. They resonated and grew until she couldn't bear it any longer. She fell to the floor of the battleship in tears.

"I love you too, Edward!"

THE END

BLACKBEARD'S REVENGE

The sequel to

BLACKBEARD'S FREEDOM

From Jeremy McLean's debut series

THE VOYAGES OF QUEEN ANNE'S REVENGE

Is on sale now through Amazon, Print and Digital.

ABOUT THE AUTHOR

JEREMY IS CURRENTLY LIVING IN NEW BRUNSWICK, CANADA WITH HIS WIFE HEATHER, AND THEIR TWO CATS, NAVI AND THOR.

Jeremy's first foray into the writing world was during a writing competition called NaNoWriMo, where the goal is to write a certain number of words in the month of November.

After completing the novel he started, and some extensive rewrites, he felt it was worthy of publishing and self-published his first novel, Blackbeard's Freedom in September, 2012.

After writing over ten books under two names, his passion for writing hasn't wavered over the years, and hopes to one day make it his primary career.

Let everyone know what you thought of his novels by leaving a review. He loves getting feedback on his books, and loves to hear from fans of his work.

Want to pirate one of Jeremy's novels? Visit http://www.mcleansnovels.com/free-book-link for a free copy of one of his books.